A Song for the Asking

A Song for the Asking

S T E V E   G A N N O N

Bantam Books
New York   London   Toronto   Sydney   Auckland

A SONG FOR THE ASKING
A Bantam Book / February 1997

Library of Congress Cataloging-in-Publication Data
Gannon, Steve.
  A song for the asking / Steve Gannon.
    p.   cm.
  ISBN 0-553-10164-1
  I. Title.
PS3557.A5184S66   1997
813'.54—dc20   96-28804
                                              CIP

Published simultaneously in the United States and Canada

PRINTED IN THE UNITED STATES OF AMERICA

BVG   10 9 8 7 6 5 4 3 2 1

For my parents

All music is what awakes from you when you are
  reminded by the instruments,
It is not the violins and the cornets, it is not
  the oboe nor the beating drums, nor the
  score of the baritone singer singing his
  sweet romanza, nor that of the men's
  chorus, not that of the women's chorus,
It is nearer and farther than they.
                                        —Walt Whitman

A Song for the Asking

August

"Travis. Wake up!"

"Huh?"

"Rise and shine, rookie. We've gotta get moving if we're gonna make it over the pass and still have time to climb."

With a groan, Travis Kane eased up on one elbow and squinted through the tent flaps at his older brother. "The sun's not even up yet, Tommy."

"Yeah, it is," Tommy insisted, reaching in and shaking Travis's foot.

"Damn, you know I hate that," yawned Travis, struggling to recover his captured foot and lashing out ineffectually at Tommy's grinning face with the other. "I swear, sometimes you're a bigger pain in the ass than Dad."

"If T. Rex were here, we'd be halfway up the trail by now," Tommy noted dryly. "How're you feeling?"

Travis gingerly tested the bridge of his nose, finding it still tender and swollen from the fight. "I'll live. Only hurts when I smile."

"You're gonna wind up with a nice shiner there, bro. Maybe two."

"Yeah," Travis mumbled glumly.

"Look at the bright side. I'll bet you're definitely in better shape than Cobb." Tommy rose and started across the campsite. "Come on, get up," he called back over his shoulder. "I've got water boiling for breakfast."

Reluctantly, Travis pushed to a sitting position. Although a hint of morning had just begun to illuminate the interior of the tent, he knew it would be hours before the sun crested the ridge behind them. Shivering, he wormed out from the warmth of his sleeping bag, then quickly donned his clothes and down jacket. Even in August, nights in the High Sierra routinely dropped well below freezing. Later that morning he'd be shedding layers; right now the extra insulation felt good.

Without leaving the tent, Travis reached outside and grabbed his boots, shaking them to clear anything that might have taken up residence during the night. As he pulled them on, he glanced across the campsite. Twenty feet away he could see Tommy kneeling beside the granite slab they'd set up as a cooking area the previous evening. He had both butane camp stoves going: one for coffee, the other heating a large pot of water for their customary trail breakfast of freeze-dried scrambled eggs, fruit, and oatmeal.

Unobserved, Travis remained in his quiet sanctuary for several minutes watching Tommy cook, feeling, for a fleeting moment, the familiar, hateful stab of resentment he'd held for his brother all his life. They'd both inherited their unruly red hair, an odious (to all four Kane siblings) genetic largess from their father, but the physical similarity between the two ended there. Like their father, Tommy possessed the natural grace, size, and physical presence of a born athlete—qualities that had earned him a football scholarship to the University of Arizona starting that fall. Tall and wiry, Travis had fallen heir to the fine bones and thin, artistic fingers of their mother. He'd never beaten Tommy at anything and had long ago resigned himself to living in the penumbra of his brother's accomplishments. Tommy played varsity football; Travis ran second-string track.

Whistling happily, Tommy dumped a generous portion of Tang into a plastic bottle, added water, shook it, and peered over at the tent. "Chow's on, cupcake," he growled in a credible burlesque of their father's autocratic bark.

"Now you're even talking like him," Travis grumbled as he

crawled from the tent. "I thought we came up here to get away from Dad."

"Right," Tommy laughed. "From what you told me, it sounds like he really topped himself on Friday. And when Mom found out about your fight . . . man, was I glad to get out of there."

"You weren't laughing at the time, Tom. You're lucky as hell to be leaving for college soon. I've still got another year to go."

"You'll survive. Especially with Mom always running interference for you."

"Fuck you. I don't need Mom to protect me."

"Come on, bro. I didn't mean it that way. Besides, Dad's usually not that bad."

"Yeah, he is." Travis poured himself a cup of coffee and took a sip, wincing at the bitter taste. "He is to me."

"Jeez, lighten up," said Tommy. "Let's just enjoy the trip and try to forget about everything at home." When Travis didn't reply, Tommy bolted the remainder of his breakfast in silence. Then, with a grunt, he jumped to his feet and began breaking camp.

Travis finished a few minutes later. After setting down his plate he gazed over thoughtfully at his brother, who by now had finished organizing his pack and moved on to filtering water for the canteens. "You realize he'd kill us if he knew we were climbing," he said, not letting it go.

Tommy turned and cracked his knuckles, shooting Travis a ferocious glare. "I gave you girls a direct order," he snapped in another startling rendition of their father. "No rock climbing till after Tom's first college season is over."

"He's worried you'll get hurt and blow the scholarship."

"Bull. Dad just wants to lead the climb himself."

"Maybe," said Travis, remembering their father's excitement when they'd first discovered the towering granite wall on a backpacking trip the previous summer. "But *whatever* his reasons, if he finds out—"

"How's he gonna find out? I'm sure not gonna tell him. Are you?"

"Shit, no. But Dad's a detective, and cops have a nasty habit of discovering things."

Tommy regarded Travis carefully. "Nobody else knows, right?"

"Well, uh . . ."

"Jesus, you told somebody? Who?"

"Arnie."

"You told Dad's partner? Damn! I don't believe this!"

"It just slipped out. He promised not to tell, and since we're here, he obviously hasn't," Travis pointed out. "Anyway, someone ought to know where we are in case something happens. Hell, we didn't even sign in with the ranger. Until the snow melts, the chances of anybody else trying to make it over the pass are pretty slim."

Tommy shook his head in disgust. "That's just great, Trav," he said angrily. "Good thinking."

"So maybe I screwed up," Travis retorted. "I still think—"

"Forget it," Tommy interrupted curtly. "What's done is done. Gimme a hand breaking camp."

"Hold on a sec. Nature calls." Irritated by Tommy's criticism, Travis tossed the dregs of his coffee, grabbed a wad of toilet paper, and headed for a copse of gnarled pines fifty yards above their campsite.

"Make it quick," Tommy yelled after him.

When he reached the trees, Travis dug a shallow trench in the soft detritus of needles and loam at their base. Still stinging from his brother's reproach, he dropped his trousers and squatted, spending several moments contemplating the placid surface of Franklin Lake far below. Although deep shadow still engulfed their camp, the snow-fields capping Tulare Peak across the water already glared in the morning sun, and as he watched, the demarcation between light and darkness began to creep down its chocolate-brown slopes, illuminating the peppering of sparse, twisted pines clinging to its flanks. Only the bright blue dome of their tent seemed alien in the otherwise pristine, beautiful surroundings.

A thousand feet above him lay the approach to the pass, with unbroken snow covering the trail for the final third of its serpentine ascent. Travis knew it would be a tough slog to reach the wall on Needleham Mountain they planned to climb, and he grudgingly had to admit that Tommy's eagerness to get moving made sense. Still, after finishing, he delayed returning to camp a few minutes more, breathing in the crisp Sierra morning and enjoying the harsh beauty of the high country.

As he looked down from his perch high on the ridge, he noticed that his brother had just withdrawn their tent's collapsible poles, causing it to deflate like a punctured beachball. Once it had fluttered to the ground, Tommy turned and scanned the slopes above. "You fall in or something?" his call echoed up.

"I'm coming," Travis called back.

It took him several minutes to make his way down. By then Tommy had the tent rolled and stowed, both sleeping bags stuffed, and the climbing rope lashed to his pack. "Damn," said Travis, shaking his head. "A couple more wipes, and you'd have had *everything* done."

"You're damn near right," Tommy sighed impatiently. He eyed the cook kit, which still needed cleaning from the morning's breakfast. "It's your turn to wash," he muttered. "C'mon, Trav. Let's get going."

• • •

When they set out twenty minutes later, Tommy quickly assumed his usual position well ahead. Since they'd been boys, each had always hiked at his own pace, with Tommy out front unless Dad was along—in which case *he'd* take the lead and neither brother would see him until the end of the day when he'd catcall them into camp, gleefully accusing them of being whiners and pussies and wimps. Nonetheless, this isolated hiking style suited Travis, who for most of the time on the trail had little energy left for chatter and found the rhythmic movement of steady walking a perfect background for introspection and daydreaming. Now, as he plodded along, his mind turned to a subject he'd found increasingly troubling as the summer had worn on: *the climb*.

Why did I let him talk me into it? he wondered for the hundredth time, angrily regretting his role in Tommy's typical rebellion against their father.

You know why, a perverse voice inside him whispered.

Travis picked up his pace, battling to ignore the voice within. *Tommy always has to play the big man—prove he's as good as Dad,* he thought resentfully. *Well, the hell with it. Why don't I just tell him to fuck off?*

You know why, the voice whispered again.

Oh, yeah? Why?

You don't want to admit to him that you're scared.

"Shut up," Travis said aloud. "That's not it at all."

Yeah, sure, the voice persisted. *The truth is Tommy tries to act like Dad and you try to act like Tom, and you know it. You also know you can't climb like him. He'll have to lead most of it, and if something goes wrong . . .*

·   ·   ·

Two hours later, after negotiating the summit snowfield by following in Tommy's posthole footprints, Travis joined his brother atop Franklin Pass, 11,250 feet above sea level. Momentarily forgetting his misgivings, he paused in silence on the Great Western Divide, gazing with awe into the heart of the High Sierra. Five hundred feet below he could see the trail emerging once again from its dazzling blanket of snow—winding down the rocky slope in a series of tortuous switchbacks to a runneled alpine meadow. Farther east the grassy fields surrendered to a dense forest of pine, beyond which lay a huge canyon, carved over millennia by the Kern River on its southward rush to Isabella Lake. And in the distance, rising silent and majestic into a sky as clear as diamond, stood the easternmost spine of the Sierra Nevada—the range's final cataclysmic upheaval before abruptly plunging ten thousand feet to the floor of the Owens Valley beyond.

Welcoming the break Travis shrugged off his pack and glanced over at Tommy, wondering whether he was still angry. "I'll bet you can see for a hundred miles," he ventured.

Tommy, who'd also shed his pack, turned from his own quiet inspection of the rugged wilderness below. "Yeah," he agreed happily, their argument apparently forgotten. "Speaking of miles," he added, "we've still got a few to go ourselves." Without awaiting a response, he shouldered his pack and started down the other side.

Just before noon, after fighting their way down the eastern snowfield and continuing north past Little Claire Lake, Tommy and Travis paused at the base of Needleham Mountain.

With a shiver of excitement Travis stared up at the peak's daunting southeast buttress, struck silent by the sheer size and scale of the granite wall before them. It rose more than eleven hundred feet from a chaos of shattered stone at its base, terminating in a broad shelf capped by a rocky outcrop. Although initially the face ascended moderately, it soon increased its pitch, turning vertical by the time it had risen a mere two hundred feet from the valley floor.

Thrilled in spite of himself, Travis studied the rock, trying to pick out the route they would climb. In the center of the wall, extending from the talus foot to within a hundred feet of the final shelf, a broad section had exfoliated over the centuries, peeling from the monolith in layers like the skin of an onion. The resulting loss had carved a giant overhanging arc, a monstrous roof looming eight hundred feet above. The right side of the wall encompassed a blank, soaring face of stone; on the left a tremendous dihedral—two flat, intersecting granite planes—formed its westernmost boundary, rising like an open book for several hundred feet to a large vertical slot. Above, after passing a huge chockstone jammed into the top, the slot gave way to a system of cracks running all the way to the summit shelf, beyond which the rock continued upward at a gentler pace—a fourth-class scramble—to Needleham's peak.

"Damn, it's a lot bigger'n I remembered," Tommy observed.

"It sure is," said Travis, still staring at the wall in amazement. "Want to bail?"

Tommy opened his pack and pulled out a Mineral King geologic survey map. "Nah. We can do it," he answered confidently. "This isn't much of a guidebook, but it's better than nothing," he added as he began comparing the rock's features to the lines on the quadrangle.

Travis quickly found himself unable to contain his growing apprehension. "Well? What do you think?" he demanded.

Tommy folded the map, smiling at his brother's nervousness. "Six pitches, maybe seven," he answered, squinting up the mammoth dihedral. "Nothing tougher than five-eleven, five-twelve at the most."

Travis felt his heart plummet. At one time the climbing community had allocated a 5.10 rating (on a scale ranging from 5.0 to 5.10) to the most difficult technical routes; since then limits had been pushed to 5.13 and beyond. Although Travis had followed Tommy and his father on a number of 5.12 climbs, he'd never led anything harder than 5.10.

"Here's the plan," Tommy continued, his eyes lighting with enthusiasm. "We ascend the dihedral to the slot, then climb the chimney to the cracks. From there we traverse right above the overhang and up. I'll lead the tough pitches; you take the easy ones."

"What easy ones?"

Tommy glanced at the sun, which by then had risen well into the morning sky. "Hell, there's bound to be at least one," he said with a smile. "Come on. If we don't want to spend the night up there, we'd better get humping."

Reluctantly, Travis dug his climbing shoes from his pack. He pulled them on and began tightening the flat nylon laces, watching as Tommy ordered the gear on the equipment rack—smallest stoppers first, larger hexagonal nuts next, finally the cam-shaped Flexible Friends—arranging the variously sized pieces of wire and metal that the lead climber would wedge into cracks for protection on the ascent. Next, after both boys had stepped into their sit-harnesses and fastened the thick protective belts around their waists, Travis passed Tommy a handful of climbing slings—lengths of nylon webbing tied in two-foot-diameter loops. As he started to close his pack, he noticed a pair of metal ascenders lying on the bottom. "Wanna take the Jumars?" he asked. Clipped to the line, the Jumars could be used to bypass a difficult section of rock, allowing one to move up the rope much as one climbs a ladder.

"What for? Think you won't be able to follow my leads?" Tommy snorted. "Leave 'em. I'll haul your ass up if I have to."

With a shrug, Travis closed his pack and leaned it against a boulder.

"Ready, bro?"

"Ready as I'll ever be," Travis lied, realizing it was too late to back out.

"Good. Let's do it."

With Tommy out front, they scrabbled over broken rock to the base of the dihedral. Once there, Travis uncoiled the fifty-meter line that would connect them until the end of the climb. Both boys tied in, and Tommy shrugged on the rack and slings. "This is gonna be great, bro," he said, grinning at Travis with unconcealed enthusiasm.

"Yeah," said Travis, attempting to return his smile.

By tacit agreement Tommy took the first lead.

As his brother moved to the base of the wall, Travis passed the rope around his back and wedged himself between two large slabs of granite. "Belay on," he said, his pulse quickening.

"Climbing," Tommy answered, slipping into a terse argot used by climbers to minimize the chances of a misunderstanding on the rock. He dipped his right hand into a bag of gymnastic chalk hanging from his sit-harness, then his left. Next he placed a foot in the crack that split the dihedral. Twisting it, he locked it in. His left hand followed, then the other foot. Alternately wedging his hands and feet ever higher, he started up the vertical face.

Ready to catch him should he fall, Travis slowly paid out the rope, watching as his brother ascended.

Using an aggressive, gymnastic style of climbing, Tommy powered through the first pitch, or rope length, placing a protective nut every twenty feet or so and clipping the line to each. Twenty-five minutes from the time he began, following a strenuous series of moves 140 feet up the dihedral, he anchored himself in. Hanging in his harness, he then belayed up his brother—pulling in slack line to ensure that if Travis slipped on the way up, he wouldn't go far.

"Man, my lats are cooked," Tommy announced cheerfully when Travis reached his airy position a good forty minutes later. "Wanna take the next lead?"

His breath coming fast, his limbs shaking with both excitement and exhaustion, Travis clipped himself to Tommy's anchor, then passed over the protective pieces he'd removed on the way up. For him the first part of the dihedral had proved extremely difficult. Several times he'd been forced to resort to dynamic lunges and risky swings for the next hold, attempting heart-stopping moves he would never have considered had he not been roped from above. Once, had he been leading, the climb would have ended right there—and the next section appeared even more treacherous. "I'll pass," he said, paradoxically both proud and terrified that he'd somehow managed to complete the first pitch.

"You sure?" Tommy chuckled, amused by his brother's reluctance.

"Yeah. I'm sure."

After a short rest Tommy led the second pitch, and then the third—his moves a study of technique and strength that bordered on physical poetry—ascending without incident to the large slot at the top of the dihedral. Although from there the following pitch up the chimney eased somewhat in difficulty, it presented little opportunity for the leader to place protective pieces.

Again Travis gave Tommy the lead.

By now their climbing had assumed a smooth, easy rhythm dictated by the rock, and as Travis belayed his brother from below, he finally felt himself beginning to relax. Shortly after Tommy disappeared over an outcrop, he let his eyes roam the valley, employing his sense of feel to maintain proper tension on the rope.

Suddenly he heard Tommy shout down from above. "Tension!"

Travis's mouth went dry. He tightened the rope around his waist and leaned out, attempting to spot his brother. "What's happening?" he yelled up the face.

"I . . . I can't . . . oh, shit. Get ready, Trav."

Travis's heart began slamming in his chest. He still couldn't see his brother. "Tom? What's going—"

"Falling!"

A split second later the rope snapped tight around Travis's waist. Several feet hissed around his back and through his hands before he managed to clamp down and stop Tommy's fall. Face slick with sweat, he stared up the taut line. "Tom?"

Nothing.

"Tommy?" he yelled again, close to panic. "Are you okay?"

"Yeah. No problem," his brother's casual reply floated down.

Travis leaned out even farther, straining to see past the outcrop. *There! Ninety feet up, dangling at the end of the rope below his last protective piece. Thank God it held.* "What happened?" he shouted.

"I fucked up, bro. I paid for it, too."

Heart still racing, Travis held the rope fast, watching as Tommy struggled to regain the rock. The fall had swung him out of position, and he had to strain to get his hands and feet back on opposite walls of the chimney.

"Okay," Tommy called down seconds later. "Slack."

Nervously, Travis eased tension on the rope.

A pause. Then Tommy's voice again. "Climbing."

Business as usual . . . for Tommy.

A little over three hours into the climb, Travis joined his brother in a tiny cave at the top of the slot, just beneath the large chockstone they'd noticed from the ground. Seeming tiny and insignificant, their packs lay at the base of the talus far below, while across the valley a thicket of clouds billowed majestically into the afternoon, casting a curious patchwork of dark and shifting shadows on the eastern reaches of the Sierras.

"Nice lead," said Travis, clipping himself to Tommy's anchor.

Tommy nodded. "Thanks, bro. That fall I took got the old adrenaline pumping, though."

"No argument there," agreed Travis. "I may have to change my skivvies when we get down," he added, attempting a smile.

Tommy grinned back. "Me, too. You think things were hairy on your end of the rope, you should've seen it from mine."

"No, thanks."

The brothers rested there, talking quietly and taking in the view. Then, all too soon to suit Travis, Tommy decided it was again time to move. But instead of taking the lead as he had before, he slipped off the equipment rack. "Last chance, Trav," he said, offering it to his brother. "After this one it's a scramble to the top, then a walk off the back."

Travis hesitated. Despite the difficulties he'd experienced during the early pitches and the unsettling memory of Tommy's fall, as the climb had progressed, he'd felt his fears gradually being eroded by a growing sense of confidence and accomplishment. Presented now with the prospect of leading the final pitch, his terror came flooding back, stronger and more pervasive than ever.

"Come on, bro," Tommy prodded gently. "You can do it."

"Guess I can't let you do all the work," Travis mumbled, wishing he could refuse but knowing he couldn't. Trying to keep his hands from shaking, he took the rack.

He spent several moments nervously arranging the equipment, sorting slings, and replacing the pieces he'd cleaned on the preceding pitch. Next he dipped his hands into his chalk bag, finding, to his embarrassment, that he had to dust them twice to dry his sweaty palms. At last, filled with a presentiment of disaster, he leaned out, placed a large stopper in a crack above his head, and clipped in the rope. He looked down. The wall fell away in a sickening plunge to the jagged rocks far below.

"On belay?" he said, hoping Tommy didn't catch the tremor in his voice.

Tommy passed the rope around his back. After checking the anchor to make sure it would take an upward tug, he braced himself in the cave. "Belay on."

Travis took one last look down, regretting it immediately. Then a deep breath. "Climbing," he said.

Trembling with anticipation and exhilaration and fear—the rock cold and unforgiving beneath his hands—Travis edged out over the void.

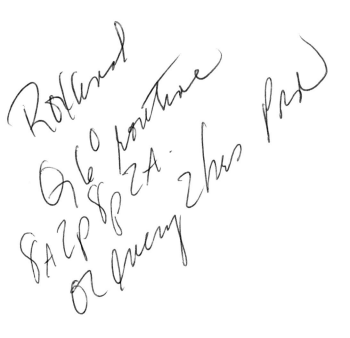

Cod Fillets with

Atlantic cod loin seasoned and baked top

Sid

Wild Ric

Lightly seasone

Sauteed Asp

Sauteed in butter and

Des

Cherry

Gluten free & Sugar fre

PART ONE

1

E arlier that year, on the final Friday of spring, Detective Daniel
Kane arose well before dawn. Without waking his wife,
Catheryn, he slipped out of bed, pulled on a tank top and a pair
of swimming trunks, and quietly descended worn wooden stairs
to the beach-level deck below his house. There he began his morning
ritual of exercise, working out for fifty minutes without pause—gradually pushing the limits of his six-foot-three, 220-pound frame. By
the time a faint palette of reds and oranges and yellows in the sky over
Santa Monica to the east heralded the birth of a new day, he'd completed a rigorous regimen of sit-ups, push-ups, bar chins, and dips,
and a sheen of sweat covered his body as he faced the dawn.

Feeling his breathing slowing and his blood-thickened muscles beginning to relax, Kane glanced back at the house, checking to see if
anyone else had gotten up. Although disappointed no lights were yet
burning, he smiled as he inspected the structure that had been his
home for the past eighteen years.

Viewed from the deck, it seemed an organic part of its environment, with towering palms flanking both sides, flowering bougainvil-
lea draping a large section of roof and upper balcony, and lush beds
of ice plant and aloe anchoring its failing foundation to the sand.

Built in the early thirties, the ancient house sat on a small Malibu cove guarding the mouth of Las Flores Canyon, located along the northernmost crescent of the Santa Monica Bay. Catheryn's mother, who'd spent most of her childhood summers there in the late thirties, had inherited the old cottage and subsequently bestowed it on her daughter and Kane as a wedding present.

Over the years the ramshackle structure had metamorphosed to accommodate their growing family, with a porch enclosed as a nursery for Tommy, rooms later added for Travis and Allison, and the defunct cistern platform atop the roof converted to a "tree house" bedroom for Nate, the youngest. And despite its scars and imperfections—termite-ridden beams, sadly sagging rafters, antiquated plumbing and wiring, and countless bootlegged additions and temporary fixes that time had lent the air of permanence—the old house was a living, if dilapidated, monument to Kane's family, embodying years of growth and change forever entangled in the milestones of their lives.

As Kane stood enjoying the first weak rays of the sun, he spotted seven Mexican brown pelicans moving in silent unison over the ocean, skimming the water in a loose V and lifting effortlessly on currents of air gusting off the waves. He followed their progress down the beach, noting that the Santa Ana winds from the desert had already begun picking up, delaying the transparent green walls of water on their march to the shore and whipping magnificent plumes of spray seaward from their paper-thin crests. The intermittent breeze felt warm and alive on his skin, vibrant as an animal's breath. It gusted briefly, stopped, then began again, bringing with it the smell of sage and the promise of another sizzling, smogless day. The press of traffic driving south into the city would increase later on; for now the intermittent sound of Pacific Coast Highway, hidden behind the single row of houses lining the beach, was barely audible, and the morning belonged to the gulls and pelicans and terns, an occasional dog padding up the clean slate of sand left by a receding tide, and Kane.

A moment later Tar, his white-muzzled Labrador retriever, scrabbled slowly down the stairs onto the deck. " 'Morning, pup," Kane greeted him when he arrived, regretfully noticing that the old dog's arthritic gait seemed to be getting worse. "Feel like a swim?"

As if to say, "No, thanks," Tar thumped his tail and sat, following with his eyes as Kane started for the beach. When his master reached the seawall, the old dog groaned in resignation and hobbled after him. Though the sand on the other side lay only a few feet down, Kane carefully lifted him over. Then, leaving him there, he retreated to the deck, returning shortly carrying a pair of swim goggles and a small buoy tied to a coiled length of polypropylene line.

Tar followed him to the ocean's edge but refused to go in. "Come on, boy. It'll loosen you up," Kane coaxed.

Again Tar balked.

Finally giving up, Kane waded into the water, glancing back at the shoreline once he'd made it past the break of a three-foot swell. Tar's black shape still sat outlined against the sand, his golden eyes watching wistfully.

Although by then the air temperature had already risen to the midseventies, the water surging around Kane's torso felt as cold as January in Idaho. Shivering, he spit into his goggles, slipped them on, and dived under the next wave. A dozen powerful strokes carried him past the shoreline turbulence, and before long he could make out broad fields of kelp covering intermittent rocky shoals twenty feet down, the sand in between rippled to a washboard appearance by the onshore currents. With the end of the buoy rope looped over his shoulder, he continued on, warming up a bit by the time he reached a point about two hundred yards from the beach. There, treading water, he adjusted his position by aligning land-side reference points, preparing to initiate his search.

The depth had now increased to over thirty-five feet. Satisfied with his position, Kane took a deep breath and dived, descending through the cool green water. He cleared his ears halfway to the bottom, then leveled off and began working his way up-current, his eyes studying the silent world beneath. Oblique shafts of sunlight filtered down from above, shifting with the undulating surface and seeming to dance with the swaying kelp and sea grass on the ocean floor below. As he passed overhead, Kane spotted a bright-orange garibaldi darting for the protection of a rocky crevice, while a school of torpedo-shaped calico bass, curious about the intruder in their midst, watched from a safe distance with cold, predatory eyes.

Kane continued to work the area for the next twenty minutes, searching in a grid pattern and taking bearings each time he rose to the surface. At last, after numerous dives, he saw it: the wheel.

Four feet in diameter and weighing over five hundred pounds, the gigantic chunk of iron lay in forty feet of water, its lower third covered with sand, the central hole serendipitously still accessible. Kane hovered a body's length above it, inspecting the rusty remnant. He supposed the old train wheel—scrap from a long-forgotten railroad spur that years ago had run up the coast—had once been used for some erstwhile mooring. Whatever its provenance, he knew it would provide a massive, unyielding anchor for a project he'd been planning a number of years.

All right, he thought, descending the final distance and running a hand over the surface. *Now, for the hard part.*

Grinning with excitement, Kane rose to the surface, took several breaths, then dived again and attempted to thread the buoy rope through the wheel's axle hole. He found the passage blocked with sand. Three dives later he still hadn't secured the line, for each time he rose, the surge refilled the hole—replacing the sand he'd laboriously scooped out on the previous attempt. Finally staying down until he thought his lungs would burst, he managed to clear the opening. Realizing he was quickly running out of time, he raced to jam through the buoy rope.

Come on, come on . . .

As a red haze began to dim his vision, he got it through. Forcing himself to stay down a few more agonizing seconds, he tied it off with cold-thickened fingers. Then, blood pounding in his ears, he kicked with all his strength for the surface, taking an explosive, gasping breath as he burst again into the morning sunlight.

Rising and falling on the incoming swells, Kane rested briefly. After he'd caught his breath, he set off once more for shore, hammering through wind and current on the return trip. When he finally stepped from the water, he found Tar still waiting for him on the sand, faithfully maintaining his solitary vigil.

•　　•　　•

Following a cold shower on the outside deck, Kane toweled himself dry and entered the house. He smiled as he mounted the stairs, considering how best to rouse his sleeping children. "Reveille, troops," he bellowed upon reaching the top landing, choosing an old standby. "Everybody on the deck for lineup in ten minutes!"

Silence. Then a plaintive cry from Nate's loft above the entry: "Dad, it's hardly light out yet."

"Ten minutes, kid," Kane warned. "And just in case you're thinking about catchin' some extra winks, don't think I won't climb up there," he added with a chuckle. "Oh, by the way . . . happy birthday."

Next he strode to his fifteen-year-old daughter Allison's room and pounded on her door. "Up and at 'em, petunia. Let's go!" Without awaiting a response he immediately moved to Tommy and Travis's room, throwing open their door and flipping on the light. "That goes for you two debutantes, too."

"C'mon, Dad," Tommy mumbled sleepily. "This is supposed to be summer vacation."

"Tough. I want every skinny butt out on the deck in nine minutes."

"Does that go for Mom's skinny butt too?" Allison called innocently from the safety of her bedroom.

"Don't push it, Allison. I may not be around much for the next couple days, and there're a few things I want to discuss with you kids before I leave. You now have eight and a half minutes."

With that, Kane turned crisply on his heel and retreated into the house. Shortly afterward the children heard the sound of Charlie Daniels blasting from the living room, followed by the dark, earthy aroma of brewing coffee. Resentfully, they started to dress.

By the time they reached the deck, Kane had changed to his work clothes: white shirt and tie, slacks, and a nine-millimeter Beretta automatic holstered on his right hip. He had his sleeves rolled up, exposing a thicket of curly red hair covering his massive forearms, and was standing with his back to the house, staring at the waves and sipping a steaming mug of coffee. Allison moved quietly to a swing suspended from the upper balcony. Nate joined her. Travis sat on the steps leading into the house; Tommy remained standing. Tar, the last one out, limped across the deck, glanced up at Nate, and sank down beside the swing.

Kane took his time draining the last of his coffee. Then, clearing his throat, he turned and regarded his children, fixing them in his gaze to impress upon each the importance of his intended communication. "Okay, rookies, listen up," he began, satisfied he'd secured their undivided attention. "I can see you're wondering why the ol' dad here's decided to schedule a little quality time with the squad this morning, so I won't keep you in the dark any longer. There're a couple reasons, but let's get the hard one out of the way first. Lately I've been tied up at work more than I'd like, and unable to provide adequate paternal supervision—especially considering how much free time you've all got on your hands. That's gonna change."

"Oh, thank goodness," Allison groaned.

Cracking his knuckles, Kane glared at her, then continued. "First off, if you think this summer's gonna be a time of lying around munchin' bonbons and improving your tans, you're mistaken."

"Aw, Dad," Tommy complained. "Why can't we just—"

"Tom, when school let out, I gave you two weeks to find a job," Kane interrupted. "There's been no progress whatsoever in that department, has there?"

"Uh, no, sir."

Kane scowled. "I thought not. If there's one thing I hate, it's seeing people fartin' their lives away, especially if those people happen to be Kanes. Now, the way I look at it, every second of so-called vacation time not spent sleeping, eating, or crappin' should be devoted to bettering yourselves, policing the premises, helping your mother, and earning money for college. Does anyone have a bitch with this?"

Sensing their father's seriousness, the children shook their heads.

"Speak up!"

"No, sir!" they answered as one.

"Good. You, Tom," Kane continued, again addressing his oldest, "probably think you're hot stuff 'cause you got a football scholarship to the University of Arizona. Now I'll admit playing for the Wildcats ain't bad, but with your talent you coulda made any college team in the country. Why didn't you? I'll tell you why. It's because you never made the decision to totally commit. As usual, you just sailed along doing barely enough to stay ahead of the game. Now you figure to cruise through the summer—lay back till you leave, surf a little, do some rock climbing. Am I right?"

"No, sir," Tommy responded.

"What, then?"

"He was planning on spending the summer chewing the buttons off Christy's blouse," Allison spoke up.

"Quiet, Allison. Tom, since you've obviously failed to come up with some constructive summer endeavor, I've taken the liberty of getting you a job myself."

"But, Dad—"

"No buts. Tony Stewart, an old buddy of mine from the department, is in the contracting business now. He's framing a bunch of houses up by Paradise Cove. You start Monday morning at seven. If I can, I'll drop you off on my way to work. Otherwise, your mom will take you." Kane shifted his gaze to Travis. "You're gonna be working there too, kid," he added.

"What about piano practice?" Travis asked. "This summer Mom wants me to—"

"Do it afterward. A little job experience won't hurt you. Hell, it'll probably get you a lot further in life than ticklin' the ivories. Is this gonna be a problem?"

"Well, I . . ."

"Is it?"

"No, sir."

"Good." Kane turned toward his youngest. "Nate, have you been giving Tar his pills like you're supposed to?" he demanded, referring to the Butazolidin tablets the vet had prescribed for the dog's arthritis.

"I . . . I forgot yesterday," said Nate, his cheeks flushing to nearly the color of his curly red hair.

"You've been forgetting more than yesterday. That's the kinda attitude I'm talking about here. That damn mutt could barely walk this morning."

"I won't forget anymore," Nate promised.

"You'd better not," said Kane. Then, to his daughter, "Allison, you've been dying to shoot off your mouth, so here's your chance. What's your plan for the summer?"

"Well, Pop, now that I hear what you've got lined up for the boys, I think I'd like to bend nails, too. You know, hang out on the job and drive all those sweaty young carpenters wild . . ."

"Make 'em puke's more like it," snickered Nate.

"Shut up, flea, before I accidentally step on you."

"Both of you shut your yaps or I'm gonna shut 'em for you," Kane ordered. "Allison, since you and Nate are too young to hold down jobs, your duty's gonna be to assist your mother in any activity she designates. In addition, I want you both to police the beach daily—all the way down to the water. That means bottles, Styrofoam, tar, seaweed, dog turds, and dead surfers. If it ain't sand, I don't wanna see it. We've got the Fourth of July party comin' up in two weeks, and I'm gonna be checking. Which reminds me—all of you start collecting driftwood for a bonfire. After the fireworks show we're gonna put together a blaze that'll give those peckerwoods in Santa Monica something to talk about." Kane paused, mentally reviewing his points. Satisfied he'd left nothing out, he said, "Okay, that's the duty roster for the summer. Any questions?"

Tommy shifted uneasily. "What about climbing? Trav and I were figuring . . . I mean, we have that trip planned to Mineral King before I leave for Arizona, and—"

"Negative. I already told you. Climbing's out."

"C'mon, Dad, that's not fair. Last summer you said we could do that wall on Needleham Mountain."

"That was before you got your slot on the U of A football squad. You wanna do some bouldering or a few easy scrambles out at Joshua Tree or Idyllwild, fine. But that's it. I can't chance your getting injured before the season starts."

"The trip's off?" asked Travis.

"The climbing part, anyway. If we go, it'll be to backpack only."

Tommy shook his head stubbornly. "Dad, you said—"

"Is that understood?"

"Aw, Dad . . ."

"Tom, is that understood?"

Tommy nodded reluctantly. "No climbing."

Kane paused again, standing with his hands clasped behind his back. "Nobody else wants to whine? Good, 'cause I've got a couple more points. But first, let me ask you all a question: What's the most important thing about being a Kane?"

The children's response was automatic. "Kanes stand together, no matter what."

"Right. So when it comes to this summer's assignments, if one of you screws up, you're all in trouble—no matter what. Tom, you being the oldest, I expect you to make sure there's no slacking off in my absence."

"Thanks for the vote of confidence," said Tommy dryly. "I'll do my best to fill your size thirteens."

"You do that," Kane muttered. He started to say something more, then stopped, glancing up as a window opened on the second floor.

"Dan, Arnie's here," Catheryn's voice floated down. "He says to come on up when you're done haranguing the children. I can get breakfast going if you have time."

Kane glanced at his watch. "Tell him I'll be right there, Kate," he yelled back. "But hold off on the grub. We'll grab something on the road."

"You sure? I don't mind."

"Yeah, I'm sure," Kane answered. Then, turning back to his children, he quickly concluded his talk. "Now, the last thing I want to cover this morning is asking you to join me in wishing your brother Nate here congratulations on his birthday," he said, placing his hand on his youngest's shoulder. "He turns nine today, and as this is his last year in the single digits, I want you all to show him special consideration. That includes you, Allison."

"Special consideration?" moaned Allison, clutching her throat. "Anything but that."

Ignoring his daughter's theatrics, Kane lowered his voice and spoke directly to Nate. "This investigation I'm on right now is keeping me pretty busy," he said softly. "I'll try, but there's a good chance I won't be attending your party tonight, so I'll say it now, just in case. Happy birthday, kid. With a little luck I may be off tomorrow, and if so, I've got something special planned. Keep the day open just in case, all right?"

"Okay, Dad."

"That goes for the rest of you, too," Kane added, turning back to the others. "Any more questions? No? Then get moving."

2

By nine that morning, although the Santa Ana winds were just beginning their adiabatic slide to the sea in earnest, the temperature had already risen into the nineties. Since the beginning of the week, searing gusts from the desert had been rocketing the mercury to triple digits and sending waves of shimmering, super-heated air rising from the pavement—baking the streets and denizens of Los Angeles alike into a torpor. Not surprisingly, the effect on the population had followed classic and predictable trends. Like similar winds throughout the world—the Mediterranean sirocco, the chinooks of the eastern Rockies, and Africa's dust-laden, suffocating simoom—the Santa Anas blasting across southern California had sent the murder rate in the City of Angels soaring.

Parked on a side street off Pico Boulevard, Kane sat in a dun-colored Chevy Impala, jammed uncomfortably behind the wheel. He stared through a pair of Bushnell seven-by-fifty binoculars, ignoring a salty trickle inching down his face. Briefly taking his gaze from the third-floor apartment down the street, he wiped his eyes, then resumed his watch. His partner, Arnie Mercer, shifted miserably in the seat beside him.

"Looks like today's gonna be another hot one," Kane noted. "Least nothin's on fire this time."

"That's 'cause everything burned the last time around," Arnie observed. "Who gives a fuck, anyway? This whole pus-bag dung-heap of a city could burn clean to the fuckin' ground and nobody'd give a shit, including me."

Kane grinned and lowered the binoculars, glancing over at the stocky man who'd been his training officer when he'd first graduated from the Los Angeles Police Academy, his partner when he'd made detective four years later, and his D-III supervisor for most of the time he'd spent on the homicide unit after that. "Jeez, don't hold anything back, amigo," he said. "Lemme know how you *really* feel."

"I just did," Arnie muttered, reaching for the radio. He paused, studying the four-story apartment down the block. "Anything?"

Kane raised the binoculars and trained them on a corner window three levels up. Through the dusty glass he could make out vague shapes in the room beyond: a floor lamp, a couch, a tacky picture of a sad-eyed clown. No movement. Next he focused on the maroon Ford parked at the other end of the street. Special Agents Tinley and Marcus. After watching the FBI operatives a few seconds, he shifted his gaze back to the apartment. "Know what the three most overrated things in the world are?" he asked.

"What?"

"Home cooking, home fucking, and the FBI."

Arnie smiled, his eyes still on the apartment. "Good one, old buddy. I'll be sure to pass that on to Kate when I see her."

Despite Kane's attempt at humor, both men knew his joke hit disturbingly close to the truth. Ever since the FBI had muscled in on the murder/kidnapping that Kane and Mercer were presently investigating, things had gone down the bureaucratic drain. Not that they had started off all that well to begin with.

Anatomy of an investigation gone awry: On Tuesday afternoon what had apparently begun as a simple mugging on San Vicente Boulevard had turned into murder when Mrs. Agnes Sellers, while struggling with three men wearing ski masks, fell and struck her head on the curb in front of the Tiny Tots Day Care Center. As Mrs. Sellers lay in the gutter dying of a cerebral hemorrhage, the men grabbed a small boy who'd been with her and fled in a late-model van, that various witnesses subsequently described as gray, light blue, orange, and tan. The first policeman there, Officer William Patterson, called the West L.A. homicide unit, and twenty minutes later Kane arrived on the scene.

Standard so far, but the seeds of what would soon become, as known in departmental jargon, a classic clusterfuck had already been sown. When the deceased Mrs. Sellers—a nanny in the home of T. J. Bradley, the senior Republican senator from California—failed to return home with eight-year-old Timothy Bradley II, the mugging turned murder became murder/kidnapping.

Senator Bradley caught the first shuttle back from D.C. Although the LAPD had jurisdiction over both the murder and the abduction, Senator Bradley insisted that the FBI be brought in on the kidnapping portion of the case. Then, to make matters worse, someone in the mayor's office leaked the story to the press, and by late afternoon the street outside the West L.A. Division on Butler Avenue resembled a media circus, with a host of network news crews doing simultaneous, side-by-side stand-ups outside the station.

That evening a ransom demand for two million dollars came in on the Bradleys' unlisted home phone. An LAPD tap on the line traced the call to a telephone switching station in Nevada, at which point—citing a technicality involving jurisdiction over state lines—the FBI assumed control of the kidnapping phase of the investigation. Even though the murder portion of the case remained his, Kane suddenly found Bureau agents Tinley and Marcus accompanying his team as observers.

Suspecting the kidnapping had been an inside job, Kane ran checks of everyone close to the family. A number of possibilities turned up, including Sylvia Martin, the Bradleys' maid. Ms. Martin, currently on probation, had served three years for burglary at CIW, the California Department of Corrections' Institute for Women at Corona. Kane also learned she had a common-law husband, Paul Escobar, whose rap sheet ranged from car theft to armed robbery. When interviewed, Ms. Martin denied having seen Escobar for months. But something—a hunch, an indefinable sixth sense Kane had developed over the years—told him she was lying.

Meanwhile, the FBI set up a ransom exchange. Following piecemeal instructions left in phone booths across the city, they placed the money in the trunk of a car that was to be driven to a Century City office tower, then left to be valet-parked in the building's subterranean garage. Unfortunately, a Beverly Hills cop inadvertently stopped the ransom vehicle for a traffic violation a mere two blocks from its destination. Seeing this, the abductors, who'd apparently been tracking the car's progress, decided to abort.

As the Bureau scrambled for a new toehold on the case, Kane took a different tack. Reasoning the kidnappers must have concocted a plan, however unlikely, for removing the money from the building without being caught, he examined every point of egress. Nothing. Then it hit him. The kidnappers didn't have to leave with the money right away—all they had to do was stash it somewhere in the building, then collect it at a later time. *But where to leave it?* The answer turned out to be laughably obvious: The First Regional Bank occupied the entire first floor.

Kane checked all safety-deposit boxes that had been opened at the bank during the previous two months. One renter's name jumped out: Ramon Estrada. The address and social-security number he'd given proved fictitious, and a clerk at the bank—when shown a picture of Paul Escobar, Sylvia Martin's common-law husband—identified him as the man who'd opened the account. Since then, lacking an address for Escobar, Kane's team had been running a twenty-four-hour surveillance on Ms. Martin's apartment. To date the stakeout had proved fruitless. Now, as they watched for the second sweltering day in a row, Kane was beginning to wonder whether he'd made a mistake.

"They got another ransom call last night," Arnie said, still squinting down the block. "It's supposed to go down later today."

"Uh-huh. Think the kid's still alive?"

"Do you?"

"It's been three days."

"Meaning?"

"Meaning I don't know, Arnie. This stakeout's a long shot, but right now it's the best we've got. Let's just hope Escobar shows up and something comes of it."

Arnie spoke into his handset. "Deluca, you got anything?"

Detective Paul Deluca was stationed in a storefront across from the

Martin apartment. He had a parabolic microphone trained on the third-floor window. "She's up. I just heard the toilet flush."

"Banowski, how 'bout you?"

John Banowski, the final member of the team, had taken a position in an alley behind the building. "Nothin'."

Arnie grunted and tossed the handset onto the seat, then reached for a large metal thermos at his feet. He filled a paper cup with coffee, handed it to Kane, then poured another for himself. Kane pointedly looked away as Arnie withdrew a small flask from the glove compartment and fortified his drink. An uncomfortable silence followed as both men continued to study the building.

Before long stakeout boredom set in once more. "Remember when you thought your life was going to amount to something?" Arnie grumbled.

"Yeah," chuckled Kane. "Thank God those days are over."

"Least you've got your family."

"For now. Tommy's taking off for Arizona at the end of August. I'll tell you, if the kid plays like he did his final two varsity seasons— Santa Monica High went undefeated this year, eight and one last year—he's gonna set the Pac-Ten on its ear. Did you know he got voted All Western Offensive End by the *Times*?"

Arnie grinned. "I know, I know. You already told me at least thirty-five fuckin' times. What's new with Allison and Nate?"

"About the same. Far as I'm concerned, Allison's grounded till the next century for that safe-sex parody she wrote in her school paper."

"You have to admit it was well written."

"That's no excuse. Considering she's the smartest one of the bunch, she sure manages to screw up. And lately all she seems to care about is reading those god-awful science-fiction stories she's got stacked in her room. She's even writing 'em now, if you can believe that."

"Are they any good?"

Kane shrugged. "Who knows? Now, as for Nate—there's hope for that one. He's a tough little bastard."

"Yeah, he sure is," Arnie agreed. "By the way, I caught some of your pep talk to the kids this morning. You got Tommy and Travis jobs?"

"Uh-huh. Workin' construction with Tony. It ought to do 'em some good. *Especially* Travis. Kate's got him all turned around with her music shit and whatnot. By God, that's gonna change."

"Have you listened to Travis play lately, old buddy? He's—"

"Yeah, yeah, he's good. So what? That and a buck'll get him a cup of coffee."

Arnie shook his head. "Now, don't take this wrong, Dan, but did it ever occur to you that maybe you're a mite hard on your kids?"

"Hell, no," said Kane. "We both know the world's an unforgiving place, and gettin' nastier all the time. I want that bunch ready for what they're gonna find when they get out here, and if I've gotta boot their tails to toughen 'em up, then that's what I'm gonna do."

"You've never had a neurotic need to be loved," Arnie noted with a grin.

"True," said Kane. "But I'll let you in on a secret, partner, just so's you don't get the wrong idea. I may grouse about 'em from time to time, but I'd stack up those kids of mine against any bunch you wanna name. If anything ever happened to one of them . . ." Kane paused, running his fingers through his hair. "I know I can't protect 'em forever," he said finally. "But I'd step in front of a bullet for any of them without hesitation, and that's the God's truth."

"Aw, hell, Dan. I know what you're trying to say. I love 'em, too. I'm their godfather, remember? I'm just saying it wouldn't hurt to let them know once in a . . . Hold on. What have we here?"

Kane and Arnie watched as a battered Plymouth pulled to the curb in front of the apartment down the street.

Kane raised his binoculars as two men stepped out. The driver was a heavyset Hispanic around six feet tall with long black hair and a mustache. The other, an Anglo, stood at least a head taller and carried a heavy coat slung over his right arm. "Pay dirt, Arnie. The driver's Escobar. I don't recognize the other guy. And what's with the coat?"

Arnie grabbed the handset. "Everybody sit tight. Deluca, start recording. Whatever happens in that apartment when they get there—I want it on tape. Banowski, be ready to roll. If they decide to leave, we'll maintain a three-car surveillance and see where they take us. And make sure that . . . What the fuck?"

Kane and Arnie stared in amazement as Special Agents Marcus and Tinley's maroon Ford executed a screeching U-turn and roared down the block, squealing to a stop inches from the suspects' bumper. Kane slammed his hand against the steering wheel. "Shit! They must've been listening in on our tac frequency."

Marcus jumped from the passenger side, FBI identification in one hand and service revolver in the other. Just as he started his routine, the front door of the apartment building opened and a young Chicano couple stepped arm in arm to the street. The kid was wearing a Dodgers jacket; his girlfriend had on a Grateful Dead T-shirt and an impossibly abbreviated pair of cutoff jeans. Tinley, who'd exited the other side of the car, attempted to signal them back inside. Without warning the coat covering the tall suspect's hand began to jump and shudder, as if some invisible force were sundering it from within.

An instant later Kane heard the unmistakable staccato of automatic-weapon fire echoing down the street.

•   •   •

"Mom . . . Allison called me a baby."

With a sigh, Catheryn Kane stopped outside the artists' entrance to the Dorothy Chandler Pavilion and set her cello case on the sidewalk. Tall and graceful, with a full, passionate mouth and a determined set to her jaw, she was an uncommonly beautiful woman of thirty-eight. Her skin was smooth and clear, except for a tiny fretwork of lines that radiated from the corners of her startling green eyes, and her long auburn hair, just beginning to show a rare trace of gray, fell to her shoulders in thick, luxuriant folds. "Allison?" she said, turning to regard her daughter. "Is that true?"

"Not exactly," Allison answered with a sanctimonious shrug. "I merely noted it might be time for him to change his diapers."

Nate glowered at his older sister with all the belligerence a nine-year-old boy could muster. "It might be time for you to get a close-up view of my fist," he warned.

"Hush, you two," said Catheryn. "I know it's hot, but squabbling isn't going to make things any better. You both know what this audition means to me. You said you wanted to come, and I expect you to behave."

"I will if the midget-sized booger factory will."

"Allison," said Catheryn sternly. "Enough."

"Okay, okay," said Allison, sensing the approach of a threshold in her mother's patience.

"This is a closed audition," Catheryn reminded them, again picking up her cello. "You're not even supposed to be here, so I certainly don't want you drawing attention to yourselves by quarreling. Now, let's go in. And no more fighting."

Catheryn led her children into the Pavilion through a pair of street-level doors on North Grand, instructing them to wait for her by the elevator while she stopped to register at the desk. Several times, as she waited for the guard to find her name on the audition list, she glanced across the room to find them, making sure they were staying out of trouble. As had all the Kane children, they'd both inherited their father's mercurial temperament, along with his unmanageably thick, wavy red hair. Compact and sturdy, with a smattering of freckles traversing the bridge of his nose and the curliest locks of the clan, Nate most reminded her of Kane, even though he'd yet to experience the explosive growth of adolescence. Allison, on the other hand, had turned fifteen that April and already embarked on an uneven rush toward maturity. Her arms and legs, graceless and gangly as a foal's, seemed too long for her torso, her sinewy chest more suited to a boy. As usual, she was dressed in a protective shell of loose, baggy clothing, her untamable mass of rust-colored hair hidden beneath a floppy-brimmed hat. Her face was freckled and plain, but behind her self-conscious smile, frequent and mischievous, lay an indomitable feistiness that warmed Catheryn's heart.

Once she'd finished registering, Catheryn joined them by the elevator. When she arrived, Allison asked, "What do you think Dad'll say when you tell him you're going to play with the Philharmonic?"

"He'll be mad you didn't tell, that's for sure," Nate piped up, smacking his small fist into his palm.

"Not necessarily. And this is just an audition," said Catheryn, nervously brushing a wisp of hair from her face. "I haven't got the position yet. If I'm lucky enough to be selected, we'll cross that bridge when we come to it. Anyway, it's only for thirteen weeks."

Allison glanced through an open door into the performers' lounge, noticing the large number of cellists already there. Several more had already lined up at the registration desk. "I thought this was just a fill-in job while your friend Adele has her baby. Seems like an awful lot of people trying for the spot."

"Playing with the Philharmonic is a great honor," said Catheryn, a trace of dismay in her voice as she too noticed the surprising number of musicians present. "I guess a lot of people want it."

The elevator door chimed open. All three entered, exiting one floor up into a busy area behind the main stage. After a short search Catheryn spotted Adele Washington, a loquacious young African-American in her early thirties. "Kate! Where have you been?" Adele called, hurrying toward them. "Cutting it close, aren't you?"

"Hi, Adele. Traffic was terrible on the Santa Monica Freeway," said Catheryn. "I've been rushing all morning, and now I'm so nervous, I don't know whether I can keep my hands steady enough to play. Is Arthur here yet?"

Arthur West, the Philharmonic's principal cellist, would be conducting the audition. Catheryn had known Arthur since her undergraduate days at USC, and in years past he had served as a source of referrals for the young cellists she tutored two afternoons a week. Catheryn knew that one of his more gifted students would be vying today for the position, along with a host of other musicians who, like her, had been invited to participate based on résumés and performance tapes submitted earlier that year.

"Arthur?" said Adele distractedly, glancing about the room. "He's around here somewhere. Listen, you'd better get warmed up. By the way, the music director will be sitting in."

Catheryn paled. "The music director?"

"Don't worry, you'll do fine," said Adele reassuringly.

"When are you having your baby?" Nate broke in, staring at Adele's bulging stomach.

"I'm due in September, honey," she answered, taking Nate's hand. "Probably right around Labor Day," she added with a smile. "Come on, I'll take you and your sister down to the performers' lounge. You're going to have to wait for your mom there."

"Can't we watch?" asked Allison.

Adele shook her head. "Rules."

"You knew that, Ali," Catheryn said firmly. "Anyway, the lounge

is right below the stage. You should be able to hear some of what's
going on from down there."

"Aw, Mom . . ."

"Go on, now. I'll see you afterward. Wish me luck."

"Okay," said Allison reluctantly. "Knock 'em dead."

"Yeah. Break your legs, Mom," added Nate.

Resisting the impulse to fire off a vitriolic comment regarding her
brother's ignorance, Allison followed Adele as she escorted them
back to the elevator. "We can find our own way down to the lounge
if you want," she offered when they reached the door.

Adele pushed the button, then glanced distractedly at her watch.
"Are you sure?"

"Positive. I've been here lots of times."

"I *do* have to get back. We'll be starting soon," said Adele gratefully. "Do you need anything? Money for the vending machines?"

"Thanks, no. Don't worry; we'll be fine."

"All right, then. See you afterward."

After her mother's friend departed, Allison pulled Nate toward a
small door set in the right wing of the stage.

"Where are we going?" Nate demanded, fighting to free himself
from his sister's grasp.

"Shhh. Do you want to hear Mom play or not?"

"Yeah, but—"

"Then shut up and follow me."

Allison swung open the stage door and peered through. The hallway outside was empty. "Come on," she said. With a guilty rush of
excitement, she dragged Nate through and hurried down the passage
to the left. A moment later, Nate still in tow, she paused at the
entrance to the darkened auditorium, her eyes sweeping over the
breathtaking expanse of the deserted room beyond.

On either side, broad wood panels soared to a distant ceiling, rising ever higher in their bold march toward the back before plunging
in graceful, unbroken curves to form three levels of raised seating in
the rear. Beneath the lowest level an encirclement of plush red seats
fanned downward toward the front, descending in measured, shallow
steps, giving a feeling of undulant motion. Allison had been to performances at the Dorothy Chandler many times with her mother, but
then her attention had always been focused on the stage, not the

room. As she viewed it now, she realized for the first time that its architects had designed the chamber to reflect the very sound it was meant to contain.

Suddenly she heard voices behind them. "Let's go," she whispered.

No longer needing any encouragement, Nate dashed up the carpeted slope, Allison close behind. The two children ducked into a row partway back just as Arthur West and the music director walked in, accompanied by Adele and three other cellists. From their hiding place the children watched as the group that would judge the audition took seats near the front.

For several moments the musicians talked among themselves in relaxed tones. Finally an elderly woman, who would act as proctor, stepped onstage. The music director signaled his assent, and a young Asian woman in her late twenties carried out her cello and seated herself on a solitary chair in the center.

As the woman set her music on the stand, Allison felt the mood in the hall abruptly shift to one of serious and deadly competition. Strangely, she felt a dampness under her own arms, a tension building in her shoulders. Nate, usually fidgety as a parakeet, leaned silently forward, his eyes focused on the stage.

Allison knew that all participants had been given a list of audition pieces to prepare, including selections from Richard Strauss's *Don Juan,* the Adagio from Brahms's Second Symphony, and the first movement of Haydn's C Major Cello Concerto. She also knew that every contestant would play only a short portion from each, lasting about a minute at most, before being stopped by the judges.

By now she was familiar with the material, having listened to her mother preparing it over the preceding months. Although the young Asian woman played flawlessly, many of the musicians who followed performed even more brilliantly, displaying dazzling levels of skill and technique, and as the morning wore on, Allison increasingly wondered how anyone would ever be able to make a choice. Occasionally she glanced down at the judges. They seemed passive, polite, making notes during each audition, but nothing in their expressions gave any hint regarding their assessment.

When Catheryn walked onstage an hour later, Nate had fallen

asleep. Allison shook him. "Wake up, runt," she whispered. "Mom's on."

Nate rubbed his eyes, brightening as he spotted his mother. Still sleepy, he stood and raised his hand to wave. With a rush of panic Allison pulled him back to his seat. "Stay down," she hissed.

Allison held her breath, hoping no one had seen them. Somehow, no one had. With a sigh of relief mixed with a growing feeling of apprehension, she watched from the darkness as Catheryn arranged her music—never taking her eyes from her mother, wishing she could be there beside her.

A nod from the judges, and Catheryn began.

Still as death, Allison listened as Catheryn's cello sang out in rich, sonorous tones that carried a weight no violin could ever hope to match, tones that for her would always uniquely and inseparably be conjoined with the voice of her mother. Some of her earliest memories were of that music, a music that struck rich chords of emotion and inspired unsettling, complex yearnings in her—strange and confusing feelings that as a child she'd found herself unable to fathom. Yet over the years, as she'd grown older, she had slowly learned their names. Pride in her mother's artistry, and wonder at the power it held over her. Resentment at the depth of Catheryn's gift, a gift that had been passed not to her but to her brother Travis, and despair at the knowledge she would never measure up to its perfection. And most of all, running nearly as deep as Allison's love for her mother, the shame of profound, unbearable envy.

When the customary "Thank you—go on to the next piece" sounded less than a minute into the *Don Juan,* Allison felt an irrational surge of irritation. *Can't they tell she's different?* she thought angrily. But as she glanced down at the judges, she suddenly noticed something had changed. And as Catheryn progressed, moving effortlessly through the Brahms selection, she saw it in their stillness and knew it for what it was. It developed slowly, just a few of them at first, but by the time Catheryn embarked on the Haydn concerto, Allison saw it in them all, and she watched in fascination as the magic of her mother's music drew them in.

The first movement of Haydn's C Major Cello Concerto, a longstanding test for virtuosity and precision, was the most emotionally transparent of all the audition pieces. Rising to the challenge, Catheryn, although incorporating the same notes performed by the other cellists, engendered a depth of feeling with her playing that to Allison seemed close to mystic. She watched as her mother played—her hands strong and sure on her instrument, her face reflecting the seductive pleasure she took in the music. Closing her eyes, Allison temporarily surrendered her conflicting pangs of emotion to the music, letting the sound lift her in its ethereal snare.

Inexplicably, the judges allowed the final piece to continue well past the customary one-minute mark. Sensing the deviation, Allison opened her eyes and glanced down at the judges, again seeing the change in their once impassive faces.

At last Catheryn stopped, realizing with an embarrassed smile that she'd been permitted far more than her allotted time. A strange silence filled the hall. Even Nate knew that something of consequence had happened. "Did Mom do something wrong?" he whispered.

"No, Nate," Allison answered. "Mom didn't do anything wrong. She didn't do anything wrong at all."

•   •   •

Agent Marcus saw it first. "Gun!" he screamed, rolling to the right. As he tried to bring up his service revolver, the first stream of bullets cut his legs out from under him, shattering his pelvis and right knee. A second burst caught him full in the chest. He slammed against the rear quarter panel of the Ford, a bloom of red soaking his shirt. He died before he hit the ground.

Agent Tinley, who'd just stepped from the driver's seat, ducked behind the hood—gun out now, trying to get off a shot. Couldn't because the Chicano couple was in the way.

An instant later a deadly barrage tore into the car, slamming fist-sized holes through the doors, windows, fenders. Both tires exploded on the other side. Unable to escape, Tinley edged toward the front, still trying for a shot, figuring he was dead if he didn't and the hell with the Chicano couple. Dimly, he was aware of a door opening in the store across the street.

Two quick shots sounded from the store. Two more. Tinley risked a glance around the headlight. The first man was backing into the apartment, dragging the couple along with him as a shield. The second man was retreating, too—spraying the storefront as he went, giving him a chance.

Determined to make it count, Tinley raised his weapon.

•   •   •

Kane hit the street running, knowing he'd never make it in time. He heard Arnie behind him in the car, screaming into the radio. Deluca was coming out of the store up ahead. Tinley working his way around the front of the Ford . . .

Bad angle. Doesn't have a shot. Jesus, Tinley, stay down, stay down . . .

Halfway up the block he saw the man with the gun drive Deluca back inside, then turn again toward Tinley. Kane brought up his automatic.

Too far. Civilians . . .

•   •   •

Before Tinley could squeeze off a shot, another deadly volley of automatic fire swept his way. A heartbeat later the Ford again began to shudder under the impact. Tinley cowered in the lee of the hood, metal and glass flying all around him and the stink of gunpowder and stale sweat and burning rubber and mindless fear thick in his nostrils, the sound of death ringing in his ears. Two slugs glanced off the engine block, finding him where he crouched behind the left front tire. One grazed his temple. The other buried itself in his throat. Gagging, he slumped to the asphalt.

•   •   •

Within minutes, in response to Arnie's officer-needs-assistance call, a thicket of LAPD black-and-whites completely obstructed both ends of the block. The FBI's bullet-riddled Ford still sat in front of the barricaded apartment, its doors ajar. Agent Marcus lay sprawled beside it, splayed out in a dark puddle of blood. Tinley had managed to squirm partway beneath the frame on the other side, but hadn't moved since then, and withering gunfire from a third-floor window precluded any thought of a rescue. Filled with a feeling of helpless rage, Kane finally retreated to his own car.

Upon arrival, he found Arnie hunched over the radio, which had just been patched through West L.A. Division communications to Sylvia Martin's third-floor apartment. Cursing under his breath, Kane slid behind the wheel, feeling his temper unraveling as he listened to the ensuing conversation between Arnie and Escobar—most of which involved Escobar's delivery of a patently impossible list of demands. By the time Escobar concluded his unrealistic spew, Kane was seething. "Goddammit, Arnie," he growled. "What do we do now?"

Arnie hesitated, thumb over the transmit button. "You already did all you could, pal," he said reluctantly. "Now we stall and wait for backup. SWAT'll be here soon. Let them handle it."

"Wait for SWAT?" Kane snorted. "What about the fed out there under the car? He could be dead by the time they get here."

"I know that, Dan. It's out of our hands."

Kane grabbed the radio mike. "Escobar? You there?"

"What, pig?" Escobar's voice crackled back.

"This is Detective Kane. I just want to make sure I've got all your demands straight. You want fifty thousand in cash, a helicopter to take you to the airport, and a plane gassed up and ready to go wherever you say. Sure you haven't left anything out, dirtbag? How about a couple hookers, some chilled champagne, and maybe a nice blow job to top things off?"

As Kane started to add something else, Arnie narrowed his eyes, signaling him to lighten up.

"Listen, asshole," Escobar replied. "I'm callin' the shots here. Unless you want more people dead, you do what I say."

Kane glanced over at Arnie.

Arnie shook his head. "There's a hostage negotiator coming out with the SWAT team, Dan. Let him deal with Escobar."

Again, Kane spoke into the mike. "Okay, *Mr.* Escobar. We want the hostages alive, but I don't have authority to grant your demands. The brass is sending somebody down."

"When?"

"Now. Meanwhile, how about letting us get those two guys off the street?"

"No fuckin' way. You get us outta here. Then you get your guys."

"Let me talk to one of the people you're holding. If we're gonna deal, I have to know they're all right."

"You ain't talking to nobody."

"Lemme see 'em, then."

"Fuck you."

"Lemme see 'em. Otherwise we've got nothing to discuss."

After a moment the young Chicano male appeared in the window. Escobar stood behind him, holding a pistol to his head. Kane studied them through the binoculars. "Looks like the kid's all right," he said after a slight pause. An instant later he saw the boy grab for the gun.

"Shit, the kid's playin' hero," Kane groaned, dropping the mike and picking up the handset. "Deluca, can you hear what's going on?"

Before Deluca could answer, the roar of a gunshot reverberated from the apartment. "Sounded like a shot," Deluca's voice came back an instant later.

"No shit," Banowski broke in, his transmission static-filled but audible. "I could tell that from back here in the alley, and I didn't need a fuckin' parabolic mike to do it."

"Drop dead, Banowski."

Suddenly the third-floor window exploded. Splinters of window frame and shards of glass flew into the morning sunlight, driven by the body of the Chicano youth. Every eye on the street lifted in shocked silence to record his final flight to the sidewalk.

Deluca's voice came back over the radio a moment later. "Look at the bright side," he said. "If they keep this up, they're gonna run outta hostages."

"What's going on in there now?" Kane demanded, ignoring Deluca's dark attempt at humor.

"The girlfriend's crying," Deluca responded. "The Martin woman's yelling at Escobar for throwing the boyfriend out the window. He's telling her to shut up. Nothin' from the other guy."

"Any mention of the Bradley kid?"

"Yeah. Not where they've got him or anything, but they're our guys."

Without a word Kane yanked the keys from the ignition, walked to the back of the car, and opened the trunk.

"What the hell do you think you're doing?" asked Arnie, leaning out the window.

Kane pulled his Kevlar body armor from the trunk. "I thought I'd work my way around to the alley, pay Banowski a visit," he answered.

"Let SWAT handle it, Dan."

Kane squinted down the street. "Tinley will probably bleed to death before they get here. And don't forget the Bradley kid. No way those scumbags are gonna give him up now. They just killed an FBI agent, maybe two, not to mention the boyfriend. There's nothing in it for them anymore."

"So what can you do?"

"I don't know yet, but we need some action now. Warn Banowski I'm on my way. I'd hate to catch him napping."

"Right. Hey, Dan?"

"What?"

"Nothing. Just be careful."

Minutes later Kane arrived in the alley. John Banowski, a large, heavyset man with a wrestler's going-to-fat physique and a crew-cut hairstyle that hadn't changed since high school, lumbered from an unmarked Dodge, joining him in the shadow of a storage shed behind the brick apartment. Both men studied the structure. Reinforced steel mesh covered every opening on the first and second floors. There appeared to be no way in—no unbarred window, service door, or fire escape. Nothing.

"Place's a fuckin' stockade," said Banowski. "They've got the shades drawn. I ain't seen anything going on up there since we got here," he added.

"How many other tenants on the third floor?"

"Hard to tell. Two, maybe three. A while back I saw an old lady sticking her head out a window on the other end. Why?"

"I want to know what to expect when I get there."

"When you get there? What are you gonna do—sprout wings?"

"Something like that. Just keep me covered. Once I'm inside, let Arnie know what's going on. And tell him not to let anybody come up till I signal."

Banowski shook his head in disbelief. "You're not thinking of *climbing* up there?"

"That's the idea."

"Jesus, Kane. Ever wonder why people think you're such a hot dog?"

"I know what I'm doing."

"You'd better," said Banowski, regarding Kane with a look of both puzzlement and respect.

Carefully staying out of view of the third-floor corner window, Kane crossed the alley, wishing he felt as certain of himself as he'd led Banowski to believe. Keeping his back to the wall, he worked his way over to a six-inch cast-iron standpipe that ran up the outside of the building. Tested it. Deciding it felt solid, he kicked off his shoes. A moment later he grabbed the pipe, placed a foot on the bricks on either side, and started up.

Using a climbing technique called a lieback, Kane walked up the vertical surface by supporting his weight on the balls of his feet, leaning back on his hands to maintain friction. It was a quick and efficient way to ascend, but as he moved up, Kane felt his fingers rapidly tiring. Forty feet up, hands cramping, sweat stinging his eyes, he began to question the wisdom of his attempt.

All at once the pipe shifted.

Jesus, it's coming loose!

Kane froze, fearing any movement might dislodge the pipe. He peered up, noticing the bolts securing the standpipe to the top of the building had almost worked their way free of the concrete.

With a cold chill Kane realized that the higher he climbed, the more he'd stress the bolts. He glanced at the street below, considering a retreat. Rejected it. His hands would give out long before he got there.

The fourth-floor windows lay six feet higher. The one nearest the pipe looked old, the caulk on the panes curling like dried mud.

By now Kane's right leg had begun to shake. Praying the bolts would hold, he moved gingerly up. Then, using a slight hopping motion, he inched his toes onto the windowsill, running over the move in his mind.

No time. Do it.

Taking a deep breath, Kane released the pipe with his left hand. As he swung backward, his fingertips found the edge of the window, slipped . . . held. He pressed until the bones of his fingers made solid contact with the brick. Then, with a grunt, he transferred his weight to the ledge, quickly reversing his right-handed grip on the pipe to keep from peeling off.

Heart slamming in his throat, Kane hung for a terrible, sickening instant, fighting the fatal urge to lean into the bricks. Seconds passed. Balanced between the window in front and a crippling drop behind, he held on. Carefully, he inched his toes farther onto the ledge. Next he brought over his other foot. Then, knowing he'd get only one chance, he leaned back as far as his handholds would allow and propelled himself toward the glass, letting go with his left hand at the same time.

He punched as he swung inward. Surprisingly, the glass didn't break. Instead, the entire window flew into the room, the weathered framework splintering under his fist. Kane's arm shot through. As his momentum stalled and he started to topple backward, he grabbed the inside edge of the wall.

A moment later he was in.

Kane glanced around the fourth-floor apartment in which he found himself. It appeared to have been deserted for some time. A rat's nest of old clothing left by a former tenant cluttered one corner, platter-sized chunks of plaster had peeled from the ceiling, and the room stank of urine, rodent droppings, mold, and age. He'd never been more glad to be anywhere in his life.

Withdrawing his automatic, Kane moved to the door. Listened. Eased it open. Outside, a deserted hallway ran in either direction. To the right, a window looked out on the street below. Doors, elevator, and a stairwell to the left.

Kane slipped into the corridor, heading for the stairs. Moving silently, he stepped onto the upper landing and glanced down the central shaft. Nothing. He descended quietly, staying to the outside of the treads. As he neared the third floor, he heard the unmistakable scratch of a match.

Halfway down the hall, the man who'd arrived with Escobar stood beside the window, facing the street. A cigarette drooped from his lips. In the backlight his figure appeared shrouded in a nimbus of smoke. Kane noticed an Ingram Mac-11 .380 machine pistol hanging loose in his right hand. Three extra clips were carefully lined up on the windowsill.

Kane braced his Beretta against the stairwell corner. His finger tightened on the trigger. *Head or heart?* He thought about the Mac-11, able to spit six rounds per second. Even a perfect shot to the heart gave a man a few moments before he dropped. *The head.* He hesitated, then relaxed tension on the trigger, resisting the temptation to end it right then.

"Police. Freeze."

The man stiffened. His shoulders pinched. He spun, dropping to the right, rolling . . . hand bringing up the pistol . . .

As the Mac-11 began its deadly stutter, Kane's first shot penetrated the man's chest a handbreadth below his neck. The second blew off the back of his skull.

"Ogden? What the fuck's going on?" a voice yelled from a partially open door at the end of the hall.

Kane backed into the stairwell, training his gun on the corner apartment. *Answer or not? Chance it.* "Nothin'," he mumbled.

"What the fuck you shootin' at, then?"

Kane left the stairwell and moved silently down the hall, Beretta extended in both hands.

"Ogden?"

Kane ran the final few feet and kicked open the door. He dived to the left, instantly taking in his surroundings.

Escobar by the window. Woman beside him. Gun.

"Police!" he yelled. "Drop it!"

Escobar looked up, his eyes widening as he saw a massive red-haired man burst into the room. Instinctively, he pulled Sylvia Martin in front of him and raised his pistol.

Ignoring Sylvia's terrified scream, Kane squeezed off a round. The shot missed her by inches, catching Escobar in the right shoulder. His pistol clattered to the floor. Bellowing in pain, Escobar clutched his arm, which now appeared attached to his body mainly by the thin fabric of his shirt. The woman glared at Kane. "You cocksucker, you coulda shot me!" she screamed.

"Keep talking. It's not too late."

Sylvia looked into the pale, dangerous eyes of the man before her and decided to save her complaints for later.

Kane motioned to the center of the room. "Both of you on the floor. Now."

His face sweaty and pale with shock, Escobar stumbled behind Sylvia to the middle of the room. Blood had already soaked through his shirt, and was running in bright rivulets from his fingers to the filthy, threadbare carpet. "I'm fucking bleeding to death," he moaned. "I need a doctor."

"Down."

Escobar and Martin dropped facedown on the floor. Kane cuffed the woman. After retrieving Escobar's pistol, he glanced over at the couch and addressed the young Chicano girl they'd taken hostage. "You live in this building?"

She nodded, eyes wide with fright.

"Where?"

"Next floor down, apartment two-C."

"Go there and wait. Some men will come for you."

The girl looked apprehensively past Kane into the hallway.

Kane's tone softened. "He's gone. It'll be okay, I promise. Just go."

As soon as she'd left, Kane backed to the window. "Deluca, if you're recording, shut it off," he said aloud. "Get the FBI guys off the street, but don't come up till I signal." Peering down, he spotted Deluca's thumbs-up from the storefront.

Kane returned to the center of the room and turned Escobar over with his foot. "I'm sure you know from watchin' TV that I'm supposed to arrest you now and read you your rights," he said. "I'm not gonna do that yet. Know why?"

"Fuck you, cop. Get me a doctor."

Kane glared down. "Look at me when I'm talking to you, punk."

Escobar's eyes traveled the room in a peripatetic search for some way of escape. He found none. Finally he looked at Kane.

Kane stared back, his eyes veiled and callous, seeming to take in the man on the floor without feeling anything at all. "I'll make this easy, so's even a boil like you can understand," he said, his voice chillingly flat. "You're going down for the two feds you shot on the street, along with the guy you just tossed out the window. But before we get to that, you and I are gonna have a little talk. Nothing you say at this point can be held against you, or used in a court of law. No attorneys will be present, so anything that takes place will just be between us girls. Now, here's what's gonna happen: I'm gonna ask you a question, and you're gonna answer."

"Kiss my ass, cop," Escobar yelled, his eyes darting to Martin for support. "We don't gotta say nothin'."

Kane nudged him sharply with his foot. "I told you to look at me!"

Reluctantly, Escobar returned his gaze.

"That's more like it. Now, what'd you say?"

"I . . . I said we don't gotta tell you nothin'."

"Wrong," said Kane softly. "Listen up, dirtbag. I'm gonna ask my question. I'm only gonna ask it once. And if I don't like your answer, you're gonna find out just how wrong you are. Ready?"

Escobar swallowed nervously.

"Where's the kid?"

3

Friday night at the Pizza Hut in Malibu seemed even more frenetic and disorderly than usual, the atmosphere resounding with a deafening mix of childish laughter, enthusiastic yelps, and piercing squeals. Adding to the chaotic ambience, uniform-clad members of two Little League teams had taken fierce possession of the video arcade lining the far wall, generating a mind-numbing din of electronic blips, beeps, and bongs, seeming the consummate accompaniment for the confusion and disorder that had achieved dominion just after six P.M. All in all, a perfect setting for the birthday party of a nine-year-old.

Lost in the kinetic bedlam, following the universal law that no human child ever walks in the company of his peers, Nate Kane stampeded a circuitous route among the tables with a group of his friends, their feet churning the sawdust on the floor into a collage of skids and swirls.

"Nate," he heard his mother call as he rounded the pinball arcade, intent on catching up with one of his buddies.

"What?" he yelled across the room.

"Bring everyone to the table, please. We're almost ready for the cake."

Reluctantly, Nate led his noisy band back to the table, reoccupying the deserted chairs across from Allison and her friend McKenzie Wallace, whose family lived a quarter mile down the beach from the Kanes. The two girls had been conversing quietly between themselves most of the evening, for the most part ignoring the rest of the party. As he sat, Nate noticed that Allison, as usual, seemed to be doing most of the talking. He also noticed that although McKenzie pretended to be listening to his sister's monologue, when Allison wasn't looking, she was stealing covert glances down the table at Travis.

Curious, Nate reached for one of the last remaining slices of pizza and moved closer.

". . . King doesn't switch perspectives like Fowles did, but he does a great job of taking the basic idea and making it his own," Allison was saying. "Heck, no one creates in a vacuum, especially a writer, so—" Allison paused, finally noticing McKenzie's clandestine glances at Travis. "Mac, do you wanna continue our conversation or just make doe eyes at my zit-faced brother?"

"I'm not," hissed McKenzie, blushing furiously.

"Hey, troll," Allison called to Travis. "If you can stop stuffing your pimply face long enough to listen, I've got a news flash."

"Allison, don't," pleaded McKenzie.

"I don't have that many zits," said Travis.

"No? What's that huge bulge on your chin hiding beneath a blanket of Clearasil?"

"What's that big obnoxious hole in the middle of your face?"

"Give it a rest, you two," Catheryn sighed. "I swear, of all my children you're the most alike, so for the life of me I can't understand why—"

"The most alike?" protested Travis. "No way, Mom. Allison and I have absolutely nothing in common."

"Sure we do," said Allison with a smile.

"What?"

"Somebody here likes us."

McKenzie slumped in her seat.

"Allison, enough," Catheryn warned sharply. "Travis, please tell Tommy it's time to bring out the cake."

"But Dad's not here yet," cried Nate. "He said he'd try to make it," he added a bit more calmly, trying to cover his disappointment.

"I know, honey. I'm sorry. It looks like he won't be coming."

Travis rose from the table. "C'mon, kid," he said sympathetically, pulling Nate to his feet. "Let's go check on dessert. You'll feel better with a little chocolate under your belt."

Sensing his brother's need to escape Allison's gibes, and glad to evade the curious glances of several of his friends following his outburst, Nate accompanied Travis across the room. As they approached the order counter, he saw Tommy talking to Christy White, an attractive blond who'd been his older brother's steady girlfriend since the ninth grade. A star on the school swim team, Christy stood a few inches under six feet, shorter than Tommy but nearly as tall as Travis, and had an archetypic swimmer's body—tanned, well-muscled arms, and a terrific set of legs. She glanced up when they arrived. As she did, Nate noticed Travis abruptly stiffening beside him.

"Hi, guys," Travis said awkwardly, shifting from foot to foot.

Christy forced a smile, seeming uncharacteristically preoccupied. "Oh, hi, Trav. And a happy birthday to you, Nate. How's the party going?"

"Okay."

"Except Allison's acting like a jerk, as usual," added Travis.

"Then all's right with the world," said Tommy lightly, seeming to welcome the interruption. "She teasing you about McKenzie again?"

"Among other things," mumbled Travis.

"Some things never change. Has Dad showed up yet?"

"No," answered Nate, this time careful to hide his disappointment. "We're not going to wait anymore. Mom says it's cake time."

"I'll bring it right over," said Christy. She shot a quick, tentative smile at Tommy, then hurried off toward the cold locker behind the counter, adjusting her Pizza Hut uniform as she went.

Travis watched her go. "Anything wrong?" he asked, glancing questioningly at Tommy.

"Nope," said Tommy. "Let's go join the party."

Nate followed his two older brothers back to the table in silence. When they arrived, Travis dropped down beside Catheryn, as far from the rowdy knot of youngsters as possible. Tommy remained standing, pensively cracking his knuckles and staring back at the order counter. Nate rejoined his friends.

"What's with the Neanderthal clone?" Allison whispered, inclining her head toward Tommy. "Having a fight with Christy?"

"I guess," said Nate.

"Well, if it's not that, it's probably some other tragic occurrence—like he forgot where he left his football cleats," said Allison. Then, peering across the room, "Ahh . . . the cake."

Nate looked up and saw Christy—her face illuminated by nine tiny, wavering flames atop the birthday cake she carried—leading a procession of Pizza Hut staff across the crowded room. Halfway to the table they broke into the traditional birthday chorus. Nate felt his face flush as the entire party joined in, followed shortly by nearly every other child in the room—their young voices happily compensating for inconsistencies in pitch and rhythm with a zealous display of ear-splitting volume.

As the song died away, Christy set the cake before him. Nate stared in amazement. From a base layer of chocolate-covered fudge rose a startlingly accurate replica of a medieval castle, complete with crenellated walls and battlements, towers at both ends, a massive keep in the center, even a drawbridge. Turning to Catheryn, he grinned with unabashed pleasure. "Rad cake, Mom."

"Gee, I wonder how she ever caught on to your childish fascination with castles," Allison mused, scratching her head. "Could it be those posters of castles you have plastered all over your room? Or maybe it's the books on castles you keep checking out from the library, or . . ."

Travis, who'd moved closer by then, elbowed her into silence. "Come on, Nate," he said. "Make your wish. Let's see if this thing tastes as good as it looks."

Nate closed his eyes. Then he reopened them and with one tremendous blast extinguished all nine candles.

"What'd you wish?" one of his friends asked.

"I wished that Tar—"

"Don't tell your wish," interrupted Travis. "If you do, it won't come true."

Allison started plucking candles from the cake. "Jeez, the little bean-brain wasted his wish on a dog," she said, rolling her eyes.

"He's not just a dog," Nate shot back. "He's special."

"The only thing special about Tar is he's so old he can barely walk."

"Well, maybe he's gonna get better."

"Yeah, sure."

"I think Trav has the right idea," said McKenzie, reaching over to pull out the last remaining candle. "Let's eat."

Allison smiled knowingly. "You *always* think dear Travis is right."

"Allison, you're impossible tonight," said Catheryn, noticing McKenzie's renewed look of chagrin. "What's gotten into you?"

"Nothing. I just get cranky when I'm surrounded by cretins."

Before Catheryn could reply, a tall boy working behind the order counter called across the room, "Mrs. Kane. Telephone. It's your husband."

Nate, who'd also been about to respond to Allison's last dig, fell silent.

Catheryn rose from the table, handing Tommy the large wooden-handled knife that Christy had brought out with the cake. "Here, Tom," she said with a look of mock admonition. "I'm trusting you to cut the cake. See that everyone gets served and nobody throws food, and if Allison keeps acting up . . . I'm authorizing you to use this on her."

Tommy scowled menacingly at his sister. "You bet. It'll be a pleasure."

•   •   •

"Here you go, Mrs. Kane," said the lanky youth who'd called, passing Catheryn the phone when she arrived at the counter.

"Thanks." Stepping past a couple waiting to order, Catheryn moved as far away as the phone cord would allow, covering her left ear with her hand to shut out the noise. "Dan?"

"Naw, it's your secret lover from the laundromat. Your powerful brute of a husband ain't around anyplace near, is he?"

"Don't worry about him. That big lug would rather work than attend his son's birthday party."

"Sorry about that, Kate. I just got done with the shooting team," said Kane, referring to a preliminary investigation immediately conducted after every officer-involved shooting.

"Shooting . . . oh, my God. Are you okay?"

"I'm fine. Unfortunately, I can't say the same for one of the FBI guys. One of the kidnappers didn't make it either. We did find the boy, though—locked in the trunk of a car in a self-storage garage off Vermont."

"So your hunch about the maid was right."

"Yeah."

"Will the boy be okay?"

"I don't know. They took him to UCLA."

"Were you the one who, uh . . ."

"It was a team effort."

"Of course," said Catheryn, accustomed to her husband's evasions concerning certain areas of his work. "Well, I . . . I'm glad you're all right. Is the case wrapped?"

"Almost. We're still missing the third guy, but the Bradleys' maid appears willing to cut a deal, so we'll get him. There are some, ah . . . procedural difficulties to clear up, though. We've got a meeting with the brass first thing Monday."

"But you're back on regular hours?"

"Yeah. Don't worry, we'll be headin' out for Nate's birthday surprise tomorrow morning, as planned. Listen, tell the kid I'm sorry I missed his party. In fact, lemme talk to the little peckerwood myself."

Catheryn covered the phone and glanced across the room. By now most of the children at the birthday table had chocolate smeared on their faces, and Nate was gleefully ripping open his gifts. "Nate!" she called. "Come over and talk to your father."

Nate looked up, then stubbornly shook his head.

"This is a bad time, Dan. He's right in the middle of everything."

"He's pissed off at the ol' dad, huh?"

"He's disappointed."

"I'll straighten that out tomorrow. Meantime, the guys and I are heading out for a little morale booster, so don't wait up."

"Instead of coming to Nate's party, you're going out drinking with the boys," said Catheryn, her voice cooling.

"Come on, Kate. You know how it is after a shooting. . . ."

"Dan, I realize you feel like unwinding, but it would mean a lot to Nate if you came."

"Negative. Hell, it would take me an hour to get there, and by then the party'd be over. Look, I know Nate's disappointed, but he'll get over it."

"Dan . . ."

"I'll make it up to him tomorrow. End of discussion, Kate. Like I said . . . don't wait up."

•   •   •

A half hour later Kane headed into the Scotch 'n' Sirloin's dimly lit bar. For years an unofficial West L.A. Division hangout, the Scotch—despite the solid and faithful support of the officers of the LAPD—had somehow avoided the stigma of becoming a "cop bar." College kids from UCLA and Santa Monica College still jammed in on the weekends, especially when there was live entertainment, and the throng filling the room was typical for a Friday night.

Once inside, Kane stopped to order a double Jack Daniel's. Then, drink in hand, he pushed through the crowd, quickly spotting Arnie, Banowski, Deluca, and two detectives from burglary sitting at a table in the back. When he arrived, Deluca was capping off a long, convoluted joke involving an elderly Jewish couple who'd shared a life of trial and tribulation—financial setbacks, a plane crash, three weeks in a lifeboat—the wife always at her husband's side. "So the husband's on his deathbed," Deluca chortled, barely able to deliver the punch line. " 'Mona,' he says, looking up at the woman who once again, at his darkest hour, he finds standing beside him. 'You're a fuckin' jinx!' "

"Jesus, Deluca. You still telling the old Jewish couple story?" said Kane after the laughter subsided. "Get some new material."

Deluca took a pull on his beer. "Screw you, hero," he said.

"Back at you," Kane replied, shaking proffered hands as he pulled up a chair to join them. "That goes for the rest of you, too."

"Nice work today," said Arnie.

"Thanks," said Kane, accepting nods from the rest of the table.

"Everybody in the squad room's talking about your little climbing expedition," noted George Lee, one of the burglary detectives. "Ballsy move."

"There *were* moments when things got a little tight," Kane admitted, feeling every eye at the table on him.

"Definitely a superhuman effort," said Banowski. "Can I touch you? Please?"

"Fuck you," Kane chuckled, beginning to relax for the first time since the shooting.

Deciding the occasion called for a formal gesture, Arnie stood and raised his drink. "Gentlemen. I'd like to propose a toast," he said. The other men fell silent and hoisted their glasses. Arnie lifted his drink even higher and continued, his voice ringing with emotion. "Here's to one of the finest detectives to have ever graced the Los Angeles Police Department, a man who has tirelessly performed his duty to protect and serve the citizens of this community without fear or complaint, who has provided a shining model of courage and self-effacing humility for everyone whose life he has touched, and a man, I might add, who is the only officer present at this distinguished gathering wearing women's underwear. Gentlemen, I give you Detective Daniel Thomas Kane."

Kane grinned and downed his drink, showing sanguine disregard for Arnie's toast and the tumult of good-natured catcalls that followed.

"How'd it go with the shooting team, *paisano*?" asked Deluca after Arnie resumed his seat.

Kane's smile faded. "I came here to relax, Paul."

"Sorry."

The group lapsed into silence. A moment later they watched appreciatively as a young cocktail waitress in a short green skirt approached—two full pitchers of beer in one hand and a tray of cocktails balanced expertly on the other. She set the pitchers on their table without spilling a drop, cleared the empty glasses, and replaced them with fresh napkins and a new round of drinks. "Anything else, guys?" she asked.

"Yeah, Arleen," said Deluca with a salacious grin. "Make my life perfect and meet me tonight after work."

Like most of the young women working at the Scotch, Arleen knew of Deluca's reputation as a lothario and had long ago decided not to take him seriously. "That sounds real tempting," she retorted, starting back to the bar. "Can I bring my boyfriend Steve along, too?"

"If that's what it takes," Deluca called after her. "Nice cakes," he added, watching her retreat. "I've got a feeling one night with her would dehydrate the average man for a week. Italians excepted, of course."

"Naturally, 'cause most Italians can't get it up in the first place—unless there happens to be a duck or a sheep somewhere in the vicinity," Kane observed. "Which reminds me, Deluca. I left my jockstrap hanging on your old lady's bedpost the other morning. I'd appreciate it if you'd tell Sarah I'd like it back. Extra large is so hard to find."

"Fuck you, Kane," Deluca shot back. "You saying you wouldn't like to get that hot little number between the sheets?"

Kane cracked his knuckles. "Now, why would I want to do something like that? One night with me and the poor girl would never be satisfied with another man for the rest of her miserable life."

The other men grinned and shook their heads. Although Kane often joked about it, everyone there knew that his attitude concerning marriage was intransigent, nonnegotiable, and straight from the Old Testament.

"Excuse me, Your Holiness," said Deluca. "I expect they'll be nominating you for sainthood before long."

"Jesus, Paul, don't get your bowels all in an uproar. You wanna screw around on Sarah, that's your business. And your problem."

"Fuck you."

Kane took a long pull on his bourbon. "Since we're swappin' humorous tales here, I just remembered an incident to toss into the kitty," he said, still looking pointedly at Deluca. "A story, I might add, that bears somewhat on the subject of marriage."

"Is that right?" asked Deluca suspiciously.

"Yeah."

"I've heard it," said Arnie.

"Tough," said Kane, continuing unperturbed. "When I first started working patrol, me and my partner at the time—a guy named Mark Smith—answered a domestic call out in Sherman Oaks. I was pretty green and made the mistake of turning my back on the woman of the house, who claimed she'd been beaten by her spouse. When she found out we intended to bust her husband, she pulled a cleaver from under her dress and tried to bury it in the back of my skull."

"Lucky she didn't aim for something vital," Banowski noted.

"Smith grabbed her just in time," Kane continued, ignoring the interruption. "Anyway, when we went into the kitchen, we found she'd already used the cleaver on her husband—which just goes to show that you just never know with a domestic disturbance."

At that point in his story Kane paused, noticing Lieutenant Nelson Long entering the bar. Long was a big man, whose square, friendly face concealed a perceptive intelligence that had earned him the rank of lieutenant and a position as detective commanding officer for the West L.A. Division. As an African-American, he'd surmounted many obstacles on his rise to his present position in the department, and was one of the few members of the brass, black or white, whom Kane truly trusted.

"Hey, Lieutenant," Kane yelled, raising his hand. "Over here."

As Long started over, Kane quickly finished his story. "Anyway, the guy checks out before the ambulance arrives, so we get the wife cuffed and stuffed and charge her with murder. All the way down to the lockup she's yellin' and screamin', carryin' on like she can't believe it. Get this: She's actually *pissed off* at her old man for dying."

Amid the reaction of skeptical amusement and outright disbelief that followed, Lieutenant Long arrived at the table. "Pull up a seat and drink awhile, Lieutenant," said Arnie, hooking over a spare chair with his foot. "You just missed another one of Kane's horseshit tales. If there was ever any doubt, this one definitely proved he is not one to let the facts get in the way of a good story."

"Thanks, but I can't stay," said Nelson. "I've got some news."

Everyone quieted.

"What?" said Kane.

"You know the Bradley kid was in bad shape when they found him. He'd been in the trunk for days, and with all this heat . . ."

"What are you trying to say, Lieutenant?" asked Kane.

"He didn't survive, Dan. I'm sorry. I thought you'd want to know."

4

Although he didn't arrive home until well after two, Kane was up early the following morning. After his workout he roused his family, then started preparing for the trip. By the time everyone joined him out front in the red Chevy Suburban, he'd already lifted Tar into the back, finished his second cup of coffee, and idled the engine long enough for the temperature gauge to have climbed to the center of the scale. "This has gotta be the slowest goddamn family on the face of the planet," he grumbled as Catheryn slid in beside him.

"Honey, you really should try to watch your language," she chided. "I listened in on a bit of your talk to the children yesterday morning, and although I generally agree with the content, I think you could set a better example in your choice of words."

"Oh, goodness gracious," said Kane. "How could I have uttered crudities like 'crap' and 'damn' around the tender young ears of my lily-white kids?"

"You said 'turd' and 'peckerwood' too," said Nate as he climbed into the rear with Tar.

" 'Peckerwood' is not a cussword. Everybody in?"

"That's right, Nate," Allison noted from her spot in the backseat between Travis and Tommy. "Jesus used to say 'peckerwood' all the time. In fact, he used it repeatedly when he drove the money changers from the temple, along with the word 'turd,' I might add."

"Nate, that's not true," said Catheryn, shooting Allison a sharp look. Then, to Kane, "See what I mean?"

"I've got an idea," Allison continued, having missed her mother's glower. "Instead of those dumb guessing games we usually play on trips, let's see who can think up the most compound cusswords that Dad can't say anymore, in alphabetic order, starting with, say . . . asswipe."

"Buttbreath," said Travis, catching on.

"Chickenshit," Tommy joined in.

"Dickhead," Nate giggled from the back.

"E-nough. You're upsetting your mother," ordered Kane, slamming the car into gear. He accelerated out onto the highway, pulled into the center lane, and completed a smoothly coordinated U-turn that put them back on the road heading north. "Besides, if you're cataloging all the cusswords I won't be usin' in the future, I can tell you right now it's gonna be one hell of a short list."

Kane pushed the speed limit, eager to leave Malibu behind as soon as possible. The road was still deserted, but he knew Saturday traffic would begin building before long, with everyone from long-haired surfers to carloads of families from the valley thronging the highway to escape the heat of the city. Minutes later the Malibu pier flashed by, followed by a steep climb to the broad manicured lawns of Pepperdine University on the right. After that the road opened up, with the signs, restaurants, and shops of central Malibu quickly surrendering to a string of ocean-side homes set far back off the highway, hidden amid lush curtains of pampas grass, eucalyptus, and ice plant.

"Where're we headed?" asked Allison.

"I already told you. I've got somethin' planned in honor of Nate's successfully makin' it out the old birth canal nine years back."

"Gross, Dad. I meant a destination."

"You'll see when we get there."

"Mom?"

Catheryn smiled mysteriously. "Your father wants to keep it a surprise."

All the children groaned.

"What's this I'm hearing from the back?" asked Kane. "You don't trust the ol' dad?"

"No!" the children screamed in unison. "Come on," Tommy pleaded. "At least tell us how long it's gonna be."

Kane glanced up to find Tommy's eyes in the mirror. "We'll get there when we get there. By the way, that's where you're gonna be working," he added, pointing to a high bluff overlooking the ocean, where a number of partially framed structures stood silhouetted against the skyline. Travis and Tommy craned their necks for a better view.

"Work. Gee, I can't wait," Tommy grumbled under his breath.

"What's that, Travis?" demanded Kane. "Bitchin' about doing an honest day's labor? Don't worry, princess. I'm sure you'll have plenty of time left for piano plinking."

"I didn't say anything," Travis protested hotly.

"I know where we're going," Allison broke in to forestall the argument. "Solvang!"

"Solvang?" Kane snorted. "Phony windmills and cutesy-pie shops sure as hell aren't *my* idea of a good time. Guess again, petunia."

"We're visiting Grandma in Santa Barbara," Nate offered from the back.

"Nate, seeing how it's your birthday, I guess I can tell you you're gettin' warm."

"The zoo at Santa Barbara?" Tommy guessed.

"Nope."

"How about Refugio State Beach?" asked Allison.

"Now, that's *really* dumb. We already live at the beach." Kane pressed down on the accelerator. "No more guessing. I will say there's more'n a couple hard hours' driving ahead, and we'll be stopping for somethin' to eat. In the meantime just settle back and enjoy the scenery."

Thirty minutes later they reached the Point Mugu Naval Air Station, and shortly afterward entered the outskirts of Oxnard. There a patchwork of vegetable fields flanked both sides of the road, many already adorned with lines of colorfully garbed stoop laborers who'd started early to avoid the heat. Kane fiddled with the radio, which until then had been tuned to a classical station. "Enough of this longhair stuff," he muttered.

"Could we stick to something soothing, Dan?" Catheryn requested.

"No problem, Kate. A little soothin' country music'll be just the ticket."

"Anything but that," said Catheryn in mock horror.

"Yeah, come on, Dad," Allison cried, immediately siding with her mother.

"Yeah," added both Tommy and Nate, jumping into the skirmish. Travis, brooding over Kane's earlier slight, remained silent.

"You kids know what I think?" said Kane, feigning dismay. "I think your mom here's turning you into a bunch of snobs. Sure, she loves her music and plays it great, but you've gotta admit classical's not exactly toppin' the charts these days. Now, country music, for instance—"

"Come on, Dan," interrupted Catheryn. "You should be proud your children are sophisticated enough to enjoy great art."

"Yeah, yeah," Kane laughed. "Spoken like a true highbrow. Lemme tell you something, sugar. To my mind there are only five kinds of music: classical, pop/rock, elevator, jazz, and country—of which classical is definitely the worst. Now, don't get me wrong. I'll be the first to admit some of the old boys came up with a good tune or two—Beethoven and Schubert, for instance. But for the most part that kinda stuff is good for only one thing," he added with a sidelong grin. "Puttin' people to sleep."

"That's incisive, Dad," said Allison. "You should consider writing the music review for the *Times*. Don't you think so, Mom?"

"I think your father enjoys jerking my chain once in a while," Catheryn said patiently. "He knows perfectly well that most of the work he's denigrating has stood the test of time, which is more than one can say for his country music."

"None of us here's gonna stand your so-called test of time, so who gives a rat's ass what they'll be playin' a hundred years from now?" Kane countered.

"You said 'ass,' Dad," Allison noted.

Kane grinned. "Allison, you and your mother can gang up on me all you want, but it's not gonna change the simple fact she's been playing classical music so long, she can't see the forest for the trees. Personally, I'd rather set my hair on fire and put it out with a hammer than listen to most of that crap."

"I'd like to see that," said Tommy.

"Watch it," Kane warned. "Now, where was I? Oh, yeah, pop/rock. I'm gonna slide right past that, along with elevator music and jazz—none of which I consider worth discussing. Which brings us to the last category: country and western, the only kinda music worth listening to. It's got clear lyrics a person can understand, a tune you can remember once it's over, and it occasionally even has somethin' to say about the human condition. Like the guy on the radio said: 'That's my opinion; it oughtta be yours.' "

"I think that's: '. . . we'd like to *hear* yours,' " said Catheryn.

"Well, *I* want to listen to some more classical," said Allison with perverse enthusiasm, grinning at her father.

"Naw, what this trip needs is some Led Zeppelin," Tommy jumped in. "Or maybe some jazz."

"Even elevator music would be better than country," added Allison.

"I see I've been tossing pearls to swine," Kane grunted. "Okay, we'll settle this fair and square. I'll think of a number between one and a hundred. Whoever hits it gets to choose the station."

"Twenty-one," said Allison, going first.

"Sixty-nine," said Tommy.

"Seventy-six," Travis guessed, slowly breaking out of his funk.

"A hundred," said Nate, poking his head over the rear seat.

Catheryn glanced at her youngest. "I thought you were asleep."

"Who can sleep with Dad talking?"

"You've got a point," said Catheryn. "Fifty."

"You're all wrong," announced Kane. "It was forty-two, my number when I played linebacker for USC. You shoulda got that, Kate," he added, tuning the radio to K-Country, a Ventura station broadcasting 150,000 watts of country music twenty-four hours a day. With a satisfied grin he cranked up the volume.

"That's not fair, Dad," complained Allison. "You already knew the number."

"Tough," said Kane, disregarding the grumbles from the back.

"You guys can pick the next station when this one fades out, if it ever does. Now, quit your bellyachin' and enjoy the music."

Forty-five minutes later, after a quick stop at McDonald's in Ventura, Kane reluctantly slowed for traffic as they entered the outskirts of Santa Barbara. By then everyone had finished eating, and Catheryn gathered up the golden M-emblazoned dross of their meal—stuffing paper plates, cups, straws, napkins, and foil wrappers into a trash bag she'd brought along for that purpose.

"Will you look at this place?" said Kane, glaring at the ubiquitous red-roofed homes blanketing the hillsides. "The mayor of this dump must own the tile factory."

"Isn't that where you and Mom spent your honeymoon?" asked Tommy, pointing to a large single-story hotel with a series of outlying bungalows along the beach.

"Yep. That's the Miramar, all right," Kane answered, recognizing the stately old hotel bordering the ocean. "What was the number of that bungalow we were in, Kate?"

"Twenty-one," Catheryn answered. "That's one *you* should have gotten."

"Yeah, yeah, I remember. Just testin'. Man, what a weekend. That first night when—"

"Dan!"

"Don't get ruffled, Kate. I was just gonna say—"

"Never mind what you were going to say," Catheryn interrupted, reaching over to take his hand.

Kane gave it a squeeze. "An unlikely pair, huh? Catheryn Erickson, innocent music student . . ."

". . . and Dan Kane, football jock on scholarship doing his best to see how much hell he could raise before flunking out," Catheryn finished.

"Don't take this wrong, Pop," Allison interjected, "but what did Mom, uh . . ."

"See in me? Hell, your mom had the hots for me right off the bat, only she didn't know it. I just had to stick around long enough for her to recognize my good points."

"Good points? Like what?" Tommy asked. "Banging heads and kicking butt?"

"Yeah. Care for a demonstration?"

"Sure, Dad. Maybe later."

"Listen, kids," Kane continued more seriously, "I know your mom here always makes our courtship sound like some kinda 'Beauty and the Beast' tale, but we've been married a lotta years. That says something."

"Especially considering I still can't stand you most of the time," Catheryn laughed.

"Hey, the ol' dad never claimed to be perfect."

"No argument there. For once we're in total agreement."

"Come on, Mom, tell us," Allison persisted. "What made you like Dad in the first place?"

"Yeah, Kate," said Kane. "Was it my good looks, my dazzlin' wit, my sophisticated sense of humor, or was it simply just a case of pure animal magnetism?"

Catheryn smiled, ignoring her husband. "To tell you the truth, Allison, when I met your father, although I knew right away he had a good heart, there wasn't much else about him I found attractive. Actually, the feelings I had for him were more like . . ."

"Irritation? Revulsion? Disgust?" Allison giggled.

"Watch it," Kane muttered.

"Sorry, Pop," said Allison. "Seriously, Mom, there must have been *something* . . ."

Catheryn paused thoughtfully. "You know," she said finally, "I think what I initially liked about your dad was his persistence. That, and discovering there's a lot more to him than first meets the eye."

•   •   •

As the Suburban left the tiled roofs and avocado groves and stately eucalyptus of Santa Barbara behind, the Kanes settled back, the steady purr of the engine and the rush of wind in their ears. Gradually, fields of western buttercup and cow parsnip and cinquefoil and California poppies began to carpet the foothills of the Santa Ynez Mountains, with occasional pockets of larkspur, columbine, and thistle nestling like mist in the hollows, their colorful presence tracing the course of drainage channels as accurately as contour lines on a map. Lulled by the gentle rocking of the car, Travis drifted in a limbo between languor and sleep, watching through drooping eyes as the scenery flowed past, the land growing more feral with each passing mile.

Allison slumped beside him, leaning against his shoulder, her eyes closed. The sound of Nate's and Tar's rhythmic breathing came from the back. Even Catheryn and Tommy seemed to have nodded off.

At Gaviota, taking a tunnel cut through solid rock, the highway turned inland and ascended into the mountains. Scrub oak soon sprang up in isolated patches of twos and threes, quickly thickening to dense stands that filled the canyon. Before long, ranches, open grazing land, and wilderness supplanted the coastal fruit groves and farms that had earlier bordered the road, and as the car progressed north, the odd notion struck Travis that they were somehow traveling back in time, retreating through the Californian landscape toward a simpler, more elementary existence.

Occasionally during the journey Travis had shifted his glance to the front of the car, secretly studying his father. Now, as he watched the way Kane's large hands moved on the wheel and the tireless manner his eyes searched the road ahead, it occurred to him that his father's entire being, even while performing a task as rudimentary as driving a car, spoke a language of decisive action, of obdurate resolution, of uncompromising force. For him there existed no confusing shades of gray.

As the rest of the family slept, Travis leaned forward, resting his arms on the seat in front. "Dad?" he said, as usual slightly uncomfortable to be talking one-on-one with his father.

"Um," Kane grunted.

"Can I ask you a question?"

"You just did."

"I mean something else. Something serious."

"It's natural, Travis. It's called a period. Don't worry about it; all the gals get 'em."

"Come on, Dad . . ."

"Okay, Travis. Shoot."

"I know you don't think much of classical music, but how would you feel if I wanted to study it in college? Mom says they've got a great music department at USC, and—"

"Hold on right there." Kane glanced over at Catheryn. Satisfied she was asleep, he lowered his voice and continued. "Look, Travis, classical music is just fine as a hobby, or when you're tryin' to get your date in the mood—but a career? Shit, look at your mom's friends. Most of 'em are losers. They bitch about their jobs, if they have one; they're narcissistic and snobbish, for the most part; and worst of all, most of 'em are poor—which is nothing new in the music world. I'd rather see you get off your ass and get something goin' for yourself than waste four more years plinking away on the keyboard. And USC? With *your* grades?"

"My grades aren't bad," said Travis defensively. "I get mostly A's and B's."

"Two years back you got C's in both math and history, and last year you got another one in English," Kane pointed out. "Plus your grade-point average has slipped the past three years running—three point five, three point forty-four, and a three point two."

Travis, who'd long ago ceased being surprised by his father's unusual memory, said nothing.

"That's not nearly in the scholarship category, and that's what we're talking about here," Kane went on. "When Tommy was your age, he already had football scouts sniffin' around. What have you got planned in that department?"

"I . . . I don't know, Dad," Travis stammered. "But isn't the idea in life to find something you love, and then do it?"

"Don't believe the horseshit you see in the movies," Kane growled. "Life ain't art. If you're poor, you're miserable. Besides, I wonder about you and music. Your mom's always kicking your butt to practice lately. Do you love playing the piano? Really love it? Is that what you honestly wanna do with the rest of your life?"

Travis wrestled silently with his thoughts, amazed that his father had somehow intuited his doubts. Unlike his siblings, who to Catheryn's disappointment had shown little musical ability, technique had come easily for him. At the age of three he'd begun sounding out songs and themes picked up from watching TV, effortlessly reproducing them on the piano. Shortly afterward Catheryn had begun his instruction, but by the time he turned six, he'd far outstripped her abilities on the keyboard. Certain he had the makings of a prodigy, she'd subsequently arranged for him to continue studying with Alexander Petrinski, one of her colleagues at USC.

From the beginning Petrinski had made it clear he believed Travis possessed the ability to become a virtuoso performer. Yet after years of instruction Petrinski seemed to be growing increasingly impatient with Travis—working him harder, pushing him toward some threshold he seemed unable to cross. Now, with a flash of insight, Travis suddenly realized that whenever he sat before the keyboard, the emotion he most strongly felt wasn't love, or satisfaction . . . or even pride. It was guilt.

"Well, is it?"

"I . . . I don't know."

"In that case maybe it's time to reassess your goals," Kane advised, still speaking quietly. "I know your mom wouldn't approve of what I'm saying, but I think you should start considering doing something productive, something you can be proud of."

"What about you, Dad?" asked Travis, surprised to be talking so freely with his father, but eager to change the subject. "Say you could have any job you wanted. Would you still be a cop?"

"Yep. Hard to believe, but true," Kane answered. "No, I take that back. There is one other thing I'd like. Being in professional sports would be great—say football, for instance—but mostly because of the money. Not that I won't be damn proud of your brother if he turns pro after college. But disregarding the money, I'd still take being on the force. Not that there aren't things wrong with it," he added as an afterthought.

"Like every time you turn on the news and see the LAPD getting a black eye?"

"Yeah, for one," Kane admitted. "Listen, kid. There are bad apples in *any* group you wanna name—politicians, teachers, Boy Scout leaders—hell, even priests and nuns. Anyone who condemns a whole organization because of a couple mutts in the pack is an idiot."

"I know that, Dad," said Travis, who'd heard it before.

"Aside from that," Kane continued, "I guess the worst part about bein' a cop is taking shit from the brass and putting up with the asswipes we gotta deal with every day—probably the same crap you've gotta eat on any job." Kane paused, seeming about to say something more.

"What, Dad?"

"Being on the force does kinda tend to isolate you," Kane admitted. "Most people are plenty glad to see a cop when they need one, but they get real uncomfortable around us the rest of the time. I see it plenty. After seventeen years on the force I consider myself a good judge of character, which is basically why I don't like many people. Most of my friends are cops, and that's just fine with me, but I guess your mom wishes I fit into her world a little better."

"So what is it you like? Helping people?"

"Shit, that's what every rookie thinks when he starts out," Kane snorted. "Granted, there *are* moments. Everybody gets a few chances to do something good like saving a kid or keeping somebody from gettin' hurt, but by the time you've been on the street very long, the idea of helping people becomes just that . . . a nice idea that doesn't match up in real life."

"What, then?"

"I'll tell you, Travis. It doesn't have anything to do with my father's bein' a cop, or helping that throng of hairballs out there called the public, or fulfillin' some dark, secret desire for bustin' heads. Or that it beats the hell outta most nine-to-five jobs. The reason's simple: I like bein' a cop 'cause I'm good at it."

"Maybe there're other things you'd be good at, too."

"Maybe."

After a long pause Travis asked, "Have you ever shot anybody?"

"Christ, Travis. What is this—twenty questions?"

"Just wondering, that's all. Have you?"

"Nobody that didn't deserve it."

"Are you ever scared?"

"On the job? Hell, yes. Any cop tells you he's not occasionally scared shitless is pissin' up your back and tellin' you it's rain."

"Then how do you . . ."

"Do what has to be done? Easy. You just do it, scared or not. Hell, everybody's afraid. Courage, valor, bravery—those are just words that don't mean spit. The guys who make the cut are the ones who can do what they have to, *despite their fear*."

"Kinda like climbing? You're afraid to make a move, but you know you have to, so you go ahead anyway?"

"Yeah," said Kane. " 'Cept in police work there's no rope if you fall. There's no rope in real life either, Travis."

"I know."

"You do, huh? Then start actin' like it." As if to signal the end of their discussion, Kane twisted up the volume on the radio. A sudden blast of static filled the car.

Catheryn sat up and rubbed her eyes. "Where are we?"

"Almost to San Luis Obispo," Kane answered, changing to another station. "Time to wake up the troops. To quote the pervert who caught his pecker in a revolving door . . ."

". . . won't be long now," Travis finished.

"Right," said Kane.

The rest of the family was stirring again by the time they reached San Luis Obispo, where Highway 101 split into two main arteries. The primary branch turned inland and followed the Salinas River north, avoiding the Santa Lucia range along the coast; the other veered toward the ocean, skirting the mountains as it wound its way up the Pacific shelf. Taking the coastal route, Kane passed through Morro Bay and continued north. Soon the road narrowed to two lanes, flashing through the towns of Cayucos, Harmony, and Cambria. At San Simeon, Kane turned right, heading into the mountains.

A few miles farther on, the Hearst San Simeon State Historical Monument, better known as Hearst Castle, came into view, the twin towers of the Casa Grande rising majestically before them. Silently, the family stared at the mammoth structures nestled like jewels in the rolling foothills.

"There she is, Nate," said Kane. "That's about the closest you're ever gonna come to a real castle anywhere around here. What do you think?"

"Awesome, Dad." said Nate, his eyes shining with excitement. "Can we . . . can we go in?"

"Oh, we're goin' in, all right," said Kane, enjoying his son's reaction. "I made tour reservations two months back, got up early, dragged you all outta bed, and endured everybody's moanin' and groanin' for over two hundred miles so's we could take in this pile o' rocks. After all that you can be damn sure of one thing: We are definitely goin' in."

5

L ate Saturday night Kane eased the red Suburban to a stop in front of the beach house. With a weary sigh of relief, he shut off the engine. The children, exhausted from the journey, had slept most of the return trip. Now, sensing they'd finally arrived, the three in the backseat roused themselves and piled slowly from the car.

"What's this? Another project?" Tommy asked drowsily as he noticed a stack of construction lumber and six fifty-gallon drums sitting on the street in front of the house.

"Yeah," Kane grunted, walking to the rear of the car. "Had it delivered today. Hit the sack. I'll tell you about it in the morning."

"Right. Good night, Dad."

"Good night, Tom. Night, rookies," he called after Travis and Allison, who were already stumbling toward the front door.

"Good night, Dad."

"Damn, when's this kid gonna put on some weight?" Kane grumbled, lifting his youngest from the luggage space behind the backseat. As he did, Tar, who'd been sleeping beside Nate, looked up and whined. "Kate, can you get the mutt out?"

"I'll take care of Tar," Catheryn answered. "You put Nate to bed. See you inside."

Kane carried Nate into the house. He stopped in the entry, shifting his sleeping son to free an arm. Then, after reaching up to flip open the trapdoor in the ceiling, he climbed a vertical ladder bolted to the wall beside the coat closet. Pausing at the top, he gently rolled the boy from his shoulder onto a single bed occupying most of the tiny rooftop chamber that had been converted to Nate's bedroom. A lambent glow from the moon spilled through an open window, dimly revealing the interior: a dresser, bedside table, lamp, desk, and a disorganized bookshelf filled with a jumble of toys and games. But most dominant in the room were the photographs, sketches, and posters of various European castles and châteaux—from crude Norman motte-and-bailey fortifications to sumptuous eighteenth-century French *châteaux de plaisance*—adorning every available inch of wall space. Even the low, sloping ceiling was completely covered.

Still perched on the ladder, Kane leaned in and removed his son's shoes. "See you tomorrow, Nate," he whispered, covering him with a blanket.

"Night, Dad," Nate's sleepy voice murmured from beneath the covers. Then, as Kane started down, "Dad?"

"What, squirt?"

"Thanks."

"Sure, kid."

When he reached the bottom of the ladder, Kane found Catheryn sifting through Saturday's mail. Without speaking, she tossed the handful of letters and bills she'd been inspecting onto a small table by the front door, then circled his waist and led him toward their bedroom at the far end of the hall. "What's his thing with castles, anyway?" Kane mused on the way there.

"I don't know. Whatever it is, he certainly enjoyed himself today. We all did, Dan. That was a nice thing you did."

"The ol' dad comes through for his kids, as usual," said Kane, unbuttoning his shirt.

"Uh-huh. Speaking of coming through for the kids, don't you think you've been a little hard on Travis lately?"

"Hell, no. That kid needs shapin' up."

Catheryn moved to the dresser and began methodically brushing her long auburn hair. "Not the kind of shaping up you've got in mind. I overheard some of the advice you gave him today."

"Uh, exactly what advice are you referring to?" asked Kane guilt-ily. "That part about gettin' off his ass and—"

"You know the part I'm talking about. Does 'classical music is just fine as a hobby, or when you're trying to get your date in the mood' ring a bell?"

"Aw, hell, you know what I was trying to tell the boy."

"I know *exactly* what you were trying to tell him. Why can't you just let him make up his own mind for a change?"

"Because he's been dickin' around for years without getting any-thing goin', that's why. On top of that, thanks to your coddling, he's scared of his own shadow. Now, Tommy, for instance . . ."

"Travis isn't Tommy, Dan. You're going to have to accept that. In his own way Travis is a strong person. Just maybe not by your stan-dards."

Kane finished unbuttoning his shirt and moved to stand behind Catheryn at the dresser. As she continued stroking her hair, he began kneading the muscles of her back and neck. "Those standards have always worked just fine for me," he said.

Catheryn put down the brush and quickly pulled off her light cotton sweater, moaning with pleasure as Kane's fingers expertly ex-plored the knots and cramps engendered by hours of riding in the car. "God, that feels good. Don't stop."

"You've gotta learn to relax more, Kate. You're carryin' a lot of tension here, and here . . ."

"Aaahh," Catheryn groaned as Kane continued to massage her shoulders with hands that knew her body as well as his own. "You do that so well," she purred. "But if you're trying to make me forget our discussion, it won't work."

"I'll tell you something, sugar. I think *you're* doing the same thing you're accusing *me* of—namely, trying to get Travis to see things your way. It's makin' him soft."

Catheryn arched and unsnapped her bra, allowing Kane's strong hands full access to her back. Feeling her muscles beginning to loosen under Kane's ministrations, she said quietly, "The words 'soft' and 'sensitive' aren't necessarily interchangeable. There's a big differ-ence."

"Not in my playbook."

"Listen, Dan. I heard someone on TV say that no matter how hard parents try, in one way or another they always manage to screw up their kids. I'll tell you what. Let's divide the guilt. You've already got Tommy. Let me have Trav."

"What about Allison and Nate?" chuckled Kane. "Who gets to screw *them* up?"

Catheryn smiled. "We'll work that out later." All at once she noticed a small black box sitting on her dresser. "What's this?"

Kane grinned.

Catheryn opened the box. Inside, sparkling on a bed of pure-white velvet, lay a pair of emerald earrings. "Oh, Dan, they're beautiful," she whispered.

Kane shifted from foot to foot, seeming embarrassed. Even though money had been difficult during the early years of their marriage, each time they'd had a child, he'd always managed to present Catheryn with a piece of emerald jewelry, and the green stones had special significance for them both. "Don't worry," he said. "I'm not suggesting we have another. It's just this being Nate's birthday and his bein' the last and all, I thought . . ."

Catheryn looked into Kane's eyes. "Dan Kane, as infuriating as you can sometimes be," she said softly, "I love you. With all my heart." And placing her arms around his neck, she kissed him.

Kane pulled her to him, his desire mounting as her supple body nestled into his. "Come to bed," he whispered hoarsely.

"Wild horses couldn't keep me away," Catheryn laughed, pushing against Kane's chest and squirming from his grasp. "Be there in a sec."

As Kane crawled under the covers, Catheryn returned to the dresser and inserted the emerald studs into her ears, inspecting them from different angles with obvious pleasure.

"They look great on you, gorgeous," said Kane. "Match your eyes."

Catheryn glanced at him in the mirror, playfully pushing her hair high on her head with one hand and resting the other seductively on her hip. Then, turning to face the bed, she slowly removed the rest of her clothes. As her hair spilled over her shoulders to her small, well-formed breasts, something in her lean silhouette reminded Kane of a cat—agile, strong, graceful.

"Come to bed," he whispered again.

She slipped in beside him, her breath warm on his lips, her mouth softly insistent as she encompassed him in her arms. Tonight she wanted to lead, and he let her, responding swiftly to her touch, her gently probing tongue, her whispered endearments. Her skin felt cool and smooth as her breasts nuzzled into his chest, moving against him in a hypnotic rhythm as ancient as life itself. Their kisses, at first tentative and exploring, quickly turned passionate, taking on a quality of sweet abandon, reflecting a hunger neither could deny. They joined and climbed as one, slowly at first, then faster, faster, until finally Catheryn arched against him and cried out softly, shuddering with pleasure. Losing himself in her embrace, Kane joined her a moment later, everything simple and perfect and flowing and complete.

•　　•　　•

Afterward, long after Catheryn had fallen asleep, Kane lay awake in the darkness listening to the gentle sounds of her breathing, and the soft, rhythmic pounding of the surf.

6

The next morning Travis found his father on the deck having coffee with Arnie. The rest of the household had just begun to stir—Allison keeping Catheryn company as she puttered in the kitchen, Tommy still in bed, Nate thumping around in his bedroom over the entry. "Hey, there's my favorite godson," Arnie said with an avuncular grin as he spotted Travis coming out the door.

Travis smiled back. "Hi, Arnie. Bet you say that to all the Kane kids."

"Only the ones with peckers," noted Kane, rocking back in his chair. "Is Tommy awake yet?"

"Morning, Dad. Tommy said he wanted to sleep in, seeing how we start work tomorrow."

"Negative. Get him up," Kane ordered. "After Mass you two are gonna hump that load of lumber sittin' in front of the house down to the beach. Now, get lost. Arnie and I have something to discuss."

"Right, Dad." Travis retreated to the stairs, briefly glancing back to watch Kane and Arnie resuming what appeared to be a serious conversation. Curious, he paused. Unable to hear what they were saying, he shrugged and continued on to the top landing. Once there, he yelled for Tommy to get up, then followed his nose to the kitchen, where Catheryn had a breakfast of pancakes, scrambled eggs, sausage, fried potatoes, orange juice, and coffee well under way.

"Good morning," she said sunnily as he entered.

"Morning, Mom. Hi, Ali," said Travis, crossing to the stove and pouring himself a cup of coffee.

"Since when do you drink coffee, young man?" Catheryn asked curiously.

"Since now, Mom. I'm still beat from yesterday, and Dad's already got a big project laid out for me and Tommy."

"So I've heard." Catheryn gave the eggs a quick stir, then grabbed a spatula and expertly flipped the pancakes she had cooking on a skillet.

"Need any help?"

"No thanks, honey. Go ahead and start. These'll be done shortly." Catheryn turned to Allison. "Ali, go call your father and see what's keeping your brothers."

Allison rolled her eyes. "Do I have to?"

"Please, Ali. I don't want the food to get cold."

"Oh, all right," Allison groaned. Reluctantly, she started for the hall.

Travis grabbed a plate and served himself a pile of sausage and eggs, covering them with a liberal dousing of ketchup. As he took his place at the table, Catheryn carried over the skillet and added a stack of steaming pancakes. "There's something I want to discuss with you," she said.

"What?"

"Despite your new job and whatever your father may have told you in the car yesterday, I expect you to keep up with your practicing."

"But . . ."

"No buts. The Bronislaw is coming up in October," she continued firmly, referring to the Bronislaw Kaper Awards—a prestigious, high-level competition sponsored each year by the Los Angeles Philharmonic for musicians seventeen years old and under. Along with a cash prize of twenty-five hundred dollars, the winner would later appear in a special concert with the Philharmonic. "That's less than four months away," she added.

"I know, Mom. I *know*."

"You realize if you do well in the competition, it will bear favorably on your application to the USC School of Music."

"Thanks for the pressure," said Travis, concentrating on his breakfast. "But I'm not sure yet if that's what I want to do."

Catheryn sat across from her son. Travis squirmed under her gaze. "Trav, there are people who would give anything to have your ability," she said.

"So you've told me," grumbled Travis, shaking his head in exasperation. "*Jesus,* Mom."

"It's just that I'd hate to see you waste it."

"Where have I heard this before?"

"You can't live your life for your father, Trav. You can't live your life for anyone."

"Not even for you, Mom?"

"That's not fair," said Catheryn, unsuccessfully attempting to mask the hurt in her voice. "I only want what's best for you."

"I didn't mean that," said Travis quickly. "I'm sorry."

Just then Allison reentered, followed by Nate. "Sorry looking," she quipped, smirking at Travis. "Hey, is that Arnie downstairs talking with Dadzilla?"

"Yes, it is," Catheryn answered. She rose and walked to the stove, ladling batter for six more pancakes onto the skillet. "He came over to help your father, who, I might add, would not take kindly to your little nickname."

"He'll never find out."

"Find out what?" Kane demanded, appearing in the doorway.

"Allison called you Dadzilla," Nate shouted gleefully.

"Is that right?" Kane growled, turning it over in his mind and carefully weighing the gravity of Allison's insubordination. "Hmmm. Dadzilla. The name strikes fear in the hearts of millions of our Asian trading partners, not to mention a few smart-mouthed kids who run like ants under my feet while I stomp 'em into greasy smears on the pavement. I like it."

"Kinda suits you," said Arnie, trailing Kane into the kitchen. "Morning, everyone."

"Hi, Arnie," said Nate and Allison in unison.

Allison breathed a sigh of relief. "Lucky for you he's in a good mood, flea," she whispered, glaring at Nate.

"You mean lucky for *you*," Nate retorted.

Ignoring their banter, Kane grabbed two plates from the counter, handed one to Arnie, and scooped a monstrous serving of eggs and potatoes onto his own. "Where's Tommy?"

"I called him," said Travis.

"So did I," added Allison. "He said he'd be here in a minute."

"When he arrives, Allison has something to tell us," Catheryn announced with a mysterious smile.

"Aw, Mom," moaned Allison, her face turning crimson.

Kane sat across from Travis and forked a stack of pancakes atop the food already on his plate. "I can't stand secrets," he said. "Spill it, Allison."

"It's no big deal."

"Sure it is," said Catheryn reassuringly. "Getting published for the first time *is* a big deal."

"One of your shorts got accepted?" cried Travis. "That's great! Why didn't you tell us?"

"It just came in yesterday's mail," Allison explained shyly.

"Well, congratulations," said Arnie. "After reading that piece you wrote in your school paper, I knew you had what it takes."

"Tell us about it," said Travis.

"*Asimov's Science Fiction* magazine bought a story I wrote last Christmas called 'Daniel's Song,' " Allison said, unable to hide the rush of pleasure she felt at her family's praise. "It's coming out in the July issue."

" 'Daniel's Song,' huh?" said Kane, drumming his fingers on the table. "You wrote a tribute to the ol' dad here?"

"Don't worry, Dad," Allison said quickly. "It's not about you."

"Too bad. How much they payin' you, anyway?"

"Three hundred fifty-two dollars."

"Whooee. Kate, book us a Caribbean vacation."

"They don't pay much at first," Allison went on, looking crestfallen.

"Money isn't the point," Catheryn interjected. "Your father's just teasing. He knows this is quite an accomplishment for a fifteen-year-old."

"Yeah. Especially a girl," said Kane, shoveling in a forkful of eggs.

"Congratulations on breaking into the big time, sport. Before long we'll be asking for your autograph."

Allison shifted uncomfortably. "Don't worry, I won't forget the little people I used to know on the way up. By the way, what was your name again?"

"Dadzilla," muttered Kane.

The table fell silent. Following a brief pause Travis spoke up, trying to fill the uncomfortable gap in the conversation. "What are you going to build with all that wood, Dad?"

"A raft."

"A raft?" said Nate. "You mean something to swim to?"

"Real good, kid," Kane grunted. "I'm glad to see all that dough I've been shellin' out for Montessori school hasn't been wasted."

"Of course it's to swim to," said Allison. "What do you think—Dad's gonna put a raft out there just so's the birds have someplace new to crap?"

"Watch your language, young lady," admonished Catheryn.

"Allison can't help herself, Mom," Travis teased. "She's just trying to be one of the boys."

"That makes two of us, huh, Trav?"

Ignoring his children, Kane turned to Arnie. "See that buoy out there?" he said, pointing with his fork to a small white shape bobbing several hundred yards offshore. "I got a line on the old train wheel yesterday. That's what we're gonna use for the anchor. Might move it closer to the house, though."

"Move it? How?" asked Travis, who'd inspected the massive relic a number of times while swimming offshore.

"You'll see when the time comes. Right now I want that wood moved down to the beach as soon as you get home from church. Go tell Tommy to get rolling."

"Yes, sir."

Travis quickly finished his meal and carried his plate to the sink. Upon returning to his room, he found Tommy still in bed, talking on the phone. "Look, I gotta go," Tommy mumbled into the receiver, lowering his voice as Travis entered. "You coming over today? Good. See you then."

"Christy?" Travis asked after Tommy hung up.

"Yeah." Tommy swung his feet to the floor and started pulling on his clothes. "What's up?"

"Dad wants that wood out front brought down to the beach right after Mass. We're gonna build a raft."

"Shit."

•   •   •

An hour after returning from church, Travis and Tommy stood on the beach beside a large stack of beams and planks, six fifty-gallon drums, a cardboard box filled with galvanized nails, and a sack of miscellaneous marine hardware that they'd struggled down from the street. During their efforts Kane had read the Sunday paper and idly supervised from the deck—shouting encouragement and an occasional exhortation to "get a move on." Finally, impatient to begin, he'd helped with the last of it, then paused to check the lumber and hardware against a list he withdrew from his pocket.

"Yep, it's all here," he finally pronounced with a satisfied nod. "Arnie, come over and look at this."

Kane turned over his material list and spread it out on the lumber. Arnie and the boys crowded closer, noticing that on the back of the crumpled paper was a rough pencil sketch of the finished raft, drawn in Kane's hand. Peering down, they listened as Kane ran a thick finger over the details, giving them an overview of the project. The design was simple and utilitarian. A triple layer of four-by-eight beams, spaced to cradle the flotation drums on all sides, would make up the main framework, with sixteen-inch galvanized bolts fastening them together at each junction. One-by-twelve redwood planks nailed on top would form the deck.

"What's gonna keep the drums from poppin' out in a big storm?" asked Arnie.

"We'll secure 'em to the underside with nylon rope," Kane answered. "But that comes later. First thing we're gonna do is assemble the framework around the barrels. When we've got it right, we'll tack 'em together with nails and drill the bolt holes. After it's bolted come the barrels; then we'll flip 'er over and nail on the deck."

"Looks easy enough," said Arnie. "Let's do it."

Although work went quickly, the sun had climbed high into the sky by the time the inverted framework stood assembled, drilled, and ready for bolting. As they'd labored, Arnie and Kane had made frequent rehydration pilgrimages to an ice chest on the deck, and a sizable collection of empty beer cans had quickly accumulated against the seawall. Predictably, as the day progressed and the pile grew even higher, the construction site took on the semblance of a swiftly degenerating party. Just as Travis had begun to wonder whether Kane and Arnie were too drunk to continue handling power tools, he heard his mother calling down from the house.

"Travis! Ask your father if he can manage without you for a while."

"Why?"

"I want you to get in some practice."

Travis glanced at Kane, expecting a bark. To his surprise his father nodded. "Go. Make your mom happy. We'll get this sucker done without you somehow."

"I can practice later, Dad. If it's okay with you, I'd like to—"

Kane interrupted with a brusque wave of his hand. "Go on. We don't need you. And take Tar up with you and give him some water. He's bakin' out here in the sun." The old Labrador had joined them earlier when it had been cool, watching as the curious new structure took shape on the sand. Later he'd been unable to climb back over the wall, and now sat panting and exhausted beside the remaining stack of decking.

"Okay," Travis grumbled, stinging at his abrupt dismissal. "Come on, boy." He waited patiently as Tar made his way to the base of the wall, then knelt and lifted him to the upper level.

"And see if Nate gave him his pill today," Kane yelled after him.

After refilling Tar's water bowl and dispensing the medicine Nate had predictably forgotten, Travis left the old dog in the shade and made his way to a bright beach-level chamber under the main floors of the house. Years back when Kane had constructed it, Catheryn had insisted he include as much glass on the beach side as possible. As a result, the room Travis now entered had turned out to be one of the most pleasant in their home. A large bay window overlooked the ocean, with a pair of French doors on either side leading out to the redwood deck beyond, giving a cheery, capacious feeling of openness and light. Rustic Mexican tiles and throw rugs covered the floor, and against the back wall, dominating the otherwise sparsely furnished space, stood an old Baldwin upright piano. A sturdy oak chair, its surface smooth and polished from years of use, sat close beside it, along with a music stand and Catheryn's cello case. Rounding out the furnishings, a couch, fireplace, and two wicker chairs formed a semicircle around an austere bar in the far corner—Catheryn's single concession to her husband in the airy space that, upon completion, had immediately been christened the music room.

Reluctantly, Travis crossed to the piano, feeling a suffocating surge of resentment as he realized Catheryn was probably upstairs listening. With a sigh, he sat at the bench and wrung his hands to loosen them. Then, as a warm-up exercise, he embarked on Chopin's Waltz in C-sharp Minor, Op. 64, No. 2. He played from memory, the complex tones seeming to flow effortlessly from his fingers. As usual, he let his mind wander, paying little attention to the exercise that had become as automatic to him as brushing his teeth. A few minutes later, after cutting short the waltz in the lovely syncopated middle section, he thumbed through a sheaf of music above the keyboard, selected the fifth prelude from Rachmaninoff's twenty-third opus, and began to practice in earnest.

Rachmaninoff's preludes, considered by many to include some of the most difficult works ever written for solo piano, abound with large finger stretches and enormous chordal sonorities, and have proved an exacting test of a pianist's ability since their creation at the turn of the century. The prelude Travis selected was no exception, possessing tremendous technical challenges from beginning to end. The first section contained bombastic, offbeat chords punctuating a stately melody, with driving sixteenth-note rhythms and extreme dynamics that lent it a harsh, militant intensity. The resulting mood of severe and unbending anger was relieved only slightly in the more evocative second section, finally returning to a recapitulation of the fierce opening melody at the end. For the next hour Travis worked on the piece, the music matching his dark state of mind as he started and stopped in fits, repeating phrases over and over in an attempt to master particularly strenuous sections.

•   •   •

Upstairs, alone in her room, Allison lay on her bed listening to Travis's playing. Angrily, she slashed over the lines she'd just written in her notebook, then tore out the page and crumpled it, letting it drop to the floor. She started to write again, then stopped. Finally she closed her notebook and tossed it onto the floor as well, and for the next twenty minutes, while Travis continued to practice, she listened in the secrecy of her room as she had for years—filled with bitter thoughts of her father's dismissive attitude that morning regarding her story. And at last, as Travis played the prelude uninterrupted from beginning to end and Allison felt her emotions rising and soaring and swelling against her will, she hated herself for her smallness and the power her brother's music held over her.

"Ali?" Catheryn called through the door as the final furious chords died away.

Allison quickly wiped her eyes. "Yeah, Mom?"

Catheryn opened the door. She glanced curiously at her daughter. "You okay?"

"Allergies," said Allison.

With a look of concern, Catheryn closed the door and moved to sit beside her on the bed. "What's wrong?"

"Nothing."

"It's about your story, isn't it? The way Dad acted?"

"No."

"Ali, he was just kidding. You know that."

"No, I don't," said Allison.

"Of course you do. Your father—"

"What I *know*," Allison interrupted, "is that Dad thinks nothing I could possibly do is worth his attention."

"That's not true. Your father loves all you children equally, and he's proud of *all* your accomplishments. Yours included."

"Oh, sure," said Allison. "Just like you, Mom?"

"What's that supposed to mean?"

"Just that you'd have never let him tease Travis like that about his music."

"If I defend Travis more than you, it's because he needs it," said Catheryn, her expression tightening. "It doesn't mean I love you any less, or that I'm any less proud of you. I don't think you realize how much more lenient your father is with you than the others, Ali. If any of your brothers said half the things you blurt out . . ."

". . . they'd be taking a one-way trip to the moon," Allison finished.

"Let's just say that in some ways you're your father's favorite."

"Lucky me."

"Oh, Allison . . ."

"Never mind, Mom," said Allison crankily. "I don't want to talk about it anymore."

Catheryn put her arm around her daughter's shoulder and gave it a squeeze. "Listen, Christy's here," she said, her voice lightening. "She brought over the rest of the birthday cake. Want to join us?"

"Ugh. After Friday I'm sick of cake."

"Why don't you come out to the kitchen anyway?" Catheryn pulled her daughter up from the bed and pushed her firmly toward the door. "You can't spend a beautiful day like this in your room."

"Watch me."

"Ali, please."

"Okay, Mom," Allison groaned. "Let's go eat cake."

When Catheryn and Allison arrived in the kitchen, they found Nate and Christy already settled like vultures around the battered remnants of Friday's birthday castle, the carcass of which now sat in ruins on a huge serving platter. Both turrets had slumped sadly on their sides; the thick walls were collapsed; even the fudge-laden keep showed evidence of a terrible, prolonged siege. Nonetheless, there seemed adequate mass, however decimated, for at least one last chocolate binge.

"Where're the plates?" asked Catheryn.

"Don't need 'em," said Nate, handing everyone a fork. "We can eat off the platter. Save on dishes."

"Good idea," said Allison approvingly, since it was her day to wash.

"Think we should call the guys?" Catheryn asked, glancing out the window. The timbers of the raft's framework had now been bolted together, the barrels lashed to the underside, and Tommy, Kane, Arnie, and a group of neighbors were struggling to flip it over in order to complete the deck. As she watched, she saw Travis joining to help.

"Who needs them?" said Allison resentfully.

"Yeah," said Nate, noticing his sister's tone. "They don't need us. Besides, it's my cake, so what I say goes. Right, Mom?"

Catheryn sighed. "Well, I suppose they're busy right now, anyway."

Nate nodded. "Yeah, too busy for us." Then, in a stern and commanding voice, he mimicked his father's time-honored order to commence. "Eat!" And for several minutes no one spoke, concentrating with single-minded resolve on the business of cake consumption.

"How's the swimming coming?" Catheryn asked Christy once the eating tempo had slowed.

Christy shrugged. "Okay, I guess. It's just . . . I don't know, Mrs. Kane. I'm thinking of taking a break."

Catheryn raised a questioning eyebrow. She knew Christy's recent performance at the western regionals—setting records in the fifty-meter freestyle and the hundred butterfly—made her a strong possibility for the upcoming Olympics, and that college offers had already started rolling in. "I thought next season was critical to your scholarship chances."

"It is, but . . . well, I guess I'm trying to keep my options open. My grades are good enough to get accepted to the University of Arizona without swimming. I've got some money saved, and maybe my folks can help. If I work until Tommy graduates—"

"Until he graduates from college?" asked Allison, her mouth dropping open in amazement.

"What's wrong with that?"

"Nothing," answered Catheryn, setting down her fork and regarding Christy carefully. "Have you talked this over with your parents?"

"Not yet, Mrs. Kane. I . . . I'd appreciate it if you wouldn't say anything to them. It's just something I'm thinking about."

Catheryn remained silent, puzzled by Christy's unexpected revelation and surprised that Tommy hadn't mentioned it. "All right," she said at last. "I will discuss it with Tom, though. He's not the reason you're thinking of quitting?"

"Of course not."

Just then Arnie stuck his head into the kitchen. "The raft's about done, and I gotta hit the road," he said with a wave. "See you kids later. 'Bye, Kate. Oh, don't let Dan forget we've got a meeting with the brass first thing tomorrow," he added. "I already discussed it with him, but I've got a sneakin' feeling that after a dozen or so more beers it may just slip his tiny little mind."

"Sure thing, Arnie. You okay to drive?"

Arnie grinned. "I'm fine," he answered. "In case you haven't noticed, I can drink that husband of yours under the table any day of the week."

• • •

Forty-five minutes later, as the cake party trooped out to the beach, Kane had just finished bolting a heavy galvanized mooring swivel to one of the main beams, and Travis and Tommy were nailing the last of the redwood planks. "What do you think, troops?" Kane demanded, giving the swivel one final twist. "Not bad, huh?"

"Yeah, check it out, Mom," said Tommy, momentarily looking up from his work. "There's room for at least fifteen people—maybe twenty. And the way it's sitting high on the barrels, the waves won't splash you when you're on it."

"It'll have a ladder, too," added Travis proudly. "It hangs down below the barrels, so we can't bolt it on till after it's floating. Pretty great, huh?"

"Terrific," said Catheryn. "When do you plan to launch it?"

"Next weekend, surf and weather permitting," answered Kane. "I'd like to get her moored before the party."

"The birds are gonna love it," said Allison coldly.

"The hell with the birds, Allison," said Kane, hopping up onto the deck and testing each board with his weight to ensure it was properly nailed. "I'll be spreadin' the word to our community of feathered friends shortly. Soon's those winged rats find out whose raft this is, they'll probably start flyin' all the way to Santa Monica to crap—just so's they don't chance havin' any stray shit land on my raft here. We'll probably wind up with the only constipated seagulls on the coast."

"That's a switch," Allison retorted. "Usually you scare the crap out of everybody."

"Yeah. And that's the way I like it," Kane declared, still striding up and down the ten-by-ten deck. "Now, quit pickin' on me, and go grab me another beer."

"Yes, *sir!*" said Allison, flipping Kane an exaggerated salute.

Kane shook his head in irritation at his daughter's retreating figure, then turned to Tommy and Travis. "You two finished yet?"

Both boys had returned to their task and were kneeling side by side—racing to pound in their final nails.

"Almost," Tommy answered without looking up.

"Done!" said Travis. With a flourish of his hammer he rose to his feet, bowed, and dropped lightly to the beach. Tommy finished thirty seconds later. He magnanimously acknowledged his brother's victory, then moved to stand beside Kane on the edge of the platform. After putting his arm around his father, he cleared his throat and solemnly addressed those sitting on the sand below.

"Mom, Christy, and others not worth mentioning," he said, winking at Travis, "on this momentous occasion, seein' how Dad's obviously weakened and wobbly from slugging down innumerable beers, not to mention the fact he's getting on in years, I've decided this is the perfect opportunity to declare myself the supreme, glorious, and undisputed king of the raft." With a laugh he pushed lightly in the center of Kane's back, unceremoniously toppling him from the deck.

A moment of shocked silence followed. Finally Kane spoke. "Think you're ready to take on the ol' man, eh?" he said with a red-faced, loopy smile.

Tommy danced to the center of the deck, signaling his response by inviting Kane forward with a waving motion of his hands. "Come get your punishment, old man," he laughed.

Just then Allison returned from her journey to the cooler. "Here you go, Dad," she said, handing her father the can of beer he'd requested. "Don't take it too hard. Everybody's gotta step down sometime."

Ignoring Allison, Kane popped the beer and took a long swallow, watching as Tommy indulged in another stutter-stepping tour of the deck. Then, after finishing his beer in one prolonged guzzle, he crushed the can and tossed it atop the considerable pile already stacked against the wall. "It's your funeral, cupcake," he said, springing to the raft.

"Come on, Tommy," cheered Allison.

"You can do it, Tom," yelled Christy.

"Yeah, knock Dad on his butt," Nate joined in. "Kill him!"

"Kids!" laughed Catheryn.

Kane crouched and advanced toward his son, hands open and ready, the cords of his massive forearms rolling under the skin. He circled slowly, moving on the balls of his feet. Suddenly he darted forward. His left hand snaked out, closing like a trap on Tommy's wrist. He yanked. Tommy dropped and went with the pull, driving his shoulder into his father's chest and reaching down with his free hand for Kane's knee, attempting to pull him off balance.

"Stay on your feet, Tom," Travis shouted.

Tommy struggled to pull Kane's leg from under him. Although Tommy nearly matched his father's height, Kane outweighed him by thirty pounds, and easily broke the hold. He spun Tommy around without releasing his wrist, gripping him tightly from behind. Then, using his superior weight and insuperable strength, he dragged his son to the edge of the raft. Tommy fought to break free. Kane tenaciously maintained his advantage. Seconds later he gleefully dumped him to the sand below.

As Tommy brushed himself off, Kane executed an elaborate, unsteady bow, blithely ignoring a maelstrom of boos and hisses from his family.

"Two out of three," declared Tommy, jumping back onto the deck.

Kane smiled. "You're a glutton for punishment, kid," he said, slurring his words. Then his smile disappeared. He advanced toward Tommy as before, weaving slightly as he approached. This time Tommy backed away warily, trying to keep from stepping off the edge, waiting his chance. It came a split second later when Kane overconfidently lunged forward. Tommy sidestepped and grabbed his father's right arm in both hands. He jerked with all his strength. Kane stumbled toward the edge, his free arm flailing wildly as he attempted to save himself. An instant later he tumbled to the beach. As he fell, the back of his hand caught Tommy in the face.

The family's cheering abruptly evaporated as blood gushed from Tommy's nose. "Tommy!" Catheryn cried, jumping to her feet. Tommy brought his hand to his face, then stared in surprise at the bright flow seeping into his palm.

An instant later Kane bounded back onto the raft, his face flushed with anger. He hesitated, noticing the blood on Tommy's face and the splatter on the redwood at his feet. "Don't worry about it, kid," he said guiltily. "A little blood ain't gonna hurt the raft."

"That's not funny," admonished Catheryn with a look of irritation. She climbed up and moved to Tommy's side. "It could be broken. Tommy, are you—"

"I'm okay, Mom," Tommy mumbled through his hand.

Christy climbed up and offered him a towel she'd brought out to sit on. "Here," she said.

"Thanks." Tommy took it and held it to his face. "I'll be okay. I don't think anything's busted."

"Good," said Kane. "Now that everybody's satisfied we're not gonna have to life-flight the kid to the hospital, how about movin' your asses off the deck so we can finish the contest?"

Christy quickly dropped to the sand, but Catheryn stood her ground. "You don't know when to quit, do you?"

"Don't start with me." Kane circled her with his arm and walked her to the edge. "You heard him. Tommy ain't hurt. It's just a nose-bleed."

Catheryn broke free. "No, Dan. That's it for today. Your little game is over."

"Kate, you're overreacting here. The kid can take it. He plays football, for chrissake."

"That's different. You and Arnie have been out here drinking all day, and I think you've overdone it."

"Jesus, Kate. I've had a couple beers, but I'm *hardly* drunk."

"You're acting like it. You know you're not much of a drinker."

"Kate, cut the crap and get out of the way." Without another word Kane roughly shoved her the rest of the way off the raft.

"Hey, don't push Mom," cried Nate.

"It's okay, honey," said Catheryn. "It's time for you to head inside. And the rest of us, too. Let's go, Tom."

Tommy glanced at his father, then back at Catheryn. "Mom, I'm okay. Really." He took the bloodstained towel from his face and tossed it to the sand. "Look, the bleeding's mostly stopped. Come on, Dad. This one decides it."

"Attaboy, Tom," muttered Kane. "I'm glad to see *all* my kids ain't turned into pussies." With a sloppy grin, he turned and dropped to a crouch. "Get ready to do some flyin', rookie."

The rest of the family watched in silence as Tommy backed from his father's huge, grasping hands, once more trying to stay out of range, awaiting an opening. He studied his father's eyes as he retreated, his back to the edge. Kane pursued him slowly, determined not to repeat his earlier error, steadily closing the distance, cutting Tommy off at every turn. At last he trapped him in a corner. Realizing he could no longer escape, Tommy feinted left and then reversed, hoping to catch his father unprepared. Kane reacted instantly, again cutting him off. Then, lashing out with lightning speed, he snagged Tommy's red-spattered T-shirt and drew him in. Triumphantly, he twisted Tommy's arm behind his back and retreated, stopping inches from the edge. "This is it, princess," he said, starting his turn.

Just as he prepared to toss Tommy to the sand, two small arms snaked over the platform and wound tightly around his ankles. Off balance and propelled by his previous momentum, Kane began toppling backward.

"Nate, no!" Travis screamed. Oblivious, Nate maintained his death grip on his father's legs, his eyes squeezed shut in blind and dogged determination.

With ponderous, almost stately elegance, Kane and Tommy's locked figures began to rotate, falling in seeming slow motion, crashing like cut timber to the sand below. Kane hit first with a sickening, hollow thud. Tommy landed on top, his 190 pounds driving the breath from Kane's body.

Nate stood frozen, horrified by what he'd done. Then, his face ashen with fear, he turned and streaked for the house.

Tommy rolled off Kane's prostrate form. "You okay, Dad?" he asked.

Kane lay unnaturally still, his breath coming in racking, choking gasps. "Where is that little thumb-sucker?" he wheezed when he could finally speak. "I swear I'm gonna kill him."

"You're going to do nothing of the kind," said Catheryn firmly. "It was an accident. And even if it weren't, you had it coming. Christy, I'm sorry you had to see this, but sometimes my husband gets a little carried away. Now it's time we all went in."

"Somebody call nine-one-one," laughed Travis. "Dad's been injured by a nine-year-old," he added, missing a look of warning from his mother. "Looks like we'll need that life-flight after all."

Groaning, Kane rose to his feet. He glowered at Travis. "Get over here, petunia," he commanded, his voice ominously flat. "The rest of you girls take a hike."

"No, Dan," said Catheryn. "Trav's coming with me."

Kane immediately started toward her, determined to quash any further sedition. When Catheryn didn't move, he spun her around and propelled her toward the house. "I mean it, Kate. Get lost. I ain't gonna hurt your little darling, but there're some things him and me gotta get straight."

Catheryn whirled. "You leave Trav out of this," she said, her eyes smoldering with anger.

"I ain't askin'. Move!"

"Dan, you don't realize how rough you can be."

"Rough? Hell, like Travis said, even Nate can take me down."

"Daddy, please," Allison pleaded. "Trav didn't mean anything—"

"I've heard enough out of you," Kane warned. "Shut your miserable snotty yap right now. Don't say another word."

Allison's eyes filled with hurt. Hand to her mouth, she turned and ran to the deck.

"Mom, please just leave," Travis begged. "We'll be up soon."

Catheryn hesitated, realizing her continued presence was making things worse. Slowly, she turned and walked toward the house, pausing when she reached the seawall. "Dan," she said quietly, looking back and holding her husband's gaze, "I'm warning you . . ."

"Don't push me, Kate. Beat it."

Cracking his knuckles, Kane waited until Catheryn joined Allison and Christy on the redwood deck. Then he turned and regarded his sons. Tommy stood quietly beside his brother. The fall from the raft had restarted his nosebleed, and he had the towel pressed once more to his face.

"That was funny seein' the ol' man get knocked on his butt, wasn't it?" Kane demanded in a voice that could cut steel.

Neither boy responded.

"I'm talkin' to you, Travis."

"Well, yeah, sort of," Travis answered.

"Quit mumbling. Speak up!"

"I said yeah, I guess it was."

"Yeah?"

"I mean yes, sir!"

"That's better. How'd you like to get knocked on *your* ass, rookie?"

"Not much, Dad."

"But it wouldn't kill you, would it?"

"No, sir."

"Good. Your mother seems to be of the opinion you're made of glass or somethin'. Are you?"

"No, sir."

"We'll see. I'm giving you a chance to show your mettle, boy. You can get up on the raft or go join the other girls up at the house. Your choice."

Slowly, Travis mounted the raft.

"You too, Tom."

Tommy blotted his face one last time and climbed up beside his brother.

"We're gonna continue the contest," Kane explained coldly. "Travis against Tommy, best two out of three. And just to keep it interesting and make sure you're both trying, the loser of each round is gonna get his tail booted by yours truly. Got it?"

Both boys nodded reluctantly.

"Good. Then go!"

The brothers circled each other, testing for weaknesses. With a sudden spring Tommy moved in and pushed hard against Travis's shoulders, sending him stumbling toward the edge. Travis barely stayed on by grabbing his brother's arm. A brief wrestling skirmish ensued, with Tommy's greater strength quickly winning out. Less than a minute after it began, Travis found himself sprawled on the beach. As he rose, Kane placed his bare foot on Travis's backside and pushed. Hard. Travis skidded on his face.

"Hey, Dad!" yelled Tommy, jumping down. "Don't do that."

"Get back up there, Tom. You too, Travis. And this time I wanna see you trying for a change," he added, glaring at Travis. "And by God you're gonna. You'd better not cave this time, bucko."

Travis rose, spitting sand. Numbly, he climbed back onto the deck. Tommy didn't move.

"Let's go, Tom. Round two," Kane growled.

"Dad, this isn't right."

"Get up there. Now."

"This isn't right," Tommy repeated stubbornly.

"Come on, Tom," Travis called, his voice strangely apathetic. "Let's get it over with."

Tommy lowered his head, staring stubbornly at his feet. "No."

With thick, cruel fingers Kane grabbed his son's chin and snapped up his head. Tightening his grip, he stared into Tommy's eyes. "Last chance. I'm givin' you an order, boy. Get up there."

Tommy stared back at his father, his vision blurring, eyes burning with hurt and defiance. "No, sir," he said.

"You're disobeyin' a direct order?"

"That's right."

"Speak up," Kane barked. "What did you say?"

"I said yes, sir."

"Yes, sir, what?"

"Yes, sir, I'm disobeying a direct order."

"You ain't gonna start blubberin' now, are you?" Kane demanded, his lips inches from Tommy's face.

"No, sir."

"You sure?"

"Yes, sir." Tommy was fighting it hard now, and not succeeding.

"I don't believe this," said Kane. With a growl of disgust he shoved Tommy away. Then he turned his back and walked slowly to the ocean's edge, where he stood staring out over the angry slate-gray waters.

Travis jumped down, warily watching his father.

"You two girls go run to your mama," Kane ordered over his shoulder. "Maybe you can all get out your hankies and have a real nice cryin' fest."

"Please, Dad. You're wrong this time," said Tommy softly.

Without answering, Kane marched off down the sand.

•   •   •

Late that night, long after lights in the Kane residence had been extinguished and darkness covered the beach, Travis lay awake listening to the waves pound the shore, feeling their rhythmic, crashing

vibrations drumming like a heartbeat through every window and timber of the house. In his mind's eye he revisited the afternoon's events.
Again he saw himself standing silent and powerless as Tommy refused
to continue the contest. Again he felt the paralyzing fear seeping into
his limbs, followed by the hateful surge of craven relief as he realized
his own test of spirit, his own crucible of courage, was unexpectedly
over. And once again he felt the burning flush of shame for allowing
Tommy to suffer their father's wrath in his stead.

"Tommy? You awake?"

"Yeah," Tommy answered drowsily. "I am now."

"I . . . I just wanted to say thanks. I don't think Dad planned on
stopping till he'd booted my tail black-and-blue."

"Aw, hell, Trav. It wouldn't have gone that far. Don't make more
of it than it was. Dad just had too many beers and got a little carried
away."

"Carried away? I can't believe you're defending him."

"I'm not defending what he did," Tommy's voice came through
the darkness. "It's just that Dad thinks you could use a little tough-
ening up. Me, too, I guess. He wants us to be more like him, if you
can believe that."

"Now, there's a scary thought. Two more like Dad in the world."

"Three. Allison doesn't count because she's a girl, but don't forget
Nate."

"Yeah. I don't envy him," said Travis, remembering the look of
terror in his younger brother's eyes as he'd fled the beach. No one
had been able to find him for hours. It turned out he'd crawled
beneath the joists of the deck, remaining hidden until well after dinner. "That kid's got a long way to go," he added.

"Maybe Dad'll mellow by then. Mom claims his temper has im-
proved a whole lot since she met him. She says he used to be worse."

"Hard to imagine."

"Yeah."

"Tommy?"

"What?"

"Thanks for sticking up for me."

"Forget it. It's no big deal. Let's get some sleep."

"Okay." A pause, then, "It is a big deal, though. To me, anyway.

When you're gone, I'm not sure how I'm gonna make out around here on my own."

"You'll do just fine, Trav."

"Tommy?"

"Yeah?"

Wondering how to proceed, Travis hesitated, attempting to find some acceptable construction of words and sentences and phrases that would allow him to ask his brother whether he loved their father. All the children had joked about their feelings for Kane at one time or another—kidding, sarcastic, tiptoeing around the edges of an issue that, like looking at the sun, none of them could view straight on. Long ago Travis had given up trying to find the answer, discovering safety in feeling nothing at all.

"What is it, Trav?"

Travis started to speak but stopped, realizing he'd already read the response to his unspoken question in his brother's eyes that afternoon, both for Tommy and for himself. *No stranger can truly hurt you; that terrible power is held only in the hands of those you love.* "Nothing," he whispered, staring out at the dark, roiling ocean beyond his window. "Forget it. Good night, Tommy."

"Night, Trav."

7

Monday morning, at a little after six-thirty A.M., Travis and Tommy stood shivering on a deserted construction site overlooking Paradise Cove. The Santa Anas had abated during the night, with the customary onshore flow of cool, moisture-laden marine air at last deposing the desert gusts. Hands thrust deep in their pockets, the boys stamped their feet against the cold, silently wishing the sun would hasten its ascent.

Around them in the chilly morning air, marching to the dead-end circle at the end of the street, rose the partially completed skeletons of seven wood-frame structures, each sequentially further toward completion than the last. The nearest was scarcely more than a foundation surrounding a concrete block chimney; the farthest had been roofed and bore the marks of the rough trades: electrical wires and copper pipes lacing the walls, sheet-metal ducts gleaming between the studs, window casements filling their appropriate openings. Here and there among the houses mammoth stacks of lumber squatted like shadowy behemoths, and piles of scrap wood and trash lay heaped everywhere. In the center of the project sat a mud-spattered trailer with a sign reading Stewart Construction, Inc.

As the sun finally rose and the construction site came to life around them, Travis and Tommy huddled by the trailer, watching a steady procession of vehicles ascending the hill to a large parking space across the street. Travis noticed that the crew appeared to range in age from early twenties to midthirties. After climbing from their cars, most of them assembled in casual groups around the lot, drinking coffee and talking in easy, unhurried tones.

Just before seven A.M. all heads turned at the throaty sound of a motorcycle climbing the hill. A moment later a leather-jacketed man riding a black Harley-Davidson roared up the street and skidded to a stop beside the trailer. He dismounted and removed his helmet, glancing curiously at the two boys.

Travis returned his gaze, looking into the creased, weathered face of the man before him, thinking he resembled a startlingly accurate throwback to the sixties—at least what Travis had seen of those years on TV and in the movies. He had a full beard and mustache and wore his curly black hair long and wild, and his muscular arms and callused hands spoke of a physical strength hardened by a lifetime of labor. But undoubtedly the man's pale-blue eyes were his most arresting feature. They crinkled now with humor as he looked from brother to brother, deepening the lattice of furrows radiating like a road map from the corners. "You must be Kane's boys," he said. "I'd recognize that fuckin' hair anywhere."

Tommy ran his hand self-consciously over his head. "Yes, sir," he said. "Dad said we were supposed to report to Tony."

"That's me." The man pulled a ring of keys from his pocket and unlocked the trailer. After tossing his helmet inside, he whistled to the men across the street. "Lemme get the guys going," he said, starting toward a large metal tool shack beside the trailer. "I'll get you two set up after that."

The crew ambled over and lined up to punch their time cards at a clock just inside the trailer. Some greeted the Kane boys as they passed. One, a heavily built youth with a pimply face and lank blond hair, smirked at Tommy. "Ain't seen your ass in a couple years," he said. "Team ain't been the same since I graduated, huh?"

"We've been doing okay without you, Junior," Tommy answered.

"Yeah?" Junior paused to stare at Travis. "Who's this? Oh, that's right, I heard you had a baby brother. What's wrong, Red? Lost your mommy?"

"No, but he hasn't seen yours in a while," Tommy cracked before Travis could answer. "If you see her, have her give us a call."

The youth's eyes hardened. Tony, who'd returned from the tool shack in time to hear this exchange, stepped between the two. "Get to work, Junior," he ordered. "I ain't paying you to gab."

"Sure thing, boss." Junior regarded Tommy and Travis coldly, then turned and sauntered off.

"Only here a few minutes and already making friends!" Tommy exclaimed cheerfully, clapping Travis on the back.

"What's with him?" asked Travis.

"That's Junior Cobb," Tony answered. "He thinks I should have hired his cousin instead of you two."

"He thinks we stole his cousin's job?"

"Somethin' like that. Junior's a good worker, but not too smart. Got a mean streak, too. Stay away from him. By the way, either of you have any construction experience?"

"Some," answered Travis doubtfully.

"Dad's had us helping around the house since we were old enough to carry lumber," Tommy added.

"Perfect, 'cause that's exactly what you're gonna be doing, at least for the next few days," said Tony. "Our forklift's busted, so there's lots of wood needs moving. You're gonna require some gear, too. Show up tomorrow with nail bags, a tape measure, and a twenty-two-ounce framing hammer. You don't have to get work boots, but I'd recommend it."

"We've already got some," said Tommy.

Tony nodded approvingly and then continued. "Here's the setup. I'm running two crews. Ron Yeats is lead man on one; Wes Nash runs the other." He checked his watch, then pointed at two large, rough-looking men across the street. "That's them over there sippin' coffee and acting like the day hasn't actually begun yet. They'll keep you busy. One more thing. Drinking or fighting on the job gets you fired. Period. Any questions?"

"No, sir," Tommy and Travis answered in unison.

Tony shook his head and grinned. "And drop the 'sir' shit. Now get to work."

●　　●　　●

At a little after nine that morning Kane rapped on the door of
Lieutenant Nelson Long's office. Hearing nothing, he raised his hand
to knock a second time, then stopped when Long's gravelly voice
boomed from the other side. "Come."

Arnie, who'd been standing behind Kane, followed him in and
closed the door behind them. Both detectives stood uneasily in the
center of the room, regarding the group of men sitting in a rough
semicircle behind the lieutenant's desk. Along with Lieutenant Long,
three others were present: Theodore Lincoln, the West L.A. Division
captain; Lieutenant William Snead, a thin man with intense, predatory eyes; and a pudgy, balding civilian neither Kane nor Arnie had
ever seen before.

Lieutenant Long looked up impassively, his dark face closed and
unreadable. "You both know Captain Lincoln," he said, glancing at
the stern-looking man with close-cropped silver hair on his left. The
captain nodded, impatiently tapping his foot.

"Morning, Captain," Arnie said. "What's this—"

"You're late," the balding man interrupted. "You were told to be
here at nine."

"Sorry, Lieutenant," Arnie said, ignoring the bovine civilian
whom both he and Kane had quickly sized up as somebody's political
flunky. "We just got a homicide call. Everybody else is out, and—"

Long raised his hand. "I know that, as does Mr. Jellup from the
mayor's office," he said, glaring at Jellup with thinly veiled contempt.
Then, turning to the final person present, "This is Lieutenant
Snead."

"I know Snead," Kane muttered.

"*Lieutenant* Snead," the man with the piercing eyes corrected.

Kane stared at Snead, then turned back to Long. "What the fuck's
Internal Affairs doing here?"

"We'll ask the questions," said Captain Lincoln. "But since you
mention it, Lieutenant Snead is here at the request of the mayor's
office, with my concurrence. Before we get into that, we've got other
matters to clear up." Reaching across Long's desk, he picked up a
thick three-ringed folder with the name Agnes Sellers taped on the
spine. Kane recognized it as the chronological log, colloquially
known as a murder book, of the investigation into the death of Senator Bradley's nanny. As the primary detective on the case, Kane had

been responsible for ensuring that it contained everything pertinent, including detailed measurements of the crime scene, a list of all persons who'd been present, descriptions, weather and lighting conditions, the crime report, death report, autopsy findings, pictures, field-interview summaries, arrest warrants, and regularly updated follow-ups. Often a murder book could swell to the size of a metropolitan phone book. Agnes Sellers's was already well past that.

Captain Lincoln thumbed slowly through the binder, stopping on the update Kane had made linking the maid's common-law husband to the recently opened safety-deposit box at the Century City bank. He looked up at Kane. "As the primary investigator in the Sellers homicide, you were instructed to inform the FBI on all aspects related to the kidnapping," he said. "When you established there was a possible connection with what's his name—Escobar—to the kidnapping, why didn't you notify the Bureau?"

"That was a judgment call," Arnie answered. "We didn't have anything definite—"

Captain Lincoln raised his hand. "I asked Kane."

Kane glanced at Arnie, then back at the captain. "Well, I'm not gonna bullshit you here, sir. There're a number of reasons we didn't bring in the Bureau. The safety-deposit box was a long shot, and at that point the feds had already disregarded our investigation of the maid—makin' it real clear they thought that approach was a dead end. Besides, there wasn't any room for an increased presence on the stakeout. And *most* of all," Kane added, "I didn't want 'em fuckin' up my investigation. Which, by the way, they managed to do anyway."

"Their two agents paid for their mistake," said Lincoln. "And now, because of it, I've got the Bureau climbing all over my ass claiming some maverick cop left them out of the loop."

"It was my case."

"That's correct, sir," interjected Lieutenant Long. "Despite the FBI's expropriation of the kidnapping phase, we still had jurisdiction on the homicide. Our cooperation on that was purely voluntary."

"Nonetheless, they're blaming the death of one of their agents and the injury of another on *our* lack of communication."

"With all due respect, that's bull," said Arnie. "Those two cowboys roared into the middle of our bust without checking with anybody and got caught with their pants down. If it hadn't been for Kane, there would've been two of 'em dead instead of one."

"Speaking of cowboys, Detective Kane," the captain continued without missing a beat, "why didn't you wait for the hostage negotiator to arrive? Who gave you permission to mount a one-man assault—endangering the lives of every civilian in that building, not to mention the hostages?"

"Hostage," Lieutenant Long pointed out. "By then they'd already thrown one out the window."

"I'm still talking to Kane," Lincoln snapped.

Kane shifted uneasily, sensing the real issue had yet to be broached. "Seemed like a good idea at the time. Like the lieutenant said, they'd already killed one hostage, plus a Bureau agent. Another one was bleeding to death in the street, and SWAT wasn't gonna get there in time. But that's not what this is about, is it, Captain?"

"Right, Kane," said Lieutenant Snead, the man from Internal Affairs. "Evidently you're not as thick as you look."

Kane smiled coldly. "Looks can be deceiving, slugger. Check the mirror."

"Keep feeding the bear," said Snead, his lips twisting in a gelid smile. "You're making my job all that much easier."

"What's going on?" asked Arnie, looking puzzled. "Kane's one of our best detectives. He just pulled in two kidnapping/homicide suspects, found the Bradley kid, and saved the life of a Bureau agent. Now you're treatin' him like garbage. What gives?"

"Just how *did* you come up with the location of the Bradley boy, Detective Kane?" Snead demanded. "The suspect simply blurt it out?"

"Is that what we're getting at here?"

"Escobar's claiming you're a racist and that you shot him in cold blood," said Jellup. "He says you interrogated him before the arrest and shot him while trying to get him to confess. He still maintains he's innocent, by the way."

"Horseshit. He pulled a gun on me. Just like the guy in the hall."

"The man you shot in the hall is no longer around to dispute your story," Jellup continued, looking distastefully at Kane. "But Escobar is, and his wife's backing him up. We can't afford another excessive-force trial in this city, for God's sake. *Especially* with racial overtones."

Kane bristled. "*Racial overtones?* What the hell are you talking about? I don't give a shit if Escobar's a goddamn Eskimo. That dirtbag had just killed—excuse me, *allegedly* killed—an FBI agent and a civilian. He wasn't about to give up the Bradley boy. I may have pushed him for the kid's whereabouts, but I sure as hell didn't shoot him to get it."

"The kid died anyway," Snead pointed out. "Your actions, *whatever* they were, didn't help one damn bit."

"It was still a good shooting," growled Kane. "Both the guy in the hall *and* Escobar."

"That's the way the officer-involved shooting team saw it," added Lieutenant Long. "There's no way the review board isn't going to rule it a good shoot."

"We'll see," Snead noted dryly. "Considering that Kane spent several minutes alone with Martin and Escobar, and then *mysteriously* came up with the boy's location, Escobar's accusations have raised some serious doubts. We intend to find out exactly what happened in that room. Everything."

"Somebody back up the truck," said Kane. "I can't believe what I'm hearin' here."

"Believe it," advised Captain Lincoln. "The chief's been fielding questions from the press all morning, and the mayor's getting nervous. Before things get out of control, we want a full statement from you, and we want it now."

"You've already got my statement, sir. It's in my arrest report."

"That isn't good enough," said Snead.

"Talk to the hostage Escobar was holding," Kane suggested. "A Hispanic girl living in the building. She saw what happened."

"Are you telling me how to run my investigation?"

"No, but—"

"We've already talked with the girl. Now we want to talk to you."

"Everything I have to say is in my report."

"IA's going to need a lot more than that," Snead warned. "A *lot* more. I'd strongly advise you to cooperate."

"Am I being charged?"

"Not at the present time."

"Then I'll tell you what, *Lieutenant* Snead," said Kane, his lips drawing back from his teeth in a humorless grin. "Let me know when I *am* being charged, and I'll come in with a city attorney and we'll have a nice long chat. In the meantime, go fuck yourself."

•   •   •

The morning passed quickly for Travis. As on any construction site, the first twenty minutes had been spent in casual, unhurried preparation—rolling out power cords that had been daisy-chained at the end of the previous workday to prevent tangles, setting up compressors and hoses for the nail guns, adjusting power tools, and drinking coffee. But once the day started in earnest, Tommy and Travis moved lumber—stacks of two-by-four and two-by-six wall studs, two-by-twelve joists, half-inch plywood sheathing, and three-quarter-inch particle-board flooring—carrying the material to various sites as needed, hustling to stay ahead of the crews. They quickly learned the technique of working in unison, especially when handling the heavy eighteen-foot joists, where a misstep by either could cause injury to both.

Throughout the morning they also good-naturedly accepted the ribbing traditionally leveled at any new worker. Travis spent fruitless minutes searching the tool shed for a left-handed hammer; Tommy likewise found himself unable to locate, among other things, an elusive board stretcher requested by one of the framers. Nonetheless, by the time the lunch wagon rolled up the hill, Travis found himself actually enjoying the work. He liked the sweet pine smell of sawdust, the sounds of the saws and hammers, the occasional thunk of a nail gun, the steady beat of the compressor, the way the framing rose almost magically from the foundations. Most of all, he liked the easy camaraderie of the crew. To his surprise, although his shoulders ached and his arms felt leaden, he experienced a pang of regret when they broke for lunch.

Both Tommy and Travis had worked up a prodigious appetite over the morning, and the food served by the wagon proved to be hot, aromatic, greasy, and delicious. Travis ordered two chili cheeseburgers, a large basket of fries, a Sprite, and a hunk of apple pie; Tommy opted for a giant chicken burrito, Spanish rice, refried beans, and a

Coke. As they retired to a stack of lumber to eat, Travis noticed Junior Cobb and a few other men gathered around a large metal trash drum across the street. Junior was laughing and poking into the barrel with a piece of scrap lumber.

"Hey, there's your new buddy," said Tommy. "Why don't you go over and say hi?"

"He's not *my* buddy," said Travis. "He's not too crazy about you, either."

"I wonder what they've got in there," mused Tommy. As he spoke, Junior again thrust his piece of wood into the trash container. A high-pitched squeal rose from the barrel. Junior laughed and poked into the container once more.

"They've got something trapped in there, Tom."

"They're not gonna hurt it," said Tommy. "Even Junior's not that big a prick."

Another squeal echoed from the barrel.

Tommy saw the expression change on his brother's face. "Don't go looking for trouble, Trav. Not the first day."

"I'm not looking for trouble. I just want to see what's going on." Travis set down his plate and crossed the street. Shouldering his way through Junior's friends, he peered into the barrel. A squirrel that had apparently become trapped while scavenging for food cowered at the bottom. Junior stabbed again, narrowly missing the terrified animal. "Slippery little sucker," he said, grinning.

"Come on, Junior," said one of the men. "That's enough."

"Says who?" Junior drove the tip of his weapon deep into the trash in another attempt to pin the small rodent. "In my book a squirrel's no better'n a rat." As he spoke, the animal suddenly streaked up the wood, clawing Junior's hand in a desperate effort to escape. Junior shook it off with a scream of surprise and pain, sending it tumbling back into the barrel.

"That little bastard bit me!" he yelled, clutching his hand.

"Hell, he only scratched you," said another of Junior's friends. "You'll live."

"Yeah, well that's more'n that fuckin' squirrel can say." With an ominous smirk Junior pulled a pack of matches from his pocket. One by one he lit them, dropping them into the barrel. Travis could hear the frightened animal at the bottom beginning to chatter in terror.

"Leave it alone," said the first man who'd spoken, clearly too daunted by Junior's size to intervene.

"Fuck you, Chuck," Junior spat, continuing to drop matches into the refuse. The other men shifted uneasily, but no one else dared to speak. Seconds later a wisp of smoke drifted up as the trash started to ignite. The sound of the squirrel clawing the metal sides became frantic. "Lookit that sucker go," Junior crowed. "Anybody for squirrel flambé?"

Travis, who'd watched silently until then, shook his head in disgust and started back across the street. But as the animal began keening in panic, he stopped. Without thinking, he returned in three quick strides and kicked over the barrel. Burning rubbish spilled onto the dirt. Singed and smoking, the squirrel raced for the safety of the brush behind the houses.

Junior's eyes glittered with rage. He grabbed Travis's shirt. "What the fuck you think you're doin'?" he bellowed.

Travis swallowed, as surprised as anyone at what he'd done. "Must have been an accident," he mumbled, nervously spreading his hands.

"You're about to have an accident of your own, pussy." Junior doubled his fist. Before he could swing, someone grabbed his arm and twisted it behind his back. An instant later a red-haired forearm circled his neck. Tommy.

Choking, Junior released his grip on Travis's shirt. He started to struggle, then quickly stopped as the pressure on his windpipe increased. One of Junior's friends moved to intercede. Travis cut him off.

"You're pretty good at beatin' up squirrels, huh, Junior?" said Tommy. "Ready to take on somebody your own size?"

"You always fight your baby brother's battles?" Junior gagged.

Tommy shoved him away. Junior stumbled, catching himself before he hit the ground. He whirled, ready to fight. Looking at Tommy, he thought better of it. Although Junior outweighed him, he recognized something in Tommy's eyes that spelled trouble.

"Don't wanna fight?" said Tommy pleasantly. "Well, you're free to tangle with my brother here anytime you want. Just so you know, though. When you get done, I'm gonna make you wish you hadn't. You hit my brother once, I'm gonna hit you twice. You sprain his little finger, I'm gonna break your fuckin' arm. Understand?"

Junior rubbed his throat. "You're lucky there's no fightin' on the job," he said. "I can't afford gettin' fired."

"You can't afford havin' me ram your teeth down your throat."

"Fuck you," said Junior, smarting under the stares of his friends. Angrily, he turned to leave. He paused briefly before Travis on his way. Travis looked down, unable to meet his gaze.

"I'll see you sometime when your brother ain't around," Junior promised softly as he shoved past.

•   •   •

At Lieutenant Long's request, Kane returned to his office shortly after everyone else had left. He stood nervously, shifting from foot to foot as Long glared at him from across his desk. Although Kane had little regard for the opinions of the others who'd been present earlier, he did care what his lieutenant thought.

"Kane, you smooth-talking son of a bitch."

"Lieutenant, I—"

"I think you've already said enough, don't you?"

"Yes, sir."

"Do you realize how much heat I just took because of you? After the way you handled yourself in the meeting, the captain wants your ass, Jellup's gonna go back and tell the mayor he's got a 'Dirty Harry' on his hands, and worst of all, you made an enemy of Snead."

"Fuck Snead."

"Wrong attitude. What's your beef with him, anyway?"

"We had a scrap when we were both working patrol out in Van Nuys."

"That long ago? What happened?"

Kane shrugged. "Snead was booking some old wino one night," he said. "The guy was so drunk he barely knew where he was and decided to relieve himself right there at the desk. He picked the nearest object, which turned out to be Snead. Snead retaliated, only way out of proportion—using his baton, stomping the guy, really bustin' him up."

"And you stopped him?"

"Yeah."

"And?"

"And he made the mistake of turning on me. I wouldn't exactly call what happened afterward a fight, seein' as how I only got to hit him once. He was unconscious after that."

"Too bad."

"Yeah."

Long sighed. "I'm afraid you've got more trouble than you think, Dan. City Hall is afraid the media coverage on this could get ugly. They're already looking for a scapegoat. Right now Internal Affairs is going over your performance reports with a fine-tooth comb, starting from the day you joined the force. I had a hell of a time keeping you from getting suspended."

"How'd you manage? After blowing my stack like that in the meeting, I figured the least I'd get was desk duty till things quieted down."

"Let's just say Senator Bradley was extremely grateful for what you did. Some friends of Agents Tinley and Marcus from the Bureau put in a good word, too. Plus with our backlog of open cases, I convinced the captain that the unit can't afford your absence. It took some doing, but he eventually saw the light. Incidentally, I just heard Tinley is going to pull through."

"Glad to hear it."

"We all are." Long paused. "You're a good cop, Dan," he said finally, studying Kane across folded hands. "One of the best. When are you going to wise up?"

"If you mean when am I gonna start kissin' ass every time some—"

"Is that what you think I'm saying? There's a big difference between kissing ass and not looking for trouble. You go out of your way to antagonize people. Jesus, Dan, you've got a family. It's time you started thinking about them."

"Maybe."

"How *is* Kate?" asked Long, noticing a change in Kane's manner.

"Fine," said Kane, looking away.

"Say hi for me when you see her."

"I will, if she ever starts talkin' to me again."

"Damn. What'd you do this time?"

"We had a misunderstanding about the kids," Kane answered,

feeling a surge of regret as he recalled Sunday's ugly scene and the terrible argument with Catheryn that had followed. "I'm bunkin' at Arnie's right now."

"Sorry to hear that."

"I'll work it out."

"Yeah. You always do." Long rocked back in his chair. "Have you ever been shot?" he asked pensively.

"No," Kane answered, puzzled by Long's apparent non sequitur.

"That slug I took last year got me thinking about what's really important," Long continued, referring to a wound he'd received while investigating a homicide in Pacific Palisades. He'd been pronounced dead upon arrival at the hospital, but somehow the emergency team had managed to bring him back. "Just between us, I'm considering taking early retirement the end of this year. What I'm saying is maybe you ought to start thinking about what's important, too. Your family, for instance. Start playing it smart. You've been tap-dancing on thin ice for quite a while; I may not be around to haul you out when it breaks."

"I'm a good swimmer, Lieutenant."

"You'd better be," said Long. "Enough about that. Let's get back at it."

"Yes, sir. By the way, that case I caught just before the meeting? The patrol unit at the scene got an ID on the body. The victim's name was Angelo Martin."

Long's eyes widened. "Martin? Any relation to the Bradleys' maid?"

"Her brother."

"Shit! Has she rolled over on the third kidnapper yet?"

Kane shook his head. "That's the first thing I checked. The Bureau guy I talked to said she clammed up Sunday after conferring with her lawyer. Acted scared shitless."

"Think there's a connection?"

"It wouldn't surprise me. I don't believe in coincidence."

"Me, either," said Long. "Look, I conferred with the district attorney about the case over the weekend. We've got Escobar cold for the death of a federal officer and the Chicano boy, but the kidnapping charges are shaky—mostly based on circumstantial evidence. We need Sylvia Martin's testimony. That, and the third guy."

"Yeah."

"Did you mention the brother when you talked to the feds?"

"No. I want to see where it goes first."

Long considered for several moments. "All right," he finally agreed. "I'll have to notify the Bureau of the situation, but at this point, unless something turns up, I can keep them off your back. Have you resumed your pending cases?"

"Not yet. I've got court appearances next week, but—"

"Fine," said Long, interrupting Kane with a wave of his hand. "I'm putting you on this full-time. See what you can come up with, and keep me informed. We'll have to bring in the feds if you do establish a link to the Bradley kidnapping—you know that."

"Yes, sir."

"One more thing."

"Sir?"

"About Friday. Good work."

8

Twenty minutes after leaving Long's office, Kane pulled up at the intersection of Pico and Centinela, just north of the Santa Monica Freeway. When he arrived, he found two LAPD patrol officers standing beside a black-and-white idling at the curb. Thirty feet in front of the squad car, enclosed within a wide perimeter of yellow crime-scene ribbon reading POLICE LINE DO NOT CROSS, lay the body of a young Hispanic male. He was curled on his side, his limbs oddly twisted, his eyes open in a look of confused, befuddled surprise often present in violent death. An open wallet lay beside him in a small pool of brown that had congealed on the asphalt at his throat.

Kane approached the patrol officers with his ID out, although from their postures he knew they'd already sized up his beige city car as one of the unmarked police vehicles assigned to the homicide unit. In the time it took him to reach the cruiser, his eyes quickly scanned the seedy neighborhood. Two hundred yards of chain-link fence ran south to the corner, apparently installed to protect the nonexistent contents of a trash-filled vacant lot paralleling Centinela. A thick clump of oleander bushes had sprung up in one corner, with a cardboard refrigerator box sporting a Westinghouse logo partially visible through the leaves. Gang writing covered the block walls of an auto-repair shop on one side of the street; similar ghetto scrawl adorned a line of low-rent apartments backing up to the alley on the other.

Both officers had seen Kane on the weekend news and extended their congratulations. Kane accepted with a shrug, then conferred with them briefly, learning that at 8:55 that morning, after responding to a call at the beginning of their shift, they'd discovered the body sprawled on the street. The younger of the two officers, whose plate read Street, had approached and felt for a carotid pulse. Finding none, he'd attempted to lift the victim's arm by his sleeve, determining by the stiffness that rigor had already set in.

"Who pulled the wallet?" Kane asked sharply.

"It was lying on the ground when we got here," answered Haggerty, the second officer. "No money in it, either."

"You picked it up?"

Haggerty shrugged. "Yeah. Had on my gloves."

"All right," said Kane, deciding the scene—with the possible exception of the wallet—was probably still clean. "Go ahead and get the crime-scene unit down here."

"We already made the call," said Street. "Do you want us to notify the medical examiner's office, too?"

"Hold off till the SID unit gets here. The coroner's investigator's gotta wait till they're done; no sense making him sit around."

"Right."

"Which one of you is gonna be keeping the crime-scene log?" Kane asked, referring to a record that would contain the name, arrival and departure time, and serial number of every official to visit the scene.

"I guess I am," answered Street, glancing over at his bored partner.

"All right, kid," said Kane. "I want you to list everybody comin' through here, and I mean *everybody*. No screwups."

"No, sir."

By now the sun had risen high enough to disperse the layer of marine fog that had rolled in overnight. Kane glanced across the alley, noticing faces staring with frank curiosity out a number of open apartment windows. Deciding to start canvassing the neighborhood for witnesses, he sent Haggerty across the street to talk to the crowd, then returned to his car and radioed for a second patrol unit. That done, he moved to the perimeter of the crime scene and ducked under the ribbon. Careful not to disturb anything as he approached, he stopped three feet from the body, squatted, and remained motionless—not looking at anything in particular as his mind began to focus. Already he could detect the faint, ripe odor of death rising from the body.

The victim appeared to have been in his late teens or early twenties. A good-looking boy with long black hair and thin, prominent cheekbones, he had on a pair of gray slacks with pleats in both front and back. A four-inch strip of fabric on the left calf was torn, the skin underneath smeared with a dark smudge of what looked like grease. Not touching the body, Kane leaned closer, noticing a purplish discoloration on the upper portion of his neck and shoulder. Postmortem lividity, caused by the action of gravity on blood after the heart stops pumping. At average room temperature it becomes too thick to move, or "fixes," in about eight hours; after that, subsequent change in body position has no effect on the characteristic port-wine staining of the skin. Since lividity was visible on the upper portion of the body—as opposed to underneath, where it should be—Kane felt sure of one thing: The body had definitely been moved.

Deep ligature marks circled the boy's wrists. His fingers were callused, his nails dirty. No signs of defensive wounds. A crust of blood covered the side of his face, appearing to have flowed from either his nose or ear. A black fuzz seemed to be growing from its surface near the cheek, like mold on stale bread.

Fibers? Have SID check it out.

On further inspection Kane noticed stippling and burn marks on the exterior tissue of the ear, and the unmistakable muzzle print resulting from a gun being discharged within inches of the skin. In addition, the characteristic star-shaped pattern of tears indicated the barrel had actually been pressed against the ear when fired. From the size and depth of the rips Kane judged the gun had probably been a small-caliber weapon. He couldn't see any exit wound on the other side of the head without moving the body, which would have to wait until the coroner's investigator arrived. He leaned even closer, noticing someone had crammed a red scarf into the kid's mouth.

A do-rag, the kid's colors.

There was plenty of room for the scarf, because the boy's tongue had been pulled through a gaping slash in his neck.

Kane immediately recognized the significance of the wound colloquially termed a "Colombian necktie." *Had someone thought Angelo was an informant?* he wondered.

After withdrawing a pair of thin plastic gloves from his pocket, Kane pulled them on and checked the wallet lying beside the body—comparing the face on the driver's license to the body's on the asphalt. Satisfied it was Angelo Martin, he replaced the wallet, then carefully lifted the boy's chin to view the neck. A ragged cut ran from beneath the left ear to the thick cord of muscle on the other side.

Definitely not enough blood for the kid to have bled out here. Shirt looks clean, too, except for a grease stain on the back. Should've been messy, unless it happened afterward.

Kane felt the stiffness in the boy's jaw and neck as he lowered his face, noting the body had already tightened in full rigor. He looked at the boy's eyes. *Milky.* He glanced at the sun, feeling its heat already beginning to rise from the dark surface of the alley. Although the Santa Ana winds had died, the city still felt the lingering effects. The variables were difficult to judge, but Kane estimated death had to have occurred sometime during the previous eight to twelve hours.

After Sylvia clammed up? Or before?

A few minutes later the Scientific Investigative Division wagon arrived, along with the second patrol unit. After organizing a widened canvass of the neighborhood, Kane spent the next hour with the three-man crime-scene unit—instructing the SID forensic technicians in their formal sketches and measurements, directing the photographer, and overseeing the criminalist's procurement of scrapings, samples, and any other evidence Kane deemed pertinent. During this time he occasionally glanced over at the crowd across the alley. Haggerty was taking statements, but Kane suspected the presence of gang members in the onlookers made it unlikely anyone would talk.

"Kane! You ready for me yet?"

Kane turned, smiling as he saw a small, smooth-headed man stepping from a late-model Ford Fairlane across the street. Art Walters, a retired LAPD homicide detective, had been an investigator for the medical examiner's office as long as Kane could remember. He was one of the best.

"Be a couple minutes, Art. Why don't you pick us all up some coffee and doughnuts while you're waiting?"

"Screw you, hotshot," Walters retorted, crossing the street. "The last thing you need is another doughnut. What've we got here?"

"Male Hispanic. Driver's license says he's Angelo Martin. We've been waiting till you arrived before trying for latents on the neck and the inside of his wrists. We'd also like to print the guy. I've got a hunch he's on file."

"Stranger things have happened."

"Uh-huh. What's the backlog at the morgue? Think we can set this one up for tomorrow?"

"Why the rush?" Walters asked, looking quizzically at Kane.

Kane hesitated. Then, "Keep this quiet, okay? There may be a connection to the Bradley kidnapping. The quicker we move on this, the better."

"Call Chang," Walters advised. "For some unknown reason he seems to like you. If anybody can get you an early post, it's him. In the meantime lemme get to work."

Kane assisted Walters and the SID print technician in an abortive attempt to procure skin prints from the body, then he remained at the coroner's investigator's side as he slowly and methodically examined the corpse—poking, prodding, recording everything. Forty minutes later, as Walters started logging his final observations, Kane directed the crime team to place paper bags over the victim's hands. He knew he was doing everything right, but contrary to the Sherlock Holmes school of sleuthing seen on late-night reruns of *Columbo* and *Kojak,* he also knew in a case like this that forensic evidence—nail clippings and scrapings, tissue samples, blood typing, hair and fiber analysis, fingerprints and ballistics—rarely led to the arrest of a suspect. Although forensics could tie someone to a murder and ultimately lead to a conviction, first one needed a suspect, and that meant finding an informant or witness.

Kane glanced again at the crowd across the alley, deciding from the look on Haggerty's face that he wasn't getting much in the way of either. Leaving the SID technicians to finish up, Kane made his way back to his car. On impulse he called over to the young officer who'd been there when he'd first arrived. "Hey, Street."

Street looked up from his notebook, into which he'd religiously been making entries with every new arrival. "Yes, sir?" he said, hurrying over.

"I'm gonna get a second detail from the P.M. watch out here to recanvass the neighborhood, starting around six. You wanna be on it?"

"Yes, sir! I'm off then, but I'll—"

"I'll talk to your sergeant and get the OT approved," Kane interrupted. "What about your partner?"

"Haggerty? He doesn't like to work overtime, but I'll ask him."

"I'll ask him myself. One more thing, Street. Come here, I wanna show you something." Kane walked to the edge of the chain-link fence and kicked aside some trash piled against the corner. Low down, where it could easily go unnoticed, a portion of fencing had been cut and then resecured with a coat hanger. The weeds on the other side had been trampled down. "I'm fairly certain we've got one of our homeless citizens campin' out over there in the bushes," Kane said, pointing to the cardboard box in the oleanders. "He probably won't be back till after dark, but there's a chance he may have seen something. You handle it?"

"Yes, sir."

Satisfied, Kane spun on his heel and returned to his car, thinking the kid was doing a good job and deciding to make sure his sergeant heard about it. Then, after sliding behind the wheel, he picked up the radio mike and contacted Detective Albert Moro from the CRASH Unit—the LAPD gang unit whose unlikely acronym stood for Community Resources Against Street Hoodlums. "Moro, this is Kane," he said once the switchboard had patched him through.

"Morning, Dan," Moro's voice came back. "What's up?"

"We've got one of your homeboys down here drawin' flies. Execution-style killing. Can you help me out?"

"Got an ID yet?"

"Yeah. The kid's name is Angelo Martin. Ring any bells?"

"Hold on, I'll check." A pause, then, "Yeah. Angelo Martin, street name Digger. A member in good standing of our very own Sotels. He's probably the latest in the retaliation killings that've been going on the past few months."

"By who?" asked Kane doubtfully, deciding not to mention the Bradley connection.

"Most likely the PBGs—the Playboy Gangster Crips from the Cadillac area over near La Cienega. Word is they've been moving drugs in what's considered Sotel turf. Could have been the Rolling Sixties or the Shoreline Crips, though. They've been working West L.A. lately, too."

Kane thought a moment. "All I need are the names of the kid's friends and associates—who he hung out with, did he have any enemies, that kind of thing. And I may be calling you real soon about rounding up some of the local gang-bangers."

"No problem. Anything else?"

"Later, maybe. Let's see what develops."

9

Monday afternoon, exhausted from his first day on the job, Travis pulled his mother's Volvo into Alexander Petrinski's driveway. After parking beside his teacher's station wagon and shutting off the engine, he nervously gathered his music, but instead of exiting, sat for several seconds gazing down on the Malibu coastline. Far below he could make out the sandy beaches of Las Flores, La Costa, and Carbon scalloping the shoreline to the Malibu pier, curving like polished bones in the afternoon sun. Farther north a smaller dock at Paradise Cove jutted into the Pacific, dwarfed by the massive headlands at Point Dumé.

Following a quick shower after work, Travis had rushed up Las Flores Canyon, making it to his music lesson with barely minutes to spare. Now, however, even though he knew Petrinski demanded punctuality, he hesitated, reluctant to enter the house. His body felt stiff and sore from the unaccustomed labor of his new job, and as he massaged the cramped knots in his hands and forearms, loosening them up for the lesson, he thought back over the events of the day. Smiling, he remembered the look of shock on Junior's face when he'd kicked over the barrel. Unfortunately, his satisfaction was marred by the knowledge that only Tommy's intervention had saved him. With a chill, he also recalled Junior's dark threat afterward. Still, that wasn't what was bothering him.

All at once Travis realized he'd been dreading this moment the entire day. As usual, he was well prepared. Nonetheless, over the past months he'd grown to hate the inexplicable signals of dissatisfaction from his mentor, subtle things he couldn't quite put his finger on: a scowl, a shake of his head, an impatient shifting in his chair—but telling.

Fighting his apprehension, Travis finally stepped from the car and made his way toward Petrinski's unassuming ranch-style house, representative for the area with its red tile roof, white stucco walls, and Mexican paver patio bordered by clumps of agaves and yuccas. As usual, he entered without knocking.

"Travis?"

"Yes, sir. It's me."

Travis closed the heavy oak door. He paused in the entry to hang his jacket on an antique brass hook. As always, what he could see of the room beyond looked as though someone had used a stick to stir it up. Clean, but messy. Books, stacks of paper and sheet music, miscellaneous articles of clothing, and an eclectic assortment of coffee cups, plates, silverware, magazines, and partially filled ashtrays covered every horizontal surface of the spacious chamber, with the notable exception of the Steinway concert grand sitting in the far corner. For as long as Travis could remember, the piano had always been the single thing in Petrinski's house that had remained unadorned with the rich clutter and confusion of his life.

"You're late."

"No, sir. My watch says I'm right on time." Travis hurried in, glancing at the older man sitting in a leather armchair across the room. Although over seventy, Petrinski had a leonine head of hair, whitened now but still thick and full, which he wore long and swept back from his forehead.

Looking up from the book in his lap, Petrinski smiled. "Then your watch is wrong. Get it fixed." Closing his book and setting it on the table beside him, he asked, "Tell me, Travis. Have you ever read Steinbeck's *East of Eden*?"

Travis took his place at the Steinway. "I saw the movie."

"The cry of the modern generation. 'I saw the movie.' It's not

even *that* anymore. Now it's 'I'll wait for it to come out on tape.'"
Petrinski shook his head. "I'll tell you something. The movie was a
classic. But the book has something to offer, too."

"What's the point? If I already know—"

"That's just it. The film is but one interpretation of the story, a
single crystallization of the diverse possibilities open to the imagina-
tion of a reader. When you read, there are no limits; with a book you
can bring vistas and textures and emotions to life in a way that has
meaning for you, and you alone. In that respect reading is much like
performing music. Do you understand what I'm driving at?"

"I think so, sir."

"I'm not certain you do," said Petrinski, watching Travis closely.
Then, changing the subject, "I submitted your selections for the
Bronislaw competition today."

"I'll be ready."

"Will you?"

"Yes, sir," Travis answered, feeling a renewed lurch of uneasiness
as he reviewed the Bronislaw requirements in his mind. For the preliminary round, along with a short discretionary piece of the performer's choosing, each competitor had been asked to prepare four
longer selections of his or her choice: a classical sonata, something
from the romantic era, a twentieth-century work, and a final piece to
be performed with an accompanist. After much deliberation Travis
had decided on Schumann's *Aufschwung* for the discretionary piece, a
Haydn sonata for the classical requirement, the Liszt transcription of
the "Liebestod" from Wagner's *Tristan und Isolde* for the romantic
period work, and a Rachmaninoff prelude—Op. 23, No. 5—as the
twentieth-century piece.

"How's the Beethoven sonata coming?" asked Petrinski, referring
to a work for cello and piano that Catheryn had offered to perform
with Travis to fulfill the final competition requirement—a test of a
pianist's ability to coordinate his playing with that of another musician.

"Fine. At least my mom thinks so."

"And what do you think?"

"I . . . I guess it's going well."

"You guess?"

"Yes, sir. I mean—"

"Never mind, Travis. We have a lot of work ahead of us. Let's proceed with the 'Liebestod.' " Petrinski rose and crossed to stand behind him. "Play. If we have time, we'll go on to the Rachmaninoff prelude."

Travis knew the lesson had not begun propitiously. After opening the music, he placed his hands on the keys, resolving to execute the strenuous Liszt piece as flawlessly as possible. And for the next few minutes he did, at least as far as he could tell.

"Liebestod," which means love-death, tells the story of two lovers and their ultimate destruction. Travis's fingers slid expertly through the opening bars of the difficult composition, running over the keys with precision. Not an advocate of passive instruction, Petrinski wove back and forth beside him like a taskmaster—sometimes pointing out a key section in the music, sometimes urging Travis on as he embarked on some particularly pivotal passage, sometimes clenching his fist in a curious grasping motion over the keyboard as if trying to pluck the complex sounds from the boy's flying fingers—all the while elucidating the rhythm, melody, and harmonic progression with a strangely atonal mix of humming and nonsense syllables and grunts.

Relentless and driving, the music rose inexorably toward a climax. The motif that had come to represent Isolde's joy at the thought of being reunited with Tristan underwent myriad harmonic contortions, constantly striving for fulfillment, struggling ever higher, at last resolving to an infinitely fulfilling tonic chord as the lovers achieved in death and transfiguration the mystic union for which both had longed.

As the final chord died away, Petrinski crossed the room and dropped into his chair. Travis hesitated, once again sensing his mentor's dissatisfaction. Not knowing what else to do, he sat nervously, hands folded in his lap.

"Travis, it's time we had a talk."

"Sir?"

"Why are you here?"

"Uh . . . well, my lessons are scheduled—"

"That's not what I mean," said Petrinski, cutting him off. "It's the same every week. You come; I listen to you play; I make suggestions; you return with the corrections mastered; we start something else. Is that what you want from me?"

Travis shook his head resentfully but remained silent, not knowing what to say.

"I'm going to tell you something, Travis. It may hurt, but I don't see any way around it. As a technician, you're *extremely* gifted. As a musician, an artist . . ." Petrinski's voice trailed off.

Travis lowered his eyes at this rebuke. "But . . ."

"I'm not saying you're not an accomplished pianist. Quite the contrary. But there's some essential, defining quality missing in your music, something holding you back from the promise of genius I know is within you. You're hiding behind technique, disguising the absence of genuine emotion with facile virtuosity. Years ago, when you began with me, I could excuse your lack of depth because of age. No more, Travis. No more."

"I . . . I'm sorry. If you'll just tell me—"

"Tell you!" Petrinski exploded. "I can't tell you how to feel! That has to come from within!" Then, more calmly, "I'm sorry, but I can't teach you something you're not ready to accept. In that respect the art of teaching is sadly overrated. The time has to be ripe, and even then all I can do is help you become a *better* musician, not a *great* one. That can't be taught. The elements of discovery must come from within, and I'm beginning to think you're afraid to look inside yourself, afraid of what you'll find. Is that it? Is it fear?"

"I'm not afraid."

"I think you are. I think you're terribly afraid." Petrinski regarded Travis closely. "Tell me something. Define music."

"It's the art of combining melody and harmony and rhythm."

"That's like saying literature is the art of combining letters and words and phrases."

Travis thought hard. "I don't understand what you're getting at."

"Okay, listen. Granted, music springs from mathematics and other measurable elements. Its component parts, the nuts and bolts of our musical prose—frequencies, decibels, durations, intervals, rhythms—are combined to form a metaphorical language, but the resultant whole is far more than the sum of those parts. Through music a composer, and later an artist interpreting his work, communicates with an audience on a wordless level, asking questions like, Have you ever experienced this shock, this surprise, this mystery, this anxiety, this release? How is music able to do that, Travis?"

"I . . . I don't know. Maybe our ability to perceive harmonic relationships is something that's hardwired in at birth?"

Petrinski leaned forward, seeming pleased. "You're still talking nuts and bolts—words, phrases, and punctuation instead of meaning—but you're getting there. You're saying we humans have an intrinsic capacity to perceive the harmonic interdependencies inherent in tonal music."

"Yes, sir."

"Good. Now you're wondering what all this has to do with you, right?"

"Yes, sir."

"Let's go back to my original question: What is music? I'll tell you what *I* think it is, Travis. Although music can be many things, in its truest incarnation, at its deepest core, *music is the power to command emotion.*"

Travis felt himself beginning to sweat.

"But if you don't feel what you play," Petrinski said quietly, "*neither will anyone else.*"

"No, sir."

"When we started this, I said I thought you were afraid of something. Do you want to know what?"

Travis sat without answering.

"I think, for some reason, you're afraid to feel. I don't know about other aspects of your life, but in music you've used your talent to isolate yourself, substituting technique for emotion. Why?"

Travis remained silent.

"Are you afraid to let yourself feel? Or are you just afraid of *being*?"

Despair descended like a weight on Travis's chest. "I don't know."

Petrinski regarded his student for what seemed an eternity. Finally he spread his hands. "I'm sorry, Travis. But until you *do* know, I don't see any purpose in going on with the Bronislaw pieces. Instead, I'm going to give you something else to work on."

"But sir, I—"

"No. I've thought about this long and hard. I know the competition is coming up and your mother will be disappointed, but this is more important."

Petrinski rose and walked to an alcove across the room. After withdrawing several pages of sheet music from a thick folder, he returned and handed them to Travis. "Here."

Travis numbly took the pages. "What is it?"

"Chopin's Étude Number Three in E Major. Are you familiar with it?"

Travis thought carefully, sensing much depended on what happened next. He remembered Chopin had written twenty-seven études, or practice pieces. In them he'd demonstrated the uttermost limits of the piano's resources, each étude exploring some particular aspect of piano technique, while at the same time creating a profound music filled with subtle and diverse emotional challenges. "Yes, sir," he said at last. "I've heard it, of course. I don't remember it, though."

"It's one of Chopin's early works, and one he considered among his most beautiful. He asked it be played for him on his deathbed." Petrinski placed his hand on Travis's shoulder. "Learn it. I think you may find things in it that will surprise you. Don't listen to anyone else's version; I want yours, only yours. Come back when you can tell me how you *feel* when you play it, and not until then. In the meantime, think about what I've said."

"Yes, sir." Woodenly clutching the music in his hand, Travis rose and walked to the door.

"And Travis?"

Travis turned in the entry, looking back at the white-haired man standing by the piano, the man who had guided his progress for the past ten years, the man who had been his friend, and the man who was now questioning the very ties of their relationship.

"Yes, sir?"

"I'll be waiting. Don't take too long."

10

Tuesday afternoon, after witnessing the postmortem examination performed on Angelo Martin at the Los Angeles County Coroner's Office, Kane returned to the West L.A. station. Shortly after arriving, he received a phone call. "Kane," he said, lifting the receiver.

"Detective Kane, this is Gary Street. I was the officer that—"

"Yeah, Street, I know who you are. What've you got?"

"Well, sir, remember last night after the canvass we checked to see whether anyone was living in those bushes? You know, inside the fence?"

"Yeah. Turned out to be a dead end."

"Yes, sir. But I went back again around midnight. Guess what? This time somebody was home."

"Lemme get this straight. You went back on your own time?" asked Kane, deciding right then to do more than call the kid's sergeant. He deserved a letter.

"I just thought—"

"Never mind, Street. I like that kinda initiative. What'd you find out?"

"Well, sir, an old lady's living there. Says she stays away till late and leaves early so nobody'll know what she's doing. When I rousted her, she was real upset about getting discovered. After I got her calmed down, I asked if she'd seen anything the other night. Turns out she did. Just before sunrise she was getting ready to leave when she heard somebody pull up. She looked out and saw two guys dumping a body from the trunk of a car. After that she got scared and ducked back into her box."

"Did you get a description?"

"No, sir. This lady, well, let's just say she won't make much of a witness if it ever comes to that. She said there were two of them, though."

"White? Black? Hispanic?"

"She couldn't tell."

"Anything else?"

"She got a look at the car. A dark-colored clunker, navy-blue or black with one of those fancy bird symbols painted on the hood. Sounds like an old Pontiac Firebird to me. And mag wheels. She was definite about that. It's not much, but—"

"It's better than nothin', kid. Good work. I'll see the right people hear about it."

"Thanks, sir. If there's anything else . . ."

"Yeah, there is. Bring this lady in. I wanna talk to her, show her some pictures of magnesium wheels and see whether we can nail down a description."

"Yes, sir."

Kane hung up, thinking about Street. The kid had shown real initiative in running down a witness, the same kind of desire that had gotten Kane moved up to plainclothes just four years from the day he'd graduated from the academy. A crooked smile creased his face. For the first time since Monday, he had a feeling the case might just possibly go down.

But by noon the next day—after interviewing the bag lady, re-canvassing the neighborhood for anyone else who'd seen the car, and spending fruitless, frustrating hours trying to run down Angelo Martin's associates and determine his actions during the final hours before his death—Kane was forced to admit he'd made little progress. Clearing a space on his desk, he hunched over the lab report that had come in earlier that day, beginning his review with the serological examination. Not surprisingly, traces of cocaine, methamphetamine, and marijuana had shown up in the serum samples taken from Angelo Martin at autopsy. He'd also tested positive for HIV—not particularly startling in light of the needle tracks, but the possibility of sexual transmission couldn't be ruled out. Kane made a mental note to have CRASH check Angelo's sexual preferences.

Continuing, he perused the rest of the report. He'd almost finished when he felt someone peering over his shoulder.

"That the stuff on the Martin kid?"

Kane glanced up. Arnie's ponderous form partially blocked the cold glare from the overheads. He looked tired. Kane noted absently that catching up on the cases shelved during the Bradley kidnapping was taking its toll on everyone. "Yeah," he said. "Just came in."

"Anything interesting?"

Both men knew the unlikelihood that the forensic reports would prove critical, but two neighborhood canvasses had been unproductive in locating a witness, no latent prints had been procured from the corpse, and a grid search of the crime scene had turned up clean—currently leaving the autopsy and forensic workup their best bet.

"Gimme a minute."

Kane quickly finished scanning the microscopic and chemical analysis of materials recovered from the body and crime scene. Then, without referring to the report, he gave Arnie a detailed summary—citing tests, lab and autopsy protocols, and all pertinent details. Well aware of Kane's nearly eidetic memory, Arnie listened without surprise.

Once he'd finished, Kane rocked back thoughtfully in his chair. "Bottom line, we've got three things," he said in conclusion. "Ballistics tagged the projectile recovered at autopsy as a twenty-two caliber short. It's fairly deformed but enough for a comparison if we find the gun. The grease smudges on the leg and shirt were identical, the composition consistent with that commonly used in light automotive applications—axle grease, car jacks, that kinda stuff. The fibers we got off the kid's face are acrylic, probably from a rug or mat."

"Like from the trunk of the car our lady in the bushes reported."

Kane nodded. "That's how I've got it figured. They took Angelo off the street, killed him, stuffed him in the trunk, and dumped him early the next morning. We find the car, we should be able to match the fibers, maybe the grease."

"Still think this is tied to the Bradley kidnapping?"

Kane shrugged. "With the gang connection it's looking less and less likely, but . . . I don't know, Arnie. It still seems way too coincidental. I talked to the Bureau again today. Sylvia Martin still isn't talking."

"Yeah." Arnie shuffled through the report, checking for something Kane might have missed. "Any progress finding the car?"

"Some. I called a local Pontiac dealer and learned the model with the bird on the hood is a Firebird Trans Am—you know, like Burt Reynolds drove in those *Smokey and the Bandit* movies. They came out in sixty-nine. Pontiac discontinued the eagle emblem when they changed the body style in eighty-two, so that narrows it down a bit. Moro's had his CRASH guys working overtime making a list of every known member of the Sotels, PBGs, Rolling Sixties, and Shoreline Crips who are old enough to drive."

"How 'bout the Eighteenth Street Crips?"

"Culver City's a little far. We'll widen the net if necessary, but if this murder turns out to be gang-related, my money's on the PBGs. Angelo Martin was a local, and word is the PBGs are muscling in on Sotel drug distribution."

"Yeah. It fits."

"I ran all the names they've turned up so far through DMV, checking vehicle registrations of sixty-nine through eighty-one Pontiacs. One of the Venice Shoreline Crips—a punk named Willie Cesko, calls himself Ratman—owns a 1979 Trans Am. I had Pacific Division check; they say Cesko's car is light green, no mag wheels. Speaking of which, I pulled in the bag lady and showed her about ten zillion pictures of magnesium wheels. She couldn't recall the design. She *was* positive about the bird on the front, though, and the color. Anyway, I'm thinking about widening the search, but before then I'm having CRASH haul in every local gang-banger they can rip for a little show-and-tell—see if we can locate the car around here first."

"When?"

"This afternoon."

"You doing the interrogations?"

"I'll tag-team it with Moro."

"Okay. Keep me informed." Arnie glanced around the squad room, then settled his considerable bulk on the corner of Kane's desk. "One other matter," he said, lowering his voice. "Your friend Lieutenant Snead from Internal Affairs wants you to drop by."

"What the hell for?" Kane demanded. Despite initial fears in the mayor's office that Martin and Escobar's charges of racial prejudice and police brutality would generate a scandal, sympathy for the Bradley boy's death had taken precedence in both media and public opinion alike, and the projected firestorm had never materialized. As a result the LAPD brass had quickly lost interest in pursuing Escobar's spurious charges—dousing Snead's investigation before it ever had a chance to ignite.

"IA may have *officially* lost interest in you, but Snead hasn't," Arnie warned. "I think you should go in."

"Not likely."

"You've got nothing to hide. Why don't you just cooperate? Granted, the guy's a hump, but he can generate a whole shitload of grief somewhere down the line if you don't."

Kane unconsciously began cracking his knuckles, starting with the little finger of his left hand and working methodically toward the thumb. "I'll think about it."

"Do that," said Arnie. "Oh, one more thing," he added as he rose to leave. "Kate phoned while you were at lunch. Wants you to give her a ring when you get a chance."

"How'd she sound?" Kane asked nervously.

"She sounded fine to me," said Arnie, shaking his head. "But then, I'm not a pigheaded Irishman like you. Not that I ain't thrilled at having you hanging around messin' up my house, but why don't you just apologize and get it over with?"

"You're full of advice today," muttered Kane. "For your information, things aren't that simple."

"Yeah, sure," Arnie sighed. "Well, good luck, amigo. And think about talking to Snead."

After Arnie departed, Kane grabbed the phone, set it down, hesitated, then picked it up again. After another hesitation, he punched in his home number. Catheryn picked up on the third ring. "Hello?"

"I'm, uh, trying to locate a big ugly troublemakin' jerk named

Dan Kane," said Kane with an abortive attempt to disguise his voice. "If you can't find him, try checking the doghouse."

"Dan Kane? Would that be the Dan Kane who makes himself scarce every time a family disagreement needs straightening out?" asked Catheryn, her tone frosty and reserved.

"That would be the one. Sorry about not coming home, Kate. I . . . I thought we could both use some time to cool off."

"You may have been right about that," said Catheryn, thawing slightly, "but I still think we should be able to discuss our problems like adults without one of us disappearing for days."

"I think we've done all the discussing about Sunday that's necessary."

"Dan . . ."

"Look, I know I took things too far, but what's there to discuss?"

"Plenty. And we're going to, whether you want to or not. When are you coming home?"

"Uh, tonight," Kane answered. "If that's okay."

"What's the matter . . . Arnie getting tired of your charming personality?" Catheryn asked with a gentle laugh.

Kane felt a surge of relief as he heard the change in her voice. "Something like that," he admitted. "Plus I miss you, sugar. Tell you what. I'll cook on Friday—kind of make things up to the troops."

"That would be nice. And how do you plan on making things up to me?"

"Oh, I'll think of something. That's a promise."

"All right. I'll hold you to it."

•   •   •

Later that afternoon Moro's CRASH detectives started hauling in local gang members, concentrating on the PBGs, the Sotels, and the Shoreline Crips. At Kane's suggestion they were sequestered in groups of three and held in interrogation rooms adjacent to the detectives' squad room, with the overflow when things got busy diverted to several small holding cells on the first floor.

Kane had worked out his interrogation system for this type of case years before. Every interview room and cell in the Butler LAPD station house was wired for sound; even the softest whisper in any of these areas could be picked up and recorded. Before and after the initial questioning Kane would monitor what went on in his absence, developing new ground to explore on the next round of questioning. Although information uncovered in this manner was not generally considered admissible in court, it had often proved invaluable for generating new leads in difficult, dead-end cases. Kane thought of it as a fishing trip.

A fishing trip, but one that necessitated the cooperation of a manifold team of highly trained individuals. Contrary to the image perpetuated by the entertainment industry of a lone homicide detective tracking down a killer, Kane estimated that so far over sixty men and women—patrol officers, communications staff, homicide detectives, SID technicians, members of the district attorney's office and the medical examiner's office, detail officers, forensic-lab technicians, CRASH detectives, secretaries, and clerks—had been actively involved in the investigation of Angelo Martin's death. The interrogations would probably add a half dozen more.

All throughout that afternoon Moro and Kane alternated interrogations, unsuccessfully using spurious lines of questioning in an effort to determine whether any of the gang members drove a dark-colored Firebird Trans Am. Although this avenue turned out disappointingly sterile, two other detectives were hunkered down in the surveillance room monitoring conversations in the holding cells and unattended interview rooms, and the hidden microphones did confirm the PBGs' drug-turf war with the Sotels. In addition, Willie Cesko, aka Ratman, was ruled out as a suspect, having totaled his seventy-nine Trans Am during a drunken spree two months earlier. Progress, but nothing putting them closer to an arrest.

Kane had just given Moro the okay to wrap it up when James Santoro, one of the CRASH detectives who'd been stationed in the listening booth, stopped him outside one of the interrogation rooms. "I've got something for you, Kane," he said.

"What?"

Santoro signaled Kane to follow him into the windowless surveillance room at the end of the hall. "Step into my office," he said. "You're gonna wanna hear this for yourself."

It took Santoro a minute to locate the pertinent section of the recording. When he'd cued up the tape, he pulled off his earphones and looked at Kane. "With three rooms to monitor and all the shit

going on, I almost missed this," he said with a smile. "I just happened to tune in some Sotels we had down in the holding cell. We
were all set to cut 'em loose." He tripped a switch, activating a small
speaker in the console.

Impatiently, Kane listened to snatches of soft, slurring conversation. "My Spanish isn't that good, Santoro. What the hell are they
saying?"

"It's coming up here." Santoro began translating aloud. "The first
guy says: 'Why'd that big redheaded *pendejo* keep asking about our
rides?'" Santoro glanced at Kane with a look of amusement, then
continued. "The other guy says: 'You dumb shit, why the fuck do
you think?' The first guy says: 'Who knows? He kept wanting to
know if anybody drove a fuckin' Trans Am. Only one I know belongs
to Miguel's old lady—what's her name? Annette? Man, I'd sure like
to get a taste of that.' A third guy laughs and says something about
his dick falling off." Santoro flipped off the recording. "That's it."

Kane rubbed his hand over the rough stubble covering his chin.
Was Martin killed by someone in his own gang? he wondered. *If so,
that would definitely rule out the murder's being the result of a drug
war—thereby increasing the chances of a tie-in with the Bradley case.
But how does it fit?* Kane's back ached and his head throbbed from the
game of rotating interrogation they'd been playing all afternoon, but
something about this seemed . . . right. "We still have those punks
downstairs?"

"Yep."

"Bring them back up separately. I want to talk to each of 'em alone
this time. Meantime, pull up any Miguels you've got on your Sotel
roster. We need a last name on him and his girlfriend Annette. If we
can't find Miguel, we'll follow her till he shows up. We're definitely
gonna be bringing them both in, so for God's sake don't do anything
to spook 'em."

"Anything else?"

"Have one of your guys get a shot of the car. I've got a hunch it's
gonna be sportin' mag wheels. It won't be enough for a warrant, but
confirmation from our witness at this point would sure help. And,
Santoro?"

"Yeah?"

"Stay on that bunch downstairs. After I'm done, we're gonna put them back in together again. I want to know every goddamn thing they say. Every syllable. If one of 'em so much as farts, I wanna hear his bowels rumblin' on that tape before his asshole even starts to pucker."

Santoro grinned. "No problem," he said. "No problem at all."

11

That Friday night Allison sat in the kitchen watching her father's thick, powerful hands carefully arranging his work space: cutting board and chef's knife in the center, vegetables in clear plastic bags and meats in white butcher's paper to the left, nested stainless-steel bowls to the right, condiments and spices lined up behind.

Kane liked to cook, and for as long as Allison could remember, her father had always prepared at least one weekend meal for the family. Not the usual daily fare of casseroles, soups, pastas, salads, and meat-and-potato dishes that Catheryn cooked during the week; Kane's creations were always unique. Occasionally his work interfered and they'd go out to dinner instead, but as a rule everyone in the house approached the end of the week anticipating a patriarchal Friday-night feast. And tonight, in keeping with the family's cautious acceptance of Kane back into the fold and the uncharacteristic solicitude he'd displayed since returning, the meal promised to be special.

Nate had been quietly watching with Allison. Finally he spoke. "Can I help, Dad?" he asked timidly.

"No."

"Dad likes to cook all by himself, Nate. You know that," said

Allison. "Except for cleaning up, of course. He trusts the little people like you and me with that."

"Come on, please?" repeated Nate, whose wary reserve around Kane since the previous weekend's fight had abated to an exaggerated need for his father's approval.

Concentrating on his task, Kane grabbed one of the meat packages and ripped open the paper. Eight split chicken breasts plopped onto the cutting board. Kane lined them up. Using a large chef's knife he started on the first, quickly removing the skin and fat, then deftly filleting the meat from the bone. Allison watched as he picked up another, struck by the incongruous, hypnotic agility of his enormous hands.

"Please?"

"Why don't you let him, Pop? The worst he can do is chop off a couple fingers and bleed to death. Think of how nice things would be without a little mutant hanging around."

Nate's face reddened. "Shut up, Allison."

"What was that I heard?" said Allison, cupping her hand to her ear. "A tiny, mouselike squeaking? Maybe we'd better set some traps."

"Speakin' of traps, how about if both of you shut yours right now?" Kane suggested. "Nate, I'll let you peel the shrimp. Do it at the sink, and don't get hulls all over like last time."

"Thanks, Dad. I'll do a good job, you'll see," he said, eager to please. "I'm the fastest shrimp peeler in the world."

"Yeah, sure. Just get the hulls off." Kane pointed the heavy knife at his daughter. "Why don't you go set the table?"

"The picnic table's already set. Mom said we're eating outside," sniffed Allison, taking stock of the assortment of food and condiments spread across the counter. "What are we having tonight? Stir-fry?"

"You'll see when it's done. Where're the rest of the troops? I want 'em ready to chow down in thirty minutes."

"Mom and Trav are downstairs in the music room, and Tommy's been on the phone for the last hour talking to the lovely Christine," Allison answered, eyeing the small incendiary peppers Kane had purchased at an Asian specialty market on Sawtelle. "Just tell me one thing. Is it going to be hot?"

"Yeah, I'm making it hot. Now, pipe down so's I can get some cookin' done."

Allison watched as Kane neatly sectioned two yellow peppers. Next he grabbed a red pepper and prepared it as he had the yellows. Then, fingers expertly curled under to avoid adding incidental flesh, he quickly reduced a pile of mushrooms to perfect thin slices, followed by broccoli, green onions, and ginger—all submitting to the precise, rhythmic ministrations of his flashing blade.

"I'm done," Nate said, pointing proudly to his mountain of hulled shrimp. "See, Dad, not one broken tail. What's next?"

"Do the asparagus," Kane ordered, scooping the shrimp into a metal bowl. "Some of the spears have grit on 'em, so wash each one carefully."

"You're not gonna believe how clean I'll get them, Dad."

"Nate, it's just asparagus, for chrissake," said Kane with a puzzled glance.

"What a suck-up," Allison whispered under her breath, innocently parrying her brother's glare with a saccharine smile.

Kane completed the last of the vegetable preparation, then butterflied the boned chicken breasts, pounded them lightly with a mallet, and cut them into thin strips. He worked in silence, seeming to enjoy the process as much as the anticipation of the meal. When all the bowls stood filled and ready, he paused, ticking off the next sequence of steps aloud. Rice on, heat the water for steaming the asparagus, bread in the oven, start the mustard sauce, blend the salad dressing, preheat the wok.

And as she watched him work, Allison suddenly realized why her father liked to cook. Unlike so many things in life, the process of putting together a meal was predictable, repeatable, and something one could totally control.

•   •   •

Twenty-five minutes later, as the sun descended over Point Dumé, the entire family assembled at a large picnic table on the redwood deck. The temperature was perfect for outdoor dining. With dusk's approach the prevailing onshore winds had reversed, bringing soft, warm gusts of inland air. On the beach below, isolated groups of terns raced the ocean's surging fingers, skittering like fleas as they pecked out their final meal of the day, while here and there, illuminated by the last slanting rays of the sun, couples strolled the water's edge—some glancing curiously at the new raft sitting high and dry on the sand in front of the seawall.

"Dad, this looks great!" said Tommy, eyeing the steaming, redolent cluster of bowls in the center of the table. He rubbed his hands in histrionic expectation, adding, "And it smells fantastic. Let's eat!"

"Aren't you forgetting something?" asked Catheryn.

Tommy smiled guiltily. "Oh, yeah. Grace."

"Well, get 'er said before the grub gets cold," said Kane impatiently.

Catheryn squinted a warning at her husband, then lowered her head to lead the family in giving thanks for the meal. During this time Allison glanced surreptitiously around the table. All eyes were closed except for Travis's, who winked at her as Catheryn requested blessings for the family and wound up the prayer with: "Dear Lord, we thank you for the delightful dinner that Dan has prepared for us, and respectfully pray it's not too hot to eat."

"Amen!" said Kane. Then he leaned across the table and served himself a huge portion of the main course—an ambrosial mix of stir-fried chicken, shrimp, mushrooms, green onions, red and yellow peppers, broccoli, and cashews—covered with a spicy soy and ginger sauce. After he'd loaded his plate, he grabbed a hunk of bread and reached for the rice. "Damn, Kate, your blessings are gettin' longer all the time," he added. "Sure you don't have some preacher blood in you?"

"It wouldn't be the worst thing in the world if I did. This family could use a little more religion."

"Yeah. We could all use a good case of the shingles, too."

In addition to the stir-fry, Kane had prepared one of his specialties, a side dish of steamed asparagus topped with a light mustard sauce so flavorful that Nate immediately devoured his serving and demanded more. And despite his family's good-natured complaints, it quickly became obvious that Kane had managed to find the perfect level of spiciness for the crisp, succulent main course of meats and vegetables—just hot enough to enhance the flavors without overpowering them. For the next fifteen minutes, as everyone dug into the meal, conversation sputtered along in a sporadic manner, occasionally punctuated by brief periods of silence.

"Some of you children may be too young to remember, but years ago when he was still hunting, your father used to make this dish with pheasant," Catheryn noted when most of the plates were empty.

"Yeah, I remember," said Travis. "Before Tar got too old, right?"

"Right," said Kane, mopping his plate with a chunk of bread. "Tar may not seem like much now, but in his day he was one hell of a gun dog. Had a nose damn near as good as a pointer, but he worked in close and retrieved over water. Handled, too. He coulda been a field-trial champion if I'd wanted." Then, with a prolonged, satisfied belch, "Any stir-fry left?"

"All gone, Pop," answered Allison. "We had a regular feeding frenzy going here. Reminds me of something I once saw on a Jacques Cousteau special."

"Yeah, I saw that one, too," Tommy said. "They were throwing huge bloody hunks of meat into the water, and—"

"It's a sad commentary on our manners to be comparing ourselves to a school of sharks," interrupted Catheryn. "Let's just say that your father's cooking managed to do for a short while something he's never been able to accomplish any other way: shut us up."

"Yeah, Pop," added Allison. "You wanna close our yaps, just keep cooking like that."

"I helped, Mom," Nate declared proudly. "I did a good job, too. Right, Dad?"

"Yeah, sure," said Kane. "Speakin' of jobs, did you give Tar his pill today? He barely made it up the stairs when I got home."

Nate ducked his head and leaped from the table. "I'll do it now."

"Damn, Kate," Kane grumbled as Nate raced for the stairs. "That kid's got a lotta growin' up to do."

Catheryn, who'd noticed Nate's restraint around his father since the fight, shot Kane a sharp look. "Dan, he's only nine," she said, unable to keep an edge from her voice.

"That's no excuse. Maybe the kid's memory would improve if I forgot to serve him some of the dessert I plan on whippin' up."

"Dessert?" Allison groaned. "I'm stuffed. I couldn't eat another bite."

"Too bad. I'll just have to eat yours."

"Why don't we wait a bit for dessert?" Catheryn suggested. "Let our food settle."

"Good idea," said Allison. "Anyway, Mom's got an announcement."

Catheryn looked over at Allison and shook her head.

"What?" asked Travis, missing the silent exchange. "Did you hear from the Philharmonic?"

"Nothing definite yet," Catheryn answered slowly. "I was going to save it for later, but . . . I may be offered the position."

"That's great!" said Travis.

"Way to go, Mom!" added Tommy.

"What the hell are you talking about?" demanded Kane.

"I auditioned for a temporary position with the Philharmonic last week," Catheryn answered. "I . . . I didn't mention it because I didn't think I'd get it, but—"

Kane cut her off. "That's a negative," he said, his tone turning peremptory. "With four kids to raise, there's no way you're taking on another job."

"Dan . . ."

"Damn it, Kate, I can't believe this is the first I'm hearing of this," Kane continued, conscious of his tenuous acceptance back into the family and fighting to control his temper. "Did you plan on doing this without discussing it with me?"

"Of course not. I thought I'd sit in on some rehearsals and see how it went before bringing it up."

"And when are these rehearsals gonna take place?"

"Tuesday through Thursday mornings at the Dorothy Chandler, with a double rehearsal on Tuesday. If I'm home late next week, I was hoping—"

"No problem, Mom," said Allison. "I'll be here to take care of Nate."

"I can take care of myself," Nate said adamantly, returning with Tar's medicine. After taking his seat on the picnic bench, he quickly scooped a bit of rice from his plate, pinched it into a ball, pressed in the pill, and tossed it to Tar. As usual, the old dog swallowed without chewing and waited hopefully for more.

"I know you can take care of yourself," said Allison with a patient smile. "I just meant I'd be here to help in case something happened—like if the neighbors' cat accidentally mistook you for a mouse and decided to have you for a little snack."

"Mom!"

"Hush, you two," reproved Catheryn. "Allison, I appreciate your offer, but let's cross that bridge when we come to it."

"That particular bridge may just get washed out," Kane observed, his face darkening despite his effort to remain calm. "When are the performances?"

"Thursday through Saturday nights at eight, with a two-thirty matinee on Sunday," Catheryn answered, adding, "That part wouldn't start till mid-August."

"And who's gonna take care of things then? You plan on letting Allison run the whole damn house?"

"I can do it," Allison declared, glancing nervously at her father.

"I'll help," said Travis.

"Me, too," Nate joined in.

"We can all pitch in," said Tommy, his voice reflecting the tension that had now descended on the table.

"You'll be gone by then, Tom. Only way you'll help is by not being around to cause trouble. How long *is* this replacement job, Kate?"

"Just thirteen weeks, but—"

"Thirteen weeks."

"There aren't any out-of-town concerts scheduled, so I wouldn't have to travel," Catheryn continued. "And I haven't accepted yet. We'll talk about it later, Dan," she added, clearly reluctant to continue the conversation in front of the children.

"You bet we will."

An ominous silence followed. In a transparent attempt to change the subject, Travis spoke up. "Uh, Dad, our new job's going pretty well."

"Yeah, I meant to ask about that," Kane grunted. "What've they got you doing? Hulking lumber?"

"Mostly. That, and sweeping up, rolling out power cords—all the drudge work. We're definitely at the bottom of the pecking order, but in between we're getting to do some nail-bending, too. Funny, I didn't think I'd like it, but framing a house is fun. One minute you've got nothing; the next all the walls are up. It really goes fast."

"What's more, Trav's already made a new friend," Tommy added teasingly.

"Who?" asked Catheryn, sounding pleased.

Travis frowned. "Nobody. Some football buddy of Tommy's named Junior Cobb who's decided he hates my guts."

"He's not *my* friend," Tommy objected. "I knew him from the team. He played defensive line—graduated a couple of years ago. He's just a loser looking for somebody to pick on."

Still brooding over Catheryn's insurrection, Kane leveled his gaze at Travis. "Listen, sport, I'm gonna tell you somethin' about guys like this, what's his name—Junior?"

Travis nodded.

"There's always at least one pus-bucket like him on every job, and they always find somebody to bully," Kane growled, venting some of his anger. "Makes 'em feel big. Take it from me, if you back away, they just keep comin'. What you've gotta do is get right in their face the first time they come at you. Otherwise they own you."

"Somehow I can't picture a guy like that ever picking on you," said Tommy.

"Dad *was* that guy," whispered Allison.

"I heard that, Allison. I'll ignore that for now," said Kane. Then, to Travis, "Believe me, kid, handling punks is one thing I know. Don't give 'em an inch, not one damn inch."

"You're not suggesting Travis fight this boy?" asked Catheryn, looking appalled.

Kane glared back. "If he has to, yeah. That's exactly what I'm suggesting." Then, turning again to Travis, "So he kicks your ass. It won't be the worst thing that ever happens to you. Just make sure you get in a few good licks. Believe me, this Junior'll come to the conclusion it's more fun to pick on somebody else."

"And if he doesn't?"

"Just do whatever it takes to *make* him change his mind. *Whatever* it takes. You understand what I'm saying here, Travis?"

"Yes, sir."

Catheryn shook her head in exasperation and angrily pushed away her plate. "That's wonderful, Dan," she said. "Any other gems you'd like to pass on? How about karate lessons? Maybe Travis should start carrying a gun?"

"Jesus, Kate. I'm just telling the kid to stick up for himself. Hell, if it were up to you, you'd probably have him kissing any mean ol' bullies who decided to pick on him."

"Dan, when I agreed to let Travis take this construction job—"

"It's okay, Mom," Travis interrupted quickly. "It won't be a problem."

"It had better not be. You could be badly hurt in a fight, not to mention the danger of injuring your hands. Contrary to what your father thinks, every difficulty in life can't be handled with fists."

"Always worked for me," said Kane.

"Fortunately for the rest of the world, everyone isn't you, Dan."

"Yeah. That's a cryin' shame, ain't it? Now, since we're all in agreement, let's drop it. Who's ready for dessert?"

"Me!" answered Nate, raising his hand.

Catheryn turned to Nate, sensing he'd been unnerved by the argument and deciding to let it go. "Okay, okay—dessert. Right after we clear the table." Then, glancing at her husband, "Not that I've got any room left, but what *is* dessert?"

Kane shrugged. "Nothin' much. Fresh strawberries, peaches, and blueberries over butter-pecan Häagen-Dazs ice cream, ringed with Pirouettes and, for those of you with discernin' palates, a little Grand Marnier drizzled on top."

Kane's description had an immediate and salutary effect on everyone's mood. Catheryn rose and started stacking dishes. "Funny," she said. "I think I just found some room."

As Kane assembled the final course, the rest of the family cleared the remains of dinner. Minutes later, when all had regathered at the table for dessert, Kane made an announcement. "I've got some things to take care of at work tomorrow, but we'll be launchin' the raft on Sunday—right after church. I checked the tables. High tide's at one. We'll shoot for that. Trav and Tom, see if you can get some of your friends down here. We'll need all the muscle we can get."

"Sorry, Dad," said Tommy. "We're working all weekend. One of the units has to be ready for inspection Monday morning. Everybody's on overtime."

"Damn," said Kane, glancing around the table.

"Don't look at me," said Catheryn. "I've got private lessons on Sunday, and after that I'm getting together with my chamber group at the university."

"I'll help," cried Nate.

"Me, too," said Allison.

"What the hell good are you two gonna do?"

"I can lift as well as anyone," Allison declared indignantly. "And so can my friends. McKenzie's already said she'd like to help." She looked over at Travis, adding, "Of course she'll be *very* disappointed Travis isn't there. Anyway, her dad has a Zodiac with an outboard motor. I'll bet I could get him to help, too. As for Nate—we could use him for an anchor."

"Real funny, butt-munch," said Nate.

"Give it a rest, you two," Kane ordered. Then, grudgingly, "Maybe you've got an idea there, Allison. Usin' Milt's boat might help. I'll call him tonight, then get ahold of Arnie and some of the guys from work."

"Now that *that's* settled, I have something to show you all," said Catheryn. "It came in the mail today." She reached under her seat, pulled out a glossy magazine, and placed it squarely in the center of the table. The picture on the cover depicted a strange, unworldly landscape in which twin moons hung suspended in a star-filled sky, their glowing crescents rising behind stark, jagged peaks that tore like fangs into a distant horizon. Across the top, above a series of domed structures mushrooming from the alien landscape, read the words: *Asimov's Science Fiction.*

"Your story!" said Travis, turning to Allison.

Allison stared at Catheryn, futilely trying to extinguish the flush rising to her cheeks. "How could you open my mail?" she managed to squeak.

"Oh, Allison, it's just a magazine, not a letter," said Catheryn. "When I saw it, I knew it had to be the issue with your story."

"Congratulations, sis!" said Tommy, thumping her soundly on the back.

Nate picked up the magazine and examined the cover. "Is it scary? Are there monsters?"

"Of course, dummy. It's science fiction." Travis grabbed the magazine and flipped it open. "Here it is on page fifty-eight," he said. "Have you read it yet, Mom?"

"Not yet. I thought I'd wait till we were all together."

"Read it to us, Allison," suggested Travis.

"Yes, why don't you, honey?" said Catheryn.

Before Allison could respond, Tommy spoke up. "Uh, I told Christy I'd meet her at the Pizza Hut after dinner," he said apologetically.

"It's a *short* story," Catheryn pointed out. "It'll be over by the time you've finished dessert. Allison?"

"Mom, I don't want to."

Catheryn took the magazine from Travis. "Then *I'll* read it," she said. "Getting published at your age is a tremendous accomplishment. You should be proud to share your efforts with your family, not embarrassed."

"Mom, please . . ."

Ignoring her daughter's look of pleading, Catheryn opened the magazine to page fifty-eight. And as the rest of the family listened, she began to read.

•   •   •

"Well, *I* liked it," Travis declared later as he and Allison stood washing dishes at the kitchen sink. "Nate was disappointed there weren't any monsters, but personally, I thought it was—"

"If you say 'touching,' I swear I'll tear out your throat with my bare hands," Allison warned.

"Touching? Hardly. I was going to say weird. The science stuff, anyway. But the story itself was great, even if Mom and Dad did look sort of . . . puzzled by it. Especially Dad."

"Puzzled? That's what you call it?"

"Well, considering how tense things got at dinner, the story was a little—"

"A little what?" asked Allison testily.

"Close to home?" said Travis. "The tale of a father who can't accept a deformity in his child and winds up losing everything because of it. You even called it 'Daniel's Song.' For anybody with half a brain, the connection isn't too hard to figure."

"Half a brain? Guess that lets you out," Allison retorted.

"Everything considered, Mom liked it—and I think Dad took it fairly well," Travis continued, ignoring Allison's gibe.

"Dad hated it."

"He said he kind of liked *parts* of it."

"Right."

"Well, I think it took guts to write it, and even more to sit there while Mom read it out loud—especially with Dad present," said Travis. "Just be glad that as a writer you usually don't have to be around when someone judges your work."

"Like you are when you play?"

"Yeah."

"Gee, Trav, you're breaking my heart." Allison grabbed a handful of utensils from the rinse water and jammed them into the rack. "The poor little prodigy's complaining about all the praise he gets."

Travis frowned and concentrated on the dishes without responding. Allison had to rush to keep up, fighting to keep her side of the sink from overflowing.

"Look, I've been trying to compliment you," Travis said at last. "Why don't you just shut up and take it? And despite what you think, I haven't been getting all that much praise in the music department lately."

"From Dad? What do you expect, Einstein? By the way, I came close to puking at your little dinner speech. 'Framing a house is fun. One minute you've got nothing; the next all the walls are up.' What a kiss-ass."

"Jesus, Allison. Why are you picking a fight with *me*?"

"I'm not."

"Okay, you're not. Look, I was just trying to say I know how it feels to be judged."

"Don't compare your music with my writing," said Allison quietly. "I'm depressed enough already."

"Join the club," said Travis.

By now the dish rack was filled to overflowing, and Allison had to dry the remaining plates and glasses with a towel and stack them on the counter. Although Travis had completed his part of the cleanup, he stayed to watch her finish.

"What's your problem?" she asked dully, looking up from the sink when she noticed he hadn't left.

"I thought I'd hang out. Anything wrong with that?"

"No." Then, returning to her drying, "So what are you depressed about? That guy Junior, Mom and Dad fighting over the Philharmonic, or just being a member of this screwed-up family?"

Travis didn't answer.

"What is it, Trav?"

Travis hesitated, trying to decide whether to confide in his sister. Finally he spoke. "When I said I wasn't getting much praise in the music department, I wasn't talking about Dad. I meant Petrinski."

"What? Mom's always said you were his prize student."

Travis shrugged. "Things have changed. That new piece I'm working on? It's get it right or don't come back."

"I can't believe this, Trav. Does Mom know?"

"Not yet. Don't repeat this, but I . . . I'm thinking of quitting."

Allison whirled. "You idiot! What're you gonna do with your spare time? Play football?" She wiped her hands on the dish towel, then tossed it angrily onto the counter. "Come to think of it, that's just perfect. With Tommy away at college, you can move up to the number-one-jock position. Really kiss the ol' dad's ass good."

"Jeez, Allison," said Travis. "What's with you?"

Allison stepped forward, her eyes darkening with fury. "I'll let you in on a secret, genius-boy. Day after day, for my whole damned life, I've been listening to you play. And for as long as I can remember, it's made me feel . . . small." She paused, embarrassed by her revelation. Then, with a wry smile, "Guess you could say I have a case of piano envy."

"Come on, Allison. You're gonna be a great writer someday."

"No. I'm gonna bust my ass to be as good as I can, and someday, if I'm lucky—maybe I'll be a *decent* writer. But great? Never."

"I think you're—"

"Shut up," Allison yelled, close to tears. "You know something? If I had your talent, I wouldn't give a damn what anybody thought, *especially* Dad. You have something unique, and now you want to throw it away. Look out, Travis. With little effort, I believe I could learn to hate you."

And, scowling, Allison turned and ran from the kitchen.

12

Following Friday's dinner, Kane and Catheryn engaged in a private and heated discussion involving matters left hanging at the table. Hesitant to worsen his already shaky position, Kane postponed a confrontation over her playing with the Philharmonic but staunchly maintained that Travis should stand up to Junior . . . *whatever* the cost. Catheryn remained emphatically opposed, and things had not ended well.

Grateful for the diversion, Kane spent most of the next day at the station catching up on cases that had been shelved during the Bradley investigation. Upon returning home he spent another restless night with nothing resolved, and on Sunday morning attended six A.M. Mass alone. Afterward, without waking his family, he made himself a cup of coffee and descended to the lower deck. There he stood for several minutes in the early-morning light, still running over the argument in his mind. Finally, with a shrug, he resolved to let it go—at least for the time being.

After kicking off his shoes, Kane stepped over the seawall and sat on the edge of the raft, sipping from his steaming mug and gazing out over the wide expanse of beach to the ocean's edge. During the past week the tides had been confined by a seasonal berm, leaving a large expanse of sand untouched, and in it Kane could now see written a chronicle of the intervening history. Scores of footprints circled the raft, giving silent testimony to one who could decipher their meaning that the latest addition to the beach had been wondered about, commented upon, walked around, stared at, jumped off, strolled past, urinated on (seventeen dogs, one human), climbed over, leaned against, and safe sex practiced under—becoming, before ever being launched, a focal point of prepositional interest for the entire shoreline community.

A sound startled Kane from his reverie. He turned. Tar's dark form stood at the top of the seawall behind him, waiting to be helped down. "Finally decided to get up?" said Kane, moving to help him over the drop. "Just couldn't hold it anymore, eh? I know the feeling, pup."

Tar wagged his tail and gratefully licked Kane's face while being lifted down. "You're welcome, but keep that tongue to yourself," Kane chuckled, thankful there was at least one member of the family whose loyalty never flagged. With a grin, he set Tar on the beach. His smile faded as he watched the old dog struggle painfully across the sand.

Upon reaching a fifty-gallon drum supporting one corner of the raft, Tar made a valiant, arthritic attempt to lift his leg. At last thinking better of it, he finally gave up and squatted like a puppy to relieve himself. His hindquarters shook pitifully as he tried to rise. Unable to regain his feet, he looked up at Kane with a poignant mix of embarrassment and pain. Finally he surrendered his dignity and, whining, settled to the wet sand, collapsing in his own urine.

"Aw, damn, Tar," said Kane softly. He knelt beside his dog, running his hand over the Lab's head. "It's that time, ain't it, boy? It's that time."

Kane climbed the stairs to the kitchen and made a phone call, waiting impatiently to leave a message with an answering service. Next he took two long-handled tools from the work shed and placed them in the back of his station wagon, along with an old woolen blanket. When he returned to the beach, Tar still hadn't moved. "Come on, pup," said Kane. When Tar didn't follow, he bent and lifted the old dog in his arms.

Kane carried Tar to his car and drove north on the deserted highway, passing the pier and climbing the incline past Pepperdine University. As he topped the hill, the rising sun glinted briefly in the mirror. After passing the manicured lawns of the university, Kane made an illegal U-turn farther on through a median break and parked on the west side of the road, stopping in an area where a geologically unstable bluff ran between Pacific Coast Highway and the ocean. Most of the undeveloped acres in this area had been deemed unsuitable for building by the county, and as a result still displayed a green blanket of indigenous coastal flora: thick native grasses, anise, sage, scrub chaparral, low bushes, and trees. It was here, years ago, that Kane had trained his dog. Each morning over those months, from the time Tar had been seven weeks old until he'd reached a year of age and was old enough to go on his first hunt, they'd worked these fields together at first light. Over those months early commuters had grown accustomed to seeing a large man and his black pup ranging the acres bordering the highway. And gradually, over those months, Tar had become a gun dog. Working with training dummies and bird wings and an occasional live pigeon, Kane had taught him to mark and retrieve multiple falls, to respond to hand and whistle signals, and to hunt in a close, quartering pattern. But most significant of the things he'd accomplished, over those months Kane had formed a bond with Tar that had lasted a lifetime.

Kane carried the old Labrador to the top of a knoll overlooking the field. To the west the endless gray expanse of the Pacific stretched into eternity; behind them the encroaching sounds of the highway crept slowly into the morning silence. Kane spread the woolen blanket on the ground and placed Tar on it. Then he sat beside him, and together they gazed out over the ocean.

For several hours that morning, drivers on their way to town who happened to glance across the field saw a large man and a black dog sitting together on the hilltop. The man appeared to be talking. Occasionally he'd gesture with his hands. Most travelers continued on without a second thought, but a few veteran commuters puzzled over it as they proceeded down the hill. And one, a lone woman in a vintage Mustang convertible who'd been driving the highway for years, even managed to remember.

She slowed as she passed, pleased with herself for recalling. Yes, she thought. It *was* the same man she'd seen many years before, working the field every morning at first light—his dog in front silhouetted black against the ocean, quartering joyfully into the wind.

•   •   •

"This is it? Nobody else?" Arnie surveyed the callow young faces surrounding the raft. "Good luck, ol' buddy."

Bending over the swivel eyelet, Kane finished twisting the shackle pin securing the mooring hawser to the raft. He examined the connection. Satisfied, he coiled the hawser and tossed it onto the deck. "You got that right. What happened to the rest of the guys?"

"Banowski's outta town this weekend, and Deluca's got a Little League game with his kid—he's the coach. The rest of the squad's busy, too. Everybody said they'd be sure to drop by next weekend for the party, though."

"Great," said Kane dryly. He turned to Allison. "I thought you were gettin' some of your friends to come."

"I did."

"I meant *boy* friends, Allison. Jeez, what's the deal? Don't you have any?" Ignoring Allison's furious blush, Kane turned and inspected the ragtag group assembled around the raft. McKenzie stood shyly to one side with her twelve-year-old sister, Nancy. Christy, the only friend of Tommy's who'd shown up, had brought a teammate from swim practice. They sat on the edge of the raft watching Kane—Christy bright and willing, her friend Marsha exuding an aura of typical teenaged surliness and boredom. Nate, the youngest there, sat cross-legged on the sand beside Arnie. All wore swimming suits.

"Anybody else gonna show? Don't any of you have older brothers?" Kane asked, glancing hopefully at the girls. All solemnly shook their heads.

Kane rubbed his chin, then turned and studied the ocean. The tide had already peaked, and sets of long, rolling waves were marching in steadily from the south. Most appeared to be five to six feet in height, with an occasional eight-footer cresting fifty to seventy-five yards out before rushing in a foamy surge to the shore. Past the breakers he could see McKenzie's dad, Milt, bobbing patiently on the swells in his Zodiac. Clinging to the hope more people would arrive later to assist with the raft, Kane had helped him launch the small boat through the waves just before noon. Milt's rubber vessel had a fifteen-horsepower outboard motor—powerful enough to tow the raft in calm water, but questionable for dragging it through the surf.

"What do you think?" Arnie asked.

"No way," Kane sighed. "I hate to give up, but you, me, and a bunch of girls just aren't gonna get it done."

"We can do it," Nate objected. "Besides, I'm a guy."

"Yeah, sure."

"Let's give it a try, Dad," suggested Allison. "The waves are still coming up. If you want the raft out for the party next Saturday, now's the time."

"Come on, Mr. Kane," Christy chimed in. "We might surprise you."

Kane shrugged doubtfully, then looked over at Arnie. "Okay, partner, let's see if we can lift this monster." He walked to the raft. Bending his knees, he grabbed the uppermost beam. Arnie moved to the other side and did the same. Using their legs, they lifted on the count of three. Although Kane managed to elevate his side a foot, Arnie's barely cleared the beach.

Unbidden, the children suddenly rushed in. Instantly, the raft rose above the sand, as if magically suspended by the sheer force of girlish giggles.

"You kids are stronger'n you look," Kane admitted, shaking his head in amazement. "Okay, put 'er down nice and easy."

"Surprised you, huh?" said Nate proudly when the cumbersome raft once more rested on the sand.

"Yeah, Pop. This is going to kill you, isn't it?" Allison added with a smirk. "Having a bunch of lowly girls launch your big manly raft."

"Hey, I'm not that way," said Kane. "I'm pragmatic. Life hands me lemons, I make lemonade."

A disgruntled murmur rose from the assembly. With a chuckle, Arnie sat on the raft and regarded his partner with a look of amusement.

"I don't know which I object to more—being called a lemon or a lowly girl," remarked Christy, glancing between Allison and Kane.

"I do," said Nate. "Being called a lowly girl."

"Aw, lighten up," said Kane, studying the surf and noticing a lull between sets. "You all know what I mean. Anyway, now that you mention it, I *would* like to get this sucker floating before the party next weekend."

"We can do it, Dad!" Nate prodded.

Kane came to a decision. "Okay, listen up," he said, his voice shooting up a notch in volume, assuming the dictatorial tones of a drill sergeant addressing a squad of raw recruits. "My insurance isn't paid up this month, so I can't afford having anybody getting their feet squished, not to mention smearin' blood all over my brand-new raft. Here's what we're gonna do. We'll pick this thing up from two sides, and nobody gets in front or behind while we're moving it. Once we've got it floating in shallow water, I'll signal Milt out there to start pulling, at which point I want everybody back onshore. Arnie and I will stay with the raft and paddle it through the waves. Any questions?"

"Yeah," said Arnie, raising his hand timidly. "Where'd you get all them great big muscles?"

Everyone laughed. "Screw you, pard," said Kane with a smile. "C'mon. Let's do it."

Kane directed his young crew to set the raft down twice on the way to the water, resting partway across the sand and again just before taking it over the berm to the ocean's edge. With the raft sitting just beyond the reach of the uprushing waves, Kane gauged the shoreline currents and then had the raft moved twenty yards south to the mouth of a dark, angry riptide flowing out through the breakers. Next he resecured all items lashed to the deck: the mooring line with metal eyelets spliced into each end, a come-along winch, a large metal shackle with ten feet of half-inch galvanized chain, the wooden ladder that would later be bolted to the raft, and two canoe paddles. Finally he uncoiled several hundred feet of light nylon rope and fastened one end to the swivel eyelet. As he slipped a loop tied in the other end over his shoulder, Christy stepped forward. "Want me to swim that out to the Zodiac?"

"Nah. I can get it there quicker."

With an innocent smile Christy's friend Marsha asked, "Feel like putting some money on that, Mr. Kane?"

"You want to bet me?" Kane snorted. "You mean real money, sunshine?"

Marsha nodded. "That's right, Mr. Kane. Real money."

"I'll take a piece of that," said Allison.

"Me, too, partner," added Arnie, grinning as the rest of the children began clamoring for a race.

Kane assumed a look of doleful, wounded betrayal at the unanimous outburst. "I guess I'm not surprised at a bunch of young pups trying to pull down the ol' dad here," he said. "That's just natural. Foolish, but natural. But you, Arnie?"

"I'm pragmatic like you, ol' buddy."

Kane scratched his head, and regarded the children uncertainly. "Well, I don't have the heart to crush your illusions right now, it's bein' such a nice day and all," he said, suppressing a smile. "That being the case, I think I'll just let Christy here swim out the line."

"Boo, Dad," hooted Allison. Nate quickly jumped in with a clucking sound, immediately spawning a rash of similar catcalls from the rest of the group, including Arnie.

"Okay, Mr. Kane," Christy laughed. "As you said, it's being such a nice day and all, I'll be glad to."

Christy entered the water, trailing the yellow nylon line behind her. Using the outflowing rip to assist her through the surf, she dived cleanly under each approaching wave just before it broke, appearing on the other side seconds later. Once she was past the break, her long, powerful strokes quickly ate up the distance to the Zodiac. Soon she and Milt had the line secured to the transom, and within fifteen minutes she'd returned to the beach.

"Good work," admitted Kane when she arrived. "Couldn't have done better myself. Now for the hard part. But before we start, I've got a question. Anybody here ever had the shore-break slam a loose surfboard into their shins?"

Several heads nodded.

"Hurts, doesn't it? Well, once we get this monster in the water, the surf'll do its best to shove it back on the beach, and if you're in the wrong spot, the result'll be a lot worse than bruised shins. Whatever you do, stay on the sides and don't get behind it." Kane regarded everyone in turn, making sure each of them understood, and then continued. "Now, listen up, 'cause once we start, I'm not gonna have time to be explaining things. First off, we'll get the raft in the water just enough to get her floatin', but not too deep. We'll hold her there and wait for a break in the sets, ready to go as soon as there's a lull. During this time we'll have to hold her steady, 'cause the incoming waves'll try to knock her back and the rip'll try to take her out in between. When I say go, the boat'll start pulling, and everybody but me and Arnie will let go and head for the sand. One more thing," Kane added, looking at McKenzie's younger sister. "What's your name, cupcake?"

"Nancy," the twelve-year-old answered.

"Once we get the raft to the water's edge, that's as far as you and Nate go."

"Aw, Dad," Nate complained.

"That's an order, small fry. Understood?"

"Yes, sir," Nate mumbled.

"I'll stay with Nate," Nancy promised.

"Good. Then let's do it."

Arnie took a position opposite Kane. The others filled in on both sides, and they quickly had the raft floating in knee-deep water. But holding it there proved more troublesome than Kane had expected. As predicted, wash from the waves pushed it shoreward, then the outflow of the increased rip quickly pulled it the other way—only much more forcefully than he'd thought. Although the group fought to maintain the raft in the shallows, it soon became apparent they'd made a mistake.

"We can't hold this mother," Kane yelled over the roar of the surf. "Get it back on the sand."

Too late. The raft surged seaward. Without warning, the entire group found themselves in waist-deep water, unable to control the formidable mass of the raft. "Let it go!" Kane bellowed. "Let it go!"

Kane and Arnie stayed with the raft as the girls retreated toward shore. Once they were there, Kane surveyed the incoming swells, spotting a break. Waving his arm, he signaled Milt in the Zodiac to start pulling. "It's now or never," he hollered over at Arnie. "Let's go!"

The yellow line tightened. As the raft lumbered slowly seaward, Arnie and Kane climbed aboard and started paddling, attempting to give it enough momentum to break through the waves.

The first swell crested forty yards out. Its wash staggered the raft without stopping it. The second broke closer in, nearly stripping away the two men clinging to the deck. Gasping for breath, Kane and Arnie strained at their paddles, fighting to propel the raft over the next wave. Suddenly Kane noticed a small head bobbing beside them in the water.

Nate!

Reaching down, he grabbed a handful of curly red hair and dragged his son on deck just as another wall of swirling foam crashed over the front. Despite the tug of the Zodiac and the pull of the rip, the raft stopped dead in the water. "Oh, shit, look what's coming!" Arnie shouted.

Kane's heart fell. The next wave, easily the largest of the day, rose before them—a mammoth wall of furious shining green, spray flying from the crest.

"Paddle, Arnie, paddle!"

But even as the two men struggled to drive the raft toward the onrushing wall of water, Kane knew they weren't going to make it. As the toe of the wave reached them, the raft staggered like a punch-drunk fighter. Slowly, it climbed the unbroken face as the surge lifted it like a toy . . . higher, higher . . . the deck tilting skyward at an impossible angle . . .

"It's gonna flip! Jump!"

Arnie bailed off one side. Kane grabbed Nate's arm and dived off the other. The last thing he remembered before going under was seeing the raft crashing over backward, disappearing under tons of angry, thundering ocean.

"Nate!" Kane screamed when he finally clawed his way back to the surface. "Nate!"

The roar of the surf drowned his calls. He strained to raise his head above the hissing foam, searching for his son.

"There he is!" Arnie yelled from his left.

Halfway to shore, a small form struggled in the surf. Kane took a deep breath. In three quick strokes he caught the next incoming wave and slid down the curling face, dropping his right arm and arching his torso, cutting toward Nate. As the huge wave closed out, he rolled through, emerging on the churning backside.

A moment later Nate surfaced beside him, gasping for breath. "You okay?" Kane yelled.

"Yeah," Nate sputtered.

With a surge of relief, Kane took Nate's hand and kicked for shore. The next wave broke outside, and the next. The four-foot wash carried them all the way to the sand. "I told you to stay on the beach," Kane growled as they stumbled from the water.

"But, Dad—"

"No buts," Kane shouted, his heart still racing. "I swear, if you pull a stunt like that again, I'll kick your butt so hard, you'll beat the ambulance to the hospital. What the hell were you thinking?"

"I . . ."

"You what?"

"I wanted to help you take it out."

"Nate, I appreciate that, but I ordered you to stay onshore for a reason."

"I wasn't scared."

"This isn't about being scared, kid. Jesus."

"I'm sorry, Dad," said Nate. "I . . . I only wanted to help."

Kane took a deep breath, watching as Arnie exited the water several yards away. "Okay, kid," he sighed. "Just don't do anything like that again, all right? If I tell you to do something—like staying out of heavy surf—it's for your own good. Understand?"

"Yes, sir."

"Good. You wanna help, help us pull the raft up on the berm and get 'er flipped. We're done for the day."

Driven by the force of the waves, the inverted raft had foundered in the boiling water, then skidded high on the sand fifty yards down the beach. With the assistance of Nate and the girls, Kane and Arnie finally managed to right it. The gear lashed to the deck had somehow survived, along with the line to Milt's Zodiac. Shortly afterward McKenzie's sister Nancy returned carrying the paddles, which had washed up a hundred yards farther down.

"Thanks for helping, kids, but that's it," Kane announced glumly as he knelt to untie the towline. "You all did first-rate work, and I'm proud of you. If the surf dies down, we'll try again next weekend after the party."

Allison stepped forward. The other children unconsciously drew together behind her. "Dad, we talked it over," she said. "We want to give it another try."

"Now? Not a chance."

"Come on, Dad. Next time we'll wait for a longer break in the sets, then float the raft when it's time to go, not before. That way the rip won't be a problem. We can do it." Allison glanced at the other children. "Right?"

"Right," they agreed.

"Absolutely not," said Kane.

"There's no danger if we time it right," Allison persisted. "I've been watching, and I think the breaks in the sets are getting more frequent. And this time *all* the kids will stay on the beach," she added with a pointed glance at Nate.

"Damn," said Arnie. "I'm impressed. Gutsy bunch you got here, Dan. Dumb, but gutsy."

Surprised, Kane studied the circle of earnest young faces. "Didn't you all get enough the first time around?"

"The first time we did it the hard way, Mr. Kane," Christy spoke up. "Allison's right. If we hold the raft out of the rip till it's time to go, we can do it without any danger."

"Let's try, Dad," begged Nate. The rest of the group joined in, clamoring their support for another attempt.

Kane watched the swells for nearly a minute without speaking, noticing that the breaks in the sets *did* seem to be getting longer. At last he turned to the children. "If we give this another go," he said, "and I'm just saying *if* . . . do I have everyone's promise you'll stay on the beach this time? *All* of you?"

"Yes, sir," they answered in unison.

"Nate?"

"I promise," said Nate solemnly.

"I'll make sure of it," said Allison. "How about it, Dad?"

At last Kane relented. "Okay. We'll give it one more try. But I'm holding you to your promise. Once we get this thing floating, you kids are back on the sand for the duration."

"No problem," said Allison.

The second attempt proceeded with military precision. Kane's team of children performed their assigned tasks flawlessly, launching the raft into the rip during a temporary lull and quickly returning to the beach as agreed. Assisted by the Zodiac, along with Arnie and Kane's determined paddling, the outflowing current quickly carried the raft through the breakers. Again, surmounting the outside waves proved to be touch and go, but they made it. Once past the breakers, Arnie and Kane stood on the deck and waved at the cheering children on the beach.

"That's one helluva bunch," Arnie noted. "They showed some guts coming back for seconds after that first fiasco."

"You got that right," said Kane. "I swear, that Nate's sure a little firecracker."

"Allison, too. By the way, ol' buddy—was she right?"

"About what?"

"About its killin' you having a pack of kids save your sorry butt."

"What kills me is listening to your pathetic attempts at gettin' my goat."

"Screw you, pard."

"Same to you, amigo. Let's get this thing moored."

Milt's Zodiac towed them to the small float Kane had placed off-shore the preceding weekend. As the rubber boat held the raft in position, Kane slipped on his swim goggles and dived in. Descending through the frigid water, he followed the float line forty feet down to the iron wheel. Once there he partially cleared the axle hole, then rose to the surface, took several gulps of air, and descended again with the length of galvanized chain, allowing its weight to carry him to the bottom. Although he was able to use the float line to pull the chain through the hole, it took four more dives to secure the moor-ing hawser and twist shut the shackle. Kane's breath was coming hard when he crawled back onto the raft.

"That's it?" asked Arnie, eyeing Kane's house a hundred yards up the beach. "I thought you were gonna park this thing closer to home."

"You thought right," said Kane, unlashing the come-along winch from the deck. "We're gonna move the wheel."

"With that?" asked Arnie, glancing curiously at the winch. "How?"

"Simple. Here, gimme a hand."

After again entering the water, Arnie and Kane secured the winch to one of the central beams on the underside of the raft. Then, while Arnie unsuccessfully attempted to avoid banging his head as the raft rolled and pitched above him, Kane swam the steel cable down and attached it to the anchor chain. Next, working from beneath the raft, both men took turns operating the winch lever. Slowly, the cable tightened. Before long, supported by the raft above, the massive iron wheel began skipping along the bottom, stirring up clouds of sand, coming to rest, lifting once more as Kane and Arnie gradually ratcheted it up. When the wheel hung well suspended above the ocean floor, Kane locked off the winch. Satisfied, he gave Arnie the thumbs-up, and together they climbed back on deck.

Milt's rubber Zodiac still had the raft under tow. At Kane's signal he twisted the throttle on his small outboard. The engine roared. Slowly, rising and falling on the passing swells, the small boat lumbered up-current, trailing the raft in a cloud of pale-bluish smoke.

Ten minutes later they arrived at a point two hundred yards directly out from Kane's house—far enough from the beach to be safe from storm surf, yet still a reasonable swim. After studying the waves, Kane had Milt move them out a little more to allow for the length of the mooring line. Then he again slipped over the side, ducked under the raft, and released the winch. The wheel dropped silently to the bottom. Two quick dives freed the cable, and the raft was anchored.

After retrieving the come-along, Kane climbed from the water for the last time. He glanced shoreward. By now the launching party had lost interest and dispersed—all except Nate, whose small figure still sat watching from the sandy berm.

"Done?" Arnie asked hopefully, his teeth chattering.

"You cold? I'd think with all that blubber you're carrying you'd be warm as toast."

"Up yours. I'm not half fish like you, ol' buddy."

"Temper, temper," said Kane, untying the two-by-four ladder lashed to the deck. "Here, gimme a hand with this. Once it's bolted, we'll head in for some warm clothes and cold beers."

Relieved now from the necessity of holding the raft in position, Milt eased the Zodiac alongside and tossed over his bowline. "Somebody mention beer?" he asked, reaching under the seat and pulling out a six-pack of Coors.

Arnie tied Milt's line to one of the beams. "Good man!" he said with a grin.

Once the boat was secure, Kane grabbed the six-pack, along with a wrench set he'd stowed earlier on the Zodiac. "Arnie, Milt. Milt, Arnie," he said, passing each a can.

"Pleased to meet you, Arnie," said Milt, stepping onto the pitching deck. A wiry man in his late thirties with straight black hair and a quick smile, he stood as tall as Kane, though not as heavily built. "You a cop, too?"

Arnie popped his beer, spraying warm foam over the deck. "Yep," he said. "Close to twenty-five years. Been partners with Kane here a good many of 'em, sorry to say."

Kane pulled the tab on his own beer, christening the deck in turn. "Hell, Arnie," he said. "Tell the truth. Every one of those years has been pure pleasure, baskin' in the warmth of my sunny personality."

"Sunny? Is that what you call it? Personality disorder's more like it."

"Twenty-five years, huh?" said Milt. "You've gotta be pretty close to pulling a pension."

Arnie shot a quick look at Kane. "Yeah, pretty close," he said. "Surprising for a youngster like me, huh?"

"You've still got a few good years left," muttered Kane. "It ain't time to pull the plug yet." Then, after setting down his beer, he selected a three-eighths socket from the wrench set and bent to the task of securing the ladder.

Milt knelt beside him to hold the wooden uprights in place. "You have any kids?" he asked, still addressing Arnie.

"Nope," answered Arnie regretfully. "My wife . . . my *ex-wife* and I never did. She had a career, and we kept putting it off. Before we knew it, it was too late." He hesitated, deciding not to mention that Lilith had left him after twenty years of marriage for a real-estate salesman.

"You want kids, take a couple of mine," offered Kane.

"Don't think I wouldn't. I'd do it in a heartbeat," said Arnie. Looking shoreward, he noticed Nate jumping to his feet as he saw his mother approaching from the house. "Those kids of yours are real pistols, too," he added, glancing back at Milt. "Nancy and McKenzie?"

"Uh-huh. The whole crew did a great job today," said Milt. "I'm glad I was out here, though. Some of those waves were huge. After that first attempt I was relieved to see you kept everybody on the beach."

Kane continued ratcheting the ladder bolts, moving from one to the next without looking up. "Yeah, well . . . I shoulda made sure they stayed there the first time, too," he said guiltily. "Things kinda got away from me. You had to be there."

"Like I said, I'm glad I wasn't." Milt chugged the rest of his beer and tossed the empty into the Zodiac. "Another brew?"

"I'll take one," said Arnie, grabbing a fresh can. "You about done, Dan? I think Kate wants you for something."

Kane cranked down the final bolt and looked shoreward. Unable to make herself heard over the surf, Catheryn was standing on the beach waving her arms. When Kane waved back, she pantomimed picking up a telephone and holding it to her ear. Then, with a sweeping gesture, she signaled them in. Kane pointed to himself. Catheryn shook her head. Next Kane pointed to Arnie, eliciting a positive response.

Kane popped his second Coors, pleased the call wasn't for him. "Looks like you've got a phone call, Detective Mercer," he said smugly, passing Arnie the wrench he'd been using, along with his empty beer can and the come-along winch. "Tell you what, pard. Go ahead and ride in with Milt. I'll swim in after I finish my beer."

"Sounds good to me. See you onshore."

"Hey, Milt," Kane said to McKenzie's father as he and Arnie boarded the Zodiac. "Thanks for the help."

"My pleasure. If I ever decide to shoot somebody, maybe you can return the favor."

An experienced boat handler, Milt waited for a lull in the sets, making it through the waves without dumping the Zodiac. Kane sipped his beer, watching from the raft as they ran the rubber boat up on the sand. He smiled as he saw Nate race down to assist. Arnie spoke briefly to Catheryn, then hurried toward the house. Again turning seaward, Catheryn waved for Kane to come in.

Kane made one final appraisal of the newly moored raft. After deciding everything was in order, he downed the last of his beer, crushed the can, shoved it into his suit, and dived into the water. Once he'd swum to a point just outside the cresting swells, he, too, waited for several sets before choosing a wave. Then sprinting for the beach, he caught a six-footer and stayed with it, riding the foam all the way in. Catheryn and Nate were waiting on the sand when he arrived.

"Damn, Kate, you look good enough to eat," said Kane as he waded from the surf, resolutely attempting to put Friday night's disagreement behind them.

Catheryn smiled. "Think so, huh?" she said, also making the effort.

"Yep," said Kane, trying to snare her in his dripping arms. "That's gotta be one of my favorite outfits."

Catheryn had just returned from her chamber-group practice. Except for removing her shoes, she hadn't changed before coming out on the beach, and still had on a flowered sundress that amply displayed her tanned figure. "Play your cards right, and maybe I'll let you borrow it sometime," she laughed, deftly sidestepping her husband's wet embrace. "I see you got the raft out," she added. "Good work, especially considering the surf."

"Dad was great," said Nate. "You should have seen him and Arnie paddling it through the waves."

"I can imagine," said Catheryn. Then, with a puzzled expression, "Who helped you launch it?"

"All us kids helped," Nate explained proudly. "Even me. You couldn't have done it without us, right, Dad?"

"That's the God's truth," said Kane. "You should have been there, Kate. Actually, maybe it's better you weren't," he added with a grin, making one last abortive try for a hug. Finally giving up, he asked, "Who phoned?"

"Somebody named Moro from the department. It sounded important."

"Hey, Dad?"

"Just a second, Nate," said Kane, still regarding his wife. "Did he say what it was about?"

"No."

"Dad?"

Kane turned. "What?"

"I can't find Tar. I looked everywhere."

"I did, too," said Catheryn. "When I got home and he wasn't on the beach, I checked the kitchen, the bedrooms, even the music room. I couldn't find him anywhere."

Kane glanced away. "I was gonna tell everybody after dinner," he said. "Tar's gone. His legs were so bad this morning, I . . . I took him to the vet. It was his time."

Stunned, Nate and Catheryn stared at Kane.

"No! Not yet," cried Nate as his father's words sank in. "Please, Daddy. I'll give him his medicine from now on, I promise!"

"Nate . . ."

"I won't forget anymore," Nate declared, his voice fierce with determination. "I promise! Just give me one more chance."

Without answering, Kane pushed past his son and started for the house. Nate trailed miserably behind, tears welling in his eyes. "Please, Dad."

Catheryn caught up and tried to place a comforting hand on his shoulder. He shook it off. "Honey, it's not because you forgot to give him his pills," she said.

"Dad, please . . ."

Kane turned and looked down. Nate stared back, his cheeks wet, his eyes filled with pleading. "Look, kid, I'm sorry," said Kane, his voice gruff with emotion. "Tar's gone. It was his time to go."

"Please give me one more chance."

"Maybe I haven't been speaking English. Tar's gone. Dead. Understand?"

"It's not fair! Tar was my dog, too!"

Just then Arnie appeared on the upper deck, the portable phone still in his hand. "That was Moro," he yelled down.

"What'd he want?"

"CRASH thinks they've got a line on that Trans Am we've been lookin' for. We've gotta go."

"Be right there." Kane turned and regarded Nate once more. "Tar's gone," he said quietly. "It's too bad, but there's nothing I can do about it. End of discussion." Spinning on his heel, he started again for the house.

Nate stood rooted to the sand, his shoulders racked with silent sobs. "I hate you!" he called after his father's receding figure. Kane continued on without breaking stride, his feet churning the sand like pistons.

Catheryn clenched her hands in frustration and anger, watching as

Kane departed. Then, with a sigh, she gently placed her arm around Nate's shoulders. This time he didn't shake it off. "You don't mean that," she said.

Nate watched as Kane jumped the seawall and crossed the deck to the house. Hot, bitter tears streamed down his face. "Yes, I do," he said softly. "I do."

· · ·

The family ate a somber dinner without Kane. Nate remained in his room, maintaining he wasn't hungry. Later that evening Catheryn climbed the ladder in the entry and knocked on the trapdoor in the ceiling.

"Go away!"

Catheryn tried the door. It rose slightly, then stopped. Nate had it hooked shut on the other side.

"Nate? Let me come up. Please."

Catheryn heard the clasp release. She flipped open the door and climbed the final rungs, finding Nate lying on his bed staring out the window. Still holding the ladder, she swung in her legs and let the hatch close beneath her. Then, without speaking, she knelt beside the bed. Resting her forearms on the mattress, she gazed with Nate out the window.

Set above the rest of the house, Nate's airy room afforded an unobstructed view of the beach. A westerly breeze had begun flowing off the land at sundown, holding up the waves and making the surf seem even larger. In the failing light Catheryn could just make out a small square object two hundred yards offshore, tossing and rolling on the swells.

Finally she spoke. "Nate, your father loved Tar, too."

"No, he didn't! If he had, he wouldn't have killed him."

"Oh, honey, I know you're feeling terrible right now, but you know that's not true."

Nate stared out the window.

Catheryn tried to take his hand. He jerked it away. Catheryn took it again, holding it firmly. "Look at me, Nate. I have something to tell you."

Nate turned, fixing red, defiant eyes on his mother. He looked down quickly, unable to hold her gaze.

"I want to tell you something about your father and Tar," said Catheryn. "There're a few things you don't know."

"I don't care!"

"Well, you're going to hear them anyway." Catheryn took a deep breath, and then continued. "Your father and that dog go back a long way, back before you were born. Every morning for over a year when we first got Tar, your father got up early before going to work, training him to hunt. And each fall after that until Tar turned nine, those two left on a hunting trip, all by themselves—Canada for Hungarian partridge, sharp-tailed grouse, and geese; Idaho for sage hen and ducks; Montana and South Dakota for pheasant. Our freezer used to be crammed full of the game they brought back. Dan claimed Tar was one of the finest gun dogs he'd ever hunted with.

"Once Tar accidentally caught some shotgun pellets. He nearly died. Your father stayed at the vet's with him all that night. He didn't sleep, just sat with Tar even though he couldn't do anything to help. The only time I've ever seen him like that was when one of you kids got sick, really sick. And then when Tar grew too old to hunt, rather than get a new dog, Dan quit hunting, too. Your father not love that dog? You couldn't be more wrong."

"Then why did he kill him?"

"He didn't want to. Tar was old. His arthritis had gotten so bad he couldn't walk, and he was in pain most of the time. Keeping him alive wasn't doing him a kindness. Your father did what had to be done."

"But . . . Tar was my dog, too. I never even got to say good-bye."

Catheryn brushed a thatch of hair from Nate's forehead, then gently lifted his chin and looked into his eyes. "I know, honey. And that was wrong. Your father was probably trying to protect you from the pain you're feeling right now. He just went about it the wrong way."

"Protect me? That's a laugh," said Nate bitterly.

"Yes, protect you," said Catheryn. "If he could, your father would gladly stand between you and all of life's hurts, and so would I. But that's not possible. I wish it were, but it's not." Catheryn hesitated, and then went on. "Listen, honey. Ever since you were little, when something bad happened, I've been telling you that everything would be all right. But sometimes . . . much as we want it, that's not true. Sometimes things happen that no one can protect us from, terrible things, things that hurt. It's part of life. It's part of being alive. Do you understand what I'm saying?"

"I understand Dad doesn't care how I feel."

"Yes, he does. More than you know. Your father isn't perfect, but we're the most important things in his life, all of us—you, me, Allison, Tommy, and Travis."

"He doesn't act like it."

"He tries, but he doesn't always know how to show it."

Turning from his mother's gaze, Nate again stared implacably out the window.

"Your father loves us, Nate. He'd be lost without us. Deep down you know that, don't you?"

Nate remained silent.

"Nate?"

Finally, in a small, tremulous voice, he answered at last. "I know, Mom," he said, burying his face in his mother's sweater. "I know."

Catheryn stroked her son's hair as an invisible dam burst inside him at last. And she held him close and whispered the old lies once more, willing them to be true, telling him things would be all right, . . . everything would be all right.

PART TWO

13

Saturday, July 3. Beer in hand, Kane surveyed preparations for the party with a practiced eye. Although certain he'd overlooked nothing, he also realized no amount of forethought could chart the celebration's final outcome, and had always considered the execution of his annual Fourth of July bash something akin to rolling a boulder down a mountainside. You could prepare all you wanted—clearing obstacles, anticipating problems, and attempting to predict the ultimate direction the event would take—but past some point a massive, irresistible inertia finally and irreversibly claimed ascendancy. After that all you could do was stand back and watch.

Kane smiled, struck with the thought that if he hadn't thrown his annual party, hundreds would have shown up anyway—especially since over the years invitations had become superfluous. As if reading his mind, Travis asked, "How many people do you think are gonna make it this year, Dad?"

Turning, Kane regarded his children, who stood lined up on the deck awaiting their assignments. "Good question," he said, scratching his head. "A lotta guys from the force'll show up. Your mom's invited all her music cronies, so they'll be mincin' their way on down, too. Then there's everybody we know on the beach and any friends you peckerwoods might have invited. Should be around two-fifty, three hundred."

"Better make that closer to five, Pop," Allison quipped. "I asked a couple hundred of my very dearest admirers to attend."

"Ali, if every one of your admirers showed up, it wouldn't increase the attendance by two, let alone two hundred," Tommy noted with a grin.

"Oh, yeah? How many of your jock buddies are coming?"

Tommy shrugged. "Fifteen, maybe twenty."

"You understand I'm not asking their IQs, right?"

"You'd better back off, Tom," advised Travis. "You're outta your league here."

"Enough yappin'," said Kane. "Let's get to work. Tom, the Porta Potti folks are droppin' off a crapper around nine-thirty. Move the cars from in front of the house to make room. There's a red Bronco across the street. Park 'em behind that. And put some sawhorses out so some idiot doesn't take the spot in the meantime."

All private homes in Malibu employed private septic systems for waste disposal; although the Kanes' plumbing was satisfactory on a day-to-day basis, experience had proved it woefully inadequate when it came to handling two or three hundred beer-guzzling guests.

"Move the cars," barked Tommy, snapping to attention and shooting Kane a crisp salute. "Yes, sir! Aye, aye, sir!"

Ignoring his oldest son's cheerful posturing, Kane glanced at the huge mound of scrap lumber and driftwood the children had piled near the seawall during the preceding weeks. "When you're done, get back down here and help Travis, who's gonna be startin' on the bonfire. Right, Travis?"

"Yes, sir."

"You check the tide tables?"

"High tide's five point eight feet, peaking around nine this morning. Low tide's in the fours later tonight. Should be plenty of beach."

"Good. Start moving the wood down, but don't set it up till the water's on the way out. Dig a shallow pit downwind of the fireworks area; then stack it like a tepee."

"I *know*, Dad. Just like we do every year."

"Just checkin'. Allison, you and Nate are on beach detail. The tide's washed in a lotta junk, not to mention the minefield of dog squeeze that's been collecting the past few days. Start rakin', rookies," Kane ordered. "My buddy Wally Sullivan and his crew are gonna be here soon, and I don't want 'em steppin' in it," he added, referring to an former–LAPD demolitions expert who'd founded a fireworks company after retiring from the force. For the past seven years Wally had provided a professional show to top off Kane's annual party—whenever possible, as they were this year, keeping expenses down by doing the shoot on the third instead of the fourth.

"Aw, Dad . . . ," mumbled Nate.

"No complainin'. The beach's gotta be clean by the time they start digging trenches for the mortars. After that you can both help your mom set up the food tables and clean the house."

"I'm always on poop patrol," Nate grumbled.

"That should tell you something, kid. Now quit bellyaching and get to it. Oh, one more thing. Tom, after breakfast you and Trav take the Suburban to the liquor store and pick up the kegs. I've got two on order—Michelob and Heineken. Not those little suckers, either. This time we're gettin' the big ones. If Pete gives you any shit about your age, have him give me a call. And don't forget pumps, tubs, and ice. I want them set up in the shade and cooled down early so they're not all foam when we crack 'em." Kane paused, mentally ticking off his list of preparations. "Am I leavin' anything out?"

Allison was quick to respond, posing the subversive question that had occurred to all the children. "Yeah, Pop. You forgot to mention what *you* plan on doing while all us poor kids are working our butts off."

"Yeah, Dad," the others chimed in, emboldened by Allison's query and caught up in her seditious spirit of rebellion.

"That kinda question hurts me deeply," Kane observed with an imperious chuckle. "Fortunately, it's also the kinda question that's liable to hurt you pip-squeaks a lot more'n me. We've got a lot to do. Move it!"

As it turned out, Kane had plenty to do, too. Wally Sullivan, a short, powerfully built man with a walrus mustache and close-cropped hair, arrived around ten A.M. Two younger men accompanied him. All three wore white T-shirts with logos depicting multicolored star bursts and the words "Astro Pyrotechnics" emblazoned in fiery red letters beneath. Following a spate of backslapping and good-natured insults, Kane conferred with Wally on the height of the evening tide and the location of the mortar trenches in relation to the bonfire—assuring him the blaze wouldn't be set until after the display. He then reviewed the fireworks program for the evening, making several suggestions concerning the grand finale.

When it came to lighting the sky, Wally knew how to please an audience. In years past the former LAPD demolitions expert had put on breathtaking shows in front of Kane's house that rivaled even the prodigal public exhibitions at the Santa Monica Pier and the Jonathan Club, for in choreographing his nonpareil displays, he always stuck to one simple rule: no dark sky. Kane learned that, along with the standard repertory, this year Wally had included a number of new shells recently available from China and Taiwan, and the show promised to be a knockout.

It took most of the afternoon to set up the shoot. Kane roped off the area, helped the pyrotechnic crew carry their equipment down from the street, and assisted in digging trenches and setting pipes— burying the mortars in the sand with only a foot or two projecting above the surface. When they'd finished, the beach bristled with a thicket of metal tubes pointing skyward, poised and ready for the evening's celebration. With the exception of the finale shots, which had to be preset to allow for rapid firing, all fireworks remained stored in the shade, locked in a stout metal container marked "Explosives."

Shortly after three o'clock Bill Flood, the fire marshal, showed up, joining the considerable number of early party arrivals who'd already drifted in. Astro Pyrotechnics had applied for a fireworks permit weeks before, with Kane putting in for the bonfire at the same time, and a preshoot inspection was a requisite part of the process.

"Bill, 'bout time you brought the family," said Kane, noticing the fireman had his wife and two kids in tow.

"I hope you don't mind," the burly man replied sheepishly. "I thought this summer I'd stick around afterward."

"Mind? Hell, no. You're always welcome, and I've been telling you to bring down the better half for years. I'm Dan Kane," he added, shaking hands with the dark-haired woman standing beside the marshal. "There's food on the tables and plenty more on the way. We've also got beer kegs tapped, wine on ice, and soft drinks for the kids in the coolers over by the steps."

The woman smiled. "Thanks. Anything I can do to help?"

"Naw, just make yourself at home. My wife Kate's upstairs in the kitchen right now, but she'll be down shortly. I know she'll want to meet you." All of a sudden Kane shifted gears, glaring down sternly at the two small boys standing behind their mother. Both wore baggy swimming trunks that extended well below their knees, and were carrying swim fins and Boogie boards—small foam kickboards used for bodysurfing. "Surfers, huh? You kids aren't planning on drowning in front of *my* house, are you? A couple deaths this early in the day might throw a crimp in the party."

"No, sir," the older boy promised seriously.

Kane grinned. "Good. See that you don't." Then, glancing at the empty plastic cup in his hand, he said, "Bill, I'm startin' to get parched. What do you say we get the inspection over with and retire to the bar?"

"Sounds good to me."

As his wife and children made their way toward the food tables, the fireman trailed after Kane to the roped-off area, noting the placement and direction of the mortars, the heavy metal explosive box in the shade by the wall, and the huge tepee of scrap lumber and driftwood that Travis and Tommy had erected twenty yards distant. "Sullivan doing your shoot?" he asked.

"Couldn't afford it otherwise. I don't know what I'm gonna do when he finally blows himself up."

"Go back to sparklers." Bill again glanced doubtfully at the unlit bonfire, where Tommy, who'd made one last scavenging run down the beach, was busily loading on a final layer. "You don't plan on lighting that till after the show, right?"

"Actually, I thought I would. See whether we can get everything to go off at once."

"In that case, we're definitely gonna need something to drink. Where'd you say those kegs were?"

"Follow me, amigo," said Kane, starting for the deck. "Follow me."

• • •

Upstairs, Travis stood at the kitchen window, watching Tommy putting the finishing touches on the bonfire. Closer in he saw his father approaching the house, accompanied by another man he recognized from years past as the fire marshal. They stopped at the beer kegs on the lower deck, just outside the beach-level music room. Travis noticed that his father looked relaxed, expansive, already immersed in the convivial good cheer he always exuded at social functions.

"Let's go, Trav. Practice time. You have less than an hour before people start arriving."

With a sigh of exasperation, Travis turned and regarded his mother. "An hour before people start arriving? You haven't looked outside recently, have you? Folks are *already* arriving."

"Oh?" said Catheryn, moving to the window.

"There's gotta be at least thirty people already out there, and more on the way. Tell you what—I'll put in some extra time tomorrow, okay?"

"All right, but see that you do," Catheryn said. "We'll be cleaning up after this one for a month," she added, surprised by the number of guests who'd already descended the outside stairway to the beach below.

"You've got that right. Did you invite anybody?"

Catheryn smiled. "Of course. I need *someone* to talk to besides your dad's beer-guzzling buddies. I asked some friends from the Philharmonic, my chamber group, and just about everybody I know at SC."

"Petrinski?"

"Uh-huh. He said he'd try to attend." Catheryn regarded Travis curiously. "I'm surprised *you* didn't invite him."

"I forgot," Travis lied, glancing away guiltily.

Puzzled, Catheryn was about to say something more when Adele Washington entered the kitchen, her brightly colored maternity dress billowing around her. "Hi, you two," she said. "I hope you don't mind my coming in the front, but I wasn't sure I could make it down the outside stairs."

"Of course not," said Catheryn, smiling at her cellist friend. "It's mostly Dan's associates I try to keep outdoors."

"Hi, Adele," said Travis, taking her hand. "You look great."

"Thanks, Trav," said Adele, planting a kiss on his cheek. "You must be *so* proud of your mom."

"Uh, sure I am," said Travis. He saw Catheryn shoot her friend a sharp look, a warning Adele completely missed in her garrulous enthusiasm.

"Well, *I* think it's just fantastic," Adele went on blithely, giving Catheryn a hug.

At that precise moment Kane bolted up the stairs from the beach. "Am I interruptin' somethin'?" he asked, poking his head into the kitchen. "You gals want me to come back, or can I get in on the action?"

"Dan! You're looking uglier than ever," said Adele, a smile lighting her face.

"And you're lookin' sexier than ever, sugar," Kane countered. "Damn, bein' pregnant must agree with you. Did you bring that worthless husband of yours?"

"Pat had to work."

"Well, I guarantee you ain't gonna be lonely." Then, to Catheryn, "Time to drag yourself down to the beach, honeybunch. There's a party startin' out there."

"We'll be there in a sec, Dan," Adele promised. "I just thought I'd congratulate your talented wife on her victory first."

"What victory?"

"She didn't tell you?"

"First I've heard of any victory."

All eyes turned to Catheryn. She hesitated. Then, staring defiantly at Kane, she said, "I got the position with the Philharmonic. They needed an answer right away. I told them I'd do it."

"That's great, Mom!" exclaimed Travis. "Congratulations!"

"Thanks, Trav," said Catheryn, carefully studying Kane's reaction. "I was planning to announce it later as part of the celebration."

"You were gonna *announce* it, huh?" Kane snorted. "If you made the cut, I thought we were gonna *talk* about it before you came to a decision. What happened to that?"

When Catheryn didn't answer, Adele jumped in. "Dan, this is a real honor for Kate. I don't think you realize—"

"What I realize is my wife's been keepin' secrets from me."

"Come on, Dad," chided Travis. "It's just for a little while. Mom deserves this."

"Shut the hell up, bucko. This is none of your business."

"That's right. This is between your father and me," said Catheryn, taking Kane's hand. "Look, I want this," she said quietly. "I'm sorry I didn't talk it over with you before accepting, but it wouldn't have made any difference. The kids have already said they'd help, and I'm doing it. That's all there is to it."

"Damn it, Kate . . ."

Forcing a smile, Adele linked her arm through Kane's and finessed him toward the door. "Let's go, Dan. As you said, there's a party starting up outside. Let's go join it."

Kane allowed himself to be led out. He glanced back when he reached the stairs. "This isn't over, Kate," he said. "Not by a long shot."

"It never is," said Catheryn softly.

•   •   •

Kane stepped outside with Adele, discovering that a host of additional guests had arrived, most carrying food. Glancing across the deck, he noticed more were on the way, with a steady river of people now flowing down the side of the house to the beach below. Swept up in the social deluge, Kane and Adele were soon washed into the center, caught like floating twigs in the turbulence of a mountain stream.

Deciding to put off thinking about Catheryn's unsettling news until after the party, Kane tossed down the last of his beer, excused himself from Adele, and bulled his way down-current—hand shaking and back thumping through a logjam of celebrants farther on. Upon arriving at a small eddy in the lee of the beer kegs, he found Deluca and Banowski elbowing for position under the Heineken tap. Happily ignoring complaints rising on all sides, Banowski had his cup tipped at a forty-five-degree angle under a barely dribbling spigot, tediously attempting to avoid a foamy head.

"Great party, Kane. Kinda reminds me of my college days," noted

Deluca, spilling half of Banowski's beer as he smashed his own cup under the nozzle.

Banowski stared at his crushed and now-leaking cup, then glowered at Deluca. "You mean your high-school car-club days, you dumb wop," he said. "Closest you've ever come to higher education is watchin' public television."

"That's more'n you can claim," Deluca retorted, turning the spigot on full and quickly filling his cup with foam. "Your old lady took the tube in the divorce, and you *still* haven't bought another one, have you?"

"Haven't had time," Banowski answered defensively. Then, turning to Kane, "What kinda beer is this, anyway? Miller extra foamy?"

Kane looked with disgust at the frothy brew sputtering from the tap. "Which one of you muscle-bound bozos overpumped this thing?" he demanded. Deluca and Banowski both looked away, guilt written on their faces. "Well, not to worry," Kane continued. With a superior smile he grabbed a large plastic pitcher from beside the ice bucket, held it under the tap, and drew several quarts of the amber liquid before foam poured over the top.

"Ah . . . the ability to use tools. Separates men from the apes," said Deluca, attempting to strike a philosophic pose.

"Not in your case," Banowski chortled. "I've *seen* the women you go out with."

"Any port in a storm," countered Deluca. "What do *you* like, Banowski? Young boys?"

Kane pulled the dripping container from under the tap. "Do you two *ever* shut up?" he asked, shaking his head. "I swear, you're worse'n my kids. Come on, let's take this pitcher elsewhere and let some of the other thirsty citizens in line here wet their whistles."

"Good idea," agreed Banowski, grabbing a fresh cup. "Speaking of miserable fuckin' divorcés, there's Mercer. Hey, Arnie, over here!"

Arnie waved, and after fighting through the crowd around the food table, joined his fellow officers near the seawall. "Beer?" Kane asked when he arrived.

"Does a bear shit on the Pope?"

"Real nice, Arnie," said Kane, filling his partner's cup. "Have you no respect for other people's feelings? There may be animal lovers here tonight."

"Sorry. Don't know what I was thinking." Arnie took a long pull on his beer, then withdrew a pint of Wild Turkey from his jacket, twisted off the top, and splashed a generous portion into his cup.

"Damn, Arnie. Hell of a way to start out."

"You're one to fuckin' talk," Arnie muttered, offering the bottle. Kane declined. "Long night ahead. Gotta save myself."

Banowski grabbed the bottle and downed a healthy swig. "Well, *I* don't," he said.

"Me, neither," chimed in Deluca, taking it in turn and amply fortifying his beer before passing the whiskey back to Arnie.

Arnie held up the pint and glared sourly at the diminished contents. "Thanks a lot, dickheads. How the fuck am I supposed to get through one of Kane's parties without any real medicine?"

Kane studied his partner, noting the dark, puffy crescents, like inverse moons, shadowing the tissue under his eyes. "Damn, Mercer. You look like shit."

"It's comforting to know I can always count on you to be tactful, ol' buddy."

Kane shrugged. "I call 'em like I see 'em."

"Right," Arnie grumbled. "Well, since there's no booze left to speak of—thanks to my two former friends here—I suggest we go grab some grub before it's all gone."

"You don't have to ask me twice," said Banowski, heading for the food table. "Did you see that spread on the way in? I'm starvin'!"

Over the years a potluck-style meal had become traditional at Kane's annual beach parties, with everyone supplying a favorite salad, entrée, or dessert. This year someone had even brought a fully cooked turkey. Wearing hot-pad mittens, Allison and Nate were scurrying back and forth from the kitchen carrying a seemingly endless supply of freshly heated casseroles, while Tommy and Trav manned two smoking barbecues at the end of the deck—tending sizzling racks of steaks, salmon, chicken breasts, and burgers. In addition, behind the entrée buffet stood a smaller dessert table loaded with a panoply of pies, cheesecakes, cookies, brownies, and tarts.

Although Banowski and Deluca quickly shouldered their way to the head of the buffet and began loading up their plates, Kane hung back with Arnie, concerned about his partner's appearance and intending to ask him about it. Before he had a chance, Milt Wallace came up behind them. "Good to see you boys," he said. "Least now I know I won't be last in the chow line."

Kane smiled. "Hey, skipper, how's it goin'? You remember Arnie?"

"Sure," said Milt, pumping Arnie's hand. "I rarely forget an ugly mug, and the sight of you diving for deep water when the raft flipped is something I'm *never* gonna forget."

"Me, neither," said Arnie. "Much as I'd like to. How're those kids of yours? McKenzie and the little one—Nancy?"

"Fine. They're around here somewhere."

"What's the holdup?" Kane yelled, haranguing a knot of diners blocking the head of the table. "You guys aren't paintin' a picture up there, you know." No one paid the least attention whatsoever except for Deluca, who winged a dinner roll in Kane's direction.

"Hear about the break-ins last night?" Milt asked. "Damn near every car at my end of the beach got hit."

"What'd they take?" asked Kane. "Stereos?"

"Yeah. I lost my fuzz buster, too. Second time this year. What pisses me off most is that they do more damage getting in and ripping up the dash than the damn stereo's worth. I'd be better off just tying a ribbon around it and leaving it on the hood."

"They'd probably bust a window and customize your dash anyway, just for good measure," Kane pointed out. "You report it?"

"Yeah. For all the good it'll do."

"I know some guys up at the Malibu sheriff's department," said Kane. "I'll make a call—ask 'em to beef up patrols on our section of the highway. Meantime, the best thing you can do is drive an old clunker nobody'll mess with. Like mine, for instance," he added shrewdly. "Speaking of which, I might consider parting with it for the right price."

"Thanks," said Milt. "I'll pass."

•   •   •

Hours later the party had swelled to over 350, dissolving by sheer mass the invisible social boundaries that had previously prevailed. Earlier, disparate groups had been the rule, with clusters of people condensing in separate, well-defined enclaves: an unruly LAPD contingent monopolizing the beer kegs, Catheryn's music associates sedately claiming the deck, Travis and Tommy's confederates methodically working the nearly moribund dessert table, and various other groups gathering in convivial clumps of ten or fifteen beside the roped-off fireworks area, the seawall, and the still-unlit bonfire. But now, as the sun slipped into the ocean with a final flash of color, everyone stood shoulder to shoulder, melded into a single homogeneous organism by pure force of numbers and lack of space.

After fighting through the crowd, Kane ducked under the fireworks barrier. There he conferred briefly with Wally Sullivan. Wally lit a highway flare, and seconds later touched off the traditional opening shot of the night. A salute rocketed high into the evening sky, exploding with a single flash followed by a sharp, deafening blast that sounded like a thousand cherry bombs going off at once.

A hush fell over the crowd. Kane stepped to the rope to address them. "Okay, everybody listen up," he shouted, his voice booming into the silence. "Pretty soon Wally here's gonna do his thing and get the fireworks show under way, but before that I'd like to ask you all to join me in a special toast—one that I mean from the bottom of my heart. I want you all to raise your glasses with me and drink to the finest son a father could ever ask for. Where's Tom? Tommy, get up here."

"Yeah, Tommy!" someone cheered from the back, followed by a chant that quickly spread throughout the onlookers. "Tommy, Tommy, Tommy . . ."

Surprised, Tommy abruptly found himself thrust into the fireworks area. "Now, you all know Tom here," Kane continued, throwing his arm around his son when he arrived. "What you may not know is that for two straight years he's led the Samo-High Vikings to the number-one spot in their division. This year they went undefeated, with Tommy gettin' voted All Western Offensive End by the *Times*."

Kane paused, allowing the barrage of whistles and cheers to die down. "Tom will be leaving home this fall," he went on at last. "He'll be attending the University of Arizona, where he'll be playing scholarship ball for the Wildcats, one of the finest teams in the Pac-Ten—soon to be *the* finest. I'm sure you'll all agree with me that with Tom on the squad, there's no way in hell Arizona won't be goin' to the Rose Bowl the next four years straight."

Again, Kane was forced to wait out renewed cheering from the crowd. Finally he lifted his hand for silence. Then, after giving Tommy's shoulders a squeeze, he forged ahead, his voice ringing out strong and clear. "So I ask you now to raise your drinks and join me in wishing my son Tom a long and happy life, four victorious seasons with the Wildcats, and that someday he has a son who makes him as proud as I am of him." Kane solemnly lifted his cup. "To my son."

In unison, everyone joined in Kane's heartfelt toast. Tommy stood beside his father, for the second time that summer struggling against an unaccustomed stinging in his eyes. Grateful the dim light hid his face, he firmly shook Kane's hand. "Thanks, Dad," he said.

A moment later Christy emerged from the crowd and stepped into the ring, handing Tommy a sudsy cup of beer she'd been holding for him. Tommy took it and touched it to Kane's. "Cheers," he said, proceeding to drain the contents in one prolonged gulp, following his intemperate guzzle with an extended and resonant belch.

"You act like you've done that before," said Kane, regarding him suspiciously.

"Maybe once or twice," conceded Tommy. "Don't worry, Dad. I never drink when I'm in training."

"Good. See that you don't." Kane smiled and reached into his pocket. With a flourish, he pulled out a set of keys. "I got something else for you, rookie. Sort of a goin'-away present. It's parked out front, across the street."

Tommy's mouth fell open in amazement. "The red Bronco? It's mine?"

Kane grinned. "Yep," he said. "Got more'n a few miles on her, but she's still in great shape."

"Gosh, Mr. Kane. What a swell present!" gushed Christy.

"You understand you're paying your own gas and insurance, right? And no joyriding when you get to school. You're gonna have to keep up your grades if you want to play football."

"Sure, Dad," Tommy agreed, staring at the keys. "I . . . I don't know what to say."

"Don't say anything, kid. You deserve it. Now, let's get the hell out of here so's Wally can get the show goin'."

"Dad? I hope . . . I hope I don't disappoint you."

"You won't, champ. You never have."

To a final round of applause from the crowd, Kane, Tom, and Christy ducked under the barrier. Then, at a signal from Kane, Wally Sullivan sprang into action. Wearing ear protection and carrying the smoldering highway flare, he started lighting up the sky—moving from tube to tube touching off quick-burning fuses in rapid succession. Occasionally he referred to a flashlight-illuminated podium in the center of the ring that held a list of the evening's prearranged sequence, but for the most part he worked from memory. His two assistants toiled behind him, running back and forth from the metal storage bin carrying grapefruit-sized fireworks with long protruding fuses and making sure the spent mortars were free of burning debris before reloading for the next shot. All three worked as a close-knit team, moving through a miasma of smoke made hellish by Wally's flare, smoothly executing the program with a sure and practiced choreography.

As the sky over the beach began to bloom with dazzling bursts of reds and greens and golds and blues, most of the guests prudently withdrew to watch from a safer distance. Kane, as usual, sat close to ground zero, savoring the powerful, bone-jarring thump of the mortars. The concussion of the larger shots actually made his clothes jump against his skin, something he'd never felt when watching a commercial show from hundreds of yards away, and as the fireworks program progressed, an odd and fanciful thought occurred to him. In the glare of Wally's flare, the men inside the ropes reminded him of an emergency crew sifting through the smoky remnants of some ongoing catastrophe, or possibly a military unit caught in a deadly artillery barrage and fighting for their lives. Enjoying himself immensely and grinning like a kid, Kane settled back on the sand and let his eyes drink in the searing magic of Wally's ephemeral artistry.

Anticipating the beginning of the show, all the Kane children except Tommy had taken their customary position on the roof outside Nate's window. Since their father had long ago forbidden them to be up there, their secret roost naturally seemed all the more enticing, and every year they assembled there, sitting silent as pigeons to avoid discovery.

"Having any fun?" Travis whispered, glancing over at his sister as the first shots of the evening rocketed into the sky.

"Oh, sure. I just *love* having hundreds of strangers troop through my house."

"Where's Tommy?" asked Nate. Sitting between Travis and Allison, he was hugging his knees and leaning against the wall beneath his window, his face illuminated by the fiery bursts blossoming like exotic flowers over the sand.

"He's probably down on the beach with Christy," Travis answered, realizing this was the first time his brother hadn't joined them on the roof.

"The chosen one's more likely out front spit-shining his new car," remarked Allison. "Just think, Trav. If you play your cards right, that could be you in a few years."

"Not likely."

"No, really. I can see it now," Allison went on, conspiratorially lowering her voice. "I'm sure all you folks out there know my son Travis," she growled, scowling fiercely and attempting to crack her knuckles. "What you may not know is that he's just about the best goddamn little piano plinker you'd ever wanna shake a stick at. Now don't wet your pants, everybody, but if he does well at the Bronislaw competition this fall, there's talk he may get to tickle the ivories at the Van Cliburn International next spring. So here's to you, Travis. I wish you a long life somewhere you're not an embarrassment to me, success in whatever profession you choose—assumin' you quit fartin' around long enough to find one—and that someday you have a daughter who makes you as proud of her as I am of you."

Travis watched the fireworks for several seconds without responding. "Screw you," he said finally. "Why are you attacking me? It's Tommy you're jealous of tonight."

Allison smiled knowingly. "Don't try to tell me *you're* not jealous of the chosen one."

"Jesus, were you just born hurtful, or is it something you work at?"

"It's not me, it's *Dad*. What are the chances he'd haul *me* up in front of a crowd like that and make everyone toast my virtues?"

"None, 'cause you don't have any," observed Nate.

"Shut up, wart," Allison shot back. "You're just starting out in this family. You've no idea what's in store for you."

"Oh, yeah?"

"Yeah."

"This is stupid," Travis intervened. "We shouldn't be fighting just because it's Tommy's night to shine. Let's be happy for him and let it go at that."

"Thanks for the sermon, Saint Travis. You're such a hypocrite, pretending you don't care. You make me sick."

"Like I said before . . . screw you."

All three children lapsed into silence, watching the fireworks until the last shot of a mind-boggling sixty-second grand finale faded away, and, following a concluding salute, the sky once more surrendered to darkness.

"Dad'll be lighting the bonfire soon," Nate said quietly after Wally and crew had taken their final bows, and the paeans, hoots, and hollers from appreciative spectators had died away. "You gonna watch, Trav?"

"Yeah," Travis answered. "I helped build the damn thing; I sure as hell want to see it lit. Let's head down."

"I'll join you later," said Allison.

"Who asked you?" said Nate.

Travis rose before Allison could respond. "Suit yourself, Ali," he said, climbing through Nate's window into the house. "Come on, Nate. Let's go."

•　　•　　•

The moon had just started to rise over the bay as Travis and Nate returned to the beach. By then Kane had already put a match to the mammoth, twenty-foot-high stack of scrap lumber and driftwood that the boys had assembled in a shallow pit near the high-tide line. Nate immediately scampered off to seek out some of his friends; Travis, alone now in the crowd, approached the fire looking for Tommy. Eventually deciding his older brother was undoubtedly cloistered somewhere dark and private with Christy, he gave up and joined the circle surrounding the blaze, slowly backing away with the others as the fire climbed steadily into the night.

Soon a roaring tower of flame danced over forty feet into the air. Driven by the heat from the raging conflagration, the ring of spectators continued to widen, retreating more than a dozen paces from the pyre's base. Before long the wood structure began to shift and settle, and then, with a series of loud creaks and pops, embarked on an arthritic, inexorable collapse to the sand.

Twenty minutes later, as many of the spectators lost interest and drifted off for greener pastures—more food, another beer, a long-overdue trip to the head—Allison, accompanied by McKenzie and three other girls from school, joined the group around the blaze. Chatting happily, they seated themselves about eight feet from Travis. Allison caught her brother's eye when her friends weren't looking. With an arch, insouciant smile, she shot him the finger.

Travis grinned and replied in kind. Then, ignoring his sister and her friends, he crossed his legs and watched as the flames gradually began to subside to a mountain of glowing coals. He'd been staring into the hypnotic, ever-changing inferno for nearly a quarter hour when a portly form settled beside him.

Travis turned. It was Petrinski, his expression unreadable in the flickering light.

"Hello, Travis."

"Hi, Mr. Petrinski," Travis mumbled. "I . . . I didn't know you were here."

"How long have we known each other, Trav?"

Travis thought back. "Uh, I had my first lesson with you when I was six. That makes it around ten years, I guess."

"My friends call me Alex. After ten years I think it's time you did, too. We're friends, aren't we?"

"Yes, sir. Alex."

"Then why have you been avoiding me all night?"

"I . . . I didn't see you."

"Travis, there's one thing above all else that I demand of my friends."

"Sir?"

"It's that they don't lie to me. Ever."

Travis stared into the fire. "I'm sorry. It's just . . . I didn't know what to say."

Absently, Petrinski picked up a small piece of driftwood and started drawing in the sand. "Listen, Trav. Whether or not we continue the didactic part of our relationship doesn't change the fact that we're friends. At least I hope not. Now, talk to me. I assume from your reticence that you haven't gotten anywhere with the Chopin étude."

Travis glanced away. "Shouldn't I be preparing for the competition?" he said evasively. "Even for the first round I have pieces far more difficult than the étude."

"You think so? Well, that's exactly why I gave it to you. I'll tell you something, Travis. Right now I'd much rather hear you play that étude with genuine feeling than win any contest I can think of, including the Bronislaw. How far have you gotten?"

"I . . . I've been working on it," Travis stammered. "The technical part was easy. Well, not easy, but I think I've got it—I just don't know where to take it from there. I don't know what you want."

"What *I* want is not the question. It's what *you* want from your playing, and what you're willing to do to achieve it."

Travis fell silent, dreading the lecture he knew was coming.

"You haven't told your mother you've reached a crisis in your music, have you?"

Travis paled. "No. Did you . . . ?"

"Of course not. That's between you and her. But I think you should discuss it with her. You owe her that, Travis. Possibly she can help."

"I don't think so."

Petrinski sighed. He continued to draw with his stick, creating a complex architecture of ridges and swirls in the sand. Travis watched, not surprised to find an element of art even in his teacher's unconscious doodling. A moment later both Travis and Petrinski looked up as they heard the sound of boisterous voices bellowing out an atonal bastardization of "The Farmer in the Dell."—"A-rafting we will go, a-rafting we will go, heigh-ho, the derry-o . . . ."

Soon Travis could make out the dim forms of Kane and Arnie marching exuberantly toward the fire, arms around each other's shoulders. As they drew nearer, he caught snatches of their conversation between verses, mostly involving which of the two men had a greater abundance of hair on his ass.

"You pussy," Kane taunted. "I say we swim out there right now."

"You goin'?" Arnie asked.

"Are you?"

"I asked you first."

"Yeah! Damn right I'm goin'!"

"Then I'm goin', too!"

"Great! Who else's got balls enough to brave them dark, shark-infested waters?" Kane shouted, spotting Travis by the fire. "How 'bout you, kid?"

"I don't think so, Dad."

" 'Fraid of gettin' your panty shield wet, eh? Come on, Arnie. Let's see whether we can talk that lard-ass Banowski into goin'. Maybe we can drown him on the way out."

"That's the first good idea you've had all night," said Arnie, executing a one-eighty and heading off with Kane toward the house.

"I'm full of 'em," Kane boasted.

"You're fulla something, all right."

"Up yours, amigo. Hey, let's find Tommy while we're at it. He'll wanna go. It'll probably take three of us to sink that fat fuckin' polack anyway."

"Such foresight, old buddy. I'm speechless."

"Damn right," said Kane, embarking once more on his off-key chant as they disappeared into the darkness. "A-rafting we will go, a-rafting we will go . . ."

"You obviously didn't inherit your musical ability from your father," Petrinski observed dryly after they'd gone.

"I guess not," said Travis, smarting at his father's taunt but half wishing he'd agreed to go along.

As though reading his mind, Petrinski asked, "You care very much what he thinks of you, don't you?"

"No!" Travis protested, surprised at his own vehemence.

"I think you do," said Petrinski gently. "I think you're stuck between two worlds."

"What do you mean?"

Instead of answering, Petrinski studied Travis for several seconds. "Tell me something," he said. "Do you think you're intelligent?"

"What's that got to do with anything?"

"Just answer. Or maybe you'd rather swim out to the raft and prove your courage to your father?"

Travis scowled.

"Jesus, Travis. Let it out. I'd rather hear 'Drop dead, Alex, you're way out of line,' than nothing at all."

"Drop dead, Alex, you're way out of line," Travis blurted.

"Well, that's a start. Now, answer my question."

"Okay, I'll play your game," said Travis guiltily. "Am I intelligent? Not especially. I get A's and B's in school, an occasional C."

With a sweep of his hand, Petrinski wiped his doodles from the sand and made two vertical lines in their place. "Look. Verbal competence here, and here, mathematics—the cornerstones of most current tests of mental ability." He drew a line connecting the marks he'd made with a circle labeled "IQ."

Travis squirmed uncomfortably, realizing his mentor's labyrinthine lectures always wound up having some cogent point, usually directed at him. As he let his eyes travel the faces ringing the fire, furtively searching a way out, he noticed his sister's friend McKenzie watching him. She quickly looked away.

"What's wrong with this picture?" Petrinski demanded, poking the drawing with his stick.

"Well, for starters the circle's lopsided, the lines are crooked, and the whole thing's out of proportion."

"Funny, Trav. No, what's wrong is this." Petrinski drew a series of parallel lines alongside the first two he'd scratched in the sand. "Verbal and mathematical reasoning aren't the only faculties of the human mind. There are others as basic and unique: a sense of spatial relations, for example, or a knack for foreign languages, or the ability to communicate using paint, music, poetry—or even the kinesthetic sense your brother Tom so aptly displays."

"You're saying Tommy's a genius because he got voted All Western Offensive End?"

"I'm saying the kinesthetic sense is a type of intelligence. As for Tommy, we'll talk about genius if he makes it to the NFL."

"And me?" Travis asked reluctantly. "I take it that's where this is leading."

Petrinski paused, his brow furrowing in thought. "I don't know about you," he said. "I suspect you have the potential to be . . . unique. Instead, I see an unhappy, confused boy."

"I'm not confused. I just don't—"

"Listen to me, Trav," interrupted Petrinski. "I believe that finding happiness in life involves discovering where one's abilities lie—your domains of intelligence, if you will—and then making the commitment to exploit them to their fullest. You have yet to do that."

"I work hard . . ."

"That's not enough."

"Then tell me what to do."

"I already did," the older man said softly. "I know you have feelings, Travis. If you won't express them in your daily life, at least let them show through in your music."

Travis fell silent once more, staring glumly into the fire. Petrinski rose. "It's getting late," he said. "I've got to be going. Please think about what I've said. And, Travis?"

"Yes?"

"You're going to have to do this on your own. No one can help you. Just remember you aren't Tommy, and you're not your father, either. You're Travis Kane."

Travis continued to gaze into the glowing mountain of coals long after Petrinski had gone, resentfully pondering his teacher's final statement. A number of times during this fruitless meditation he felt as if he were being watched. Finally looking up, he found McKenzie's eyes on him once again. As before, she quickly glanced away. Then she looked back shyly. Travis nodded and returned his attention to the fire, groaning inwardly as he saw her rising to join him.

"Hi, Trav," she said with an ingenuous smile when she arrived.

"Uh, hi, McKenzie."

She dropped down on the sand beside him, curling her long, coltish legs neatly beneath her. "It's a beautiful fire, isn't it?"

Travis shrugged, in no mood for company.

"Notice how yellow the flames are? That's from salt in the driftwood."

Travis stared into the fire without responding, absently noticing the flames *were* more yellow than usual.

"It's the sodium in the sea salt that gives it the color," McKenzie went on quickly. "You know, like when we did the flame test in chemistry lab—dipping a wire in different solutions and sticking it in a flame. Sodium burns yellow, copper blue, zinc has a greenish tinge . . ." Her voice trailed off. Confronted by Travis's monolithic wall of silence, she sat quietly, unable to fill the glacial void.

"I'm sorry," she said at last. "I didn't mean to jabber on about some stupid chem class. You look like, well . . . is something wrong? Who was that man you were sitting with?"

"Alexander Petrinski. My piano teacher." Travis tossed a piece of driftwood into the fire, sending an angry storm of sparks spinning into the darkness. "After ten years he drops me as a student and then tells me to call him Alex," he added bitterly.

"But why? What did you do?"

"It's what I *didn't* do—play as well as he thinks I should," answered Travis, feeling small and mean for his simplistic misrepresentation.

"But . . . you play beautifully. I can't imagine why he would—"

"What the hell do *you* know?" Travis lashed out cruelly. "Look, my sister sent you over to bug me, and you've succeeded. Now take a hike. Get lost."

McKenzie rose slowly to her feet. "Is that what you think?"

"That's what I *know*," said Travis. He glanced up, surprised to see tears shimmering in McKenzie's eyes.

She turned to go. "I'm sorry," she said.

"Wait," Travis said quickly, feeling more despondent than ever. "I'm the one who should be sorry for taking out my problems on you. Please don't leave."

McKenzie hesitated.

"Please? Can we start over?" Travis smoothed the sand beside him in a gesture of conciliation.

After a brief hesitation, McKenzie wiped her eyes and sat back down. Both stared uncomfortably into the flames, not knowing what to say.

Finally McKenzie ventured, "It really *is* a beautiful fire."

"Yeah. See how yellow it is? A reliable source told me that comes from sea salt in the driftwood. You know, sodium burns yellow, copper blue, zinc green—like in chem lab."

"If you're trying to impress me with some stupid trivia you picked up at school, it won't work," McKenzie laughed, her voice rising like a bright, lovely bird into the night.

In the glow of the fire Travis could just make out her fine patrician features: intelligent brown eyes, high cheekbones, a strong jaw framing a mouth slightly too large to be called beautiful, a smattering of freckles accenting the bridge of her nose. Her long ebony hair, parted in the center and worn in a thick French braid for the party, seemed to shine like silk in the darkness.

McKenzie stared into the shifting coals for several moments, then looked up to meet Travis's gaze. "I meant what I said," she said quietly. "About your music. I think you play beautifully. I want you to know that."

"Thanks," said Travis, embarrassed by her unexpected sincerity. "But I don't recall ever playing for you. When was it?"

"Oh, I've spent hours listening to you," McKenzie confessed. "Up in your sister's room. Ali listens too. She's your biggest fan, next to me."

"Are we talking about the same Allison?"

"The very one."

"I didn't know you liked classical music. Do you play?"

"Uh-huh," McKenzie answered self-consciously. "Flute. I'm in the school band. Nothing like what you do."

"Maybe we could play something together sometime."

"Oh, I'm not good enough for that," said McKenzie quickly. "I'd rather just listen."

"Okay." Travis hesitated, running out of words. "Then, McKenzie? You know something?"

"What, Trav?"

"It's just that, uh . . ."

"What?"

Travis opened his mouth, intending to say something about not expecting to find he actually liked one of his sister's friends, and that he regretted never giving her a chance. But when he finally spoke, what came out surprised him nearly as much as it did McKenzie.

"Do you want to go out with me?"

14

Like clockwork, every morning at 11:45 A.M. the aluminum-sided lunch truck with elaborate indigo lettering on the side reading "Arturo Domingo" made its appearance on the job site, and Monday was no exception. Travis had spent the morning helping one of the older men nail siding and, from his position high on the scaffold, was the first to spot it lumbering to the top of the hill. *You can damn near set your watch on Arturo,* he thought, his stomach rumbling at the prospect of food.

Arturo's truck boasted an imaginative and diverse selection of heart-clogging options: deep-fried chicken, half-pound burgers dripping with juice, a tantalizing selection of tempting Mexican dishes, polish dogs smothered in cheese, chili, and onions, and a huge inventory of junk food—cupcakes, Twinkies, Cokes, chips, and Ding Dongs. To his surprise, Travis found he couldn't get enough. Although health purists might have condemned some of his dad's dinner extravaganzas as unhealthy, for the most part Catheryn did the routine cooking in the Kane household, preparing low-fat, high-carbo meals. Arturo's lunch wagon had proved a revelation for Travis: He loved grease.

Travis grabbed his T-shirt from the safety bar and pulled it on.

During the long, hot days of summer he'd been laboring in boots and shorts only, and the past weeks had turned his skin a deep, ruddy brown. "Chow time," he yelled over at Pete Wilson, the grizzled carpenter with whom he'd been working.

Pete looked up from the other end of the twelve-foot plank. " 'Bout time," he said brightly, abandoning a clip of galvanized nails he'd been shoving into the pneumatic gun. "Let's get 'er down. I hate bein' last in line."

Using the toe of his boot, Travis began ratcheting down his end of the plank, carefully matching his movements to Pete's at the other end as they slowly descended the metal support columns. Getting too far out of sync could cause the scaffold jacks to bind, or worse yet—slip. By the time Travis and Pete had painstakingly lowered themselves to within jumping distance of the ground, the lunch truck had already opened for business and most of the crew stood queued up beside it. As he joined the line, Travis found himself behind Tony Stewart, the owner of the company and his father's friend from the force. "Hey, Kane," said Tony, touching a match to an unfiltered Camel. "Great party Saturday."

"You were there?" said Travis. "Somehow I missed you."

"Not surprising, considering the crowd. I saw you, though. Sitting by the fire next to a cute little number with a long braid."

"Uh-huh. She's one of my sister's friends."

"Right. Looked like you were working on making her one of yours."

"Well . . . yeah."

Tony grinned. "Can't say's I blame you." Then, noticing Travis's flush and deciding to let him off the hook, "How's work going?"

"Great," Travis answered. And it was. With houses in various stages of completion, plenty of variety existed on the job—especially for Tommy and Travis, who filled in wherever needed. For the past two weeks Tommy had been working on Ron Yeats's framing crew, and Travis had recently joined Wes Nash's smaller finish unit—running siding on one of the nearly completed buildings. The system they were using was simple. Wes cut the prestained tongue-and-groove cedar on a table down below, beveling the ends and varying the runs so the joints wound up staggered. Using a length of half-inch rope, Travis pulled up stacks of cut siding to the scaffold plank, then assisted Pete in nailing. At first Travis had only been hauling and holding; lately Wes had begun letting him use the gun—a vote of confidence that hadn't gone unnoticed by the rest of the crew.

"Shot yourself with that nail gun yet?"

"No, sir. Not yet, anyway," answered Travis, realizing that not much on the job got past the boss.

"Good. Keeps the insurance premiums down. I like that. How's your brother doing?"

Travis spotted Tommy near the front of the line ordering his current favorite: a huge burrito stuffed with cheese, beef, and beans and buried beneath a mound of sour cream and guacamole. "Fine, 'cept he's gained about ten pounds since starting here."

"We probably aren't working him hard enough. I'll see what I can do to correct the situation. Thanks for the tip, Trav."

"Anytime, boss."

By now the line had shortened. Tony stepped under the aluminum flap and grabbed a plastic liter of Coke, two Ding Dongs, and a fresh pack of Camels. Like most of the men on the crew, Tony was an inveterate smoker. For some reason Travis couldn't fathom, carpenters seemed a subculture that had somehow never gotten the word on cancer. Nonetheless, with few exceptions, everyone there looked lean and trim and glowing with health, ostensibly thriving on a daily ration of carcinogen and grease.

"Art, my man, I think I'll have the special today," Tony announced as he arrived at the head of the line.

Arturo flashed a gold-filled smile from beneath the bill of his Dodgers' baseball cap. "Extra bacon?"

"Absolutely."

Travis checked the small blackboard listing the special of the day. Grilled pastrami and fried egg on a French roll with bacon, tomato, jalapeño peppers, melted cheese, and fries on the side. "Make that two," he said.

Minutes later Travis joined Pete and some younger members of the crew who were eating on a stack of two-by-sixes. He glanced around as he unwrapped his sandwich, spotting his brother talking on the pay phone beside the equipment trailer. Tommy had his burrito balanced on top of the phone box, cooling and apparently forgotten. Twenty minutes passed before he finally joined them on the lumber pile.

"What's up?" Travis asked.

"Nothin'." Tommy stared glumly at his lunch, poking the now-glutinous burrito with his fork.

Travis shrugged and dug back into his sandwich, looking up after several bites to see Tommy wadding up his food, uneaten. "Not hungry?"

"Not really."

"Better watch out, bro. Keep skipping lunch and that Arizona line's gonna eat you alive."

"Never happen." Tommy checked his watch, then rose and arced the remains of his lunch into a metal rubbish drum ten feet away. "Catch you after work."

Shortly afterward, as he finished the last of his fries, Travis heard the high-pitched whine of Wes's Skilsaw rising into the heat of the afternoon. He balled up his trash, tried to match Tommy's toss, missed, made the second shot, and headed back to work. When he arrived, he found Junior Cobb standing on the plank.

With a surly grin Junior looked up from toying with the nail gun. "Well, well, lookit who we got here," he said, enchilada sauce from lunch still smeared on his chin. "It's Howdy Doody."

Wes Nash, who'd just finished beveling a stack of cedar, laid his saw on the cutting board. "Knock it off, Cobb. Kane's working with you this afternoon. Let's get to it."

"Where's Pete?" asked Travis.

"I needed him inside running trim," answered Nash. "The owners are coming by Friday, and Tony wants the interior done. Now, if you two don't mind, I'd appreciate seeing some of this cedar gettin' nailed."

"No problem." Junior looped the air hose around the safety bar, securing the gun. "Come on, red. Going up."

Travis reluctantly mounted the plank and moved to one end, placing his foot in the jack stirrup. Glancing over, he saw Junior had done the same. Without speaking he began to pump.

It took a number of minutes to raise the scaffolding to the spot where Pete and Travis had quit for lunch, over twenty feet from the ground. The hillside at the base of the wall fell away sharply, making it seem even higher, and Travis noticed that for some reason Junior had remained strangely silent on their ascent. He also noticed that the higher they got, the more carefully Junior had matched his movements on the jack. With a feeling of satisfaction, Travis suddenly realized Junior was terrified of the vertical environment in which he himself felt completely at home. "You aren't afraid of heights, are you?" he asked, locking off his jack.

"Fuck you, pussy. I ain't scared of nothin'."

"Whatever you say." Travis moved to the center of the plank to select the first length of cedar. In transit he pretended to stumble, causing the scaffold to shake. He smiled as he saw the blood drain from Junior's face.

For the next two hours Travis and Junior worked steadily, nailing up the cut lengths Wes sent from below. Travis hauled wood and helped place the pieces, occasionally sending down a board to be recut. Junior nailed. Neither spoke more than necessary. They progressed smoothly up the wall, ascending another eight feet by early afternoon, and despite his dislike for the man sharing the plank, Travis grudgingly had to admit that Junior was a skillful carpenter. If it hadn't been for his sadistic game with the nail gun, the afternoon might have even been pleasant.

Two things must happen for a pneumatic nail gun to fire: The trigger must be depressed, and the nose of the gun must be shoved against a surface to trip a safety mechanism in the tip. It's possible to circumvent this dual triggering feature by manually holding down the safety catch in the tip, something Junior amused himself by doing from time to time when Wes wasn't looking—shooting at birds, the equipment trailer, and various other objects within range. But as the day wore on, he found another target: Travis.

At first it had merely been irritating. The small finish nails they were using tumbled as soon as they cleared the barrel, rarely hitting point first. But from close range—say, twelve feet, the length of the scaffold plank—they stung, especially when they hit bare skin.

Several nails had pelted Travis before he figured out what Junior was doing. He'd slapped at his legs, thinking he was under attack by a persistent bee. The third time it happened, he caught Junior in the act. "Knock it off," he warned.

"Or what?" said Junior with a smirk. "Gonna go cry to your big brother? Or maybe you wanna call your mommy."

"Just cut it out."

Junior considered the situation, obviously enjoying himself. "Tell you what," he said. "Let's make it interesting. A hit scores one for me; a miss one for you. First to a hundred wins. Ten bucks says it's me."

"Gee, that sounds like a lot of fun. Maybe some other time."

Junior feigned disappointment. "Okay, then we'll call it an experiment. I'll say *move*. If you get outta the way in time, you don't get hit. I predict by the end of the day I'll have you jumpin' like a trained dog. What do you say, pussy?"

"I think I'll pass."

"Not an option," Junior chuckled, pulling the trigger. The nail caught Travis on the back of his hand. "Oops, forgot to say move."

"What's going on up there?" Wes called from below.

"Nothin', boss," Junior shouted down. "Just training the new guy. Right, pussy?"

Travis rubbed the growing welt on his hand.

"Quit fuckin' around and get to work."

"You got it. Let's *move*, Red," Junior barked, grinning as Travis flinched.

Ignoring Wes's warning, Junior continued his game, taking shots when he couldn't be seen from below, aiming at Travis's legs, arms, the back of his neck. Travis tried to avoid the nails as best he could, miserably waiting for day's end. But otherwise he did nothing, telling himself it would be too dangerous to start a fight on a plank thirty feet above the ground. Besides, a fight would get him fired, and losing his job was something he didn't want to explain to his father. But deep down, he knew the real reason he didn't retaliate: Junior was just too damn big.

Every time Wes left to check on the rest of his crew, Junior resumed his puerile diversion in earnest, gleefully inflicting his stinging depredations on Travis. The longer it went on, the more humiliated Travis felt, and the bolder Junior became. To make matters worse, Travis realized with a flush of shame, Junior's prediction was coming true. He *was* beginning to cringe involuntarily every time Junior yelled.

"You know something?" he said finally, burning with frustration and anger. "You're sick, Junior. You're nothing but a sadistic fuck."

"You gonna cry for me, Red? Come on, let's see some tears."

"Fuck you."

"Okay, you don't wanna cry, then *move!*"

Travis fought not to react.

Junior laughed. "Damn, your trainin' seems to be undergoin' some kinda relapse." He sprayed more shots at Travis's legs. "I said move!"

Toward the end of the day a pattern of angry welts covered most of the exposed skin on Travis's arms and legs. The only thing detracting from Junior's enjoyment was a progressively mounting bout of stomach cramps that had increased in frequency and severity as the afternoon wore on. "Man, I'm never eatin' them fuckin' enchiladas again," he groaned after a particularly acute attack. "I gotta hit the crapper. Let's get this thing on the ground."

Travis glanced down at the cutting table. Wes was gone. "We aren't finished for the day."

"Now, pussy," Junior ordered, hurrying to his end of the plank. "We're goin' down." He placed his foot in his jack and looked over, waiting for Travis to do the same.

Travis hesitated, noting the urgency in Junior's tone. Stinging from an afternoon of ridicule and abuse, he came to a decision. As he turned and walked to his jack at the other end, he deliberately kicked the half-inch hauling line over the side. It dropped to the ground, uncoiling as it fell. "Now look what I did," he said. "Guess I'll have to go get it."

Without another word he grabbed the metal support pole and placed his feet firmly against the wall, bridging the four-foot gap with his body. Alternately moving his hands and feet while maintaining outward pressure on both, he rapidly chimneyed to the overhanging eaves.

"Hey, where the fuck you going? Get down here!"

"Be back in a flash," Travis promised, shifting a hand to one of the rafters. Smoothly, he swung over a leg and mantled to the roof.

"Goddamn you, you little shit! Get back here!"

Without answering, Travis crossed the sloping surface. He dropped over the side again just past the chimney chase, hanging by his hands from the eaves in a section where the exterior wall had yet to be sheathed. Quickly, he kicked through the paper and insulation, then swung through the studs into the house. By the time he exited on the ground floor, a small crowd had already gathered at the base of the scaffolding, drawn by Junior's angry calls. They stood in a loose semi-circle, laughing and jeering at his predicament.

"Slide down the pole, Junior," someone hollered.

"Climb up to the roof like the kid did," advised another who'd witnessed Travis's scramble.

"Jump!" offered a third.

"Fuck you," Junior bellowed down, holding his stomach as he raced across the plank from end to end—first cranking down one jack and then the other—tediously lowering himself.

Wes, who'd returned to investigate the cause of the boisterous yelling, moved to stand beside Travis. "What happened?" he asked, glancing curiously at the welts on Travis's arms and legs.

Travis shrugged. "I knocked the rope off the plank. I climbed down to get it, then couldn't get back. Guess Junior's nervous up there without me."

"Looks worse than nervous. More like desperate."

"Yeah, he does, doesn't he?"

Quitting time was fast approaching. Welcoming any diversion to consume the last of the work day, the rest of the crew rapidly joined those already gathered below Junior, and a festive atmosphere soon pervaded the mocking assembly. Inch by inch Junior lowered himself, all the while reviling those below, saving his most minatory threats for Travis.

By the time he'd dropped the plank to within sixteen feet of the ground, he'd grown frantic and had resorted to hunching over in a curious crouch to ease his cramps, his simian posture inspiring a whole new generation of imaginative heckling. Driven by his distress and able to wait no longer, he finally hung by his hands from the edge of the plank. His boots still dangled eight feet from the ground when he let go.

Junior hit the dirt in a low squat, dropping heavily on his hands and feet, his ignominious landing accompanied by the prolonged, sonorous resonance of a noisy and distinctly wet-sounding fart.

"Damn, Junior," one of his friends hooted over the laughter. "You got the Hershey's squirts! You sure as hell ain't riding home with me!"

Glaring furiously, Junior pushed through the crowd and waddled toward the outhouse, a telltale smear of glistening soggy brown ooz-ing through the seat of his jeans, clearly evident to everyone there. Travis laughed with the others, trying to ignore a plunging presenti-ment of doom.

At last, as the obstreperous assembly drifted off, Pete Wilson joined him by the cutting board. "Good one, Trav," he sputtered, wiping away tears of amusement.

"Yeah," said Travis dully.

"I saw the whole thing. Cobb had it coming, all right. He's a mean one, though," the older man added somberly. "He don't forget nothin'. Hope it was worth it, kid."

15

The following evening Allison answered McKenzie's knock at the front door. Her friend was wearing a pair of crisply pressed jeans, Nike tennis shoes, and a soft cotton cardigan. Allison also noticed that for tonight's date McKenzie had applied a careful hint of makeup to her eyes and lips, and her thick raven hair hung loose and full on her shoulders. Despite her nervousness, McKenzie looked radiant.

"Uh . . . hi, Ali," she said. "I thought I'd walk down early, save Trav a trip. Is he ready?"

Allison pursed her mouth in a prudish parody of disapproval and regarded her friend critically before replying. "You know, Mac, if you're gonna date, you could at least pick someone from your own species."

"He's *your* brother, Allison."

"Only by some cruel twist of fate. I've got the hospital checking the records," said Allison, still not quite sure how she felt about the situation.

Hearing voices, Travis emerged from his room down the hall. "Ali, where's Tommy? I don't want to be late the first time I—" He stopped when he saw McKenzie. "Oh. Hi."

"Hi, Trav. I walked down," said McKenzie shyly. Then, with a roll of her eyes, "Dad wants me home by eleven-thirty."

"In answer to your question, handsome," Allison interjected, "Tommy already left to pick up Christy. He said he'd be back for you soon. I hope you guys have a good time," she added.

"Who *are* you, and what have you done with my sister Allison?"

"If you look carefully, brother dear, you'll find big green pods under *all* the beds in the house, including your own."

Travis grinned. "Get rid of 'em all except Dad's. His is liable to be an improvement."

As if on cue, Kane strode in through the front door. "Damn, did Kate have another kid when I wasn't lookin'?" he asked, scowling at McKenzie.

"Hi, Mr. Kane," laughed McKenzie, long inured to Kane's rough brand of humor.

"You're not staying for dinner again, are you?"

"No, sir. We're grabbing a pizza in Westwood before the movie."

"Good. I'd hate to have to start sendin' your dad a food bill."

Just then a series of impatient honks from Tommy's Bronco sounded outside. "Come on, McKenzie, we've gotta go," said Travis. "See you, Dad."

"You girls have fun," Kane called after them. Then, bellowing into the house, "Kate. I'm home. Start whippin' up some chow."

"Mom's not here," said Allison. "She started rehearsals with the Philharmonic yesterday, remember?"

"That's only supposed to be during the day."

"Tuesday's a double rehearsal. She decided to eat dinner with Adele afterward and attend a special performance they're having at eight. She left a note for you by the fridge."

Muttering to himself, Kane stomped into the kitchen, finding Catheryn's note on the counter beside a partially eaten vegetable casserole. He quickly scanned her neat, Catholic-school penmanship. "She wants us to heat up some crummy leftovers for dinner?" he called to Allison.

"Just you, Dad. Nate and I already ate."

"Hmph. Where the hell is Nate, anyway? Hey, Nate!" Kane returned to the entry and slammed his hand on the trapdoor in the ceiling. "Damn—the little peckerwood's got it locked. What the hell you doin' up there? Chokin' your chicken?"

"I don't think Nate's old enough to have discovered his chicken yet," noted Allison, who by then had retreated to her room.

"Don't be concerning yourself with your brother's privates," Kane warned. "People might get the wrong idea. Like me. Hey, Nate!"

"I'm coming, I'm coming," Nate's voice drifted down. The trapdoor lifted, and his head poked through the hole. "Hi, Dad."

"What were you doin' up there?"

"Reading," answered Nate, who'd recently discovered L. Frank Baum's *Wizard of Oz* collection at the library and over the past weeks had been spending most of his free time discovering its whimsical pleasures.

"Reading? When'd you learn to do that? Never mind. Go back to your book. I just wanted to see what you were up to."

"Sure, Dad."

Still grumbling over Catheryn's absence, Kane returned to the kitchen. Not feeling particularly enthusiastic about eating the vegetable casserole she'd designated as dinner, he opened the refrigerator, discovering a number of other Saran-wrapped dishes jamming the shelves. Deciding the Fourth of July parties were worse than Thanksgiving for generating unwanted leftovers, he selected the best of the lot: a chili con carne ringed with soggy tortilla chips and covered with melted cheese and jalapeño peppers. After reheating it in the microwave, he retired to the table.

Kane had never liked solitary dining. In an attempt to complete his unaccompanied meal as quickly as possible, he ate directly from the Pyrex dish, scooping huge spoonfuls of meat and beans into his mouth and washing it down with a cold Coors. A second beer and a hunk of leftover cherry pie followed. A quarter hour later, his stomach pleasantly full, he rocked back and gazed out at the raft bobbing offshore in the failing light.

As he sat, his mind turned to the vexing question of Catheryn's new job. He'd always been content to condone her music career as long as it didn't interfere with their home life, especially since raising four kids on a detective's salary had often been a stretch, and the money she'd earned from her private lessons had pulled them through difficult times. Nonetheless, this was different. Her recently acquired position with the Philharmonic promised to disrupt the household severely for the next thirteen weeks, and because she'd have to curtail her tutoring, which actually paid better, it wouldn't change their financial situation one iota. The way Kane saw it, the only result that could possibly derive from her temporary stint with the Philharmonic was the offer of similar work in the future, maybe even a permanent position. In other words, more trouble. To be fair, he wouldn't have stopped her from doing it if she'd asked. The trouble was, he thought with a surge of resentment, she hadn't.

Kane grabbed a third beer, then crankily resumed mulling over Catheryn's unexpected insurrection, trying to arrive at a course of action. He ran over various scenarios in his mind—often speaking aloud to his absent spouse as he assayed protean rationales, tacks, and stratagems—becoming progressively more irritated as he realized he could argue her side better than his own. When the phone rang a half hour later, he rose with a sigh of relief.

"Yeah?" he answered, picking up the phone beside the kitchen table.

"Kane, Detective Santoro from CRASH. Is it snowing down there?"

"Snowing? Why?"

" 'Cause when you hear my news, you're gonna think it must be Christmas."

Kane leaned forward. "You got some action on the Trans Am stakeout?" Although CRASH had located the 1981 Pontiac belonging to Annette Ramos, a sometime-girlfriend of Sotel gang member Miguel Voss, they'd been unable to find Voss. A CRASH surveillance team had been sitting on Annette ever since.

"Yep," said Santoro.

"The gang-banger boyfriend showed up?"

"The one and only. She met him in West Hollywood after she got off work. From there they picked up her kid brother and drove to the Liberty Theater on Wilshire and Doheny. We didn't want to move without checking with you."

"You did right," said Kane. "They go in?"

"Yeah."

"When's the movie over?"

"Eight."

"Okay, don't do anything till I get there."

After making calls to both Arnie and Lieutenant Long, Kane grabbed his coat and started for the door. He stuck his head in Allison's room on the way out. "How's it goin', princess?"

Allison looked up from her desk, noticing Kane's coat. "Fine, Dad. You going out again?"

"Yeah. Something came up at work," Kane explained apologetically. "I don't like leaving you kids here alone, but . . ."

"Don't worry, we'll be all right," said Allison. "Mom'll be home soon, and I'm sure we can manage not to burn the house down until then."

"Your mom oughtta be home right now," grumbled Kane.

"We'll be fine," said Allison patiently. "Go."

•   •   •

The Firebird Trans Am, mag wheels and all, sat taking up two spaces near the front of the theater parking lot—deliberately angled so no one could ding the dark-blue paint. Kane, Arnie, James Santoro, and another CRASH detective were in an unmarked car fifty yards down the block—Kane at the wheel, Santoro sitting shotgun, Arnie and Santoro's partner in the back. Two-Adam-Six, a black-and-white backup unit from the Beverly Hills police department, was parked around the corner.

Kane glanced impatiently at his watch: 7:53 P.M. The movie, billed on the seedy marquee as the last and final episode in a long-running series of horror-thrillers, would let out in a few minutes.

"What's the drill here?" asked Santoro's partner. "Take him down soon as he shows?"

"No. We let him drive out of the lot, then have the uniforms pull him over," Kane answered. "Lemme see that picture of Voss again."

Santoro pulled a booking photo of Miguel Voss from his pocket. "Punk goes by the street name El Galgo," he said, passing it to Kane. "His juvenile folder runs three pages long—assault, robbery, and drugs. When he turned eighteen, he became one of the Sotel seniors, then promptly pulled a two-year stretch at Tehachapi State Prison. He got out four months back."

"Anything on the girlfriend?"

"A shoplifting bust when she was fourteen."

Kane studied the photo without comment, then passed it over his shoulder to Arnie. As he did, he stole a glance at his partner, noticing Arnie looked even worse than he had the previous weekend. His eyes were red-rimmed and bleary, his motions slightly unsteady. Although no one else seemed to notice, Kane detected the smell of bourbon coming from the backseat.

"El Galgo," Arnie mused aloud, his words slow and deliberate. "What the fuck's that mean?"

"Greyhound," Santoro answered. Then, "Why let him out of the lot? Why not just grab him right away?"

"And what? Haul him in for questioning, then cut him loose?" said Kane. "We don't have anything substantial on him yet. Hell, we don't even have enough for a warrant on the car—just the word of some old sauce-head living in the bushes who can barely remember her own name."

"Then what—"

"We let him get in the car," Kane continued patiently, "establishing the link between him and the Trans Am. Once he's cleared the lot, the patrol pulls him over, leans on him a little, sees what comes down. Maybe he's holding, whatever. What we're going for here is PC to search the car."

"You already run this by your lieutenant?"

"Long says it'll fly provided we have probable cause for the search."

"What if you don't?"

Kane cracked his knuckles. "Then we find some reason to impound the car and drag 'El Greyhound' and his girlfriend in while we work on a warrant."

"I heard the feds still haven't picked up the third guy in the Bradley kidnapping," said Santoro. "You still think Angelo Martin's murder is connected? So far Voss just seems like some two-bit gangbanger to me—hardly the type to get involved in anything as complicated as kidnapping."

"He's involved, all right," said Kane, retrieving the photo from Arnie. "I'm not sure how, but he is. If he's not the third guy, he sure as hell knows where to find him."

Just then a theater employee wearing a shabby burgundy coat

opened one of the theater's front doors, and people began trickling in twos and threes onto the street. Kane scanned their faces, trying to spot Voss in the glaring light of the marquee.

"There he is," said Santoro, pointing down the alley toward a man accompanied by a tall woman and a small boy. "Must've come out the side exit."

Kane glanced at the photo in his hand, then back at the trio. The man was definitely Miguel Voss. Older than his picture, but him. Tall, skinny, with pockmarked cheeks and black hair worn in a stubby ponytail. He was joking with the woman, a chesty blond in her midtwenties. The boy, maybe about ten or eleven, followed behind—kicking rocks and sending them skittering up the alley. When they got to the car, Voss unlocked the driver's side and slid behind the wheel, then reached across and opened the passenger door. Kane waited until the boy and the woman hopped in, then picked up the mike and alerted the patrol unit around the corner.

After exiting the lot the Firebird turned left on Wilshire. Kane followed, easing into traffic three cars back. A few blocks up the black-and-white cut over from a side street and slipped in behind. Together they followed Voss for several minutes, waiting for an excuse—giving him time to run a light or break the limit, anything. It didn't really matter. They were going to pull him over anyway, but it would have been nice. Finally Kane got tired of waiting and radioed the uniforms to hit their lights.

A moment later Two-Adam-Six raced past, their red-and-blues flashing as they dropped in behind Voss. When Voss showed no sign of slowing, they tweaked the siren and used the bullhorn, ordering him to pull over. Instead, the Trans Am slammed forward with a burst of speed and wove dangerously in and out of traffic, slamming into the side of a taxicab as it shot through a red light one block up.

"Gracious, what have we here?" said Kane, stomping on the accelerator. "Felony evading? How accommodating."

The black-and-white skidded sideways into the intersection, getting hung up between the taxi Voss had clipped and a Mercedes driven by a panicked older woman with blue hair. Kane swerved left, careening past the jam-up just in time to see Voss turning off Wilshire four blocks up. Hunching over the wheel, Kane smoked into the side street he'd taken twenty seconds later.

Voss hadn't gotten far. The Firebird had come to a stop beside a large metal Dumpster—one wheel up on the curb, the driver's door flung open. The left front tire had been shredded by the fender, which had evidently been jammed against it during the accident. The woman sat alone in the front, her terrified face illuminated by the dome light.

"Anybody see him?" Kane yelled.

"There!" Arnie pointed down a narrow alley forking to the right.

Kane saw a dark figure slipping into the doorway of a burned-out building. He sent Santoro to cover the back, then spoke briefly into the mike—giving Two-Adam-Six their position and requesting backup. Leaving Santoro's partner with the woman in the car, Kane and Arnie piled out and proceeded down the alley on foot, guns drawn—Kane moving quickly, Arnie working to keep up.

Arnie was red-faced and breathing hard when he joined Kane at the entrance of what appeared to have once been a service garage. An indecipherable scrawl of gang writing covered the door's metal surface. The rusted padlock beside the knob had been jimmied sometime in the past, and dangled now, sad and useless, from a rusted hasp.

"Damn, I thought my days of busting through doors were over," puffed Arnie.

"Yeah. Me, too," said Kane. Both men had gone through countless doors when they'd worked the street, never quite sure what lay on the other side. It was always one of the most frightening aspects of police work; common wisdom on the force held that if you went through enough doors, sooner or later one would have your name on it.

Kane regarded Arnie carefully, trying to assess his condition. "Voss could be anywhere by the time backup arrives," he said. "You want to wait?"

"Do you?"

"Hell, no."

"I was afraid you were gonna say that." Briefly, Arnie spoke into the handset he'd brought from the car, advising Two-Adam-Six of their intentions. Then, "Okay. Let's do it."

Kane counted down from five. He kicked open the door on one.

He went in low, moving to the right. Arnie followed a moment later, slipping to the left. Weak rays from a streetlight filtered down from a boarded-up window high on the opposite wall, revealing a large, cavernous room that smelled of smoke and mildew. The two men moved forward in a silent, efficient pattern they'd established over the years, each covering the other as he worked his sector. The drill came back with unconscious ease, etched in their minds by a lifetime of experience.

Staying in the shadows, Kane crept through a litter of twisted metal and rotting drywall. He approached a ruined line of service bays, some with lifts and others with recesses under the ramps. He checked each bay carefully.

Nothing.

On his right a number of rooms branched off the main chamber. Straight ahead, a metal staircase led to a loft and more doors fifteen feet up. Kane hesitated, then started up the stairs.

Suddenly, in the corner of his vision, he saw a burst of light. He felt the slug whine past his head an instant before he heard the shot.

Small-caliber weapon, he thought as he hit the floor.

A split second later Arnie's gun thundered in the darkness. Two quick shots, then another. Footsteps crashing over a piece of sheet metal. The screech of hinges as someone forced open a door . . .

Silence.

"Arnie?"

"Over here. You okay?"

"Yeah." Kane peered across the darkened chamber, wishing he'd taken time to put on his vest. "He get away?"

"I think so. Out the back. He won't make it far. The uniforms'll pick him up."

"I'm getting too old for this shit," Kane muttered, finally spotting Arnie's dim shape across the room. He listened as Arnie spoke into his handset, advising the backup officers that shots had been fired and an armed suspect had left the west end of the building on foot. Kane started to rise. Then he froze, his senses straining. "You hear that?"

"What?"

Kane listened.

Someone still there?

He could just make out a low, scraping sound, as though some-thing were being dragged. It seemed to be coming from a burned-out office in the back. "Movement. Far wall."

"Yeah. Got it."

The noise stopped. "Give it up, Voss," Kane yelled into the shad-ows. "You can't get away. Come on out."

No response.

Kane motioned with his gun, signaling Arnie to circle left. Moving in a low crouch, Kane worked his way right, keeping as much as possible between himself and the far wall.

Arnie got there first. Seconds later he called through the darkness, his voice strangely urgent. "Dan. Dan . . . over here."

Kane quickly crossed the remaining distance. He found Arnie kneeling beside a young boy, the kid who'd followed Voss and his girlfriend from the theater. A dark stain covered the boy's belly. It had soaked through his shirt and was rapidly seeping onto the rub-bish-strewn floor. He was still conscious, his eyes uncomprehending and wide with fright.

Kane checked the boy, then the surrounding area. No gun.

Arnie handed Kane the radio. His hands were shaking, his face mottled and sweaty. "Call for an ambulance," he ordered. "Advise them we've got a gunshot victim who doesn't have much time. And tell them . . . tell them . . ." Arnie's voice broke.

Kane made the call, watching as Arnie rolled up his jacket and pressed it against the boy's abdomen. The kid was losing conscious-ness, starting to twitch. Blood quickly covered Arnie's hands. "Aw, damn, Arnie," Kane whispered.

"I fired at the muzzle flash. I didn't know . . ."

"It wasn't your fault."

Shaking his head, Arnie continued applying pressure to the wound.

As he watched, Kane noticed that Arnie's lips were moving—mur-muring something that sounded like a chant. All at once he recog-nized it. Kane stood silently, not knowing what to say. Halfway through Arnie stumbled, forgetting the words, then started over. "Our Father, Who art in heaven, hallowed be Thy name. Thy king-dom come, Thy will be done . . ."

"It wasn't your fault, Arnie," Kane repeated softly as Santoro and the two backup officers slammed into the garage at the far end. "It wasn't your fault."

* * *

Allison heard the sound of breaking glass.

"Nate?" she called.

No answer.

She checked the clock on her desk, surprised to see so much time had elapsed since her father's departure. Suddenly she heard it again.

It sounded as if it had come from the street. Allison stood and stretched, welcoming a diversion from the story she was writing— even if it was only chasing away one of the neighborhood dogs perusing trash cans in front of the house. A moment later she heard a heavy thump, and again the tinkle of glass. With a sigh, she walked to the front door and stepped outside, wondering which of the local canines she'd find with his snout buried in a tipped-over pile of garbage.

She glanced to the right. The Kane trash cans, enclosed in an open wooden frame between their house and the next, appeared undisturbed. Puzzled, she turned and walked to the left. Stopped. Crystalline shards of glass littered the pavement beside a BMW parked next door. A pair of Levi-clad legs protruded from the window.

"Hey!" she yelled. "What do you think you're doing?"

Faster than she would have thought possible, a powerful-looking youth in his early twenties scrambled from the car. Surprise and anger twisted his face, transforming it into a mask of rage. His eyes took in Allison at a glance, then darted like weasels up and down the deserted highway. Once again they settled on Allison.

Allison turned and ran. He caught her before she reached the front door. She struggled but he held her easily, twisting her arm behind her back and clapping his hand over her mouth.

A van screeched to a stop beside them. A white face appeared in the open window. "Cal, what the fuck you doin'?"

"The bitch caught me. Open the slider."

"You crazy? We're after stereos, remember?"

"Fuck you, Joey. If we let her go, she's gonna call the man. How far do you think we're gonna get?"

"I don't give a shit. She ain't comin' in my van."

The youth holding Allison hesitated. "Anybody in the house?" he hissed, his breath warm and fetid on her cheek.

Allison nodded.

"Bullshit. Where're the cars? There was two of 'em out front when we came by earlier. Your folks left for the evening, right?"

Allison shook her head, groaning as her assailant wrenched her arm even higher behind her back. "Don't lie to me, cunt. You're doin' a home-alone scene, right?"

Allison shook her head again, tears stinging her eyes. She felt the coarse hand over her mouth relax slightly so she could speak. Twisting in his grasp, she caught a finger between her teeth and bit down hard.

"Shit!" the youth screamed, releasing his hold. "You fuckin' bitch!"

Allison broke free and raced the final few steps to the house. As she flung open the door, a strong hand grabbed her hair, snapping back her head.

Enraged, the powerful youth circled Allison's throat with his forearm and squeezed, choking her into submission. He held her immobile and listened through the open door. Allison clawed at his arm, beginning to black out.

"Jesus, Cal, let's get the hell outta here!" begged the man in the car, his voice cracking with urgency.

"Nobody's home," Allison heard the first one mutter. "Gimme a hand gettin' her inside."

"What for?"

"So's we can tie her up, stupid. Give us some time to get down the road. Besides, there's probably cash in there, maybe jewelry."

"I hope you know what you're doin'," the driver said.

"Don't worry," the first one answered. As Allison felt herself descending a long tunnel into unconsciousness, she heard him add, "While we're at it, we can have some fun with the bitch."

16

An hour after the shooting Kane stepped from an interrogation room on the second floor of the West Los Angeles station, fighting to control his anger. He'd just given his testimony regarding the accident to the lead detective of the officer-involved shooting team, a senior officer from the Robbery-Homicide Division. It was Arnie's turn next. After the questioning he'd just experienced, Kane knew it wouldn't go easy. None of the others present at the scene had heard the initial shot, and the possibility of an unreasonable-force charge being levied against his partner, although ridiculous, was becoming more and more a reality. Hoping Arnie would be all right, Kane nodded to his friend as he brushed past. From the expression on Arnie's face, it didn't look good.

Taking a deep breath, Kane swallowed his rage and decided to concentrate on the problem at hand. Purposefully, he entered another interrogation room two doors down. Miguel Voss sat at a small table in the center—eyes closed, head slumped on the green metal surface, cheek resting on his forearm. Although he'd managed to slip out the back of the garage past Santoro, Two-Adam-Six had picked him up later at a bus stop five blocks from the burnout. No gun.

Kane slammed the door. Voss stirred groggily, looking up with half-lidded, surly eyes. From his pocket, Kane withdrew a fresh pack of Camels and tossed them onto the table. "I'm Detective Kane, Los Angeles Police Department, West Los Angeles Division," he said, pointedly failing to mention the unit in which he worked.

Voss scooped up the Camels and shook one out. "Fuck you, cop. I ain't sayin' nothin'."

"Fine," said Kane, watching as Voss searched for a match. "You do that. In fact, that's *exactly* what I want you to do. Just for the record, though, your name's Voss, right? Miguel Voss?"

Voss grunted.

"Speak up," Kane ordered. Since the interrogation was being recorded down the hall, he wanted Voss's verbal affirmation on tape.

"Yeah. Miguel Voss."

"Good, Miguel. Now, just sit there and listen to what I've got to say." Kane dropped into a chair across from the sallow, pockmarked youth. He pulled out a pack of matches and tapped them on the table. "Don't get up, don't ask questions, don't even open your mouth. Got it?"

"Yeah."

Kane skidded across the matches, giving Voss time to light up before launching into his routine. He knew if Voss asked for an attorney at that point, the interrogation would effectively be over, and thanks to *Arizona v. Miranda*, Kane had to advise him of this—along with the fact that he was under no obligation to respond to any questions he might pose. An imposing hurdle, but one which Kane had developed his own method of sidestepping.

"I ain't gonna bullshit you here," he began. "That stunt you pulled tonight could land you in a lotta trouble, so think before you say anything or make any decisions you're gonna regret later."

"I didn't do shit."

"Shut up till I'm done. I may be able to help you, maybe not. It depends on you. But before we continue, there's a formality we've gotta go through. I know the cops who brought you in probably read you your rights, but I want to make absolutely sure you understand. First off, I'll tell you right here and now that I can't *make* you say anything. If you decide to talk, that's fine, but anything you say can and will be used as evidence against you in court, so don't lie. You wanna keep your mouth shut, that's fine too. I can't do anything for you if you do, but it's your decision. Understand?"

Miguel shrugged.

"Speak up," Kane ordered again.

"Yeah, I understand."

"Good. Now, the second thing: You can have a lawyer anytime you want. If you don't have the money, we'll get you one. We'll trot a public defender right on up here whenever you say. Course, soon as that happens, our conversation's over, and once again I can't help you. It's up to you. You understand what I'm telling you, Miguel? You gettin' all this?"

"I'm not stupid, cop."

"I didn't say you were. I just want to make certain you understand your rights, because next I'm gonna tell you how we see things from our end. Then you can tell me how you wanna play it. Fair enough?"

Voss took a long pull on his Camel. "I get a lawyer anytime I want?"

"Correct. You want to hear what we've got on you or not?"

Voss considered. "Can't hurt to listen, right?"

"Right," Kane said. "One thing, though. If you lie to me, all deals are off."

"There ain't gonna be no deals, 'cause I didn't do shit."

"We'll see about that. I'll be talkin' to a deputy DA first thing tomorrow morning about what charges to file, and he generally goes with what I say. There're a lot of ways of lookin' at this, Miguel. For instance, right now you've been brought in on a charge of felony evading, referring to the bumper-car scene you pulled on Wilshire. On the other hand, a word in the right place and felony evading turns into reckless driving. You followin' me?"

Voss nodded suspiciously.

"We'll be able to prove you were driving the Trans Am. Know how?" Kane went on, monopolizing the conversation but drawing Voss out a little at a time.

"You tell me."

"One: We're gonna find your prints all over the steering wheel, the car keys, and the driver's-side door. Two: We've got your girlfriend's testimony. She's in the next room, singin' like a fat Italian." Actually,

Annette Ramos had proved less than cooperative but, confronted with her limited options, had named Voss as the driver. Without divulging the reason for his questions, Kane had also established that Voss had borrowed her car the day of Angelo Martin's murder.

"Three: Your darling Annette also says you had a gun tonight. A twenty-two revolver. Why a twenty-two, Miguel? I thought you guys went in for the big stuff—forty-fives, nine-millimeters, autoloading scatterguns. A twenty-two's a toy. A woman's gun." Despite his question Kane knew that a .22 was the preferred weapon of professional hit men for close work, and at short distance was as lethal as an Uzi.

Voss remained silent.

"Four: We followed you into that burnout. We know you and the kid were the only ones in there, and *someone* fired a shot. We've already recovered a twenty-two-caliber slug from the scene," Kane lied. At his insistence a search team was presently looking for it, along with the pistol; so far the results had been negative. "We'll find the gun too," he continued. "It's somewhere between the garage and the bus stop where we picked you up. We've got teams out looking for it right now. It's just a matter of time."

"I don't know what the fuck you're talkin' about."

"Sure you do. Now, I know what you're thinking. You're patting yourself on the back for dumpin' the piece, right? You're also thinking you wiped it down good, so how can we tie it to you? Lemme ask you something. You take out the bullets and wipe off the casings?"

Voss was sweating now, looking nervous.

"So, let's see, what've we got here? Felony evading, possession of an unregistered firearm, and assault on a police officer with attempt to commit murder."

Voss stubbed out his butt. Nervously, he shook a fresh one from the pack, then peered shrewdly across the table. "You wouldn't be tellin' me all this if you didn't want somethin'."

Kane hesitated, pretending to be caught off guard. "You're a smart kid, Miguel," he said at last. "Yeah, maybe I've got something in mind, something everybody can live with. You wanna hear my deal?"

Voss nodded.

"I can't hear you, Miguel."

"I said let's hear your deal, cop."

"Fine," said Kane, ready to set the hook. "I already ran this by my lieutenant, so there's no problem gettin' it through. You're a lucky son of a bitch, you know that?"

"Is that right?"

"Yeah. The mayor, the brass, and every police officer involved is gonna want this situation with Annette's kid brother cleared up as fast as possible. That's the key here, Miguel. As fast as possible. I'll tell you how it's gonna go down if I take this case as it stands to the DA tomorrow morning. You'll be arraigned, plead innocent, get a trial date, won't make bail, and sit in custody till your date comes up. The whole thing'll drag on forever, but in the end you'll go away for seven, eight years. Meantime, if there's any question regarding my partner's returning fire tonight, the press is gonna make our life miserable. Nobody'll be happy."

"Tough."

"But maybe it doesn't have to be that way," Kane went on, deciding the time had come to offer Voss "the out." "Maybe tonight was all a big mistake. Maybe you didn't actually shoot *at* us in that burnout. Maybe you just fired into the ceiling to slow us up, givin' yourself time to make it out the back. Hell, maybe the gun went off accidentally. You didn't hit anybody, right?"

Voss shook his head, looking as though he couldn't believe his ears.

"Here's the deal. You admit shooting the twenty-two—plead to accidentally firing an unlicensed gun within city limits—and we forget the attempted-murder charge. Since other officers were involved in the car chase, the best I can do on that is gettin' the felony evasion bumped down to reckless driving. You're gonna lose your license, Miguel."

Voss smirked. "I ain't got one," he said. Then, "What kinda guarantee do I get on this?"

"Guarantee?" Kane exploded. "Guarantee? You want me to notarize something? Jesus! I'm offering you a traffic ticket and a probationary offense for takin' a shot at a cop, and you're asking for guarantees."

Kane glared at Voss, then continued more calmly. "Look, you

plead to the lesser charges. We give it to the DA first thing tomorrow all wrapped up neat; he's glad to get it off the books without a trial; and that's that. On the other hand, if we find the gun before you cut a deal with me here and now, there's nothin' I can do for you. Personally, I don't give a shit what happens to your sorry ass, but I'll level with you, Miguel. My partner's in hot water over shooting that kid. You play it smart and take advantage of the situation, fine. You don't, you deserve what you get. It's up to you.''

Voss vacillated. "If I admit accidentally shootin' the pistol, the twenty-two . . . that's it?''

"The *unlicensed* pistol. We can't get around that, Miguel. Plus reckless driving . . . also without a license.''

Voss considered a moment more. "You got a deal,'' he said finally. "It happened just like you said.''

"*I* didn't say how it happened, Miguel. I just guessed at how it *might* have happened. You're the one who has to say what went down.''

"No problem. You guys chased me, and I pulled my gun 'cause I was scared. I tripped on somethin' and it accidentally went off. I never tried to shoot nobody.''

"Now we need the gun. Where is it?''

"Why?'' Voss demanded, suspicion suddenly gleaming in his eyes.

"You don't think we're gonna let you keep it, do you?'' Kane answered patiently. "We need to match it with the slug we found in the garage and prove things went down like you said. Besides, we'll find it sooner or later anyway, and it'll look a lot better for you if you give it up. Where is it?''

Voss hesitated. Then, with a shrug, "I dropped it down a street drain.''

"Where?''

"Uh . . . a couple blocks from the bus stop. Near Robertson.''

Kane rose. "You're doin' the smart thing here, Miguel. I'm gonna send somebody to pick it up right now before the search team finds it. It better be there.''

"It's there.''

"Good. I'll type a statement for you to sign. One more thing,'' Kane said, staring intently across the table. "I'm going way out on a limb for you here. If there's anything else I should know, anything you want to tell me—about the shot you fired, the gun, *anything*—now's the time."

"I ain't got nothin' else to say, cop. Not a fuckin' thing."

•   •   •

Fifteen minutes later Kane pulled a sheet from his typewriter, adding it to others on his desk. He'd been working steadily since leaving Voss in the interrogation room, during which time he'd contacted the Beverly Hills search team with the location of the pistol, fielded several calls, and gotten a start on Voss's statement—at least as much as he'd need for the next step of his questioning. A moment later the assistant watch commander phoned from downstairs, informing him one of the search units had just recovered the pistol. After establishing that strict forensic and custody procedures would be maintained all the way to the evidence room, Kane got the names and serial numbers of the officers who'd found the weapon. He also made a mental note to have the gun transferred to Parker Center first thing in the morning for printing. He'd also need a ballistics comparison with the slug taken from Angelo Martin's skull.

Deciding to let Voss stew a little longer, Kane grabbed the phone, intending to call home and make sure Catheryn had returned. Certain she must have, he replaced it, electing to put off a discussion of her unscheduled absence until later. Instead, he rocked back in his chair and mulled over the first round of the interrogation.

It had gone pretty much according to plan, not that one could ever precisely forecast how an interrogation would progress. Kane realized he'd overstepped acceptable bounds by offering Voss a deal without first clearing it through Long and the DA—not that it would make any difference in the long run. *And part of it* was *true,* he thought. *Everybody in the courts system* would *rather see Voss plead to a lesser charge than go to trial. Wanting to clear the cloud over Arnie and get the heat off the department as fast as possible—that was true, too. Just not the way Voss figured.*

A few minutes later, having run through a mental blueprint of the second phase of the interrogation, Kane levered himself up from his chair, grabbed Voss's partially finished statement, and headed back.

This time Voss was awake. Wide-awake. He stubbed out his cigarette, watching as Kane stomped in and disgustedly flipped the typed pages onto the table. "What's wrong?" he asked.

"We've got a problem."

"The gun wasn't there? I swear I threw it down the sewer."

"The problem, Miguel, is that you've had me wasting my time workin' on a statement that's never gonna see the light of day."

"What the hell are you talkin' about?"

"I'm talking about your gun. We found it, all right. I just got a call from ballistics. Seems your twenty-two was used in a murder two weeks back. One of your Sotel buddies named Angelo Martin turned up in an alley with an unsightly hole in his head. The slug we dug out of his brain matches your revolver. Big surprise, huh?"

"I just bought that piece three days ago. I don't know nothin' 'bout no murder."

Kane stared at him. "No, I don't think you do," he said, gathering his duplicitous pages and placing them on the corner of the table. "But this is something we're definitely gonna have to clear up."

"How'd you test the gun so fast? That takes time, don't it?"

"You watch too much TV, Miguel. Everything's computerized nowadays. We get this kinda stuff done in minutes." Kane took a small notebook from his coat and looked at Voss expectantly. "Well?"

"I told you, I don't know nothin'."

"Then where were you three Sundays back? Let's see . . ." Kane pretended to refer to his notebook. "That would have made it June twentieth. Where were you?"

"Who the fuck knows?"

"You wanna get clear of this, you'd better start remembering."

Voss squirmed in his seat. "Three Sundays back? Oh, yeah. I was with my old lady. Me and Annette always spend Sundays together."

Kane scribbled in his notebook. "You were with her all evening?"

"Yeah."

"What'd you do?"

"We went to the movies."

"What'd you see?"

"Uh, some horror flick. A good one, too. This bitch could make people do anything she wanted—swap bodies with 'em, that kinda shit. It was playing at the Aero on Montana."

"Fine. You go to the seven or the nine o'clock show?" asked Kane, continuing to work the edges of Voss's story.

"Uh . . . the nine."

"What'd you do after?"

"I dunno. Got something to eat."

"Where?"

"McDonald's, Jack in the Fuckin' Box. What difference does it make?"

"It makes a difference, Miguel. I'm tryin' to help you here."

"Okay, it was McDonald's. Yeah. We had some Big Macs and a basket of them chicken balls."

"McNuggets?"

"Yeah."

"Anybody see you, someone who might recall your being there?"

"I didn't see nobody."

"Okay, you ate. Then what?"

"We went back to my place and did the deed."

"You're doin' real good, Miguel. Annette stay all night?"

"No. She hadda be at work the next morning."

"So she left around . . ."

"One, one-thirty."

"And you went to sleep."

"No, I went out and robbed a fuckin' liquor store. Yeah, I slept. What the fuck else am I gonna do?"

Kane closed his notebook, ignoring Voss's sarcasm. "Okay, that takes care of where *you* were. Now let's talk about the gun. Since you didn't use it that night, it must've been somebody else—one of your friends, maybe. I know how you feel. It pisses me off when I lend people stuff and they fuck it up. Or worse, leave me holdin' the bag like this guy did to you. Whoever used your gun fucked you, Miguel," said Kane sympathetically, giving the "I know how you feel" approach a shot. *I know how you feel—I used to shoplift myself; my brother got caught boostin' cars; I've got a buddy who's a child molester . . .*

"I don't know who shot Angelo. It wasn't me."

"Then how'd they get your gun?"

"I told you, I just picked it up a couple days ago."

"Yeah. You told me." Kane pushed to his feet. "I've gotta check some things."

After returning to his desk Kane made a call to the Aero, killed several minutes catching up on paperwork, then returned for a third session with Voss. "You fucked up, Miguel. I told you not to lie," he growled as he entered the room.

"What're you talkin' about?" Voss demanded, a sheen of sweat glistening on his forehead.

Kane pulled out his notebook. "First off, you told me you were at the movies. I just called the theater. That horror flick, *Nocturne Seven: The Final Chapter,* didn't start till last Friday. I talked to Annette down the hall, too. She says she wasn't with you that night. Says she lent you her wheels that afternoon and didn't get 'em back till the next morning."

"Fuckin' bitch is lying."

"Why should she? And what about the movie?"

"Maybe we saw another one. Who can remember that far back?"

Using his thumb, Kane started cracking the knuckles of his right hand. The wet, portentous sound of popping cartilage filled the small room. "I'm gonna level with you. I know you were there when your buddy Angelo got whacked. Maybe you didn't pull the trigger, but you were there."

"No! I told you—"

"Shut up. I've been trying to help you, and you've been jerkin' me around. Know why we were following you tonight? We've got a witness who saw two guys dumping Angelo Martin's body in the alley that night. They were driving a Trans Am with mag wheels, just like your old lady's. We're gonna match the grease stains and fibers found on the body to those in the trunk of her car. We also got a description of the guys. Guess what? One of 'em matches you. Why'd you kill him?"

Voss paled. "I don't know nothin' about that."

"I think you do. I even know why you did it," said Kane. "Angelo ratted out your partners on the Bradley kidnapping, right? Or maybe killing him was just a way to make sure his sister Sylvia kept her mouth shut."

"Kidnapping? I don't know what the fuck you're talking about," said Voss, clearly shaken by Kane's words.

Kane knew Voss was lying, but his instincts also told him the youth across the table wasn't the third kidnapper. "Let's clear the air here," he said. "This isn't about Angelo Martin. We're not talking about some worthless gang-banger getting capped. That kidnapped boy was the son of a senator, Miguel. A *senator*. We know for a fact that Angelo Martin's death is connected, and we know you're involved. You've got one slim chance of comin' out of this without pulling a death sentence, and that's telling me everything you know right here and now. I want the other guy. Who was with you in the car that night?"

Voss glanced away.

Kane's hand shot across the table, grabbing Voss's chin. "Look at me when I'm talking to you."

Jerking free, Voss balled his fists and glowered at Kane with red-eyed, unadulterated hate.

Slowly, Kane stood up and took off his watch. Carefully, he laid it atop the typed pages on the corner of the table. "You gonna take a poke at me, Miguel?" he asked. "I can tell from the look on your pimply face you're thinkin' about it. Go ahead. Nobody can hear anything outside. It's just you and me."

Voss's eyes shot around the room. No weapon, no place to hide. Just the huge cop with a short fuse.

"Over here, Miguel. I'm not gonna tell you again."

Voss reluctantly turned his gaze back to Kane.

"I'm sick of your lies," Kane said. "There's nothin' I'd enjoy more right now than subduing a hemorrhoid like you who made the mistake of attacking me during an interrogation. Go ahead. Do it."

Voss opened his hands. "I ain't doin' nothin'."

"Yeah, you are. You're gonna tell me who pulled that trigger on Angelo. We know everything else. I don't think you were the one, but if you don't gimme a name, we're gonna hang it on you, and the kidnapping along with it. That friend of yours used *your* gun to whack that kid, *your* car to dump the body, and left *you* holdin' the bag. He fucked you, Miguel. You don't owe him shit. You were there, but you didn't pull the trigger, did you?"

"No."

"I didn't think so. Who did? Gimme a name."

"I . . ."

Time to go ballistic. With blinding speed Kane jerked Voss to his feet. "I'm done fuckin' with you," he bellowed, nose to nose with Voss. "Gimme a name!"

"I don't know no names."

"Bullshit! Talk!"

"Jimmy."

Kane watched with arctic satisfaction as Voss began to fold. "Jimmy who?"

"Kearns. Jimmy Kearns."

Kane shoved him back into his seat. "I'm gonna give you one more chance, Miguel. I may be able to help you yet. You done lying?"

Voss stared numbly at his hands.

"You'd better be," Kane warned, lowering his voice. "Lie to me again, I'll make you wish you never heard my name. Understand?"

"Yeah."

"Good. Now start at the beginning," Kane ordered. "And this time, don't leave anything out."

•   •   •

Nate looked up from *The Road to Oz*. Dorothy had just discovered her homeward journey had somehow landed her in the curious town of Foxville, and the Fox-King she'd met there had advised, "Be content with your lot, whatever it happens to be, if you are wise," and of course Dorothy had come to the conclusion that she might as well explore the magical city of Foxville a bit before returning to Kansas, and that Auntie Em wouldn't be angry if she didn't stay *too* long. . . .

There it was again.

Nate sat very still, listening.

He'd heard Allison at the front door some time back, probably letting in one of her friends. Since then the house had been quiet except for an occasional bumping sound, as though someone were moving furniture. Figuring Allison had decided to rearrange her room, he'd ignored it. But lately a new and puzzling noise had begun. Now it sounded as if Allison had grown tired of simply *rearranging* furniture and had graduated to *breaking* it.

He heard a sudden crash from Tommy and Trav's room, then the squeak and thump of drawers being pulled from a dresser.

What's Allison doing?

Nate moved to the trapdoor. He opened it partway, then stopped as an unfamiliar voice sounded beneath him in the entry. "Cal, you done yet?"

Another voice from deeper in the house. Agitated, breathless. "Don't rush me, Joey. You'll get your turn."

Nate considered easing the hatch closed. *No. Might make him look up.* Holding his breath, he peered through the opening. A man with skinny, hairless arms stood below. He'd cracked the front door and was peeking nervously out at the street. "I got a bad feeling about this," he called into the house.

Seconds passed before the other man answered. Nate heard a sharp slapping noise, followed by the muffled sound of someone crying. Then, "Ain't nobody home but sweet-cheeks here. Keep checkin'. There's bound to be cash somewhere." The man below studied the street a bit longer, then closed the door and retreated into another part of the house.

Nate listened until he heard the door to his parents' bedroom bang open. Silently, he closed his hatch and latched it shut.

Stay here till they leave? They haven't found me yet. Maybe they won't. But what about Allison?

Nate remembered the sobbing he'd heard. He tried to drive it from his mind. Couldn't. Clenching his teeth to keep them from chattering, he unlatched the hatch.

Crashing in his parents' room. And an odd grunting coming from deeper in the house. The living room.

Nate opened the hatch. Trying to ignore the trip-hammer pounding of his heart, he climbed down the ladder to the entry.

Get to the phone, call nine-one-one, wait till the cops come.

He hesitated. There were two phones in the house: a portable in his parents' bedroom, another in the kitchen. The first was out. That left the kitchen. But to get there, he'd have to go through the living room.

Hugging the wall, he crept silently down the hall. He paused when he reached the door to the living room. The grunting had grown louder. "You like it, don't you, bitch?" he heard a voice laugh. "Oh, yeah. You *love* it."

Nate eased his head around the corner, risking a glance into the

room. He could see the kitchen on the far side, the phone tantaliz-
ingly out of reach.

More of the room coming into view . . . TV, coffee table . . .

His eyes widened in horror when he got to the man on the couch.

He had his jeans down around his knees. Allison lay trapped beneath him, her skirt shoved up around her waist, torn underwear
bunched around one ankle. Tears streamed down her face. A strip of
duct tape sealed her mouth, another bound her hands. Blood ran
from her nose. A grotesque artwork of red smeared her thighs, hideously finger-painted on the white canvas of her legs. But most chilling, the expression Nate saw in his sister's eyes—the hopeless,
heartrending look of pleading, terror, and worst of all . . . despair—
would stay with him the rest of his life.

"Damn you. Move!" the man on top commanded. His muscular
buttocks thrust hypnotically, pounding with virulent fury at the helpless girl beneath. He stopped to deliver a backhanded blow, sending a
spatter of blood gushing from Allison's nose onto the back of the
couch. "I said move!"

Nate's heart plummeted as he saw his sister's pelvis begin to jerk
spasmodically, grinding in obscene lockstep with her attacker's.
"That's better. Keep it up, bitch," the man ordered.

Suddenly a sound from behind.

The other one's coming!

Fighting a surge of panic, Nate glanced down the hall. He couldn't
retreat. As quietly as possible, he slid behind the door and held his
breath. An instant later the second man burst into the living room. "I
found some jewelry in the big bedroom," he said. "That's all there is.
Let's go, Cal."

"Joey, get the fuck outta here till I'm done," the first man snarled.
"There's gotta be cash. Find it."

"There ain't none. I looked."

Cal grabbed Allison's hair and jerked her head from the couch.
"Where's the money?" he demanded.

Allison moaned.

"She might be able to talk better if you took off the gag," Joey
pointed out.

Cal ripped the tape from Allison's mouth. "Where's the money?"

"There isn't any," Allison sobbed. "My father doesn't keep cash in the house."

Cal doubled up his fist. Coldly and deliberately, he hit her in the mouth. Grinning, he drew back his arm and hit her once more, transforming her face into a mask of blood. "Where is it?"

Nate crept from his hiding place and backed into the hallway, swallowing hard against the bitter gorge rising in his throat.

"She don't know, Cal. You're gonna kill her!"

"Bullshit! She knows and she's gonna tell."

Nate could hear them arguing as he retreated toward the entry.

The phone in Dad's room? No time. Run to the neighbors for help? Stop a car on the highway?

All at once he remembered the gun.

It was a .38-caliber Smith & Wesson, his father's service revolver before he'd switched to the Beretta automatic. Nate knew he kept it on the top shelf of the entry closet, supposedly out of range of prying hands. He also knew from experience that he could reach it from the ladder to his room.

Nate padded quietly to the front of the house. He ascended the ladder in the entry, stopping two-thirds of the way up. Resisting an urge to climb the final rungs to his room and lock the hatch behind him, he leaned out and groped through the clutter on the closet's top shelf.

It has to be here somewhere. Please be . . . There!

His trembling fingers closed on the gun. Then the box of .38 hollow-point cartridges.

Hurry . . . hurry . . .

Struggling to control his shaking hands, he opened the cylinder, jamming in shells as he'd seen his father do many times at the academy qualifying range.

One, two, three, four . . . That enough? No. Fill it. Don't want to come down on an empty cylinder . . .

A cartridge slipped from Nate's fingers. He froze as it hit the floor.

•   •   •

Cal looked up from the couch. "What was that?"

"I didn't hear nothin'," Joey answered.

Cal listened carefully. "Guess you're right." He sucked his finger. It still throbbed from the bite, not to mention slapping the bitch around. *Maybe she really doesn't know where the money is,* he thought. *If she does, she sure took a lot of punishment without talking.*

Cal decided he could search the rest of the house later. It wouldn't take long, and besides, all the rough play had made him hot. *Christ, I'm hard. For some reason Joey watching made it even better.* "Oooohhh, baby, get ready," he panted, picking up his rhythm and closing his eyes, straining now. "I can't wait no more!"

"Get off my sister."

"Huh?" Cal opened his eyes. A kid around nine or ten with curly red hair stood just inside the room. He was holding a pistol.

"Where the fuck'd you come from?"

"Get off my sister," the boy ordered again, his voice shaking.

"Christ, Joey," Cal laughed. "Lookit this. They're givin' the diaper patrol guns now." He rose from the couch. Using Allison's torn underwear, he wiped himself and then pulled up his jeans, stuffing his swollen penis into his pants.

Joey noticed the cocked pistol in the kid's hands looked too real for comfort. He backed away. "Let's go, Cal. There ain't nothin' here anyway."

"You nuts?" Cal demanded, glancing at the girl on the couch. "We won't get two miles down the road 'less we tie up baby brother here along with his sister. Besides, I ain't finished."

"I wanna get out now."

Cal grinned, watching as the boy motioned with the gun toward the door, noticing he could barely hold the pistol in his trembling hands.

"Both of you get out," the boy pleaded, so scared he'd begun to cry.

Cal smirked. "You've got guts, kid," he said, moving forward. "I'll grant you that. Now, gimme the gun."

• • •

Kane had nearly finished taking Voss's statement when a knock sounded at the interrogation-room door. "Sorry," said Santoro, sticking his head into the room. "Phone."

"Can't it wait?" asked Kane.

"The desk said to get you right away."

Leaving Santoro with Voss, Kane returned to his workstation. "Kane," he said, lifting the receiver.

"Detective, your son's on the line," a voice informed him. "He sounds . . . upset."

"Tommy? Put him through."

A slight pause. Then, "Dad?"

"Nate? Jesus, I thought Tommy'd wrecked his car or something. You know you're not supposed to call me here unless it's an emergency."

"Dad, can you come home?" Nate sobbed. "Please?"

"Jesus, are you crying? What's wrong, kid?" asked Kane softly. "Talk to me."

"Please, Daddy. Just come home."

•   •   •

When Kane arrived, he found the front door locked. He fumbled in the darkness for his keys. After coming up with the right one, he inserted it and twisted open the dead bolt. The light was off in the entry.

"Dad?"

Kane stepped into the unnaturally quiet house, feeling an electric prickle of alarm as he smelled the odor of burned gunpowder.

"Nate?" he called, flipping on the light.

Nate emerged from the darkened hallway. He lowered the pistol in his hands and ran forward, stopping short when he saw the look in his father's eyes. He stood numbly, gun at his side, tears of relief wetting his cheeks.

"What the hell's goin' on?" Kane demanded. Without waiting for a reply he ripped the revolver from his son's hand and opened the cylinder. Two shots had been fired. "Damn it, kid, I told you never to touch my guns. Never."

Nate swallowed. He opened his mouth to speak, but couldn't.

Kane shoved the pistol into his belt. Then he grabbed Nate and shook him. "Start talkin', bucko. You've got some explaining to do. What happened? What the hell were you doing with my gun?"

"I . . . I thought the other one might come back," Nate choked.

"What other one? Quit blubberin' and talk!" All of a sudden Kane saw the blood. A trail led up the stairs from the beach.

Smears on the lower door, more on the walls, a spatter down the hall . . .

"Christ, did you . . . ? Oh, sweet Jesus! Allison! Where is she?" Kane's fingers dug into Nate's arms, closing like coiled springs. With growing dread he shook his son again, trying to rattle an answer from the panicked child. Receiving none, he started down the stairs to the beach. "Allison! Allison!"

"In here, Dad."

The living room.

Kane bolted past Nate, thundering down the hall. He found his daughter on her hands and knees beside the couch. She had a sponge in her hand. A pail of soapy water sat beside her, along with a pile of towels from the bathroom. More were scattered around on the carpet, soaking up blood.

Allison glanced up as Kane entered, then returned to her work. "Don't worry," she said dully. "There's a lot, but I think I can get it up before Mom comes back."

Kane pulled his daughter to her feet, brushing back her long, damp hair from her face. "Oh, sweet Jesus," he whispered again, horrified by what he saw.

Allison's eyes were bruised and dark and purplish; one had already completely swollen shut. Crusts of dried blood ringed each nostril. A deep, ragged laceration traversed her cheek. But the worst damage had been done to her mouth. Cal's blows had split her lips, making it difficult for her to talk. Seeming strangely ashamed, she looked up at her father, then back at the stains on the rug. "Lemme go, Dad. I've gotta get this finished."

"Leave it." Kane put his arm around her and led her toward the couch. "Come over here and sit down."

Allison twisted away, her eyes round with panic. "No!" she cried, staring at the couch. Then, struggling to control herself, she stammered, "I . . . I don't want to sit."

"Okay, okay, you don't have to," said Kane gently. He looked at the dark pool seeping into the carpet in the center of the room, the smaller puddles by the door, the trail of red leading into the hall.

Can't all be from Allison . . .

"Honey, try to get ahold of yourself," he said, unable to control the tremor in his own voice. "Tell me what happened."

Folding her arms over her chest, Allison took a deep breath and began speaking in a monotone—barely moving her distended lips, her leaden words sounding as if she were describing something that had happened to someone else. "There was a noise on the street. Some guy was breaking into Evelyn's BMW. He came inside. There was another one, too. They wanted money. They wouldn't believe there wasn't any. They . . . they beat me up."

"Did they do anything else?" Kane asked, his fists balling at his sides. "They didn't—"

"No."

Kane let out a small sigh of relief. "What happened then?"

"I . . . I got away and grabbed your gun. I told them to leave. When they didn't, I . . . I shot one of them."

Nate had followed his father from the entry. He stood mutely by the door, carefully watching his sister.

Kane's eyes narrowed. "Where are they?" he demanded, his tone turning hard as granite.

"One guy ran. The second guy . . . I think he crawled out back."

Kane withdrew his automatic. "Nate? You see where he went?"

"Nate was asleep in his room the whole time," Allison answered quickly. "He didn't see anything."

"Did you get a look at the car?"

"No," Allison lied.

"Nate, go to the kitchen and call the Malibu sheriffs' office. The number's by the phone. Have 'em get a unit down here right away."

"Yes, sir."

Kane looked at Allison. "Is he armed?"

"I'm not sure. I don't think so."

"Good. Nate, go make the call."

Gun extended, rage swelling in his chest, Kane followed the trail of blood down the stairs and onto the deck outside. He found the body on the far side of the seawall.

The kid hadn't gotten far. He lay collapsed in a circle of dark sand, his right leg twisted at an unnatural angle to his torso, his jeans soaked with blood. *Slug must've broken the femur, caught the artery at the same time,* Kane thought. He felt for a carotid pulse. He found none.

After returning to the house, he searched the music room for the other intruder, then climbed the stairs to the entry. "Nate. You call the sheriffs?"

"They're on the way, Dad," Nate answered from the kitchen.

Kane checked his watch. *Four miles to the Malibu station. At sixty miles per hour they'll be here in four minutes.* Moving from room to room, he rapidly searched the remainder of the house. He found only smashed lamps, spilled drawers, and broken furniture. At last he returned to the living room.

Allison looked up as he entered. "Did you find him?"

"One of them. He's out on the beach."

"Is he . . . ?"

"Yeah," Kane replied. "He's dead."

Nate gasped, releasing a flood of sobs. Fighting back her own tears, Allison took her brother's hand.

Kane put his arms around his children and held them both. "I'm so sorry, Allison," he said, his voice thick with emotion. "You too, Nate. I don't apologize for much, but I'm apologizing for this. Your mom and I should never have left you alone like that. It won't happen again."

"It wasn't your fault, Daddy," Allison whispered. "It wasn't Mom's fault either," she added quickly.

"Yeah, it was. But I blame myself a lot more than your mom," said Kane, regarding Allison closely. "I won't be taking it out on her, if that's what you're worried about."

"Nobody's to blame," Allison repeated numbly. "It just happened."

Outside, Kane heard the sound of approaching sirens. "The sheriffs will be here soon," he said. "You're both going to have to talk to them. After that we'll head up to the emergency clinic," he added, glancing at Allison. "Take care of that face."

"I'm okay. I don't want to go anywhere."

"Honey, those cuts need looking after."

"Dad, I don't—"

"We're going soon as we're done here," said Kane firmly. Puzzled by his daughter's reluctance, he looked at Nate, then returned his gaze to Allison. "Is there anything you forgot to tell me? Something you left out?"

"No."

"Nate?"

Nate raised his eyes to his sister. Still holding his hand, she stared back for a long and silent moment.

"Nate? You have something to say?" Kane asked again.

"No, sir," Nate finally answered. "It happened like Allison said. The shot woke me up. I didn't see anything."

Kane heard a squeal of tires in front of the house, accompanied by the sound of dying sirens. The sheriffs' cruisers had arrived. "Allison, they're here. If there's anything else, I've gotta know right now. I want to help you, honey—more than I've ever wanted anything in my life. Please trust me."

Allison's tortured eyes unwaveringly held her father's. "There's nothing else to tell."

"Allison . . ."

"Dad, I just want to get through this," she said in a small, quavering voice.

"But—"

"Daddy, please," Allison begged. "Leave me alone. There's nothing more to tell."

With a surge of utter, overwhelming desolation, Kane dropped his hands to his sides, for the first time since childhood feeling completely powerless and unsure of how to proceed. "Okay," he sighed, unable to shake the conviction he was missing something, but not knowing what else to do. "Let's go talk to the cops."

17

The following morning, still immersed in thoughts of Allison's attack and blaming himself for not having been home to prevent it, Kane pulled into the police parking lot behind the courthouse. As he twisted off the radio and killed the engine, he noticed a Channel 2 mobile news wagon parked across the street on Butler, right in front of the West L.A. station house. In a red zone, too.

Kane hesitated as he slid from behind the wheel, momentarily considering parking behind the station to avoid running the news gauntlet. He wasn't surprised to see them; the media had picked up the previous evening's accidental shooting in time to get it on the morning news, and he suspected the Channel 2 crew was just the first of many. To make matters worse, an election was coming up, and the mayor had predictably promised a thorough investigation. Kane had a feeling that, as usual, the politicians of the city of Los Angeles would be lining up to stand firmly behind their beleaguered police department. Way behind.

Scowling, Kane slammed the door and strode across the lot. As he approached the corner, he realized with a renewed surge of irritation that the news team had already begun taping, and he couldn't have picked a worse time to arrive. A cameraman wearing a heavy battery belt had positioned himself so the sign reading West Los Angeles Police Station would be prominently displayed in the background, and Lauren Van Owen, an attractive blond news correspondent with whom Kane had crossed paths on numerous occasions, was standing in front reading from a large cue card held by an assistant. She had the microphone gripped in her right hand and was occasionally gesturing with her left toward the building behind her as she spoke. Kane couldn't make out her words, but he knew one thing for certain: She definitely wasn't lavishing encomiums on the department.

Years ago Lauren Van Owen had carved a niche for herself as a crack crime reporter, but in Kane's opinion she routinely used, as did many in the media, the excuse of "giving the public what they wanted" as license to file sensational, biased reports, often prejudicially slanted against the police. He groaned as she spotted him crossing the street.

"Detective Kane! Detective Kane! Can we have a word with you?"

Kane stopped when he reached the sidewalk, cursing under his breath as Van Owen hurried toward him. As the newswoman drew near, he grudgingly conceded that even that early in the morning she looked great—silk blouse, every blond hair impeccably in place, her slim, aerobically maintained figure fashionably clothed in an expensive-looking gray suit.

"Ms. Van Owen. What a pleasure," Kane said with a mordant smile when she arrived. "Universe still revolving around you all right?"

The young woman stopped in front of him, slightly out of breath. "Good one, Kane," she retorted. "Especially coming from you. Mind giving us a statement?"

Kane pointedly checked his watch. "I'd love to, but I'm late for an intimate breakfast with the chief. He wants my opinion on some new policy changes he's considering."

"Would they include one about not firing on unarmed civilians like the ten-year-old boy your partner shot last night?"

Kane bristled. "That's bull and you know it," he growled, realizing she was deliberately pushing his buttons to gull him into talking, but—still furious with the way the previous evening had turned out—unable to stop himself. "That kid getting shot was a justifiable accident."

"Uh-huh. According to your department's preliminary investigation. A case of the foxes guarding the chicken coop, wouldn't you say?"

Instead of answering, Kane turned and started down the sidewalk.

Van Owen followed. "Isn't it true no gun was ever found at the scene?"

Kane whirled. "Yeah, it's true. We found it four blocks away in a sewer. We've also got a suspect who admits firing it, which is something you people have so far forgotten to mention."

"And you think that justifies your partner, Detective Arnold Mercer, shooting an unarmed ten-year-old? Just a little over two weeks ago you and Detective Mercer were involved in another shooting, correct?"

"For once you've got something right. I blew away some dirtbag after he and his partner shot two feds and tossed a kid out a third-floor window. I'd do it again."

"Yes, I'm sure you would, Detective. But isn't there a pattern here? Allegations of excessive force came up concerning your treatment of one of the suspects in that case. In view of this, will Detective Mercer—"

"Those *allegations* never went anywhere for the simple reason there was nothing to 'em," Kane interrupted. "As for what happened last night, my partner was completely justified in returning fire. Hitting the kid was an accident."

"But according to—"

"Another thing," Kane continued. "Here's a news flash for all the bleeding hearts out there watchin' your show. You shoot at a cop, he's gonna shoot back." With that, he turned and again strode toward the station.

Lauren smiled, signaling the cameraman to cut. "I've got a proposition for you, Kane," she said, hurrying after him.

"What?" Kane asked, noting with mounting anger that the newswoman seemed extremely pleased with herself.

Lauren touched her hair, smoothed it, then let her hand drop demurely to her side. "I'm more than willing to listen to your side of things," she said. "Meet me for lunch and we'll discuss it."

Kane kept on walking. "Not in a million fuckin' years, honey," he muttered.

•   •   •

After climbing the stairs to the second floor, Kane slouched into
the detectives' squad room, mentally kicking himself for letting Van
Owen goad him into an interview. With some judicious editing at the
studio, he knew he'd undoubtedly come off sounding like some trig-
ger-happy killer on the evening news. In fact, it probably didn't even
need editing, he decided miserably.

Kane took off his coat, hung it on the back of his chair, and slid
behind his desk. Groaning inwardly, he surveyed the mountain of
paperwork piled on his workstation, momentarily daunted as he considered the tedious task of correlating files, chronological logs, and
forensic evidence on the Bradley kidnapping with the more recent
murder of Angelo Martin—cross-indexing the two wherever possible
and bringing both up-to-date.

Following Kane's interrogation of Voss, the Bureau had immediately been notified of the tie-in to the Bradley case, as agreed. A
subsequent search of the Department of Justice computer database,
along with a check of the California Prison Index and calls to the
prison authorities involved, had revealed that James Kearns—aka
Shorty Kearns—and Miguel Voss had been cellmates at Tehachapi
State Prison. Kearns was currently on parole, but hadn't checked in
with his parole officer for months. Barring something unforeseen,
Kane knew it was just a matter of time until someone—either the FBI
or members of the local police—picked him up, and at this point in
the investigation it was essential to update everything in both bur-
geoning murder books.

Although it was a chore that would probably take more time than
he cared to consider, it had to be done, and Kane threw himself into
the work, gratefully suspending thoughts of the previous evening—as
well as his more recent and ill-advised talk with Lauren Van Owen.
He worked steadily, but had only made a small dent in the task when
Arnie arrived a half hour later.

Kane looked up. "You all right?" he asked.

Arnie slumped wearily at his desk. He looked as if he hadn't slept
all night. "Just got back from the hospital," he said. "The kid's out
of surgery. It was touch and go for a while, but he's gonna pull
through."

"That's good. I'm glad, Arnie."

"Yeah. Me, too." A pause, then, "Listen, Dan. I just heard about what happened at the beach last night. Is Allison gonna be okay?"

"Yeah," Kane answered. "Kate got home from her damn concert about the time the sheriff finished up, and we took her up to the emergency clinic together. She needed some stitches. Nothin' was broken."

"Lucky."

"Yeah."

"How's Kate handling it?"

"As well as can be expected. She's taking some time off to spend with Allison, help get her over the hump. The kid's acting kinda withdrawn, which I guess is natural after something like that. She's tough, though. She'll get over it."

"And Nate?"

"He's fine."

"Any luck finding the second guy?"

"Not yet," said Kane angrily. "The sheriff's detectives got a positive ID on the dead one, though. Right now they're going through every one of that punk's associates with a fine-tooth comb. Don't worry, they'll find him. And if they don't, I will," he added ominously.

"I'm sure you will. Lemme know if you need any help."

"Thanks, but if it comes to that, I'll handle it myself." Then, abruptly changing the subject, "When you got here, was the news team still out front?"

"Lauren Van Owen? Yeah. Good-looking broad, for a ghoul."

"You talk to her?"

"Hell, no. Did you?"

"Well, uh . . ."

"Jesus, Kane, that's great. That's just great. What'd you say? Never mind, I don't wanna know. I'm sure I'll be hearing about it soon enough."

"Sorry. She got under my skin."

"Right," said Arnie.

Just then Lieutenant Long entered the squad room. With a wave he signaled Arnie into his office. Every head in the room turned, following the senior detective as he rose from his desk and crossed to the door.

Five minutes later he returned.

"What?" asked Kane.

"I'm being placed on administrative duty until the Shooting Review Board makes its ruling," Arnie said simply. "Long said it came from the top. Nothing he could do."

"But why?"

"Who knows? Whatever it is, I'm riding my desk till this thing blows over. Long wants to talk to you next."

"Good. 'Cause I definitely wanna talk to him."

Kane stomped from the room, ignoring questioning looks from Deluca and Banowski as he passed. A moment later he banged on Long's door. "Come," the lieutenant's voice boomed from the other side.

"What's this crap about Arnie bein' taken off the roster?" Kane demanded as soon as he'd entered.

Lieutenant Long looked up, his dark eyes registering a seething impatience barely under control. Hunching his shoulders, he motioned to a metal chair beside his desk. "Sit down and shut up."

"What happened last night was a justifiable accident, and you know it," Kane continued. "The review board's gonna clear Arnie. What the hell are you—"

"Lemme ask you something, Kane," growled Long. "You may have the thickest head on the force, but you still comprehend English, right? Just exactly what part of 'shut up' don't you understand?"

Sensing he'd gone too far, Kane slouched over to the chair and sat.

"That's better. You ready to listen?"

"Yeah. I'm all ears," said Kane, impatiently cracking his knuckles.

"Good. I've been on the phone the last hour with both the mayor and the chief. Do you have any idea what the press is going to do with this?"

"Fuck the press."

"Unfortunately, everyone doesn't share your simplistic view of the situation. Things could get a lot worse."

"What do you mean, worse?"

"Between you and me, IA's going after Mercer for being under the influence while on duty," Long said. Then, lowering his voice, "Was Arnie drinking last night?"

"If he was, I didn't see him," Kane hedged. "And even if he did have a pop or two, it sure as hell didn't affect his judgment. That punk was shooting at us, for chrissake."

"Whether or not Arnie's drinking played a part in the accident isn't for us to decide. Right now the best thing you can do to help your partner is lose the attitude. Understand?"

"Yeah. I understand just fine. Shit flows downhill. The mayor wants the press off his ass, the brass want the heat off the department, and Arnie's on the hot seat."

"It sucks, but that's how it's going down. I'll go to bat for you and Mercer, but you'll have to help."

"How?"

"Internal Affairs wants to talk to you this morning. I suggest you put a lid on your sunny disposition and cooperate."

Kane hesitated. "Sure, I'll cooperate," he said at last. "We did everything by the book. There's no way they can screw Arnie."

"I hope not. There's something I didn't mention."

"What?"

"The investigation's being headed up by an old friend of yours. Lieutenant Snead."

•   •   •

Two hours later found Kane impatiently pacing the confines of a small alcove outside Lieutenant Snead's office. At that point Snead had kept him waiting more than fifty minutes, which Kane took to be a crude demonstration of who held the upper hand. "This is bullshit," he grumbled, turning to leave. Just then one of the IA secretaries stuck her head around the corner and motioned him in.

Snead didn't look up as Kane entered, pretending instead to study the contents of a thick folder on his desk. Kane stood quietly for several seconds, then began inspecting an eclectic assortment of pictures covering Snead's walls: Snead with the chief, Snead with his arm around the captain, Snead with members of the city council, Snead standing beside the district attorney. In each he had the same officious, obsequious expression plastered on his face.

Tiring of being ignored, Kane picked up a brass-framed picture sitting on the bookcase. Snead and ex-Chief Gates. "Where's the one of you and Mayor Fitzpatrick?" he asked.

"I beg your pardon?"

"There're plenty of shots here with you kissin' everybody else's ass. I figure you oughtta have one with your lips planted on the mayor's butt, too."

"Put that down."

Kane flipped the eight-by-ten of Chief Gates facedown on Snead's desk. "No problem. Let's get on with it. You recording this?"

Snead smiled with unconcealed, sardonic guile. "Why, Detective Kane. What makes you ask that?"

"Never mind, slugger. What do you want?"

Snead's face darkened. "Don't push it, Kane. One more crack and I'll have your badge for insubordination."

"What is it, Snead? Cramps? Or is that pesky yeast infection back?"

Snead paused. He studied his fingernails, then glowered at Kane. "You don't get it, do you?"

"Get what?"

"You fucked up bad this time, cowboy. This one isn't going away."

"Cut the crap. What happened last night was an accident, and that's the way the review board's gonna see it."

"You think so? I've got two words for you, Kane: excessive force."

"I've got two words for you too, champ."

Snead stared at Kane, his anger barely in check. "Let me spell it out for you," he said tersely. "We've got two detectives here. One has a history of ventilating suspects whenever he feels like it. A real maverick. He's been up on charges more than once, but nothing has ever stuck."

"Nothing's ever stuck 'cause the charges were all horseshit."

Snead resumed shuffling through the file on his desk. "His partner's a different story," he continued, ignoring Kane's objection. "Worked his way up to D-three, twenty-five years on the force, only fired his gun twice in the line of duty before this. The only questionable area in his record seems to involve covering up for his hotshot partner." Snead looked up, starting to enjoy himself now, getting into it. "So guess what? The D-three *accidentally* shoots a ten-year-old kid—says it was dark, he fired at the muzzle blast, that kinda shit—and this time his cowboy partner covers for *him*. A little payback, Kane?"

"We were fired upon. Mercer returned fire. Period."

"If that's true, why didn't you fire, too?"

"I didn't have time."

"Is that right? Or was it that in your judgment the use of lethal force didn't constitute an appropriate response to a single shot from a twenty-two—especially when you knew there was a child in the building?"

"I told you, I didn't have time to shoot. And we didn't know the kid was in there."

Snead snorted derisively. "That's what you told me. Speaking of judgment," he went on, "here comes the interesting part. We do some checking and find out this D-three's taken to uncorking his lunch every day."

"What?"

"You heard me. We know Mercer has a drinking problem. We also know he was under the influence last night at the time of the shooting."

"We all take a drink now and then. It doesn't mean—"

"Was Mercer drinking last night when he shot the kid?"

"Let's lay our cards on the table here, Snead. This isn't about Arnie, is it?"

Snead's hand moved to a partially open drawer. Kane heard a click. He'd been right—Snead *had* been recording.

The IA officer closed the drawer and carefully folded his hands. "I don't like you, Kane," he said slowly. "We don't need your kind on the force. Mercer, either. He's history, and I'll let you in on a secret. If you try to cover up for him, so are you."

"Yeah? How do you figure?"

"I'll find a way," Snead snarled. "Last chance, Kane. Mercer was drunk last night. He screwed the pooch when he shot that kid, and I want your testimony to that effect. If you don't cooperate, I'm gonna take you down, too—if not *this* time, then the next. I can't think of anything that would give me greater pleasure."

"This interview's over."

"Is that right?"

"That's right, *Lieutenant*. Like I said before, you wanna talk to me, call my attorney."

Snead shot Kane a malevolent grin. "Sure thing, cowboy. Play it that way. It's your funeral."

Placing his thick, big-knuckled hands on Snead's desk, Kane leaned across. "You know something, slugger?" he said. "I don't mind cops checking on cops. I really don't. It's gotta be done. Just not by tight-assed, small-minded, chickenshit little pricks like you."

18

Catheryn sat at the kitchen table, watching as Allison toyed list-lessly with her lunch. The stitches in her daughter's cheek and lip had come out weeks before, and the bruises were finally beginning to fade—turning from an angry purple to a sickly yellow-gray. The doctor had assured them the scars would be minimal. Nonetheless, Catheryn suspected that Allison had sustained a deeper wound in the attack, something that had not yet begun to heal.

Following the break-in Catheryn had canceled her tutoring lessons and skipped rehearsals as much as possible to be with her daughter, spending long hours walking with her on the beach, taking her on shopping excursions to Santa Monica and Westwood, and often simply joining her in the solitude of her room—trying without success to comfort her and at the same time draw her out about the incident. At one point, concerned with Allison's reticence, Catheryn had insisted she visit a psychiatrist. Allison had gone once, then abruptly terminated the sessions.

"What's new with McKenzie, honey?" Catheryn asked, attempting to pry open a conversation.

"I don't know," said Allison. She shoved away her tuna sandwich, adding, "We haven't talked much lately."

"You should start getting out more," advised Catheryn, trying to keep her tone light. "See some of your friends, maybe catch a movie—"

"I don't feel like it."

"I know," said Catheryn, powerless in the face of her daughter's obstinate withdrawal. "But, honey, you've been through a terrible experience. The best thing right now would be for you to start picking up the pieces—even if you don't feel like it."

Allison gazed pensively out the window.

"Allison, please talk to me."

"I don't feel like talking. Nate's back from day camp. Talk to him."

"Allison, don't shut me out. I'm trying to help you."

"Help me do what, Mom?"

"I . . . I don't know. I just know you're unhappy, and I want to—"

"I'm *fine*, Mom," Allison interrupted. "Kane kids are tough, re-member? It takes more than a little slamming around to keep us down."

"You're not fine, honey, and it's killing me that I can't make things better."

"I'm all right," Allison repeated angrily. "Some guy beat me up, and I shot him. Happens to kids all the time. I'll get over it."

"Allison . . ."

"Jesus, Mom! I'm sick and tired of everyone fawning all over me. Why don't you just get off my back?"

Tears of helplessness sprang to Catheryn's eyes. "Ali, I know you don't really feel that way."

"The hell I don't," Allison declared defiantly. She was about to add something more when she saw the look of desolation on Catheryn's face. Ashamed, she glanced away. "I'm sorry," she said softly.

"It's okay, honey. Please tell me what's wrong."

"Nothing's wrong. Look, I just want to forget what happened. I never want to think about it again."

"Ali . . ."

"Please, Mom," said Allison. "Stop worrying about me. I'll call some friends, start going out again, whatever you want. Maybe McKenzie would like to come over for dinner tomorrow. I'll invite her, okay?"

Catheryn took a deep breath, then let it out. "That sounds like a great idea."

Just then the front door banged open. "Anybody home?" Kane's voice boomed into the house. "Kate! Allison! Nate!"

Allison and Catheryn made their way to the front of the house, where they found Kane setting down a large cardboard box in the entry.

"Dan. What are you doing home so early?" Catheryn asked, regarding him curiously.

"Just taking a long lunch hour, honeybunch," Kane answered. "Hadda make a delivery. There's more stuff in the back of the Suburban," he added, smiling mysteriously at his daughter. "Bring it in, okay, Ali? Have Nate give you a hand. Where is he, anyway? Hey, Nate!"

"Up here, Dad," said Nate, answering from his room above. "What do you want?"

"Come help your sister unload some stuff from the back of my car. And don't drop anything. It's fragile."

"Okay."

"What's going on, Dan?" asked Catheryn. "I haven't seen you this excited since the fireworks show."

"Yeah, what is this?" asked Allison, bending to examine the box.

"You'll see, petunia," said Kane, closing the box and firmly placing his foot on top. "Get the rest of the stuff in the house first."

Minutes later, after Allison and Nate had completed several trips to Kane's Suburban, a desktop computer, mouse, ink-jet printer, and a Gordian tangle of cables lay on the entry floor beside the carton Kane had first brought in.

"A computer?" said Allison, struggling to lift a fifteen-inch color monitor from the cardboard box. "Jeez, Dad, I never thought you'd buy one of these."

"I picked it up cheap from one of my buddies at work. What do you think?"

"It's great," Allison conceded with a shrug. "Where do you want to put it?"

"How about your room, sunshine?"

"My room? This is for me?"

"Yep. I figured if you're gonna keep pecking away on those stories of yours, you might as well do it on something quieter'n that old Smith Corona."

Allison stared in shock at the equipment strewn across the floor. "You got me a computer? I . . . I can't believe it." Bursting into tears, she threw her arms around Kane's neck and kissed him on the cheek.

"Now, don't get all mushy on me," Kane said gently, exchanging a quick glance with Catheryn. "Come on, let's get 'er into your room. You know how to set it up?"

Allison stepped back and nodded, trying to cover her embarrassment. "We use Macs at school," she said, quickly wiping her eyes. "This is an IBM clone, but they're similar. I'll figure it out."

"Good, 'cause I don't have the faintest idea."

"Do you know the specs? How about a manual? Did you get one?"

"The manual's in the box with the monitor, sugarplum, and the guy I bought this sucker from said it's got all the software you'll need already loaded."

"Thanks, Dad," said Allison, still blinking back tears. "I . . . well, thanks."

"Forget it. Just do me one favor. Never again, under any circumstances, put the ol' dad here in one of your stories."

Fighting for control, Allison took a deep breath, let it out, and then shook her head somberly. "You're safe, Pop," she said with a small smile. "That's one genre I've given up."

"You're giving up science fiction?"

"No. Horror."

•　　•　　•

After lunch Kane spent the rest of the afternoon in court testifying—or more accurately, *waiting* to testify—on a case he'd put together more than a year before. It proved a frustrating experience, with a legal technicality threatening to blow the entire prosecution.

Although at the end of the day he'd have liked nothing better than to climb into his car and start for home, earlier that morning Arnie had asked him to stop by before leaving, saying he had something to discuss.

Reluctantly, Kane headed back to the station. Walking briskly, he took a shortcut through the Municipal Courts parking lot and entered the Butler station across the street. Most of the day-shift detectives had gone when he arrived upstairs, where he found Arnie at his desk shuffling through a huge pile of paperwork. As Kane crossed the deserted squad room, he saw his friend make an entry in a thick three-ring binder, then add it to a swelling mound on the workstation opposite his own. Kane's.

"What the hell's goin' on?" Kane demanded, staring with dismay at the files and folders strewn across his desk. "I just got this thing cleaned up."

Arnie rocked back in his chair. "Sure you did," he said, glancing up wearily.

"Well, maybe not clean, but at least I *used* to know where everything was."

"Right."

Kane looked carefully at his partner. He appeared tired, deflated, the past weeks he'd been restricted to desk duty seeming to have aged him. Although Kane had been quickly exonerated in the accidental shooting, Snead's IA investigation of Arnie showed signs of dragging on interminably, and the media's interest in the case—still occasionally fueled by Kane's ill-chosen words to Lauren Van Owen following the accident—showed no signs of flagging, either.

With a sigh Arnie picked up a murder book labeled "Bradley," initialed it, and stacked it on the pile. "By the way, I got a call from the Bureau today."

"What'd they want?"

"They phoned to let us know they finally picked up the third kidnapper."

"They found Kearns? Where?"

"Vegas. Evidently he stopped off in L.A. just long enough for him and Voss to whack Angelo Martin, then headed back. Turns out you were right. Kearns thought Angelo had ratted out the kidnapping, and he wanted to make sure Angelo's sister Sylvia didn't get any similar ideas. Threatened her family, said he'd kill them if she talked. With Kearns in custody Sylvia cut a deal with the feds. Voss is turning state's evidence, too. Everybody involved should be goin' away till the middle of the next century."

"Martin and Voss'll probably do less than ten."

"Yeah. That's the way it goes. Anyway, I heard the captain was real pleased with your work on that. You'll be getting a commendation letter."

"Swell," said Kane dryly, glancing again at his workstation. "Look, Arnie, you didn't ask me to stay late so you could pat me on the back. What'd you want to tell me—that you decided to turn my desk into your very own personal junk pile?"

Arnie picked up another file. "Nope."

"What, then? Jesus, you're actin' like a virgin on her first date. Spill it."

"I put in my papers today," said Arnie quietly. "You're gonna be the new ranking detective around here, at least till they get a replacement. Who knows?" he added. "Play your cards right, this could all be yours on a permanent basis."

"You're retiring over that thing in the garage? Damn it, Arnie, don't do anything rash. Snead couldn't touch me, and sooner or later he's gonna have to give up on you, too."

"I don't think so. Anyway, that's not the only reason."

"Bullshit," said Kane, sinking into a chair behind his desk. "Look, I know you're fed up with IA breathin' down your neck. I've got news for you, pard. Every job—and I'm talkin' any one you wanna name with the possible exception of bein' a *Penthouse* photographer—is gonna have its downside. If you leave, you'll probably wind up trading the brand of shit you've gotta eat now for a new and undoubtedly less tasty variety."

"Let's just say I'm ready for a change of diet and let it go, amigo."

"I'm not buying that. C'mon, Arnie. Take a couple weeks off, go fishing, whatever. Things'll look better when you get back."

Arnie shook his head. "It's not just the ass-duty they've got me on, Dan. I'm sick of the whole fuckin' thing: the press, the brass, the bodies, the paperwork, and most of all the unending parade of butt-wad shit-eatin' scumbags we've gotta deal with every day."

"You already mentioned the brass and the press."

"You know something?" Arnie continued pensively, ignoring Kane's attempt at humor. "All my years on the force, I never shot anybody before. Never."

"Arnie, put it behind you. It was an accident."

"Yeah."

"The kid's gonna be fine, right?"

"Right," Arnie replied. "He's making a full recovery." Then, ruefully, "His parents are suing the city for three and a half million."

"I heard. The brass'll probably take it outta your paycheck."

"Fuck the brass."

"I'll drink to that," said Kane, immediately regretting his choice of words.

Arnie saw it in his eyes and quickly looked away. "You know I've been thinking about retiring for a while now," he said. "I'll have twenty-five years in at the end of the month."

Kane did the calculations aloud. "Forty percent base salary after twenty years; three percent per year after that. You'll barely be getting over half pay," he pointed out. "Can you live on that?"

Arnie shrugged. "No kids, the house is paid for, and Lilith isn't around anymore to blow it on clothes. Plus I've been offered a job with a security service down on Crenshaw. Hell, with my pension I'll be making more than I am now."

"You can't start drawing till you're fifty-five. That's still a few years off."

"Not so many, partner. Anyway, I've got some money saved."

"Aw, Arnie . . ."

"Let it go, Dan."

"It's the kid, isn't it?"

Arnie looked away.

"Listen to me, pard. Shooting that kid was an accident. A terrible, unfortunate, unavoidable fuckin' accident. That's *all* it was. An accident."

"I wish I could believe that."

"What are you talking about? It was dark in there. That dirtbag was shooting at us, and—"

"We both know I'd had a couple drinks that night," Arnie interrupted. "More than a couple. Maybe Snead's right. Maybe my judgment *was* off. The kid wasn't in the car; I should have known he followed Voss into the garage."

"I forgot about him, too. That's no reason to shoulder this kind of blame."

"You may have *forgotten* about the kid. I *shot* him."

"Arnie, we can fight Snead on this thing. We're not talking criminal charges here, so even if the investigation doesn't go your way, what's the worst that can happen? A suspension—maybe getting sent back for retraining. You can handle that."

"Yeah," said Arnie slowly. "What I can't handle is pulling other people down with me. That's not the way I want to end my career, Dan. If I retire now, the whole thing goes away. No more Snead, no more IA, no more hassles."

"Arnie, if you're worried about my getting dragged in—"

"It's more than that. It's about being able to face myself in the mirror every morning. I'm processing out a week from Monday."

"Jeez, Arnie, I . . . I don't know what to say."

"How about wishing me luck?"

"Well, sure," said Kane. "If I can't change your mind, then I . . . I hope it works out."

"Thanks."

Kane stared at his hands in resignation. "Arnie, I've gotta ask one more time. Is there any way I can talk you out of this?"

"I'm afraid not, partner."

"Are you sure?"

Arnie sighed. "Yeah. I'm sure."

19

That night Kane arrived home to find Catheryn, Allison, and Nate gathered in the kitchen. For some reason he'd never been able to understand, the entire family always seemed to prefer the ambience of a crowded kitchen to that of any other room in the house. Catheryn theorized it stemmed from man's prehistoric desire to huddle around a fire for safety and warmth; Kane suspected it was simply a good way to keep an eye on the food.

"As you were, troops," he said as he entered, attempting to shake off the dejected mood he'd been in since learning of Arnie's decision. Although a detectable current of tension still charged every family gathering, during the weeks since Allison's attack all the Kanes had struggled to get things back to normal, and Kane was determined not to hinder the nascent recovery with his own problems. He bent to kiss Catheryn, checking the contents of the simmering pot she was stirring. "Mmm, smells good. What're we havin'?"

"Lentil soup," Nate answered, looking up from his task at the cutting board. "Mom let me chop all the vegetables."

"You *let* him, huh?" said Kane. "Kate, sometimes I underestimate you."

"I did all the potatoes, celery, onions, garlic, and tomatoes. Now

I'm doing the carrots," Nate continued with a smile. He raised his hands and wiggled his fingers. "And look. Still got 'em all."

Since the break-in Kane had noticed that Nate had been strangely distant, his normal high spirits dampened to the point of cautious reserve. Glad to see him smiling again, Kane said, "Damn. I like some meat in my soup. Kate, since we're not having fingers, you got anything else to put in?"

"Lamb. It's already in, along with a secret ingredient Nate forgot to mention."

"What secret ingredient?" Nate demanded suspiciously.

"Spinach," Allison answered from her perch on the counter across from the stove. "Mom always puts it in."

"Spinach? Yuck. She does not."

"Yes, she does. And you always eat it."

"I do not!"

"Whatever you say," said Allison, uncharacteristically backing away from the skirmish.

Noticing this, Kane glanced at Catheryn, then continued. "I'll tell you somethin', Nate," he said, trying to keep the conversation on an upbeat note. "Spinach is one hell of a lot better'n *some* secret ingredients you find in food. Take Chinese, for example. Anybody care for a cocktail?" he added, crossing to the refrigerator.

"I'll have something with an umbrella on it," said Catheryn.

"Gee, sure thing, Kate. Comin' right up. How about some apple juice for you, Ali?" Kane pulled out a gallon jug and slid it across the counter. "Pour some for your brother, too."

"What *about* Chinese food?" persisted Nate, not letting it go.

Kane popped the tops off two Red Hooks. He looked at Nate thoughtfully, then returned to the stove and handed one of the bottles to Catheryn. "I'll tell you this," he advised sagely, lowering his voice in sepulchral confidence. "Never, under any circumstance, send your food back at a Chinese restaurant."

"Why not?"

Kane took a long pull on his Red Hook. "Why not? Well, the first thing that happens when your food gets back to the kitchen is some skinny Chinese cook starts cussin' out the barbarian infidel who had the nerve to complain about his culinary masterpiece. Then he hocks a lunger right in the middle of your plate."

"Dan! That's not true," protested Catheryn.

"It sure as hell is," Kane insisted. "Your stir-fry comes back with a big ol' Chinese oyster on it."

"I don't believe you," said Nate, looking slightly green as he tried to remember the last time he'd eaten Chinese food.

"Believe it, squirt," Kane went on. "I'll let you in on another little secret—"

"I think it's time we changed the subject," Catheryn said firmly. "I'm cooking a nice dinner, and you're talking about lunkers."

"That's lungers," corrected Kane. "And I totally agree. Let's talk about something else. Did you hear on the news a while back where some lady died in the emergency room and her body gave off this cloud of poison gas? Half the doctors who breathed it are still laid up."

"Really?" asked Nate, his eyes widening in credulous amazement. "What do you think she was eating?"

"Chow mein," said Kane.

Just then the front door banged open. Travis wandered in, followed by Tommy and Christy. "Somebody say we're having chow mein?"

"No, lentil soup," answered Catheryn with a petulant glare at Kane.

Spotting the Red Hook in his father's hand, Tommy walked to the refrigerator and pulled out one for himself. "Great. One of my favorites. You put lamb in this time?"

"Yeah," said Nate. "And tonight yours is gonna have a secret Chinese ingredient, too."

"Nate!"

"Sorry, Mom."

"What's the midget over there babbling about?" asked Tommy.

Although Nate was inured to Allison's habitual denigration, his face fell at the unaccustomed taunt from his older brother.

"Never mind," said Catheryn. "And that wasn't a nice way to say hello to Nate. You shouldn't—"

"You know something, Tommy?" Allison broke in. "Every ninety minutes a teenager commits suicide. Why don't you try upping the stats?"

The entire family stared at her in surprise.

"Jeez, sis," said Tommy, taken aback by her venom. "Since when did you start sticking up for Nate?"

"Drop dead."

"That's enough, both of you," warned Catheryn.

"Allison defending someone besides herself," said Travis, trying to break the tension. "This momentous occasion calls for a beer. Okay, Dad?"

Catheryn answered before her husband could respond. "Absolutely not," she said. "No matter what you think, Travis, sixteen years old doesn't make you an adult."

Following another uncomfortable silence, Christy spoke up. "Your soup smells wonderful, Mrs. Kane."

"Thanks, Christy. You're more than welcome to stay for dinner."

"Oh, I don't want to impose."

"Don't be silly. You're family. Anyway, you won't be imposing. You can help with the dishes."

Christy smiled. "Okay, I'd love to stay. I'm starving."

Catheryn looked up from the stove, noticing a change in Christy she couldn't quite place. Tommy's girlfriend had always been a beauty, but tonight she seemed nearly luminescent. "You look great, honey," she said. "But what's different about you? Your hair . . . ?"

"She's puttin' on some ell-bees, that's what," said Kane. "Looks good on you, sugar. I always said all that swimmin' made you too skinny."

Christy ducked her head self-consciously. "Thanks." Then, quickly changing the subject, "How's your job with the orchestra going, Mrs. Kane?"

"Fine," Catheryn answered, glancing at her husband. Her position with the Philharmonic had become even more of a sore subject since Allison's attack, and she and Kane had pointedly avoided discussing it. "Rehearsals have been going extremely well, and I'll be joining the performances starting mid-August. Arthur West, the principal cellist, just moved me down to the second tier," she added.

"What's that mean, Mom?" asked Nate. "Is that good?"

Catheryn turned to her youngest. "Yes, it is, Nate. You know how we all sit on those raised platforms that step up toward the back? The principal cellist is down in front, right by the conductor, with the associate and assistant principals occupying the other two titled positions. Everyone else is arranged behind them according to ability— the most inexperienced high up in the back. It's quite an honor to be moved down this soon."

"Sounds to me like the new kid on the block's screwin' up the pecking order," Kane observed. "Movin' you forward means everybody else got moved back, right? Bet that caused a few catfights."

"Some," Catheryn admitted.

"Well, congratulations anyway, Mrs. Kane," Christy said. "I can't wait to come and hear you play."

"Thanks, honey." After grabbing an insulated glove from a drawer beside the stove, Catheryn checked a loaf of French bread she had baking in the oven. "This'll be done shortly," she announced. "Let's all get cleaned up and sit down."

Minutes later the entire group squeezed around the circular kitchen table and, following grace, turned their attention to the steaming bowls before them—industriously dipping bread and spooning up the thick, delicious soup. The only sound heard for several minutes was a noisy slurping from Kane and his youngest son. After he'd finished his first bowl, Kane looked over at Travis. "Been seein' a lot of that Wallace kid, huh?" he said. "Kissed her yet, Romeo?"

A flush crept up Travis's neck, quickly spreading to his cheeks. "Jeez, Dad! What kinda question is that?"

"Just asking," said Kane. "Seems like a spunky little broad. You like her, huh?"

Travis shrugged. "McKenzie? Yeah, I guess so."

"He's been out with her every night this week," offered Allison. "He sees her more than I do."

"That's not saying much," countered Travis. "McKenzie says you hardly call anymore. Lately you barely even leave the house."

"Hey, Mom? Check this out," said Nate, cleaning his spoon with a napkin.

Ignoring Nate, Catheryn looked over at Travis. "You could start spending more time at home yourself," she said sharply. "Like in the music room, for instance."

"Trav's practicing not meeting up to your specs, Kate?" Kane interjected. "This calls for severe punishment. Allison, go get the cattle prod."

"Dan, this isn't a laughing matter. He hasn't been putting in *nearly* the time on the piano he should."

"Hey, the kid's got other things to do. He finally decides to stand on his own two feet, and you—"

"*I'll* decide when Travis can start making his own decisions."

"Jesus, Kate. Listen to yourself. Can I make a suggestion here?"

"No. You stay clear of this. I don't try to tell you how to beat a confession out of a suspect, do I? Trav's music is my concern."

Kane quickly backtracked. "Sure, Kate. Whatever you say." Then, to Travis, "Watch out, kid. When it comes to trouble with your mother, it's a lot easier to stay out than get out."

"That's wonderful, Dan," said Catheryn. "Thanks for the support. Did you think up that little aphorism all by yourself?"

"He stole it from Mark Twain," said Allison.

"I figured as much. Travis, I want to speak with you after dinner."

"What about?"

"After dinner, Travis," Catheryn repeated.

Travis lifted his shoulders in a puzzled shrug. "Yes, ma'am."

"Look, everybody!" Nate said urgently.

"Nate, try using your mouth to eat," suggested Catheryn, still regarding Travis sternly.

"That's right, Nate," added Kane, regarding Catheryn curiously. "Can't you see your mom's busy pickin' on your brother?"

"Dad, please look," Nate cried insistently. "Neat, huh?"

Kane finally turned to his youngest, noticing he had his soup spoon dangling proudly from the tip of his nose. "Gee, Nate, that's swell," he muttered. "Damn, Kate. You have any mental infirmity on your side of the family? He sure as hell doesn't get it from me."

Nate quickly removed the spoon.

Christy, who until now had sat with the slightly embarrassed air of someone forced to eavesdrop, smiled thinly and rose from the table. "I'm going for more soup. Anybody else want some while I'm up?"

"I'll take a little more," answered Tommy.

"I'll take a *lot* more," said Kane.

"Can you bring me back the big serving spoon when you come?" asked Nate.

"No!" yelled everyone in unison.

After Christy had collected Tommy's and Kane's bowls and disappeared into the kitchen, Kane laced his fingers behind his head and looked across the table at Catheryn. "I got some bad news today," he said. "Arnie's retiring."

Catheryn looked up. "I thought something was bothering you," she said sympathetically. "Is it because of the shooting?"

"That has a lot to do with it," Kane sighed.

"I'm sorry, Dan. I know how you must feel. You two have been partners for a lot of years."

"Yeah," Kane said glumly. "Things won't be the same."

"He's been talking about retiring for quite a while now, though, hasn't he?"

Kane nodded. "I knew it was coming; I just hate to see it go down like this."

Catheryn remained silent for several seconds. "Why don't you invite him over for dinner next week?" she said at last. "I'll make something nice."

Kane shrugged. "Sure."

"Hey, Dad?" said Tommy, glancing at Travis as he spoke. "Guess what? Our job's ending next week, too. Remember you promised we could hike the Mineral King loop before I left for training camp? That's just two weeks off, so how about it? Think you can break away from work for some backpacking?"

"No way."

"Can Trav and I still go?"

Just then Christy returned from the kitchen. She set Kane's and Tommy's refilled bowls before them, along with a second basket of bread, then went back to the kitchen for hers.

No longer hungry, Kane ignored his soup. "Mineral King, eh?" he said. "When do you plan on leaving—assuming I give my okay?"

"Early Saturday, right after our last day at work," Tommy answered. "We want to get to the lakes by late afternoon and over the pass the next morning."

"You two wouldn't be thinking about climbin' that wall, would you?"

"After you told us not to? Don't worry, Dad. Our gear'll stay right in our room."

"Okay. See that it does." Kane paused thoughtfully. "Your last day at work is comin' up, eh? Hmmm. I just had an idea."

"Strange . . . you're not due for another one of those till next month," Catheryn joked, trying to nudge her husband out of the funk he'd been in since discussing Arnie.

"Funny, Kate." Then, to Tommy, "What time do you get off?"

"Three-thirty. But by the time we roll up and get the equipment stowed, it's usually closer to four. Why?"

"Never mind," said Kane mysteriously.

•   •   •

Following dinner, Kane and Catheryn moved to the living room for coffee and a more private discussion of Arnie. Tommy grudgingly agreed to help Christy with the dishes, leaving Travis, Allison, and Nate to clear the table. After finishing the cleanup, Travis spent a half hour reading in his room, then ambled down the hall in search of his mother—morosely deciding nothing was to be gained by a continued avoidance of the after-dinner meeting she'd so pointedly requested.

Not finding Catheryn in the living room, Travis made his way downstairs. He found her in the music room. She was sitting on her chair by the piano, her left hand traveling the strings of her instrument, her bow quietly teasing out short, muted phrases that Travis recognized as some of the more difficult sections of the Beethoven sonata they'd been practicing together since spring. With Catheryn spending so much time with Allison, they hadn't played it, or anything else, for weeks. Feeling a surge of regret, he realized it was a lapse that hadn't occurred since he'd first started taking lessons.

More than any other part of his long hours spent at the keyboard, Travis loved playing with his mother, whose presence had always seemed intimately woven into the fabric of his music. From the very beginning she'd been there beside him at the piano, guiding his hands through endless scales and chords and exercises, and he remembered her joy at each step of his progress—mastering his first piece, performing his first recital, winning his first competition. Throughout she'd celebrated his triumphs as though they had been her own, and over the years their hours spent together in music had formed an enduring bond between them that none of the other children shared. He missed it.

Catheryn glanced up. "I think it's time we started working on this again, don't you?"

Glad to postpone whatever lecture she had in store for him, if only temporarily, Travis nodded. "Sure, Mom," he said.

"Then let's begin."

Travis took his place at the old Baldwin. He paused to massage his hands and loosen the joints of his fingers, then opened the sheet music.

Beethoven's Sonata for Cello and Piano, Op. 5, No. 1, the composition they'd been working on for the Bronislaw competition, was one of two for cello and piano that the master had written during his "early period." Unlike most of the accompanied keyboard works of the time, the F major sonata constituted a virtuoso collaboration, with neither instrument subordinate. The first movement followed the classic sonata form and encompassed a wide range of contrast and resolution—with two differing themes presented in the initial exposition, expanded and elaborated in the development that followed, then ultimately reconciled in the final recapitulation. A spirited rondo imbued the second movement with a mood of cheerful abandon, concluding a piece that was one of Travis's favorites.

Placing his hands on the keyboard, he looked over at Catheryn. She tipped her head slightly, and they began. Before they'd progressed very far into the Adagio, Catheryn stopped. "Let's go to bar thirty-three," she suggested, flipping ahead in her music.

Travis found the place and resumed, playing from memory once he'd established the starting point. They jumped around in this fashion for the next hour—each one calling changes in turn, repeating problem passages until both were satisfied. At last they played the work straight through from the beginning, with Travis matching his notes in an intricate dance of tone and rhythm to the joyous sound of his mother's cello.

As the final chords of the blissfully self-regenerating rondo died away, Catheryn sat back in her chair. "That's enough of that for today," she said. "It's coming along, Trav. You're playing beautifully."

Travis felt a flush of pride and allowed himself a small smile. "Thanks, Mom."

Instead of returning his smile, Catheryn placed her instrument in its case, then carefully folded her hands in her lap. "I saw Petrinski today," she said.

"Uh, really?"

"Yes, really. I asked how your preparation for the Bronislaw was coming. Do you know what he told me?"

Travis looked away. "No."

"He told me I'd have to ask you. What's going on?"

Travis lowered his head, guiltily recalling the Chopin étude that Petrinski had given him to learn. For the past month he'd been sporadically laboring on the puzzling and difficult assignment, and although he'd initially discovered and overcome various mechanical difficulties, the exposition of the work's deeper meaning that his teacher demanded had grown progressively more remote, and his after-work practices correspondingly more difficult to face. Eventually, discouraged by his lack of progress, he'd given up.

"Travis?"

"I'm not playing in the competition," he said, feeling sick.

"What? You're withdrawing?"

"That's right."

"You haven't seen Petrinski for weeks, have you?"

"No. I . . . I'm thinking of quitting the piano."

Catheryn stared. "You can't be serious."

"Look, Mom. I know how much you want me to succeed, but I'm just not sure I'm cut out to be a musician."

"You're *already* a musician. What's gotten into you?"

Travis felt his palms beginning to sweat. "I . . ."

"Relax, Travis. I'm not going to bite."

"I know, Mom. I . . . I guess I'm just afraid of what you're going to say."

"And what do you think that is?"

"That you're disappointed in me. That I'm letting you down."

"Letting *me* down? This isn't about me. It's about *you*."

"Are you sure about that, Mom?" Travis rushed on, ashamed of what he was about to say but unable to stop. "You never went as far in your music as you wanted, having a family and all, and now—"

"Is that what you think?" Catheryn asked. "You think I could be that selfish? You think I want to relive lost opportunities through you?"

"Don't you? Why else would you push me so hard?"

"Oh, Travis, you couldn't be more wrong."

"Really, Mom?" said Travis stubbornly. "I know when it came to your music, you gave up a lot to have a family. You made sacrifices, and . . ."

"I sacrificed nothing." Leaning forward, Catheryn took her son's hands in hers and held them tightly. "Travis, I think a life in music is the finest existence anyone can experience," she said. "It's charged with beauty, inspiration, art, discovery—all the things that make being alive truly wonderful. And although things didn't work out for me as I originally planned, I've had all that, all of it, more than I ever hoped. I have no regrets about having a family. None." She paused, looking intently at her son. "But now it's your turn. I want the very best for you, Travis. I want you to be as happy as I have been."

"I know, Mom."

"Then promise me something. Promise you'll think long and hard about this before coming to a decision."

"I've already thought about it, Mom."

"Please, Travis. Promise."

Travis hesitated, torn between his doubts and fears and his mother's iron will. He thought back to the night of the party, hearing Petrinski's words ringing in his mind. *To find happiness one must first discover where one's abilities lie, then make the commitment to exploit them to their fullest.*

But what if his talent was just an accident of nature, signifying nothing?

Again he heard Petrinski. *You aren't Tommy. You're not your father, either. You're Travis Kane.*

"Trav?"

Travis knew his mother's request was not to be taken lightly. He hesitated a moment more. And then at last, with a conviction he longed to embrace . . . he gave his word.

•   •   •

Afterward, miserable and confused, Travis retreated up the stairs. But instead of returning to his room, he knocked on Allison's door— partly to apologize for his impolitic comment during dinner regard-

ing her reclusive behavior and partly to discuss his troubling talk with
Catheryn.

"Ali?" he called. "It's me. Can I come in?" Assuming from the
silence that she'd decided to ignore him, he turned the knob.

Allison's room was deserted. Travis glanced around, noticing she'd
left her bedside light on, as well as her new computer. He started to
leave, but hesitated when a slight rustling caught his attention. He
turned. As he watched, the printer slowly ejected a sheet of paper.

Travis crossed to the desk. He glanced at the door, then picked up
a thin pile of sheets that had collected in the printer tray. It was
Allison's latest story. Although she'd refused to discuss it, he knew
she'd been working on it for weeks. Apparently she'd spent the afternoon typing it into her computer.

Feeling strangely guilty, he began to read.

Titled "Jessie," it told of a nine-year-old boy named Paul who,
following the death of his parents, had gone to live with his aunt and
uncle on their dairy farm in Minnesota. Although they accepted him
wholeheartedly and loved him as their own, their teenaged daughter
Jessie did not. Travis quickly flipped through the pages, realizing his
sister's most recent work contained a dark, brooding intensity he'd
never noticed in her earlier writing. He glanced again at the door and
then continued reading.

We had a four-mile walk to a crossroads where the bus picked us up
for school. In winter we could shave the distance by taking a path
through the pines, then crossing the frozen river. We were forbidden
to go that way, so naturally we always took it, provided the snow
hadn't drifted too deep. That day we'd gotten off the bus after school
and Jessie had headed into the woods, taking the shortcut home. By
then the ice covering the river had thinned in spots, and I worried
every time we crossed it. Nonetheless, I trudged along behind, keeping my customary distance. I figured Jessie knew what she was doing—
after all, she *was* fifteen.

When we reached the river, the sun had already begun to slip behind the mountains flanking the western bank of the valley, and a
chilling wind had picked up. Eager to get home, I increased my pace.
All of a sudden I noticed a man following Jessie, paralleling her course

along the river's edge. He looked like one of the pulp-mill workers who'd drifted into town earlier that winter, hoping for work. I fell back and shadowed him, wondering what he was doing.

He stayed in the trees, stalking her, taking care to remain hidden until she broke into a clearing by the river. I should have done something—called out, warned her, run for help—but I didn't. I was too frightened.

And then it was too late.

He caught up with her in an instant. I trembled in the shadows, unable to move. Jessie struggled, fought like a cat. I heard him laugh as he doubled his fist and hit her. Then he jerked her jacket over her head, covering her face and trapping her arms. Brutally, he pulled her jeans down around her ankles and ripped off her underwear.

Jessie was crying but she kept on fighting, kicking out blindly. The man held her down with his knee and punched into her jacket, smashing at her until she lay still. Then he undid his belt.

It was over in minutes. Although I couldn't move, I couldn't tear my eyes from the horror of the scene before me, either. I just . . . watched. As long as I live, I'll never forget my feelings that day of helplessness, self-loathing, and despair.

When he finished, the man pulled up his pants and fastened his belt. Jessie lay crumpled at his feet, her legs smeared with blood. He lifted her, hefting her over his shoulder like a sack of garbage, and set out on the frozen river toward a hole fishermen had cut the previous weekend. We'd passed it every day on the way to school, and I knew only a thin film of ice now covered it. With a sinking feeling, I realized the man didn't intend to let Jessie go.

I had to do something . . . *but what?* I was no match for him. And if I revealed myself, he'd kill me, too. But whatever happened, I knew I couldn't simply watch as he took her life. Without thinking, I grabbed a baseball-sized chunk of river rock and slipped onto the ice behind him.

Disturbed, Travis went to the door and peered into the hall. "Ali?" he called. Receiving no response, he returned to the printer and picked up several sheets that had accumulated in the tray as he'd been reading. Flipping ahead, he scanned the final few pages.

The stone glanced off his temple. It hurt him, but not enough.

I stood dumbfounded as he whirled to face me. "You little bastard," he snarled, wiping blood from his face. Then he grinned, and I knew we'd both had the same realization: *I was out of rocks, and I couldn't outrun him.*

He covered the last few yards to the hole in a heartbeat. Jessie screamed as he threw her in. With a cracking sound, her body broke through the crust. Then he turned to me. I glanced at the shoreline, knowing I'd never make it. Even if I did, he'd quickly catch me in the woods. I hesitated, then sprinted for the center of the river, heading toward the thin section we'd been avoiding all week. I hoped he'd follow.

He did.

He'd nearly caught up when the ice abruptly gave way beneath him. Narrowly avoiding going in myself, I stood on the creaking surface, watching him thrash in the freezing water.

Then I remembered Jessie.

Praying she'd still be there, I made a wide circle around the broken section and returned to the hole where he'd thrown her in. I found her clinging to the edge. The river was flowing sluggishly beneath the ice, but with enough force to drag her legs under the perimeter. "Jessie, hang on!" I yelled, scrabbling through a pile of firewood the fishermen had left. I needed a piece long enough to span the hole. The best I found was a three-foot length of two-by-four.

Too short. Maybe onshore.

"Hang on!" I yelled again, starting for the woods.

"No time," Jessie mumbled, her teeth chattering. "Get me out."

The current had begun to pull her under.

Stretching out on the ice, I extended my hand. She took it. Her grip felt weak, her skin as cold as death. "My wrist, Jessie," I shouted. "Grab my wrist!"

"Wha . . . ?"

"The fireman's grip. I can't hold you otherwise."

She shifted her hand. She grasped my wrist, and I hers. It felt solid, but I knew I didn't have the strength to pull her out.

"You've gotta help."

"I can't."

"Yes, you can. Throw a leg over the edge. You can do it."

Inch by inch Jessie struggled from the hole. Finally she rolled onto the ice. Shivering violently, she pulled on her wet clothes, covering her nakedness. Without warning a loud crack sounded on the ice behind us, and something else. Something moving.

Jessie wasn't the only one who'd made it out.

Somehow the man had managed to pull himself up on the shelf. Moving on his hands and knees, he started working his way toward us.

After all that, I thought bitterly, *we're no better off than before.*

All at once the frozen surface gave way beneath him again.

"Jessie, let's go! Run!"

"No."

"Please," I begged, pulling at her arm.

"No, Paul. He'll get out again. He'll catch us before we get to the road."

I knew she was right. The best we could do was split up; maybe one of us would escape. "What should we do?" I asked, my voice trembling.

She picked up the two-by-four I'd discarded. "Stop him."

I followed her out on the ice. By the time we reached him, he'd moved to a thicker section and already had a leg over the edge. I watched as Jessie raised the two-by-four high over her head and brought it crashing down.

She drove him back. Blood poured from his nose, staining the water around him. But he was strong. He wouldn't give up.

Every time he came close to making it out, Jessie was there.

He lasted fifteen minutes. I saw the fury in his eyes turn to surprise, then pleading, and finally despair as he realized he was going to die. In the end, the current simply took him under the ice. We watched as his shadow moved slowly downriver beneath the surface.

"Jesus," I said, trying hard not to cry.

Jessie threw her bloody club into the water. It bobbed a second; then the current took it away, too. After it disappeared, she put her arms around me and held me tightly. I could feel her body shaking under her wet clothes. "You saved my life," she said.

I looked away, feeling a rush of shame. "I . . . I wanted to do something earlier, but . . ."

"You saved my life. I'll never forget it. Never." Then her voice

hardened. "I had to do what I did. He would have caught us and . . .
I couldn't let him get out. You understand, don't you?"

I nodded, not trusting myself to speak.

"Then it's over. We're not going to tell anyone about this."

"But you're hurt. What will you say to your folks?"

"I'll make up something. Please, Paul. I don't think anyone would
understand, not really. And even if they did . . . Look, I just want to
put this behind us. Will you promise?"

I thought for a long, searching moment. "I promise," I said at last.

• • •

Neither of us ever spoke of that day again, but it wasn't forgotten. I
kept that promise, and it became a silent covenant of trust between us,
a bond that drew us together, something we shared alone. And
through all the years that followed, after Dad died and Mom sold the
farm to one of the big conglomerates that took over in the sixties, after
Jessie moved to California and I to New York, it held us still.

Travis paused, puzzling over the grisly scene his sister had described in such detail, almost as if . . . Suddenly he felt a presence
behind him.

"What are you doing here?"

Travis turned to see Allison standing in the doorway.

"Oh, hi, Ali. I, uh . . ."

Allison saw the sheets in Travis's hand. "Damn you," she cried,
rushing across the room and tearing them from his grasp.

"I . . . I'm sorry. I came looking for you. I didn't mean to pry."

Allison shoved the papers into a desk drawer, then whirled to face
him. "You didn't, huh? Well, you did. Now, get out."

"You write stories for strangers to read in magazines. I didn't think
you'd—"

"You thought wrong," Allison yelled. She crossed to the door and
flung it open. "Get out."

"Ali, I'm sorry." Travis tried to say something more, but before
he could, she shoved him out and firmly closed the door behind
him.

Travis hesitated. Then, instead of leaving, he knocked softly on the door. When Allison didn't answer, he reentered. He found her sitting on her bed, staring with angry, swollen eyes at the beach below her window.

"What now, Trav?" she said. "Come back to paw through my underwear drawer? Maybe you'd like to read my diary while you're at it."

Travis regarded her for several seconds. "Ali, I never thought I'd say this, but I'd rather see you angry, even at me, than so depressed."

Allison didn't answer.

"That guy did a lot more than beat you up, didn't he?"

Still Allison said nothing.

"Didn't he?"

"Shut up."

Travis stared in bewilderment. "Why didn't you tell?"

Ignoring her brother's question, Allison began lethargically plucking invisible pieces of lint from her bedspread, worrying the fabric with dull, mechanical precision.

"Why, Ali?"

Finally she raised her eyes. "Why should I tell? So Dad can fly off the handle and take it out on Mom? So Mom can drown me in sympathy and make me feel like shit? So everybody at school next year can point and stare? The guy's dead, Trav. What are we gonna do—dig him up and shoot him again?"

"You can't keep something like this secret."

"Oh, yeah? I've already got enough problems fitting in around here. I sure as hell don't need any more."

"Ali—"

"Would *you* want to live with everyone's pity the rest of your life?"

"No, but—"

"Right. Neither do I. Besides, what good could possibly come from telling?"

"I don't know, but something's wrong keeping it all inside. I mean . . . maybe you should talk to someone."

"I am talking to someone. You."

"I meant somebody more qualified."

"Like that shrink Mom took me to?" asked Allison bitterly. "Hell, why spend good money to have some creep ask me how I *feel* about pluggin' that dirtbag?" she muttered, dropping into a rancorous lampoon of their father. "I feel shitty about it. That's natural. I'll get over it. I'm a Kane."

"This may be hard to imagine," said Travis, "but there *are* people who know slightly more than Dad about things like this."

"I'm not talking to anyone. And if you tell, I swear I'll kill you. Or myself. I'm not kidding, Trav."

"I'm supposed to keep quiet like the kid in your story? This isn't make-believe, Ali. This is real."

"No one else is ever going to read that story, and you're going to keep your mouth shut. If you don't, I'll—"

"You made Nate promise, too," Travis interrupted as the pieces suddenly slipped into place. "I didn't buy his sleeping through all that. Here I thought you were lying to protect him. You weren't protecting him at all. You were protecting yourself."

"You don't know anything," Allison spat. "I haven't told you anything, not one damn thing, and I'm not going to. And if you ever open your mouth about tonight, you'll be sorry. Now, get the hell out of here and leave me alone."

"Allison, you're acting as though what happened was your fault. You don't have any reason to be ashamed."

"I'm not ashamed!"

"You're sure acting like it."

"Fuck off, Travis," Allison shouted. "I don't need an amateur psych evaluation from you."

Travis paused, staring in open bewilderment. "I don't understand you," he said. "I don't understand you at all."

"Who asked you to?"

"Nobody. I . . . I just want to help."

"You and everybody else."

"Listen, Ali—"

"No, *you* listen," Allison yelled, tears now shimmering in her eyes. "I won't be a victim, Travis, I won't."

At that moment Travis was struck by how much his sister, in her fierce determination, reminded him of their father. He shook his head, surprised he'd never seen the resemblance before.

"The only thing you can do for me right now is keep your mouth shut," Allison continued, angrily palming away her tears. "Can you do that?"

"Ali, I . . ."

"Please, Travis."

Not sure what to do, Travis thought carefully. Finally he folded his arms and sighed. "I think you're making a big mistake, but if that's what you want . . . I'll go along," he said. "For now, anyway."

"Forever. Say it, Travis."

"Not forever. But until you come to your senses—which you will—I'll keep quiet."

Allison briefly held Travis's gaze, then resumed her vigil at the window.

Numbly, Travis walked to the door, thinking it had been a night for promises. He turned, struggling for words. "Ali, I'm so sorry this happened to you," he said. "I wish you would—"

"Enough. We're done talking. Get out of here."

"Okay. I'm leaving." Still Travis hesitated. "If you ever, well . . . just don't forget you have a family, and we love you."

Allison flung herself facedown on the bed. "I know that, Trav," she said, her voice muffled by the pillow. "Thanks. Now get lost."

20

Early Friday morning Travis punched his work card for the final time. Filled with a bittersweet feeling of regret, he stepped from the construction trailer and stood outside for a moment, breathing in the cool ocean air. Then, shaking off his feeling of nostalgia, he headed across the street to pick up his tools. He'd be working that day with Pete Wilson, as he had for weeks, running trim in one of the nearly completed houses.

Travis enjoyed assisting the amiable older man, with whom he'd formed an easygoing friendship over the past few months. They worked together now as a smoothly functioning team—Travis pulling his share of the load and concurrently serving a time-honored apprenticeship in the techniques of woodworking. He'd picked up a lot from Pete, a master carpenter, which gave him a gratifying sense of accomplishment. The assignment to Pete had also conferred another benefit—it had kept him away from Junior Cobb.

Since the affair on the scaffold Travis had avoided the surly youth as if his life depended on it. *And it might*, he thought grimly. Two weeks back Junior had "accidentally" dropped his hammer while working on the roof, narrowly missing Travis as he'd passed beneath.

And a week later someone had cut partway through the underside of a two-by-ten plank he'd been using to span a gap on the second floor. Luckily Pete had spotted it, saving him a dangerous fall.

Despite their father's warning to let Travis fight his own battles, Tommy had confronted Junior after the second incident. Although he'd denied everything, Junior had subsequently restricted his animus to tormenting Travis verbally whenever he got the opportunity. "*Move*, pussy," he'd growl whenever he approached the younger boy, much to the amusement of his friends. Travis had reacted by giving Junior a wide berth, and so far had been able to avoid an out-and-out fight.

"Last day, eh, kid?" said Pete, looking up from a stack of trim as Travis struggled in with the chop saw they'd be using that morning. "Gonna come visit sometime?"

"Morning, Pete," said Travis. Setting the heavy saw on the cutting table, he glanced with satisfaction around the wood-rich interior of the house. "Yeah, I might just do that. See how the place finishes out. What do you think it'll take—another week or so?"

"Yeah, probably."

"Good. We'll be back from our trip by then."

"You're leavin' tomorrow?"

"Uh-huh. But Tommy and I will definitely stop by before he takes off for Arizona."

"Do that. Meantime, let's get to work. This stuff ain't gonna nail itself up." Pete glared at a number of trim pieces he'd been inspecting, then tossed them back onto the pile. "Which reminds me. Tell Wes we're gonna need more wood. Half this shit's crooked enough to run for Congress."

The morning passed quickly, and at eleven-thirty Travis joined Tommy for lunch. Since the brothers now worked on different crews, they rarely ran into each other during the day but usually managed to get together during the break. As they ate, Travis noticed his brother seemed strangely preoccupied. After wolfing down his burrito, Tommy made his way to the pay phone, finally returning just as lunch period ended. "You seen Tony?" he asked, glancing around the site. "I've gotta take off."

"He's in the trailer. What's up?"

"I have to drive Christy somewhere."

"Now?"

"Yeah."

"Can't her mom do that?"

"She's working."

"Is Christy all right?"

"She's fine. Look, I've gotta go. Just tell Tony something came up. I probably won't be back by quitting time, so catch a ride home with one of the guys." Tommy turned and started for his car, adding, "Grab my paycheck for me too, okay?"

"Sure. But you'd better keep tonight open," Travis called after him. "Remember what Dad said last week at dinner? I've a feeling he's got something planned."

"No problem, bro. See you at home."

At the end of the day Travis arranged to get a ride with Roland Grisham, who lived in Topanga and agreed to drop him off at the beach on his way home. After returning the chop saw to the equipment shed, Travis waited as Roland loaded his tools into a lock bin on the back of his truck. Because it was Friday, most of the crew had skipped their customary after-work bull session, but nearly everyone had taken time to say good-bye to Travis—clapping him on the back and wishing him luck. Now, as he stood watching a steady stream of cars heading down the hill, Travis felt strangely depressed. With a shrug he turned and started back through the project, deciding to take one final tour.

•   •   •

At the bottom of the hill, Kane and Allison sat in the Suburban. Irritably drumming his fingers on the steering wheel, Kane surveyed the dusty exodus of cars and trucks winding slowly past. "Where the hell are they?" he grumbled. "They better not have left."

"I still don't understand why you didn't just meet them back at the house," said Allison dully.

"I want to surprise 'em, that's why," said Kane. "Plus we're goin' someplace from here. Now quit your bellyachin'. We'll give it a few more seconds, then drive on up. Besides, it's time you got out of your room," he added. "Do you good."

"Dad, even if they are still here, I've only got a learner's permit. I'm not old enough to drive the Bronco home alone."

"Don't worry, cupcake. It's only a couple miles. You'll be back home havin' dinner with your mom before you know it."

"But—"

"Quit worrying, kid. If you get stopped, I'll bail you out."

"Gee, thanks," said Allison with a sigh of exasperation. "You know, Pop, Tommy and Trav might already have plans for tonight."

"Then they can change 'em. Tom's not gonna be around much longer. Him and me are gonna do some celebrating, whether he likes it or not. Travis too, of course."

"Of course," Allison noted dryly. "Tell me, Dad. What wonderful male-type activities do you have scheduled for tonight? Load up at the liquor store, then hit the nudie bars in Oxnard?"

"Nah," said Kane. "Your mom wouldn't approve of that." Impatiently, he slammed the Suburban into gear. "Time to go find 'em. We've waited long enough."

"So what *is* on tonight's agenda?"

"Have you seen the waves that've been rolling in since yesterday?" asked Kane, his voice rising a notch with excitement. "Five- to six-footers. We're headin' down to the beach right here at Paradise Cove—do a little bodysurfing, use their outside showers—then throw on clean shorts and grab some steaks at the Sand Castle restaurant. I brought the guys a change of clothes, along with a few other necessary items," he added, glancing at the cooler in the back.

Earlier Allison had seen her father loading it with ice and beers. "Should be quite a night," she observed without enthusiasm.

Kane topped the hill and pulled into the dirt parking lot. "I still don't see Tom's car," he said, looking disappointed. He twisted off the engine. "C'mon, let's go find out where they went."

"I'll stay here, Dad."

"Suit yourself."

Allison watched as Kane crossed the parking lot. A moment later she saw him stop to talk with a man she recognized from the party. Before long Kane and his friend had their heads stuck under the hood of a customized Chevy pickup. Hot, bored, and realizing her father would probably be gone longer than expected, Allison stepped from the Suburban and started toward the edge of the bluff, hoping to catch a breeze from the ocean. Partway over she passed a small knot of men gathered by the construction trailer.

"Lookin' for somebody, miss?" one of the younger men in the group asked politely.

"Uh, yeah," Allison answered, disarmed by the worker's pleasant demeanor. "I'm trying to find my brothers Tom and Trav. Tall guys—red hair, brown noses. Seen them around?"

"I haven't seen Tommy, but Trav's around here somewhere," the man chuckled. "Hey, anybody know where Travis is?" he called out.

"Who wants to know?"

Allison turned to see a huge, muscular youth with a pimply face and stringy blond hair stepping from a cul-de-sac formed by the equipment shed and a metal Dumpster beside the trailer. Two men followed him out, one holding the smoldering remnant of a hand-rolled cigarette. Allison smelled the sickly sweet odor of marijuana.

"This is Kane's sister, Junior," the first worker answered nervously, stepping aside as the heavily built man bulled his way through the group. "She's lookin' for her brother."

"She is, huh?" Junior stepped in front of Allison, crowding in just a little too close. Allison retreated a step. Junior moved closer, then reached out and felt her hair, running it between his fingers as though he were examining a piece of cloth.

"This red shit makes your brothers look like a couple of fags, but I kinda go for it on you," he said with a grin. Then, cupping his crotch, "Speakin' of redheads, I've got one right here that'd like to make your acquaintance. What do you say?"

Allison pulled free, a cold trickle building under her arms.

"Aw, don't go, Red," laughed Junior, grabbing her arm. "We're just gettin' to know each other."

The men who'd been standing by the trailer shifted uncomfortably. "Hey, Junior, take it easy," said the soft-spoken one who'd greeted Allison earlier. "Leave her alone."

"You gonna make me, Roland?"

Roland spread his hands. "Come on, Junior—"

" 'Cause if you ain't, shut the fuck up. We're just havin' a little fun. Right, babe?"

Just then Travis rounded the corner, making his way back from his final survey. Quickly assessing the situation, he hurried over. "Knock it off, Cobb," he ordered.

"Well, well. Baby brother to the rescue, eh?" Junior released Allison and regarded Travis with a mixture of menace and surprise. "Didn't think you had it in you, pussy."

"Allison, get out of here," said Travis quietly.

"Yeah, go on," said Junior. Then he shoved Travis, sending him stumbling toward the cul-de-sac beside the trailer. "Me and the pussy here got some unfinished business."

Allison turned and ran. "I'll get Dad," she yelled back.

"No!" Travis called after her.

"That's right. He'd rather have his mommy." Junior shoved Travis again, this time sending him sprawling to the ground. "Is this how you defend your little sister, pussy?" he demanded. "Lying down?"

"Fuck you," Travis grunted, scrambling to his knees.

"Fuck me?" Junior snorted, taking careful aim and smashing his boot on Travis's hip. "You'd like to, wouldn't you, faggot?"

Travis scrabbled away on his hands and knees, narrowly avoiding a second kick. As he rose, he realized that Junior had him trapped in the alcove.

Junior moved forward, bracing him against a stack of lumber. "Maybe you just want to suck my dick," he suggested, spraying spittle as he spoke. "Say it, pussy. Say you want to suck my dick." He backhanded Travis across the face. "Say it."

"No."

Junior hit him again. His high-school football ring opened a cut on Travis's cheek. "Say it."

"No."

As Junior drew back for another blow, a heavy hand descended on his shoulder and spun him around. "What's goin' on here?"

Junior's eyes narrowed as he sized up the man who'd grabbed him. He took in the suit coat and tie, the black wing-tip shoes, and the thick, unruly shock of red hair. Unfortunately, he missed the choleric gleam in the man's eyes.

"I'd take that off, 'less you want to lose it," Junior warned.

"Is that right? Okay, no problem." Kane thrust his hands into his pockets. "Now, tell me what's goin' on."

Junior smiled as his two pot-smoking friends moved to stand beside him. "Sure," he said, glancing at Kane's hair. "By the way, old-timer, it's sure easy to see where your kids get their shitty looks."

"Dad, let's just leave," Travis begged, attempting to push past Junior.

"You ain't going nowhere," Junior hissed, blocking his way.

Kane stared at Junior. "I asked you something," he said. "I'm not gonna ask again."

"Back off, gramps," said Junior. "What's goin' on here is I'm teachin' your chickenshit kid he can't hide behind his big brother forever. He's been beggin' for trouble all summer. Now he's gonna get it. Unless, of course, he'd rather suck my dick to apologize."

"Shut up, Junior," said Travis.

Kane glared at his son. "Is that true? You been dodgin' a fight with this turd?"

"Dad, nothing happened," said Allison, tugging at her father's arm. "Please, let's just leave."

Kane shook off her hand. "Is what he said true?"

Travis glanced at Junior, and then back at his father. "I, uh . . ."

"I want an answer, Travis."

Travis shrugged. "I guess so."

"You *guess* so?"

Travis straightened. "Yes, sir. It's true."

Kane's expression tightened. "Are you gonna let this asshole push you around?"

"Dad, I—"

"He's begging to get his ass kicked. What are you gonna do about it?"

"Fuck off, old man," Junior ordered. Then, to Travis, "This is between you and me, pussy. Or are you gonna hide behind your daddy here now that Tommy ain't around?"

Travis felt his father's eyes burning into him.

"Maybe I should just whip your old man's ass instead," Junior continued, placing his hand on Travis's chest and giving him another shove, pushing him back into the alcove. "What's it gonna be, chickenshit?"

An agitated silence gripped the onlookers.

"Yeah Travis," said Kane slowly. "What's it gonna be?"

Junior smiled, pleased with the unexpected turn of events. "Yeah. Show your old man what you've got," he said. "I'll tell you what— I'll give you the first shot. Hell, I'll even keep one hand behind my back."

Travis met his father's cold, inscrutable stare. With a look of resignation, he raised his hands.

Grinning, Junior circled in. Travis feinted and threw his left, unexpectedly connecting with a short jab. A low snarl ripped from Junior's throat. He stormed forward, descending on the younger boy with a whirlwind of blows. Seconds later Travis lay at his feet, blood gushing from his nose.

"Get up," Kane commanded.

"That's right, pussy," crowed Junior. "Come and get it."

Travis rose to his feet. Again he raised his hands. Junior rushed in once more, easily driving through Travis's ineffectual defense. Two hard blows landed in rapid succession, flattening Travis's nose and splitting his upper lip. A punishing right cross to the temple sent him down.

"Get up, pussy. Plenty more where that came from."

Travis shook his head to clear it.

"Get up, Travis," Kane repeated, ignoring looks of disapproval from everyone present. Everyone but Junior.

Bleeding from the nose and mouth, Travis wobbled to a standing position. Junior stepped in again.

"No!" screamed Allison, thrusting herself between the two. "Daddy, stop this!"

Before anyone could react, Junior pushed her to the ground. "Be patient, honey," he laughed, moving to stand over her. "You'll get your turn next."

Kane started forward. Before he could intervene, Travis drove in from the side, throwing with everything he had. A solid right caught Junior full in the mouth.

Junior staggered back, wiping his bloodied lips with the back of his hand. With a bellow of rage, he again smashed past Travis's feckless resistance, all thought of toying with his smaller opponent gone. His knuckles connected with devastating results.

Barely conscious, Travis slipped to the ground. Not satisfied, Junior knelt on his chest and drew back his fist for another blow. Before he could throw it, Kane pulled him off.

"Enough."

"Fuck you, old man. *I'll* say what's enough."

Ignoring Junior, Kane dragged Travis to his feet. Allison rushed forward to help.

Junior's face darkened with rage. "I told you to stay out of this," he barked at Kane. Without warning he threw a roundhouse right. Kane reacted with blinding speed. His thick fingers closed on Junior's fist, stopping it inches from his face.

Junior's eyes widened in surprise. He tried to retrieve his hand. Couldn't. An instant later, still holding the youth's fist trapped in his left, Kane's right hand flashed out and latched onto Junior's nose. Using a pinch that could easily crack walnuts, he began to squeeze.

"Get him off, get him off," Junior squealed in agony.

One of Junior's friends moved in from behind. Without turning, Kane released Junior's fist and threw his left elbow. The man's head snapped back. Groaning, he sank to his knees, holding his smashed and ruined mouth in his hands.

"You cocksucker! Lemme go!" Junior pleaded, tears now mixing with the unction of blood running down his face.

The sinews of Kane's right forearm rolled under his skin like steel cables as he increased the pressure between his thumb and forefinger. Grinning coldly, he shook Junior's head with the brutal, mindless jubilation of a terrier killing a rat. Blood squirted through his fingers as if he were pulping a fruit. Everyone present heard a sickening crack as Junior's nasal bones crunched beneath his fingers.

"Oh, Jesus, lemme go, lemme go," Junior blubbered, a gush of red spattering the dirt at his feet.

Kane twisted, forcing the burly youth to his knees in a genuflection of agony.

"Let him go, Dad," said Travis. "Please."

"You and your sister get in the car."

"Don't, Dad," begged Allison, who from long experience recognized the unmistakable signs, as did Travis, that their father had crossed a cruel and dangerous limit, an irreversible portal past which anything could happen. "Please let him go."

Kane ignored his daughter's plea. "You wanna fight me, punk?" he asked, glaring at Junior.

"No, no, no," Junior shrieked. "Just lemme go."

"I think you do. I'll tell you what—I'll give you the first shot," Kane snarled, echoing Junior's earlier offer. "Hell, I'll even keep one hand behind my back."

"Please, please. No more."

"You don't wanna fight?" Kane released Junior's nose. Roughly, he wiped his bloodstained hand on the youth's chest. "Fine," he said. "But by way of apologizing, you're gonna do something for me."

Still on his knees and trapped in the alcove with no hope of escape, Junior lowered his head, unable to meet Kane's icy gaze. "What?"

"I can overlook your comments regarding my son Travis," Kane said slowly. "I can even overlook your callin' me a cocksucker. What I can't overlook is what you did to my shoes."

"Huh?"

"Look at 'em."

Junior glanced down. His nose had dripped on Kane's shoes, staining the surfaces and filling the ornate perforations in the leather wing caps with blood.

"Clean 'em."

"You want me to clean your shoes?"

"That's right," said Kane, his voice as hard as steel.

Holding his gushing nose in one hand, Junior clumsily wiped at the stains on Kane's shoes with the other.

"Not that way. Use your shirt."

"What?"

"Use your shirt."

Junior hesitated. His eyes darted past Kane, searching some avenue of retreat, some hope of assistance. He found nothing. Slowly, he removed his shirt.

A deadly quiet fell over the group. Sick with fear but unable to look away, Travis and Allison stood mutely with the others, watching in queasy fascination and shameful horror as Junior Cobb cleaned their father's shoes.

•   •   •

Later that evening, long after the rest of the household had settled in for the night, Travis and Tommy lay awake in their room. "Dad did that?" Tommy whispered from the darkness.

"Yeah."

"Must've been something to watch. I'm sorry I missed it."

"No, you aren't, Tom. It was, I don't know . . . scary. Everybody was afraid to stop it. In the end Junior was down on his hands and knees, sniveling like a baby. His nose kept dripping on Dad's shoes as he cleaned them, so every time he'd about finished, he had to start over. I've never seen Dad like that. I don't want to ever again."

"Junior had it coming."

"Yeah. But you want to hear something weird? I never thought I'd say this, but . . . I almost felt sorry for him. It was like watching a live disaster happening on TV. You know, where people are dying and all kinds of shitty things are going on and it's turning your stomach but you can't look away; and all the time, though you're ashamed to admit it, you're secretly congratulating yourself it isn't you."

"Fuck Junior. I'm still sorry I missed it."

Travis remained silent, realizing Tommy couldn't truly comprehend what had occurred on the job site that afternoon without actually being there. His brother had arrived home late that evening and had missed most of the bitter confrontation between Catheryn and Kane that had followed, too.

"Did Dad say anything to you on the way home?"

"Not a word," said Travis, his stomach churning as he remembered Kane's ominous silence on the ride back. All at once he recalled the reason his brother hadn't been present. "How's Christy?" he asked. "Did you get her to wherever she had to go okay?"

"We never made it."

"Why not?"

Tommy hesitated. "We had an argument on the way over," he said finally. "She decided she didn't need to go."

"Go where?"

"Never mind. It doesn't matter." Then, quickly changing the subject, "Sounds like Dad really lost it today."

"Yeah. I wonder what it would take to get him that mad at one of us."

"Who knows? Burn down the house, wreck his car, say something bad about the Chicago Bears . . ."

"How 'bout tellin' him we plan on climbing that wall?"

"Shhhh. Jeez, Travis, do you have a death wish or something?"

"He can't hear us in here. What do you think? Would that do it?"

"Probably," Tommy conceded. "Think Dad'll check to see whether our climbing gear's still in the closet?"

"Definitely. But since we're borrowing Brian's, he'll never suspect," Travis answered, referring to a friend with whom he and Tommy occasionally climbed. "By the way, have you got that lined up?"

"Yeah. He's leaving it in his garage. We'll pick it up on the way out."

"Brian's gonna be up at five in the morning?"

"You kidding? He said he'd leave the side door unlocked. We'll just grab his rope and rack and be on our way."

"Are you sure you want to do this? Dad wasn't kidding when he ordered us not to."

"Jesus, Trav," muttered Tommy. "Do you plan on doing exactly as Dad says for the rest of your life? I sure as hell don't."

"I'm just saying—"

"I know what you're saying. And I'm saying I don't give a shit. Dad thinks he can plan out my whole fucking life, but he's wrong."

"I thought we were talking about climbing the wall."

"We are. Are you in?"

"Yeah, I'm in," said Travis reluctantly. "If nothing else, it'll get us out of the house," he added, again recalling the fierce argument that had raged between his parents over his fight with Junior.

"Right," Tommy agreed. "Things are gonna be pretty tense around here for a while. You feel okay enough to climb?"

"I think so. Junior didn't bust me up that bad."

"Ali said you got in a couple pretty good licks yourself."

"A couple," Travis admitted.

"Good. I'm proud of you, bro." Then, in an apparent non sequitur, "What do you think Dad's reaction would be if I told him I'd decided not to go to college? What if I told him I'd decided to apply to the police academy instead?"

"Huh? Oh, I get it. We're still on 'What would it take to push Dad over the edge,' right?"

"I'm serious. What do you think he'd say?"

"You're not really thinking about it, are you?"

"I don't know. I mean, what's the point of my spending four more years in school? The only reason I got accepted to college in the first place is 'cause I can snag a football. You and Ali and Nate are the ones with the brains. I'd just be spinning my wheels, and when I graduated—assuming I did—I'd be no further ahead. At least if I start now, I can get going on some kinda career."

"Like being a cop?"

"What's wrong with that?"

"I don't know. Look what it did to Dad."

"I'm not Dad," Tommy said stubbornly.

"He's dead set on your going to college, Tom. You know that."

"So?"

"Jesus, Tommy, you can't really be—"

"Look, it's just something I'm thinking about. Forget I said anything."

"But—"

"Don't worry, I'm not gonna do anything crazy."

"Are you sure?"

"Yeah, I'm sure," Tommy said firmly. "Now, let's get some sleep. We've got a long day tomorrow."

"Okay," said Travis—still bothered by his brother's words, but sensing the subject was closed. "Good night, Tommy."

"Night, Trav."

•   •   •

Within minutes Travis could hear the sound of Tommy's rhythmic snores drifting across the room, mixing in syncopated counterpoint with the waves crashing on the beach. The moon had risen, and cold slivers of light now reflected from the ocean's surface, sending an arctic phantasm of light and shadow dancing into their room. Instead of sleeping, Travis lay in bed watching the ghostly flickerings on the ceiling and pondering the events of the day, trying to decipher the brutal images that had been indelibly burned into his mind, struggling with questions of courage and cowardice and fear.

He lay awake a very long time.

PART THREE

21

"Belay on."

"Climbing."

Heart pounding, Travis edged out from the safety of the embrasure, his back to the drop. Using opposing pressure on the flaring walls, he moved out carefully—eyeing a handhold higher up. He swung his left foot onto the face, finding a toehold on a small nubbin. Gingerly, he transferred weight to his foot. Attempting to ignore the vast, sickening plunge beneath, he squinted up the sheer vertical expanse. After surmounting the chockstone he'd have a respite on top, then a face climb using a series of small finger cracks to the ledge above the main overhang.

"I assume you'll need plenty of slack for this move—say, fifteen or twenty feet," offered Tommy from his perch in the cave, clearly enjoying his brother's apprehension.

"Screw you. Just keep that rope tight."

"Hold on a sec. I gotta pick my nose."

Although irritated by Tommy's cavalier humor, Travis recognized it for what it was: an attempt to decrease the anxiety level and, at the same time, goad him into making the difficult and exposed move. Thanks to his hesitation, Travis's left leg had already begun to tire.

He realized he had to do something. Soon. He considered placing a second piece. Rejected it. No time. Besides, the first nut looked solid, and Tommy would recognize another placement as a patent indication of fear, as manifest and unmistakable as writing on a billboard.

"Anytime, bro."

His leg trembling now under the strain, Travis knew he'd reached a pivotal moment. He either had to proceed or retreat. Nervously, he placed his hand high in the slot and wedged his fingers between the chockstone and the wall. Leaning back on his arm, he brought his right foot to his waist, smearing his toe against the granite.

Weight on his right leg now . . . moving up through an adrenaline rush of excitement and fear, jamming a fist, his other foot finding a small flake, left hand scrabbling, searching for a hold . . . finding one, right leg up again . . .

. . . and over.

"Nice move, Trav. I missed the last part, though. How's about doin' it again?"

"Not a chance," Travis replied, cramming a small stopper in the crack above him. "I plan on enjoying the rest of this pitch."

"Don't let me stop you. I'll be down here takin' a little nap."

A moment later Travis started out once more, the sun warm on his back. He moved up smoothly on a nearly invisible series of nubbins, using tiny cracks in the surface for finger jams and an occasional piece of protection. Twenty feet higher the climbing relented to 5.9 or 5.10—still tricky and demanding, but within his ability—and with a surge of relief Travis felt the knots in his stomach beginning to loosen. He was leading the best pitch of his life, climbing as well as he'd ever climbed—moving surely, eyes and fingers exploring the rock above, his body following with fluid and unconscious grace.

A half hour later he traversed right to the sloping bulge, then shortly afterward gained the narrow shelf over the main overhang. He peered over the edge. The granite fell away to a small outcrop thirty-five feet down, past which it dropped in a dizzying plummet to the talus eight hundred feet below.

"You there yet?"

"Yeah. Off belay," Travis called down. "Gimme a minute to get in an anchor."

Glancing at the rack, Travis saw he'd used most of the small wired nuts and stoppers on the ascent, and, unfortunately, that was exactly what he now needed for the new anchor. Working with the equipment remaining on the rack, he finally got in two fairly good pieces: a medium stopper and a large Friend. As an afterthought he looped a nylon sling around a rock horn and added it to the system. Next he took a ten-foot bight at his end of the rope, tied a figure eight, and clipped it to his anchoring setup—securing himself to the rock at the end of a short tether. That done, he hauled in slack rope until he felt Tommy's weight at the other end.

"Belay on," he yelled down.

"Climbing."

Although from the ledge Travis couldn't see his brother, he could easily follow his progress by maintaining tension on the belay. Over the years he'd learned to read the rope, deciphering a rich texture of meaning in the pauses and hesitations, the rapid ascents and sudden strains, and the occasional jarring tugs. He concentrated as he felt Tommy pause at the chockstone, then shook his head in silent wonder as he took in rope seconds later, realizing Tommy had easily surmounted the overhang. A brief interruption followed for piece removal, then again rapid progress. Barely fifteen minutes had passed by the time Tommy's head topped the base of the ledge.

"Nice lead," said Tommy as he mantled onto the shelf. "Off belay."

"Thanks," said Travis. He stepped out of his belay, then tied a second figure eight in the rope near Tommy's belt, preparing to secure him to the anchor. "I gotta admit getting over the chockstone got my heart pounding a little."

Tommy grinned. "Me, too," he agreed, offering the wired nuts he'd retrieved on the way up. "Here."

Instead of taking the pieces, Travis clipped a carabiner through Tommy's figure eight. "Lemme anchor you in first."

Impatiently, Tommy shoved the hardware at Travis. "Just take 'em, Mr. Safety. We're standing on a ledge, for chrissake."

Shrugging, Travis took the nuts. As he did, a large stopper slipped through his fingers and skittered across the ledge.

"I've got it." Tommy grabbed, missed, then dropped to his knees and lunged. His hand closed on the stopper just before it slipped over the edge. "Like they say," he chuckled, holding up the piece triumphantly as he rose, "the hand is quicker than the—"

As he stood, Tommy cracked his head on the rock horn. He stumbled, nearly dislodging the anchor sling Travis had placed. He tried to catch himself, teetering for a long, terrible moment. In the passing of a heartbeat his expression changed from surprise and irritation to numb, mindless terror as he realized he was going over. "No . . ."

Travis's eyes widened as Tommy disappeared over the edge. He grabbed for the rope, watching in horror as the loose coils snaked after his brother. Trying for a belay, he whipped a loop of rope around his back. Too late.

His hands burning now as the rope shot through—faster, faster . . .

Tommy's scream grew distant. Heart in his throat, Travis braced for the final jerk, praying the anchor would hold. An instant later Tommy's weight hit the end.

The rope snapped tight, sweeping Travis over the edge.

•   •   •

"Tommy!"

No answer.

Fighting panic, Travis hung a body's length beneath the ledge, eight hundred feet above the valley floor. He peered wildly down the rope. "Tommy!"

Something running into his eyes.

Blood.

Travis squeezed them shut to clear his vision, then wiped his face on his shirt. Finally able to see, he stared into the sickening abyss.

The rope disappeared past the small outcrop thirty-five feet down. Tension on the line told him his brother was still at the other end.

Travis glanced up at the ledge. His breath caught in his throat. Both the stopper and Friend, the two pieces he'd placed as belay anchors, now dangled uselessly from the figure eight he'd tied in his end of the rope. Placing his feet against the wall, he leaned out on his short tether, noticing that only the sling he'd looped over the rock horn had held. With a chill, he saw it had slipped precariously close to the tip.

"Tommy!" he called again.

He heard only the rush of wind from across the canyon.

Once more Travis wiped his eyes. Exploring gingerly with his fingers, he felt a ragged gash on his forehead. That would have to wait. He had to get back onto the ledge.

Abruptly, the sling shifted.

Travis froze, realizing the slight swinging motion he'd initiated by leaning out on the rope could easily cause the last tenuous anchor to give way—sending both him and Tommy crashing to the rocks below. He held his breath. Then, sensing he had no other choice, he moved hand over hand up the rope and hooked his left ankle over the ledge. Gingerly, he tried to get a handhold on the wall.

No good. Sling won't hold much longer. Move!

All thought of style forgotten, Travis pulled with his left leg and jerked himself the rest of the way up, praying his movements didn't dislodge the anchor sling. They didn't. With a shudder of relief, he rolled over the lip and back onto the ledge. Quickly, he removed a Friend from the rack and crammed it into a crack above the rock horn, then attached a sling and clipped a carabiner through the figure eight he'd tied earlier. Not satisfied, he added another piece, also replacing the original two that had pulled out. At last he surveyed his work, ruefully thinking his beefed-up anchor smacked of locking the barn after the horses had already bolted. Fortunately, at least one had remained in its stall.

Travis spent the next several minutes shouting his brother's name down the granite face. Receiving no answer, he finally gave up.

What now?

Huddled against the rock, Travis stared at the snow-covered peaks across the valley. The sun had already crested and begun its descent to the west, shifting lengthening shadows up the canyon, and the billowing cumulus formations that had risen earlier in the afternoon were already beginning to disperse with the cooling of the land. Travis wrapped his arms around his chest, trying to stop his shaking.

Cold? he wondered. *Or just scared?*

He realized Tommy must be hurt—either unconscious, or worse. He refused to consider the latter. An entire rope length was a long drop, but survivable. Climbing ropes were designed to stretch during a fall, softening the jolt like a bungee. Tommy could have made it without sustaining serious injury, unless he'd hit something on the way down. Suddenly Travis remembered the outcrop he'd seen projecting from the face.

Feeling hopeless, he toyed with the metal descender hanging from his belt, tracing the two unequal circles of the rappelling device that, under different circumstances, could have allowed him to execute a controlled slide down the rope to his brother. Tommy's weight on the line now made its use impossible.

Go for help?

Good idea. But how?

Down-climb?

Impossible without a belay.

Wait for someone to come?

Could be days, if at all.

Bring Tommy up, then use the rope to descend in stages to the ground.

Bracing, Travis grabbed the rope and tugged for all he was worth. It didn't budge.

"Tommy! Say something, goddammit!"

His call echoed back unanswered.

One final option.

Gripped by a paralyzing wave of dread, Travis suddenly knew what he must do. But could he? *Admit it,* his inner voice whispered. *You're scared. More scared than you've ever been in your life. . . .*

Maybe I am. So what?

So this. Tom's hurt, and you're too afraid to help him.

No!

Admit it. You're so terrified you can't—

"Yeah, I'm scared," Travis said aloud. "But I know what I have to do, and I'll do it."

Trembling, he leaned over the edge, his mind roiling with fear. "Tommy, hang on," he yelled. "I don't know whether you can hear me, but hang on. I'm coming down."

Ignoring the blisters on his rope-burned palms, Travis quickly stripped the nylon laces from his shoes and tied together the ends, forming two separate loops. A short length of cord from the chalk bag provided a third. Next, lying on his stomach, he hung over the edge and wound the first loop around the climbing rope twice, then back through itself, creating a prusik knot—a type of slipknot that grabs under tension. If he used it carefully, Travis knew it could provide a primitive means of descending the rope. Primitive . . . and dangerous.

He repeated the process with the other loops he'd formed and attached nylon slings to all three—double lengths on the lower two for his feet, a single sling on the top knot running to his sit-harness.

A moment to check the setup. A deep breath. Time to go.

A rush of mind-numbing terror washed over Travis as he swung his right foot into the lowest sling. The prusik held. The left foot next. Then, conscious of the shaking in his hands and the vast plunge beneath his feet, he untied the bowline at his waist and freed himself from the anchor. A moment later he started his descent.

Moving as quickly as possible, Travis worked his way down—using the inchwormlike process of standing in one sling while he slid the two unweighted prusik knots lower on the rope, then standing in the opposite sling and repeating the process. After what seemed an eternity he reached the outcrop thirty-five feet down.

He paused without taking his feet from the slings. As he rested, he felt a slight current of air rising up the towering face to meet him, wafting up the sappy smell of pine from the valley floor. Carefully, he leaned out and peered over the edge. The granite dropped endlessly beneath him.

A little farther . . . Suddenly he could make out Tommy's body hanging at the end of the rope. "Tommy!" he called.

Travis's heart soared as he saw his brother look up.

Alive! He's alive!

Tommy raised one hand, then let it drop to his side.

Tommy's weight had the rope jammed against the outcrop, preventing the prusiks from slipping past. After several heart-stopping attempts, Travis got all three knots by the obstruction and swung out once more over the void.

The overhanging wall quickly receded as he descended. Before long it lay completely out of reach. Dangling in space, Travis concentrated on the motions, keeping up a steady, methodic rhythm—forcing himself to ignore the jumble of talus far below, spinning now in sickening, hypnotic circles.

Fifty minutes later he finally arrived. Below him Tommy hung limp and unresponsive at the end of the rope. "Tommy!" he yelled. "Come on, wake up!"

Slowly, his brother opened his eyes. He swung listlessly in his sit-harness, making no attempt to grasp the rope. Dried blood covered the left side of his face, matting his hair in a thick dark-brown crust. "Hit something," he groaned, raising his hand to his head.

"There's an outcrop higher up," Travis said, trying to sound cheerful. "You managed to bounce off the only projection on the whole damn wall. Don't worry, you're gonna be all right."

"Can't move my legs."

"That's from hanging in the harness so long," Travis said doubtfully, hoping he was right. "Must've cut off the circulation. You'll be okay." He reached down and pulled his brother upright. "Here, grab the rope."

Tommy attempted to hold himself up. Exhausted, he barely managed to do more than maintain a sitting position. "I screwed up bad, Trav," he said.

"You're gonna be okay."

Tommy closed his eyes, straining to form the words. "Hope you're right."

"I know I'm right. We're getting out of here."

"Don't think so," Tommy croaked. "Not together, anyway."

"What's that supposed to mean?"

"Nothing." Tommy stared at the makeshift descenders Travis had fashioned from his shoelaces. "Told you to bring the Jumars," he added with a feeble grin.

"The hell you did." As he'd been talking, Travis had joined several nylon slings and clipped one end to the locking carabiner on his harness. Reaching down, he clipped the other to a similar carabiner on Tommy's harness, linking them together.

"Trav, what . . . ?"

"We're getting off this face before the sun goes down. Just hang on." Standing in the foot-stirrups, Travis slid the top prusik as high on the rope as he could. Then, sitting in his harness and transferring weight to the top knot, he drew up his knees and moved up the bottom two prusiks—reversing the procedure he'd used to descend.

Again he stood in the stirrups, lifting Tommy as he rose. The operation gained just two vertical feet. But it worked.

Hours later, burdened by his brother's weight, Travis had ascended less than half the distance to the outcrop. His legs were shaking and beginning to cramp. Gasping for breath, he paused to gaze up at the small projection still sixty feet higher. It seemed an impossible distance. Even if he made it, he realized getting past would be a problem. He set out once more, the image of a spider ascending a silken thread with a trussed-up burden in tow popped into his mind. Angrily, he thrust it away as he heard Tommy mumbling something below him.

"What's that?" Travis asked, glancing down.

"Won't work."

"You got a better idea?"

"Take the rope . . . rappel down alone."

"Take the rope? What about you?"

Tommy didn't answer.

Travis stood abruptly in the slings, jerking his brother another two feet up the face. "Forget it. We're making it together, or not at all."

"The outcrop . . ."

"I'll figure out how to get past it when I get there."

Ninety minutes later they reached a point just beneath the jutting outcrop. The wall in front still lay out of reach. Travis knew the overhang eased significantly above the outcrop, and once there and able to get his feet on the face, he might be able to pendulum left to the sloping bulge below the final ledge—circumventing the last thirty-five feet of the tedious ascent up the rope. But first he had to get there.

As a chilling wind signaled the approach of dusk, Travis scrutinized the projection above. To proceed, he'd once again have to lift the rope clear of the rock to slide past the prusiks. It would be an impossible task with Tommy weighing him down.

After a few seconds he found what he'd been searching for. Just below the outcrop a small crack split the granite face. Quickly, Travis wedged in a wired stopper. A downward tug locked it in place. Remembering his failed anchor on the belay ledge, he jammed in a second piece higher up, then passed a sling through both.

Travis glanced down at his brother. He'd been slipping in and out of consciousness for the past hour. "Tommy!" he shouted. "Come on, I'm gonna need your help for this."

Tommy's eyelids fluttered open.

"You okay?"

"My head," he groaned, peering up myopically. "Dizzy."

"How're your legs?"

"Numb." Tommy closed his eyes.

"Stay awake."

"Huh?"

"You've gotta stay awake."

"I'll try."

Travis secured Tommy's tether to the temporary anchor he'd placed, then retreated down the rope, allowing the wired stoppers to take his brother's weight. Carefully, he opened the locking carabiner at his waist. Tommy swung free.

Briefly, Travis rested. Then, "Listen, Tommy. I'm going to leave you here while I climb past the outcrop. I'll pull you up once I'm there, but you'll have to help."

"How?"

"When I start hauling, unclip from the anchor and fend yourself off from the rock. Can you do that?"

Tommy nodded weakly.

"Good. See you in a minute." Travis unclipped the top prusik from his harness. Then, grabbing the rope, he shook his feet free of the slings, once again conscious he was just a slip away from death.

Three quick hand-over-hands up the rope got him high enough to get his dangling legs into play. Smearing his right toe on the granite, he leaned back over the drop. His movement raised the rope off the rock, allowing him to move up his grip. Suddenly his foot slid off the face. The rope snapped back against the outcrop, pinning his hands.

The blisters on Travis's palms had ripped open hours before and were now slick with blood. With a feeling of horror, he felt them beginning to slip. His right leg was hopelessly out of position. Frantically, he scrabbled with his left foot, trying for a purchase.

No good. Can't . . .

Easy. Don't panic. You can do this.

Travis fought for control.

No time.

Taking a deep breath, he thrust himself backward, pushing off with his left foot.

Hang on . . .

He swung outward for a heartbeat, twisting in space. His lunge again lifted the rope from the rock, momentarily freeing his hands. Praying his grip would hold, he brought in his right leg, getting it beneath him just as he dropped back on the face.

Can't hold on much longer . . .

His toe found a nubbin. It felt solid.

Left hand up. Now the right. Smear the other foot. Hands up once more . . .

Got it.

Gasping with exertion, Travis rose to his knees atop the outcrop. Quickly, he hauled in slack rope and clipped it to his harness when he felt the tug of Tommy's weight at the other end. Heart still racing, he reset his rudimentary ascenders on the rope above. Then, using his legs to lift, he began pulling his brother over the outcrop. But by the time he'd managed to drag Tommy up to join him, the light had started to fail.

Travis peered to the left. In the growing dimness he could just make out the sloping incline he'd traversed near the end of his pitch. He studied the intervening wall, considering a horizontal run across the rock face to the relative safety of the incline. "Tommy?" he said at last.

"What?" Tommy groaned.

"I think we can pendulum across to the bulge. I'm gonna give it a try."

"Too heavy," Tommy mumbled. "Tie me off . . . go down alone."

"No way." Travis stepped up in the ascenders, lifting Tommy clear of the rock.

"Trav . . ."

"I'm not leaving you up here. I told you I'd get you down, and I will." Leaning back, Travis placed his feet flat against the wall, preparing for the pendulum. "Besides, aren't you forgetting something?"

"What?"

Travis smiled grimly. "Hell, Dad's been pounding it into us since we were old enough to listen. Don't you remember? Kanes stand together, Tom. No matter what."

•   •   •

Flushed with excitement, Kane climbed the ladder to Nate's room. "Nate! Get up!" he shouted, banging on the hatch.

A thump as Nate rolled out of bed. Then the hatch slowly lifted, and a tangle of red curls appeared in the opening. "Is it time for church already? It's still dark out."

"Naw, we're not goin' to church, least not right now," Kane chuckled. "Come on, get up. I've got something to show you."

"Are Tommy and Trav getting up, too?" asked Nate, wary of his father's early-morning summons.

"Your brothers left yesterday to go backpackin', kid," said Kane, feeling a stab of regret that he hadn't talked with Travis about the fight before he'd left, and making a mental note to do it as soon as the boys returned.

"Oh, yeah, that's right," said Nate, sleepily rubbing his eyes. "I forgot."

"C'mon. Get dressed and meet me downstairs."

"Now?"

"Yeah, right now. I've got a surprise for you."

Still groggy, Nate stumbled outside a few minutes later, joining his father on the lower deck. Kane was sitting in a beach chair, his back to the ocean, a giant-sized mug of coffee in his hand. He grinned as Nate descended the final few steps from the house.

"Well, I'm here," said Nate. "What, uh . . ." He looked down. At his feet, tugging at his cuffs with resolute, single-minded determination, was a seven-week-old black Labrador pup.

Speechless, Nate knelt and cupped the pup's head in his hands. The pup licked his fingers and then resumed her attack, shifting to the laces of Nate's tennis shoes.

"She's got a lotta spirit," said Kane proudly. "I got her from the same guy who bred Tar. She was the best bitch of the litter. According to her papers she's got some of Tar in her, too. He's her great-granddad."

At the mention of Tar, Nate stood and shoved his hands into his pockets. "What's her . . . What's your new dog's name?"

"Ain't my dog."

Confused, Nate glanced down once more at the tiny animal. She had her rump high in the air, shoelaces firmly gripped between her teeth. The pup looked back, the white crescents of her eyes gleaming in startling contrast to her coal-black fur. "She's not yours? Whose is she?"

"We'll discuss that later," Kane answered mysteriously. He stood and headed for the stairs. "Pick her up," he ordered without looking back. "We're goin' someplace, just you and me."

"What for?" Nate asked numbly, kneeling to scoop up the pup.

"You'll see."

Cradling the pup in his arms, Nate hurried up the stairs after his father.

After following Kane out to the car, Nate sat in silence as they drove the deserted highway north. The pup nestled quietly in his lap, content to be held. Nate stared straight ahead during the ride, seemingly paying little attention to the small animal, but by the time they'd parked on the ocean side of Pacific Coast Highway just past Pepperdine University, his hands had begun to travel with unconscious and proprietary interest over the dog's soft fur.

"I used to train Tar in this field," said Kane as he turned off the engine. "That was before you were born, so you probably don't remember."

Nate shook his head.

"That was a joke, kid. Come on, let's take a stroll up to that knoll. Bring the mutt with you."

Nate followed his father along a path that wound through knee-high grass and sage toward a low ridge. Just as the sun broke over the horizon, they reached a promontory overlooking the field below and the ocean beyond. Kane sat, indicating for Nate to join him. The boy sank down beside his father. Quickly, the pup squirmed from his arms. Kane absently picked up a small stick and tossed it a few feet down the hill. Immediately warming to the game, the pup scampered down to retrieve it, but refused to relinquish it upon returning. Kane snagged her and reclaimed the stick, then threw it again. "She's got plenty of fetch in her," he said with a nod of approval.

"Uh-huh," Nate agreed. Sensing the game was over after several more throws, the pup settled at their feet and began happily reducing the stick to splinters.

"You know Tom's leaving for college soon."

"I know."

"He's not gonna be around much after that, and Travis and Allison won't be far behind. Soon it'll just be you, me, and your mom." Kane looked at Nate carefully, then went on. "That's why I've decided if we're to own another dog, it's gonna have to be yours."

"Mine?"

"That's right. Think you can handle it?"

"I . . . I don't know," said Nate, taken aback. "I mean, I want to . . ."

"That's a good answer, Nate. I like to see you think before you commit to something. Shows you're growing up. And you're right; there may be more to owning this pup than you realize."

"Like what?"

"Well, first off, I'll help you train her, but it's gonna mean getting up early every morning for the next year or so, just you and me."

"That's no problem," Nate said seriously. "We'll train her to be a bird dog, just like Tar?"

"That's right. By the time she's twelve weeks old, she'll be doin' simple retrieves and know 'sit,' 'stay,' 'come,' and 'heel'—both on and off the leash. After that we'll move on to steadying her, whistle commands, multiple retrieves, and handling, then the gun and live birds when she's ready."

"Can she learn all that in a year?"

"Sure. I'm a good teacher. It's no different from raising kids: repetition, consistency, patience, and discipline."

"And letting her know when she does something right," added Nate protectively, bristling at his father's reference to discipline.

"Of course," Kane said with a smile. "That's the most important part, but it won't take much. You'll see. Labs are the finest dogs in the world, and once we get goin', you're gonna find she'll do anything to please us, unlike kids. It's built into the breed. When we're done, I'm gonna want to take her hunting a couple times a year, if that's okay with you. By then you'll be old enough to handle a gun yourself. Maybe you'll want to come along."

Nate shook his head. "I'm not sure about that."

"We'll see when the time comes," said Kane firmly. "Now, second off, feeding and cleaning up'll be your job, too."

"Okay."

"Well, do you want her?"

Nate hesitated. "She'll really be mine?"

"That's right, kid. She'll be all yours."

"And you won't ever hurt her?"

Kane studied his son. "Like I did Tar?"

Nate stared at Kane without answering, his lips compressed in a silent slash of defiance and anger.

Kane took a deep breath and gazed out over the ocean. "You know, Nate," he said, "when you came along, Tar had already been part of the family for a whole lotta years. By the time you were old enough to notice him, he'd gotten pretty old."

"I loved Tar," said Nate quietly.

"I know you did, kid. I also know how much you miss him, and how mad you are at me for what I did. I know I screwed up in the way I went about it, but it was his time, and putting him down was my responsibility. It was something I had to do. Do you know why?"

"No."

"Because I loved him, too."

Nate glanced away, refusing to look at his father.

"I'll tell you something, son. If you take this pup, she's gonna be with you long after everybody else leaves 'cept me and your mom. She's gonna become your best friend in the whole world, and you'll love her more than you can imagine. Maybe even as much as you loved Tar."

"Maybe."

"You're afraid of that, aren't you?"

Nate stared at his hands without answering.

"I thought so. Look, there're a lot of great things about having a dog, but there's a hard part, too. The hard part is being responsible for her, and sooner or later it's something you're going to have to take on. One day somewhere down the line it'll be her time to go. It may be a year from now; it could be fifteen, but it's going to happen.

And when that time comes, it'll be the responsibility of the people who love her to do whatever's necessary to help her out."

"You mean like giving her pills, taking her to the vet?"

"You know what I mean, Nate. Having this pup means accepting that someday we're gonna lose her . . . just as we lost Tar. Can you do that?"

"I . . . I don't know."

"Nate, before you make up your mind, lemme tell you something," said Kane sympathetically. "Some people might think you're too young to hear this. I don't. Considering what happened a few weeks back, I think you're ready—not to mention the fact you're a Kane. So here it is: A lot of crappy things like losing Tar and that guy breaking into our house are going to happen to you before they plant you in the ground—things you can't do anything about. But a lot of good things will happen, too. Growing up, falling in love, having a family of your own. Unfortunately, there's a hard part to that, too. You're gonna discover that some of the very best things in life, the ones you want more than anything else, often carry a heavy price. But unless you're willing to pay that price, you're going to miss out."

Nate nodded slowly. "Mom told me something like that, too."

"She did, huh? I'm not surprised." Kane paused, regarding his son carefully. "Well, what do you think? Do you want this pup or not?"

Nate thought for a long time. Finally he answered. "I want her," he said.

Kane smiled. "Good. You just took the first step toward bein' a man. What're you gonna name her? And for God's sake, don't pick some pansy name like Princess or Fluffy or Daisy."

Nate considered. "Ruby," he declared. "I'm naming her Ruby."

"Ruby Begonia. Has a nice ethnic ring to it for a black dog. I like it."

"Just Ruby, Dad."

"Okay, kid. Ruby it is." Kane laughed, tousling Nate's already disheveled hair. Then his smile faded. "Now that we've got *that* settled, there's something else I've been meaning to bring up."

Nate sat quietly, waiting for his father to continue. Ruby, who by now had tired of her stick-chewing, yawned, stretched, and trotted over to curl up in the boy's lap.

"It's about the night those punks robbed our house. I've already had a private little talk with your sister about it. I've been waiting for the right time to go over it with you."

"You talked to Allison? What did she say?"

"Not much. She still claims it happened just the way she told the sheriffs. But from the way you two have been acting, I've got a suspicion that more went on than you're telling."

Again, Nate looked away.

"Do you know why I didn't push Allison about it?"

"No," said Nate in a small voice.

"I'll tell you," said Kane. "I figure whatever else happened that night, that scumbag broke into *our* house and got what he deserved. The investigation is closed, and the DA has no interest in pursuing things, so I'm sure as hell not gonna open it up again—*especially* since the only reason I can think of that might explain your not telling all you know is that you and Allison are ashamed of something. And Nate, I can see from looking at your face right now that I'm right."

Nate sat numbly, wishing he could hide.

"Son, you and Allison are Kanes. I know you'd never do anything wrong, but since that night you and your sister have been acting . . . I don't know . . . *different*. So I'm asking you once more. Is there anything you want to get off your chest?"

Miserably, Nate shook his head.

"She made you promise, didn't she? Don't answer; I figured that already." Kane thought a moment and then continued. "I'll tell you what. I'll respect your promise to Allison, but I definitely plan on getting to the bottom of things. Sooner or later I'm gonna find out what you're hiding, but I'd prefer if you and Allison came to me on your own. Will you think about it?"

"Yes, sir."

"One more thing. Look at me, Nate."

Nate turned, reluctantly lifting his eyes to his father's.

"You're a good kid," said Kane slowly. "I sense you may be having doubts about that right now—with this secret or whatever the hell it is—and I can see how it's affecting you. That's all I care about, Nate . . . how it's affecting you. Whatever it is, it could never change the way I feel about you. Not one damn bit. You're my son, and I'm always going to stand by you. No matter what. Okay?"

Nate felt the sting of tears. He tried to hold them back and failed. Torn between embarrassment and desolation, he sat before his father, furiously wiping his cheeks with his small fists, unable to stem the long-overdue flow. "I . . . I'm sorry, Dad," he sobbed. "I can't help it. . . ."

"It's okay, Nate. It's okay." Kane put his arm around his son and drew him close, and for several minutes they sat without speaking as the boy cried himself out, their two figures joined on the hilltop in the hush of early morning. At last Ruby, who'd grown tired of the strange new game her humans had decided to play, yapped and tugged at Nate's sleeve.

"I guess it's time to go," Nate sniffed, looking down at the insistent pup. "She's probably getting hungry."

"Me, too," said Kane, giving his son a final hug. "Let's go home and have your mom scare us up some breakfast. What do you say?"

"Okay, Dad." Nate took a deep breath, then slowly let it out. "Let's go eat."

•   •   •

Night. Travis paused, searching the rock below, barely able to make out the dim outline of his own hand in the darkness. Feeling a shiver of alarm, he suddenly realized that finding his way back down to his brother might be more difficult than he'd thought.

The pendulum had been difficult with Tommy in tow, but he'd eventually managed to swing over to the small sloping incline. Precious minutes had slipped past as he'd again temporarily anchored Tommy to the rock, after which he'd untied his prusiks, relaced his shoes, and climbed the remaining distance up to the final belay ledge alone. Once there, he'd repositioned the anchor to a better rappel point, fighting to use the final seconds of dusk. Working as quickly as possible, he'd then passed the climbing rope through a rappel sling—knotting together the ends and leaving equal lengths dangling from the middle. But by the time he'd clipped in his figure-eight descender and again started back down the rope, the light had failed, leaving the rock cloaked in complete and unfathomable darkness.

Now, as Travis rappelled slowly down the rope, he resisted the urge to rush, realizing if something went wrong, there would be no second chance. After fifteen feet he stopped and pendulummed to each side, calling Tommy's name.

Why doesn't he answer? He can't be that far below me. He must be able to hear. Unless . . . No! He's all right. He has to be all right.

Travis let another ten feet of rope pass through the figure-eight descender, fighting a realization that Tommy's periods of unresponsiveness had become more frequent as time went on. With a chill, he remembered that a friend of his who'd suffered a concussion in a car accident had seemed fine for hours, then had slowly deteriorated as the swelling and pressure in his cranium gradually increased.

"Tommy!"

Still nothing.

Have I already gone by him?

Travis stopped his descent and initiated another exploratory pendulum, groping with his free hand as he swung across the granite. Suddenly his toe encountered something.

Tommy!

It took several frustrating passes to return. Finally Travis could make out the dark shape of his brother on the incline where he'd left him. "Tom! Come on, Tommy, wake up."

It took Tommy a long time to answer. When he did, his voice sounded weak and drained. "That you, Trav?"

"Who else would be dumb enough to be up here with you in the dark? How're you doing?"

"Not good . . ."

"Just take it easy. I'm gonna get you down."

"How? Can't see a thing."

Travis hesitated, considering their options. He did a quick mental calculation, figuring it would take a minimum of ten sequential rappels to reach the ground—each stage of the descent presenting its own opportunity for misplacing an anchor, snarling the rope when retrieving it, or simply misjudging the distance to the next stopping point—any of which could prove fatal. With Tommy's weight dragging him down, it would have been difficult enough during the day. To attempt it in darkness would be suicide.

Alone, however, Travis realized he might be able to make it—even in the dark. Once on the valley floor, he could go for help. But without Tommy to lead the climb back up to their present position, the only way to reach him upon returning would involve a time-consuming hike up the backside and another multiple rappel from above. *Would Tommy still be alive when I returned?* As it had the night before, the temperature promised to drop well below freezing later on, and in all probability his brother was already in shock. Travis knew he had to get him down, and the sooner the better.

But how?

All at once Travis remembered the moon, recalling it had risen just before they'd turned in the previous evening. He tried to recollect how much later it came up each night, deciding it had to be somewhere around an hour. "Listen, Tom," he said. "The moon'll be up before long. We'll wait till we can see, then rap down."

Tommy nodded that he understood. "Cold."

"Yeah. Me, too."

Estimating he'd already descended half of the doubled rope to rejoin his brother, Travis secured himself to Tommy's anchor, then unthreaded the descender. Next he retrieved the remaining line dangling below, untied the knot at the bottom, and carefully pulled on one end—watching as the other end snaked up into the darkness. Seconds later it cleared the rappel sling and hissed down from above.

Okay so far, he thought, numb with exhaustion. He smiled ruefully, recalling the story of a man falling off the Empire State Building who'd been heard repeating those very words all the way down. With a determined effort, he drove the morbid joke from his mind and proceeded to set up a new rappel. Satisfied they were ready to embark as soon as they had enough light, he huddled next to Tommy and waited.

They sat without speaking for the next hour. A thousand stars glittered in the night sky above them, but still no sign of the moon. Travis stared impatiently at the eastern horizon, feeling Tommy shivering uncontrollably beside him. At times he couldn't tell whether his brother had slipped into unconsciousness or was merely asleep. Fearing the former, he talked, saying anything that came to mind, anything to maintain contact. After a while he found himself relating his run-in with Petrinski, his doubts regarding his music, and his persistent fear that he'd disappoint their mother.

"Know how you feel," Tommy whispered.

"I thought you were asleep."

"Heard part . . . know how you feel."

"I doubt that, Tom. You've never disappointed anyone."

Tommy laughed weakly. "I will."

"Don't worry about it. Dad'll be pissed about this when he finds out, and we'll have to listen to his 'I told you sos' from now till doomsday, but he'll get over it."

"No," said Tommy, struggling to get out the words. "I mean college."

"What? You weren't serious the other night about not going, were you?"

"Yeah. I was."

"But . . . why?"

" 'Cause you're gonna be an uncle."

Thunderstruck, Travis mulled over his brother's revelation. "But why?" he asked again. "Christy doesn't have to have the baby. You could wait till later, at least till you both graduate from college . . ."

"She wants it," said Tommy, his teeth chattering so hard he could barely talk. A noticeable slur had crept into his speech, but still he continued. "We're getting married."

"Tommy, I know you've thought about this, but you're only eighteen. You're too young to get married, and—"

"I'm doing it."

"What about school?"

"Later . . ."

"What about Christy's swimming and *her* going to college? Hell, what about her finishing high school?"

"She'll finish."

"Oh, Jesus, Tommy," Travis sighed. "I hope you know what you're doing."

Tommy put his hand on Travis's arm. "Listen," he said, a sudden urgency rising in his voice. "Tell her I'm sorry about . . . what I said. Tell her I'm happy. Happy about the baby. Not sorry."

Travis covered Tommy's hand with his. "We're both making it down," he said. "Deliver the message yourself."

Tommy nodded feebly. "In case I don't . . . tell her."

Travis noticed a faint glow had finally begun lighting the sky over the eastern peaks. He felt a lurch of apprehension, knowing they'd soon begin their dangerous descent. "Here comes the moon."

"Trav . . ."

"Okay, Tom. It won't be necessary, but I'll tell her."

•   •   •

It took Travis twelve rappels and most of the night to bring his brother down off the rock. In the first exiguous glimmerings of dawn, they reached the talus slope at the foot of the wall. By then Tommy was unconscious.

Trembling with cold and fatigue, Travis scrambled the rest of the way down and retrieved their camping gear. After returning, he quickly set up their tent on a flat slab of granite and dragged Tommy inside. "Hang on, Tom," he whispered, struggling to get his brother into his sleeping bag. "You're gonna make it."

After covering Tommy with the second bag as a blanket, Travis placed a full water bottle by his head. Then, taking only a canteen, he headed up the trail, maintaining a steady lope back toward Mineral King. Eighteen long, arduous miles stretched between him and the ranger station. It had taken ten hours of steady plodding to cover the distance on the way in. If he ran, Travis figured he could get out in four.

He stopped once as the trail turned sharply upward. He paused to look back, his breath coming in ragged sobs. Still visible in the distance, alien and forlorn, the blue dome of their tent sat at the base of the scree. "You're gonna make it, Tom," he whispered once more, fighting a terrible premonition that had settled like a stone in the pit of his stomach.

And, turning, he started again for the pass.

22

Monday afternoon Kane quit his shift early and drove Arnie downtown to LAPD headquarters, arriving at Parker Center a little after three P.M. There, under the guise of running latents through the ALPS print computer, he killed several hours visiting friends while Arnie underwent his final processing-out procedures. At last, his shield relinquished, termination forms signed, exit interview completed, and retirement ID in hand, Arnie joined Kane on the mezzanine. He looked strangely forlorn.

Kane thumped him on the back. "You're a free man, amigo," he said in a transparent effort to cheer him up. "How's it feel?"

"Like I need a drink. My hand's about to cramp from signin' all that shit."

"A drink?" said Kane. "Jeez, Arnie. This bein' a weekday and all, I don't know. Some of us gotta work tomorrow."

"Well, I ain't one of 'em. You coming?"

"Maybe just this once."

"Where to?"

Kane pretended to think. "How 'bout the Fox Inn? Some of the guys mentioned going over there after work."

"I don't want to get into some big crowd scene," protested Arnie, looking at Kane suspiciously. "My official send-off's gonna be bad enough."

"It's just Banowski, Deluca, maybe two or three others," Kane assured him. "No big deal."

"It better not be," Arnie grumbled.

An hour later, after bucking after-work traffic and wishing for a siren all the way across town, Kane and Arnie pulled up to the valet station at the Fox Inn, a rambling, Tudor-style restaurant with leaded windows, green shutters, a gray slate roof, and single-storied wings fanning from a semicircular entrance in opulent disregard for economy of space. With a grateful sigh, Kane killed the engine and slid from behind the wheel, tossing the keys to a youngster wearing a mint-green jacket and matching bow tie. "I spent years gettin' them dents just right," he warned the attendant. "See you don't mess 'em up."

"No, sir," the youngster promised, regarding Kane's Suburban with unconcealed amusement. "I won't."

Kane grinned and started for the restaurant. "Then my mind's at ease," he laughed. Calling over his shoulder to Arnie, he added, "Get a move on, partner. We've got some celebratin' to do."

"Right behind you, ol' buddy. Right behind you."

The two men pushed through a pair of heavy oak doors and made their way inside, skirting a spacious dining area with white-linened tables and cozy, intimate alcoves. At the end of a short hall they turned left into a comfortable-looking bar, pausing to inspect a sumptuous interior that had been designed to resemble an old English pub.

Kane shot a quick glance toward a room in the back that could be reserved for private parties. "See any of the guys?" he asked.

"Nope," Arnie answered, appreciatively eyeing a long-legged cocktail waitress in a skimpy outfit who was wending her way through the crowded tables. "They're probably stuck in traffic. Come on, let's go stomp some brain cells."

Kane followed Arnie to a pair of vacant stools at a four-sided mahogany bar dominating the center of the room. One of the young bartenders looked up as they took their seats. "Detectives Kane and Mercer," he said brightly, flipping off the blender and expertly pouring a row of frothy-looking strawberry daiquiris from the pitcher. "How're you two gents doing tonight?"

"Not bad, Jerry," said Kane, "with the exception of this terrible thirst we somehow contracted on the way over."

"You came to the right place. What'll it be?"

"I'll start off with a Jack Daniel's, straight up," replied Kane, thinking the kid didn't look old enough to crack a beer, let alone tend bar. "My friend Arnie here, in keeping with his sexual preferences, would appreciate something with lots of fruit on it—maybe some pineapple and a nice red cherry. And stick one of those cute little flags on top, too."

"Not likely," rumbled Arnie. "I'll have a Wild Turkey, beer back. And keep 'em comin'."

Jerry placed the daiquiris on the service counter and slid a bar tab alongside the frosty glasses. "You got it," he said.

When their drinks arrived, Kane and Arnie quickly downed them and ordered a second round. "Damn, Arnie. I can't believe you're a civilian now," Kane said after a long moment of silence.

Arnie nodded. "Join the club."

Again they lapsed into silence as Jerry placed fresh drinks before them.

"I saw that prick Snead last Friday," Kane noted, trying to kick-start the conversation. "He was madder'n a constipated duck about your retiring. Blew his witch hunt right out of the water."

"Fuck Snead."

"I'll drink to that," said Kane, lifting his bourbon.

"Yeah."

Kane regarded Arnie carefully. "Are you gonna be okay with this?"

"Retiring?" Arnie stared into his drink. "I don't know, ol' buddy. To tell the truth, it's hittin' me harder than I thought."

Kane hesitated. Although they'd discussed Arnie's retirement on several occasions after that evening in the squad room, this was the first time he'd seen a crack in his partner's thorny determination to put the LAPD behind him. "Aw, hell, Arnie. You're better off," he said, making another effort to cheer him up. "No more departmental crap, no more IA, no more Snead. And like you said, once you add your pension to the paycheck from your new job, you'll be making a lot more money than you were."

"Right."

"I'm gonna miss you, but it's not like we won't be seeing each other. Hell, you're practically part of the family."

"Yeah, I know," said Arnie with a small smile, the first since he'd left Parker. "And it means a lot to me. A whole lot. Thanks, Dan."

"How about coming over next week for some chow? I'm cookin' up some bouillabaisse for the troops on Friday."

"Sounds good. Will Tommy and Trav be back from their climbing trip by then?"

"Climbing trip? Those two are backpacking. I told 'em no climbing."

Arnie looked away. "Oh, yeah. Right."

Kane's eyes hardened. "You know somethin' I don't, pard?"

Arnie studied his drink before answering. "Well, uh . . . a while back Trav did mention something about climbing. He asked me not to mention it, and I guess I sorta put it out of my mind. Sorry."

"Jesus fucking Christ. How could you forget to tell me something like that? If Tommy gets hurt and blows his scholarship . . ."

"I know, I know. I should've said something."

"You're damn right you should have said something. I swear, when I get my hands on those two, I'm gonna kill 'em."

"Don't be too hard on them," said Arnie. "They're just kids."

"Yeah, and I know just how to handle 'em," Kane muttered. Then, changing the subject, "I wonder where the hell the guys are. Hey, Jerry, you seen Deluca or Banowski around tonight?"

Jerry looked up from washing beer mugs at the sink. "Nope," he said.

Just then a crash sounded from the private room in the back, followed by a prolonged, raucous ovation of hollers and cheers. "What the hell's goin' on?" asked Arnie.

"Just a bunch of doctors having some kind of reunion," Jerry answered. "Proctologists, I think. They've got a couple strippers scheduled for later, some stag films, that kinda stuff."

"Asshole specialists, you say?" Kane narrowed his eyes at Jerry, then turned toward the source of renewed whooping and laughter. "What're they drinking?"

Jerry referred to one of the tabs on the spike. "Mostly beer and tequila."

"Hmmm. Strippers and stag films." Kane flipped out his ID and hung it on his coat. "What do you say, Arnie? Think they could use a little police protection?"

Crashing disorderly gatherings under the auspices of keeping the peace had always been a favorite pastime of Kane's, particularly during his early days on the force. Unless drugs were present, an off-duty cop with the right attitude usually found himself welcomed—especially if he had a drink in his hand instead of a gun—and over the years Kane had made a number of friends that way, not to mention a host of memorable busts. Regardless of the outcome, it usually proved entertaining.

With a shrug Arnie slid from his stool. "Why not? Beats the shit outta sittin' here getting chewed out by you."

Drinks in hand, the two detectives threaded their way toward the back. As they approached, one of the cocktail waitresses emerged from the room, blushing as an effusion of whistles chased her out.

"Ready, pard?" Kane asked with mock seriousness when they arrived at the door. He placed his hand on the knob. "I go right, you go left."

"Just like always," Arnie chuckled. "Guns?"

"Nah. It's just a bunch of pansy doctors. Now if it were dentists, that'd be different. One, two . . ."

On three, Kane flung open the door and burst into the room.

Arnie tumbled in close behind. He froze as he looked around the crowded room. Jammed in the small chamber, packed into an area designated for a maximum occupancy of twenty, were over forty-five of LAPD's finest: Deluca, Banowski, and the rest of the men from the homicide unit; a healthy turnout of detectives from robbery, burglary, auto theft, and juvenile; a handful of sergeants and patrol officers from the day shift; and friends of Arnie's that Kane had invited over from other divisions.

Lieutenant Long, the single member of the brass who'd been asked to attend, raised his glass amid the ensuing din. "Hey, Mercer," he called, yelling to be heard over the turmoil. "Here's to you. And to making it out in one piece."

"Hear! Hear!" everyone shouted.

Stunned, Arnie continued to stare around the room in shock and disbelief. Finally he composed himself enough to speak. "I was led to believe by my lyin', two-faced partner," he said, glancing from face to face with obvious pleasure, "that this was supposed to be a convention of butt-hole specialists. At least he was partly correct. You guys sure as hell ain't doctors, but I haven't seen this many assholes since boot camp."

Kane raised his hands to quiet the boisterous outburst following Arnie's declaration. "Before things go too far," he announced, "there's a guy here who some of you may not know. I want to introduce him 'cause he was Detective Mercer here's TO about a hundred years back, and he may be able to shed some light on Arnie's meteoric rise in the department. Let me present Sergeant Thorpe 'Gasman' McGowan from the Foothill Division, that imposin'-lookin' stud over there hoggin' down a pitcher of beer. Stand up and take a bow, Gasman. Oh, sorry. You are standing."

"Eat my shorts, Kane," a steely-eyed man with a flattened nose and the dulcet, mellifluous voice of a drill instructor shot back across the room.

"Sergeant McGowan got his nickname from somethin' that happened a lotta years back when him and me were working SWAT together," Kane continued. "It was an unfortunate incident during which he accidentally lobbed a tear-gas canister right into his own command post—gassing the shit out of half the unit. He made history with that act, rivaled only by the notoriety he received by being the first person to ever be accepted on the force after havin' a sex-change operation—something I'm sure Gasman doesn't mind my disclosing since it's a known fact he's a confirmed homosexual. Gentlemen, I give you one of the meanest, ugliest, toughest bastards you ever wanna meet—Gasman McGowan."

The compact officer stood and waited for the vociferous ovation sparked by Kane's introduction to abate. At last he spoke. "As you all know," he began in reprisal, his sepulchral growl cutting through the room like a saw, "aside from being the most disorganized detective on the force, Dan Kane is also a notorious liar. To set the record straight, I didn't fire the gas gun accidentally. I *will* admit hitting the command post was unintentional—I was aiming for the press down the street."

Laughter forced McGowan to pause for almost a minute. "What's more," he finally continued, his pugilistic features returning to their previous elegiac mien, "Detective Kane was not even present at the time of the gassing. He'd just suffered a small emergency of a personal nature and had run to a local drugstore to buy some tampons."

Everyone again raised his voice in full-throated approbation. Mc-Gowan waved his hands for silence. "Kane's right about *one* thing, though," he said. "It is true that I was Detective Mercer's training officer when he first came on the force, and right from the start I sensed he'd go a long way. Beneath that thick skull is a razor-sharp mind, as the following will demonstrate: Arnie and I were working a series of robberies over in Baldwin Hills. These guys were mugging drunks comin' outta the local bars, so Arnie and I started trading off hangin' out in various sleaze joints, acting as decoys—with the other guy in a car around the block ready to swoop in for the bust. About a week into it I exit some shit-hole late one night, and these two punks step out of an alley next door.

"They brace me up against the wall. One of 'em has a knife; the other's hefting a brick. The one with the knife says, 'Gimme the money.' I'm stalling, waiting for the cavalry to show, wondering if my wire's still working. When Arnie doesn't make his appearance, I figure I'm on my own. 'No problem,' I say real pleasantlike, reaching under my coat. As soon as they see my piece, they take off. I grab one. The other guy gets away.

"Just then Arnie comes flying blind around the corner with his lights off. He accidentally hits the runner doin' about thirty and knocks him halfway down the block. I've got the first guy down; Arnie jumps out and collects the track star. He can't believe how far the guy flew and all he's got is a dislocated shoulder. The perp's moanin' and groanin' when Arnie drags him back—why are we hassling him, he didn't do shit—the usual. 'Didn't do shit?' says Arnie. 'Didn't do shit? Hell, even if we don't nail you for robbery, we've got you on something that'll stick in any court of the land.' 'What's that?' the guy asks."

McGowan paused. Then, "It was at this point that I realized Arnie had a true genius for police work," he said, coming to the end of his story. "Anybody guess what charge he came up with?"

"Leaving the scene of an accident!" Kane yelled from the back.

"Give that man a cigar," said McGowan, grinning at the renaissance of laughter inspired by his story. Kane joined in the ovation.

Then, knowing from past experience how much Arnie hated to speak at public gatherings, he started chanting, "Speech! Speech! Speech!" Others quickly echoed his call. Arnie scowled at Kane, then rose reluctantly to his feet.

"Gentlemen," he said self-consciously, his eyes sweeping the room. "First off I want to thank Gasman for that horseshit tale. I'd also like to express my heartfelt appreciation to all the rest of you for attending. I realize all too well the sacrifice you made tonight of not bein' with your wives and children to come down here and drink with a bunch of degenerate fellow officers."

At this point Arnie was forced as others had been to wait out a cacophony of whistles and foot stomping.

"A lot of you have expressed wonder," he continued when the noise had died down, "that someone so obviously in the prime of life as yours truly would choose to retire. To that I can only reply: When it comes time to cash in your chips, hardly anyone ever complains about not having worked enough. I, for one, don't plan on making that mistake. Nonetheless, I've gotta admit there *are* some things I'm gonna miss about the job. There're a few things I'm not gonna miss, too."

"You're shittin' us. There's a downside to bein' a cop?" Deluca hollered.

Ignoring the interruption, Arnie took a long pull on his drink and plunged ahead. "I remember bein' a P-two graduatin' the academy, green as they come—thinkin' I was gonna make a difference, do some good. Superman with a badge and a pension plan. Like all of you, I got over that real quick, put my ideals behind me, and did the best I could. Why? I don't know myself. Maybe just because somebody has to. But after twenty-five years I'm not gonna miss bein' stuck at a desk shuffling papers, takin' shit from the gold braids, and puttin' up with departmental bullshit. I won't miss overtime cutbacks and last-minute scheduling changes, second-guessing myself 'cause I think I might do something wrong and wind up lookin' like an idiot, drinking stale coffee on stakeouts, worrying about my clearance rate, and seein' people's eyes glaze over at parties when I tell 'em I'm a cop. Last of all, I definitely won't miss a couple areas of our profession that nobody talks about much: drinking, divorce, drug abuse, and losing friends who happen to go through the wrong door."

Arnie hesitated, seeming lost in thought. Finally he continued. "I know some of you younger guys are bucking for homicide. The cream of the crop, the top of the heap, right? Well, if you succeed, lemme tell you what you'll find when you get there. Most of your cases will be stupid, brutal, and uncomplicated. Eighty percent will be domestic—husbands killing wives, mothers killing children, kids killing kids. The motivations will range from who's-screwing-who to a fight over somebody changin' the TV channel. The weapons will include just about anything you can name: guns, bricks, knives, shovels, fists, scissors, frying pans. Of the five to ten percent of your cases that turn out to be true whodunits, you'll be lucky if somebody, probably a fellow officer, hasn't screwed up the scene by the time you get there. And once you've got your suspect in interrogation, you're gonna discover that after a little lying they can't keep their mouths shut. Then, when you get to court, you'll watch your case plea-bargained away, placed on the inactive docket, or maybe the guy'll just walk on a technicality. On the rare occasions when everything goes right, the press will step in and make you look like shit anyway. Those are the things I'm *not* gonna miss."

An uncomfortable silence had fallen over the room. With some embarrassment, Arnie realized he'd thrown a damper on the proceedings with his vitriolic speech. Nonetheless, he plowed on. "Now, having got that off my chest, and so's you don't get the impression I've been bellyachin', which I guess I have, lemme say there *is* one thing I'm gonna miss."

"What's that, Mercer?" Lieutenant Long shouted from the back. "Badging your way outta traffic tickets?"

"Nope," Arnie answered, glancing around the room. "It's working with you guys. That's what I'll miss. And with that said, I ask you to join me in a toast." Arnie raised his glass.

Every officer in the room lifted his drink. "Here's to the Los Angeles Police Department," Arnie said solemnly. "And to you, who despite all its failings, make it one of the finest law-enforcement institutions in the world."

After everyone to a man had drained his glass, Arnie continued in a lighter tone. "Now, last off, I want to thank my longtime friend and partner, Dan Kane, for organizing this little shindig. Although most of you don't know it, Dan's had a lot on his mind lately—medical problems and such—but he's not a man to trouble others with his worries. As always, he puts his friends before himself, so I ask you to once more raise your drinks and join me in wishing Detective Daniel Kane a long life, continued success in his career, and the best of luck on his upcoming hysterectomy." Arnie sat amid a tumult of laughter and cheering, satisfied he had properly reset the mood of the evening.

And so, the business of speeches and testimonials behind them, the men of the Los Angeles Police Department began drinking in earnest. As expected, the evening quickly deteriorated to a debacle of rising volume and sinking propriety, with chairs toppling and glasses breaking amid an atmosphere of good-natured roughhousing.

Having quietly switched to soda water, Kane ran interference, acting as the group's liaison to various restaurant personnel periodically sent to seek an abatement of the noise, which grew more deafening and obnoxious as the night wore on. He brushed aside all complaints with universal good humor. Along with a continuing supply of booze, he directed that platters of potato skins, nachos, and salsa be brought with each round of drinks to sober the men. He also promised to pay for all damage, tip well, and never return.

Undaunted, the levity continued. Their cocktail waitress, increasingly terrorized as the party slowly spiraled toward anarchy, became conspicuously absent during the later hours. As a result, the group routinely required someone to run to the bar for fresh libations, and being one of the few celebrants steady enough to make the trip, Kane was unanimously elected.

As he elbowed his way through the crowded bar on his fourth refueling mission, a waitress timidly plucked at his arm, informing him he had a call from his wife.

23

Exhausted, Travis sat in a small alcove on the fifth floor of the hospital. Down a broad green corridor to the left he could see the nurses' station; to the right he could just make out a pair of wide swinging doors marked Authorized Personnel Only. In one of the sterile, brightly lit chambers beyond, he knew Tommy lay under the surgeon's knife.

Excepting brief and fitful snatches, Travis hadn't slept for nearly thirty-six hours. He ached with a bone-deep weariness of total fatigue, both physical and mental. Running, walking, and jogging the eighteen miles of mountainous terrain back to the Mineral King ranger station had taken much longer than he'd expected, and he'd then been forced to wait another frustrating forty-five minutes until the emergency medical team from the Ash Mountain station arrived. Praying Tommy would still be alive, he'd ridden back in the helicopter and shown them where he'd left his brother.

They'd found Tommy still unconscious. All attempts to revive him on the flight to the hospital had failed. Travis had seen the look the park medic had given his assistant when he'd folded back Tommy's eyelids and checked his pupils. Even from where he'd been sitting,

Travis had noticed that one appeared many times larger than the other, as vitreous and unchanging as death.

The pilot had radioed ahead on the flight in, advising the hospital they were bringing in a head-injury victim, and an emergency crew had been waiting on the helipad when they'd arrived. Travis had followed the gurney as they'd wheeled Tommy into emergency admitting. While others tended his brother and a hospital official called their parents, an ER doctor had bandaged Travis's hands, then sutured the gash on his forehead. By the time he'd finished, the triage unit had already transferred Tommy to an operating room on the fifth floor. Travis hadn't seen him since.

Now, as he fought to stay awake, Travis reviewed his actions. *Could I have done more?* he wondered miserably. *Gotten to him quicker, rappelled down faster, made better time on the way back? Even a few minutes might have made a difference. Just a few minutes . . .*

Around him, as doctors in green surgical scrubs paused for charts at the central station and white-clad nurses wheeled trays of medications down the hall, Travis sat in his alcove, watching the clock above the door ticking out the seconds and minutes and hours of his nightmare. And gradually, as the night wore on, his eyes began to close. He slept.

And as he slept, he dreamed.

• • •

"Come on, Trav. You can do it."

He looks up.

Tommy is forty feet above, his hands and feet jammed into the crack. He's younger somehow, can't be more than twelve or thirteen. "Come on," he calls again. "Try."

He puts his hand in the crack, feeling the rough crystals of quartz monzonite digging into his fingers. Joshua Tree National Monument, *an isolated part of his mind observes with surreal detachment.* We're in Indian Cove campground, doing one of the climbs Dad started us on when we were kids. *But how . . . ?*

"Forget Travis and get movin', Tommy," another voice commands. "We don't have all day."

He glances over at his father. He's belaying Tommy, has the top-rope he set up earlier wrapped around his waist. It ascends to a fixed bolt above the first belay ledge, then down to Tommy's harness. Kane squints up the face. "Let's go!"

"What about Travis? Doesn't he get a turn?"

"He can have one right now. Go ahead, boy. Give 'er a try."

He stares up at Tommy, then turns to his father. "Don't I need a belay?"

"You'll be okay. Just don't go up too far."

Travis tries the crack, jamming his hands and feet into the rock the way he saw Tommy do it. Slowly, he moves up. The break in the face is narrow at the beginning, providing excellent support for his small hands and feet, but before long it widens. He looks down. He's eight feet up without protection. "That's it for me, Dad," he says, dropping clumsily to the ground. He tears the skin on his knuckles as he slips from the rock.

"Not bad for a first try," Kane says. "And you'll do better next time. I'll rope you up when Tommy gets to the ledge."

"I'm not sure I can do this one, Dad. Can I try an easier climb?"

"You're gonna do this one, kid. You're better'n you think."

"But—"

"No buts. You can do it, and you will."

"Yes, sir."

"Attaboy." Then, to Tommy, "Damn it, Tom. Move!"

Tommy grins and starts up once more, heading for the belay ledge. As he's about to surmount the final difficulty, his left hand slips. His right can't hold him. He topples backward. The rope catches him, but he winds up inverted, one foot still stuck in the crack.

"Shit!" Kane yells, pulling hard, vainly trying to lift Tommy and dislodge his trapped foot. The rope drag against the rock is too great.

Tommy screams in pain. "Help me!"

Kane's eyes search his surroundings. The picnic table is too far away. So is the car. "There's nothing to tie to," he yells. "I gotta stay on the rope. Travis, climb up and help him."

"Dad, I . . ."

"Get up there!"

"Please help me," Tommy screams.

"Goddammit, Travis! Get up there!"

He places his hands on the rock, his mouth filling with the coppery taste of fear. He starts up. He hesitates at the first difficulty, then forces himself to continue. He peels from the face and lands on his back. Hard. Both hands are bleeding. He can't breathe.

"Get up, Travis. He's your brother."

"Dad, I can't . . ."

"Get up!"

Again he tries. Again he fails.

Inexplicably, Petrinski is now belaying the rope. "What are you afraid of, Travis? Get up."

"I can't."

"He's your brother, Travis. Don't you want to help him? Do you hate him so much you won't help him?"

"I don't hate him!"

"I think you do."

"No!"

"Then get up!"

"Please, Trav, help me . . ."

"Get up!"

His eyes fill with anger and frustration. He rises from the ground and lowers his head, feeling helpless and small, hating himself for his weakness. He trembles as he places his hands in the crack . . . knowing his efforts will never succeed, knowing he'll never reach Tommy, knowing he'll never forgive himself for his cowardice. As though sensing his terror, the rock itself begins to shudder beneath his hands, quivering with the same fear that has locked him in its hateful grip, shaking . . . shaking . . .

"Wake up, boy!"

Travis opened his eyes. He found himself staring into the angry face of his father. Kane released Travis's shoulders, allowing him to slump back into the chair. "You've got some explaining to do, bucko."

"Dad . . ."

"Talk. What the hell's goin' on?"

Travis's mouth went dry. "Where . . . where's Mom?"

"She's over there trying to get some news," growled Kane. "Talk."

Travis peered past the looming bulk of his father, spotting Catheryn speaking to an older woman at the nurses' station. She glanced over at him and smiled reassuringly, then resumed her conversation. Travis returned his gaze to his father. He shook his head, wondering where to start.

Construing his son's action as a refusal, Kane grabbed Travis's shirt and jerked him from the chair. "Are you gonna tell me what happened, or am I gonna have to knock it outta you?"

Travis's eyes blurred. "Tommy fell, Dad. He fell. I did the best I could, then went for help . . ."

"You left him? You chickenshit little bastard."

"Dad, you don't understand . . ."

"I understand fine, bucko. I understand just fine. You and your brother lied to me. You climbed that wall anyway, didn't you?"

Travis lowered his head.

"Look at me when I'm talking to you, boy."

Travis raised his eyes.

"Answer."

"Yes, sir. We climbed the wall anyway."

"Then, when something went wrong, you turned tail and ran."

"No, sir. That's not the way it happened."

Kane continued as if he hadn't heard. "I swear, if this screws up Tommy's football scholarship, I'm gonna wring his neck."

Travis remained silent, wishing Tommy's football season were the only thing in jeopardy. Kane glared for several seconds without speaking, inspecting Travis's bandaged hands and the dressing on his forehead. For some reason the injuries inflamed him even more. He tightened his grip. As he started to issue another warning, Catheryn rushed over. With surprising strength she wrenched free Kane's hand. "Don't," she said, her voice smoldering with fury.

"I'm just trying to—"

"Not now!"

Kane hesitated, struggling to control his temper. Then, glancing again at Travis's wounds, he backed away. "Okay. But I'm not done with you, kid," he said.

Travis retired to a bench on the far side of the alcove, watching as Catheryn conferred with her husband in a low voice. Minutes later she joined him. Horror flashed across her face as for the first time she noticed his bandaged palms. "Travis! Your hands!"

"They'll be all right."

Catheryn knelt and took her son's hands in hers, concern welling in her eyes. "Oh, Travis, Travis . . ."

"Please don't worry about me," Travis begged, fighting his own tears. "I'll be fine. Have you . . . have you heard anything about Tommy? Is he going to be all right?"

"They don't know yet. He's still in surgery."

"He'll be all right. I know he will."

"Oh, God, how could this happen?"

"I don't know, Mom." Travis rose and helped his mother to the bench. Then, burning with shame and guilt, he took his place beside her. Catheryn put her arm around him, and together they waited in silence.

Slowly, the minutes dragged past. Unable to remain still, Kane paced the dimensions of the room like a caged animal, moving back and forth with mechanical precision, again and again.

At last the doors at the end of the hall swung open.

All three watched as a tall, razor-thin man in green surgical scrubs approached the nurses' station. He consulted briefly with the nurse Catheryn had questioned earlier, glancing toward the alcove as he spoke.

Without a word Kane strode to the desk. Catheryn squeezed Travis's arm, then hurried after her husband. Instead of following, Travis remained on the bench, watching from self-imposed isolation as the wordless tableau played out before him.

In seeming slow motion he saw his father stop before the doctor. The surgeon shook his hand, then Catheryn's. Suddenly, to Travis, the light in the hallway seemed painfully bright. He narrowed his eyes as if squinting into the sun, wishing more than anything to look away. Instead, he forced himself to watch. With a feeling of bottomless despair he saw the doctor fold his arms and speak his words of regret, saw his mother's hand fly to her mouth as she received his heartbreaking epiphany, saw his father encircle her with his arm as the message inflicted its terrible hurt.

Tommy was gone. As though examining a coin found in the gutter, Travis turned it over in his mind, numbly struggling with the reality of his brother's death. He wanted to cry. Strangely, he discovered he could not. The tears he'd felt earlier had now evaporated, leaving his eyes hollow and empty and dry as dust.

Desolate and alone, he sat . . . listening to the slow, inexorable ticking of the clock.

24

Travis lay in bed, staring at the ceiling. Sounds filtered in through his walls: Allison getting ready in her room next door; Catheryn admonishing Nate to get dressed for the service; Kane stumbling upstairs from the music-room bar, where he'd been drinking for most of the past three days. A moment later Travis heard his parents arguing over how much time to allow for the drive.

What difference does it make? he thought woodenly. *Tommy isn't going anywhere. And they sure as hell won't start without us.*

Rolling over on his side, he let his eyes listlessly roam the room. Tommy's things were right where he'd left them—work clothes hung on the back of his chair, Friday's sports page spread across his desk, a book he'd been reading open facedown on the nightstand. Over the weekend someone had made his bed.

Mom never could stand a mess, Travis thought, surprised she hadn't cleaned up the rest.

After returning home Travis had shunned the family as much as possible—preferring the solitude of his room to the guilt of accepting their comfort. Abandoned by their older sibling, Allison and Nate had drawn closer together than ever before, seeking solace in each other's company. Catheryn had shouldered the burden of making arrangements, notifying relatives, calling friends. Throughout this time, as she'd stepped into the vacuum of Kane's drunken withdrawal, Travis had watched his mother impose upon herself a yoke of control and discipline that to him seemed nearly superhuman. But he'd also witnessed, on the rare occasions her mask had slipped, how costly this quiet subjugation of her anguish truly was. And it was during those moments, infrequent though they were, that he'd realized the true bedrock on which their family's strength had always resided.

Turning, Travis shifted his gaze out the window. A marine layer had moved in overnight, and a blanket of fog now hung low in the sky, shrouding the coast in a cloak of damp and dismal gray. He watched for several minutes as a lone dog proceeded with measured purpose along the water's edge, exploring his invisible world of smell and leaving his mark when the occasion arose.

Down the hall, he heard his parents' argument shifting from the entry to their bedroom. He tried to shut it out, detecting the soft slurs of alcohol embedded in the meter and syntax of Kane's staccato phrases, feeling his stomach lurch at the harshness in his father's voice. Kane hadn't spoken a single word to him on the plane ride back, and it had been that way ever since. For a while Travis couldn't decide which was worse: his father's glacial, impenetrable wrath, or the pit of drunkenness into which he'd descended. Finally, as the days wore on, he'd told himself he didn't care.

Outside, a squeal of brakes sounded as a car pulled up, then the muffled clunk of a door slamming shut.

"Mom, the car's here," Allison called out.

"Please tell him we'll be out shortly," Catheryn called back.

"Yes, ma'am. I'll tell him."

Ten minutes later, as the rest of the family gathered in the entry, Travis left his room. Head down, feeling as if he were stumbling through some dark and terrible dream, he followed them out to the limousine and took his place in the backseat beside his mother.

The family made the short journey up the coast to Our Lady of Malibu Church in silence. The limo parked in a small lot adjacent to the chapel. Travis stepped with the others from the car, then followed them up the steps to the small stone-faced building. Inside, mourners filled the pews. Heads turned as they entered. Present among the immediate family were Catheryn's mother, who'd driven down that morning from Santa Barbara, and Kane's younger sister, who at the last minute had flown in from Chicago. Christy sat with her parents behind Petrinski and members of the USC Music Department; Tommy's friends from school took up two other rows. But by far the largest group there consisted of members of the Los Angeles Police Department, with a wall of broad-shouldered, thick-necked men in dress-blue uniforms occupying most of the benches on one side of the nave. Conspicuous in his civilian attire, Arnie sat in their midst.

Tommy's casket lay at the head of the congregation, just inside a low Communion rail running the length of the altar. It was closed, at Catheryn's request, for she'd maintained that she wanted to remember Tommy as he'd been in life, not death. At the time, Travis hadn't seen what difference it made. Now, as he regarded the polished wooden box before him, he understood. More than anything, he wished his own final images of his brother could be forever expunged from his mind.

Travis sat with his family in the front row during the requiem Mass that followed. As the service droned on, his mind drifted back to earlier, simpler times, remembering the brother who had always been with him, always been his touchstone, always led the way. At the midpoint of the long Mass, after a short summation of Tommy's life and a lengthy sermon concerning the immortality of the spirit and the transience of the flesh, the priest asked whether anyone would like to speak. Travis forced his attention back to the present.

Seconds passed, yet no one stepped forward. The congregation shifted uneasily. Many looked toward Kane. Travis, too, glanced over at his father, realizing from his ethanolic scowl that he didn't intend to rise. Fleetingly, Travis considered ascending the pulpit himself. He hesitated, guiltily wondering how to speak of a brother for whom his feelings of jealousy and envy had always run nearly as deep as his love. In that instant, in a crystalline moment of clarity, Travis suddenly realized what he truly felt. Inside, in a secret place he seldom dared to look into, he felt . . . empty.

"I've got something to say."

Everyone turned. There, in the ranks of the LAPD contingent, stood Arnie. Angrily, Kane started to rise in the pew. Catheryn pulled him down, silencing him with a glare. Missing this interplay, Arnie edged his way to the center aisle. Then, looking neither right nor left, he proceeded to the front of the congregation and entered the chancel through a small gate in the Communion rail. The priest stepped aside, and Arnie took his place behind the lectern.

Once there, he paused briefly to collect his thoughts. Finally he spoke. "Eighteen years ago," he began, his voice strong and clear, filling every corner of the church, "I was asked by a friend to act as godfather for his firstborn son. That man was Daniel Kane. The boy was his son Thomas. Of course I felt honored, but back then I was a relatively young man and didn't think too much about it. But as the years went on, I had the privilege of becoming godfather to all the Kane children who followed: Travis, Allison, and Nate. And as the years went on, being a part of their lives came to mean more to me than I'd have ever suspected.

"It seems like yesterday that we stood in this church and baptized Tommy. Many times, in the past few days, I've asked myself this question: If on that morning eighteen years ago I could have looked into the future and seen how brief Tommy's life would be, would I have done anything differently? I'd like to think I would've spent more time with him, but I probably wouldn't have, things being the way they are. I'd like to think I'd have told him how much I treasured his friendship, but I probably wouldn't have gotten around to that either. But most of all, I'd like to think I'd have found the right time to tell him how much I loved him." Arnie's voice broke. He stopped, unable to go on.

Travis straightened in his seat. Even from where he sat, he could sense his father inexplicably seething with fury.

Arnie stared down at the lectern, struggling to compose himself. At last he continued, his eyes burning, his voice filled with sorrow. "Those of you who know me, and there're a few of you out there, realize one of my main regrets in life is not having children of my own. I always thought I would, along with a couple other things that didn't work out, so being a part of Tommy's life, being a part of all the Kane children's lives, means more to me than I can express in words. If I could have had a son of my own, I would have wished for one like Tom. I'm going to miss him."

• • •

After the service Travis sought out Christy, with whom he hadn't talked since the accident. He found her standing near the chapel door, despondently watching her parents conveying their sympathy to Catheryn and Kane in the parking lot below. Although during the service Christy had maintained a brave facade, her grief over Tommy's death was plainly visible in her face, her swollen eyes, the dejected slump of her shoulders. Joining her, Travis put his arm around her and stood without speaking, gazing down at the mourners below.

"I'm so sorry, Trav," Christy said, trying hard not to cry.

"I am, too. I . . ." Travis's voice trailed off.

Christy blinked back her tears, also at a loss for words. She glanced at Travis's forehead. "Does it hurt?" she asked, gently touching his face. The dressing was off, but an angry black lattice of sutures still crisscrossed the stigma Travis carried from the fall.

"Not really," mumbled Travis, his expression tightening as he revisited the horror of Tommy's accident.

"It wasn't your fault," said Christy, sensing his thoughts.

"I wish I could believe that," Travis said. "I was so scared. I keep thinking if it hadn't been for that, maybe I could have done something differently. Got him down faster, reached help quicker. I keep thinking if only I'd—"

"Don't, Trav."

Travis looked away. "Tom was barely conscious most of the time I was bringing him down," he went on. "We talked some, though. He told me about . . . about you and him. He gave me a message, just in case he didn't make it. At the time I wouldn't accept the possibility, but . . ."

Christy placed her hand on Travis's arm. "What did he say? Please, Trav. I have to know."

Travis took her hand. "He wanted you to know that he was happy about the baby, that he wasn't sorry at all," he said quietly. "He said you and the baby were more important to him than college . . . or anything else. He was planning on applying to the academy and becoming a cop so you could all be together."

The tears she'd fought earlier sprang to Christy's eyes.

"Are you still going to keep it?" Travis asked softly.

Christy gave the slightest nod.

"You're sure?"

"Now more than ever."

"Have you told anyone? Your parents, anyone?"

"No."

"What about school? What about the swim team, your chances for a scholarship?"

"I don't know."

"But . . ."

"I'll be all right," Christy said, wiping her eyes. "I don't have everything all wrapped up in a neat little package, but I'll work it out. I don't know how, but I will."

"I hope so," said Travis.

"I will."

As they'd talked, Travis had been marking his parents' progress across the parking lot. They'd paused occasionally to receive condolences and words of solace, but at last Kane had ushered Catheryn, Allison, and Nate into the waiting limo. Then he'd turned. Travis's heart fell as he saw him start back across the lot.

From a long and arduous apprenticeship as a child in the Kane family, where even the youngest quickly learned to decipher the ominous portents of a falling barometer in a father prone to violence, Travis recognized the aura of danger now enveloping his father like a cruel and unyielding armor: the aggressive tilt of his head, an odd stiffness in his back and limbs, a belligerence in his gait as real and tangible as a backhanded slap.

"I've gotta go," said Travis, giving Christy's hand a final squeeze. "If you ever want to talk, or there's anything I can do—anything at all—I want you to call me."

Christy leaned over and kissed Travis lightly on the cheek. "Thanks, Trav. I . . . I guess I'll see you around."

"Count on it."

By the time Travis arrived at the parking lot, Kane had already reached Arnie. He stood before him now in blind and unreasoning rage, repeatedly jabbing a thick, accusatory finger into his friend's chest. "You *knew*!" Kane shouted. "You *knew* they were gonna climb, and you didn't say a goddamned thing. Not one goddamned thing."

Arnie stood with his head down, arms loose at his sides. "Dan, I . . ."

"One word from you and we wouldn't be here."

"I know," Arnie mumbled. "I'm more sorry than I can say."

"Sorry? You're sorry?" Kane bellowed, giving Arnie a shove. "Sorry doesn't cut it, pal. Get the fuck out of my sight."

"Dan . . ."

Kane shoved him again.

"Please, Dan—"

Another shove. Harder this time, sending Arnie stumbling backward.

Driven by guilt and shame, Travis stepped between them. "Dad, stop it. It's not Arnie's fault."

Kane glared at Travis, seeming to notice him for the first time in days. "It ain't, huh?" he muttered, the dark, earthy smell of whiskey heavy on his breath.

"No. If it's anyone's, it's mine. I made him promise not to tell."

"Horseshit," said Kane, moving again toward Arnie.

Again, Travis blocked his way. "Dad, don't!"

Kane hesitated, surprised by Travis's defiance. "Outta my way, boy. Get out of my way or I'm gonna knock you out."

"No."

"Don't fuck with me, kid. Move!"

"Dad, you're wrong about this. Blaming Arnie is—"

With a powerful swipe Kane sent Travis sprawling. "Get lost, princess," he snarled. "I'll deal with you at home. Don't think I won't."

"Come on, pard," said Arnie, spreading his hands. "Go easy on the kid. I know how you feel, but don't take it out on him."

"You know how I feel?" Kane exploded. "That's funny comin' from a guy with no family of his own. How would you know how I feel? What the hell do you know about anything except lyin' to your friends?"

"I'm just saying you've been drinking, amigo. Maybe you should—"

"*You're* talking to *me* about drinking? That's a laugh. I've been carryin' your worthless ass at work for longer'n I can remember. *You're* the one hadda retire, you fuckin' lush."

Arnie regarded Kane with a look of profound desolation but said nothing.

"One more thing, *amigo*," said Kane brutally, giving Arnie a final shove. "We're quits. I don't want to see you at the burial. In fact, I don't ever want to see you again." Without another word he turned and started toward the limo, pushing through a crowd of embarrassed mourners who'd witnessed the ugly confrontation.

Travis began to follow, then looked back at Arnie. "Dad didn't mean that," he said.

"You don't have to apologize for your old man," Arnie replied evenly. "He had a perfect right to say what he did. He meant every word, and I don't blame him one bit."

"He's wrong. He's just taking it out on you because he doesn't know what else to do. He'll see things differently when he sobers up."

"Maybe," said Arnie, anguish clearly manifest in his gruff features.

"He will. I promise."

"Travis!" Kane's voice boomed from across the lot. "Let's go, bucko. Now!"

"I'll . . . I'll talk to Mom. She'll straighten things out."

"Forget it, kid. Don't make things worse than they already are."

"Travis! Get your ass over here."

Reluctantly, Travis started again for the limousine.

"Hey, Trav?" Arnie called after him.

"What?"

"Thanks for trying."

·   ·   ·

The burial took place later that afternoon at a cemetery in the San Fernando Valley. Fog still shrouded the coastline when the Kanes returned home. Once there they splintered apart, each going his or her own way to deal with the loss in private. Kane continued to drink, holing up in the downstairs bar like a wounded animal. Catheryn retired to her bedroom; Allison and Travis to theirs. Nate, the smallest and most sensitive of the children to the dark storm building in their father, completely disappeared from the house.

As the sun made a brief appearance under the clouds in time to touch the horizon, Travis heard a timid knock at his door. "Come in," he said, not feeling like company but curious to see who had sought him out. It was Allison. She entered, crossed to Tommy's bed, and sat staring out at the dying sun. Her face looked drawn and pale. Travis realized that the events of the day had taken a terrible toll on his sister, as they had on the rest of the family. "Are you all right?" he asked.

"Yeah. How about you?"

"I'm okay."

"At least Dad's talking to you now," said Allison, concern evident in her voice.

"I liked it better the other way."

"Amen to that."

"Is he still downstairs?"

"Uh-huh." Allison extended her thumb and little finger, bringing her hand to her mouth in a gesture Travis understood all too well.

"No wonder Nate decided to make himself scarce. Maybe we should do the same."

Allison smiled sadly. "He's a lot smaller than we are, Trav," she said. "I don't think we can all fit under the deck. We're stuck here."

"Speak for yourself, sis. If things get rough, I'm gone."

"My fearless brother Travis," said Allison gently. "At least Tommy stood up to him once in a while."

"Yeah, and got his ass kicked for his trouble."

"Nobody said he was smart. Maybe that's why we were never close, not like . . ." Allison stopped. She glanced at Travis, then returned her gaze to the fading sunset. "We never really connected," she went on quietly. "Aside from being older, Tommy just thought of me as a girl, some lesser species that happened to be part of the family. Sort of like Dad does. Exactly like Dad does, actually. I'm going to miss him, though. I . . . I'm going to miss him a lot."

Travis nodded slowly. "I know," he said.

Allison took a deep breath and turned from the window. "I saw you talking to Christy at the church. How's she holding up?"

"She seems okay, considering. By the way, you're going to be an aunt."

"Huh?"

"It's not public knowledge yet. Her folks don't even know, so don't say anything. They were going to get married. Tommy was going to skip college and go straight to the academy—join the force just like Dad."

Allison shook her head. "Just like Dad. Somehow that doesn't surprise me."

"It's gonna surprise Dad."

"You've got that right."

"Just keep your mouth shut."

"Sure. At least till school starts, anyway. The news will probably be public domain by then, along with all the other wonderful occurrences this summer," Allison said bitterly. "I can see my first English composition: 'My Summer Vacation,' by Allison Kane. No, I need something with more weight. I know . . . I'll throw in some literary references and pull out a title, like, say . . . 'Once Upon a Summer Dreary,' or—"

"That sucks, Ali."

"I'll admit it's pretentious, but a lot of authors do it."

"I'm talking about your sense of humor. You just don't know when to shut up, do you?"

"I . . . I'm sorry. I have a bad habit of joking when I don't know what else to do. I just can't believe Tommy's gone. I don't know how to handle it."

"You're not the only one," said Travis.

• • •

Later that evening Travis heard the sound of Catheryn's cello filtering up from below. He descended the stairs, finding his mother alone in the music room. She was sitting in her chair beside the old Baldwin, her instrument case open beside her, her cello between her knees. Not knowing what to say, Travis hesitated in the doorway. As he turned to go, Catheryn glanced up. "Come in, Travis," she said. "Please."

"Sure, Mom."

As Travis entered, Catheryn stopped playing and placed her bow in its padded notch in the case. Listlessly, she continued moving her left hand over the neck of the cello without depressing its strings, but said nothing.

"Where's Dad?"

"Your father's on the beach somewhere," she answered without looking up.

By force of habit Travis sat at the piano, taking his customary place on the wooden bench. *How many hours have we spent like this?* he wondered, glancing over at his mother and thinking back on the wealth of wordless communication that had passed between them in that room.

Absently, he placed his hands on the keyboard. The bandages had come off the day before, and although his hands still felt stiff and sore, they were healing far more quickly than he'd expected. A moment later, after sounding out a few tentative notes, he removed his fingers from the keys and looked over at Catheryn.

Other than recounting the bare facts of the climbing accident and the subsequent rescue, details in which Kane had perversely shown little interest, Travis had avoided discussing Tommy's death with anyone. And despite his mother's repeated efforts to draw him out, he'd steadfastly refused to open up to her—irrationally dreading, in his guilt and shame, the thought of suffering through her knowing lectures, her probing questions and silken recriminations, her logical excoriation of the nightmare he longed to forget. But most of all, he'd feared a sympathy and understanding he knew he didn't deserve. And so, realizing he was wrong but unable to stop himself, he'd hidden his feelings—from himself as well as from her—retreating into a shell of silence and denial. Now, no longer able to abide the barrier he'd erected between them, he finally spoke. "Mom?"

"What is it, Trav?"

"Do you hate me?"

Catheryn glanced up in surprise. She studied her son, recognizing the self-accusation in his eyes. With a sigh she leaned her cello against the wall. Then, shaking her head sadly, she reached over and took his face in her hands. "Oh, Travis," she said gently. "I love you. I'll always love you. Don't you know that?"

Travis swallowed, fighting the stinging flow that threatened to blur his vision. "Mom, I'm so sorry for what happened."

"I know." Catheryn's hands dropped to her lap. "But it was an accident, a terrible accident. It was no one's fault."

Travis shook his head and looked away.

"Listen, Trav," Catheryn continued, her voice filled with compassion. "I talked with one of the rangers. He said he couldn't believe what you went through to bring Tommy down. He said what you did was nearly impossible. No one could have done more."

"I keep telling myself that," said Travis. "It's just . . ."

"Don't do this to yourself, honey. You did everything you could. Let it go."

"I want to, Mom. But I can't."

"You must. Tommy's gone, and now we have to go on."

"I know he's gone," Travis sighed. "I . . . I'm just having trouble accepting it."

"All of us are," said Catheryn. She paused, gazing pensively out at the beach. "Especially your father."

At the mention of Kane, Travis once more fell silent. Without thinking, he again placed his hands on the piano and struck the opening chords from Chopin's third étude, the frustratingly elusive work Petrinski had designated as his rite of passage.

"That's a beautiful piece," Catheryn said, watching him carefully. "Truly beautiful."

Travis withdrew his hands. "Yes. It is," he said dully, staring down at the keys.

He could feel his mother's sympathetic eyes upon him. With a renewed surge of guilt he realized that, despite her own sorrow and the staggering depth of her loss, she was still trying to comfort him, still trying to soothe his hurt. Suddenly, more than anything, Travis wanted to give something in return.

But what?

All at once he knew.

Feeling strangely nervous, he placed his fingers on the keys once more. A slight hesitation. Then, taking a deep breath, he started the étude from the beginning.

The piece opened with the right-handed statement of a simple, heartbreaking melody that slowly raised its voice over the chords of the left. Travis played softly, feeling an unaccustomed chill pass through him as the poignant theme unfolded, rising for several bars without embellishment, then falling back. The song progressed and once more the right hand spoke, restating the lyric theme with melting elegance . . . climbing higher, promising more, then falling back again, trailing off in a curious, stillborn silence leading to the middle section.

As he steeled himself to embark on the difficulties of the next passage, Travis's thoughts traveled back, remembering his brother Tommy and a lifetime of shared experience that had served as a nexus to bind them. He thought back to the night after the fight on the raft, hearing his voice drifting ghostly through the darkness of their room.

"Tommy?"

"What?"

"Thanks for sticking up for me."

"Forget it. It's no big deal. Let's get some sleep."

"Okay. It is a big deal, though. To me, anyway. When you're gone, I'm not sure how I'm gonna make out around here on my own."

With a strange sensation of effortless power, Travis embarked on the middle passage of Chopin's moving composition, his fingers finding their way flawlessly through a study of contrasting fourths and sixths, building tension, relaxing, then soaring anew, higher, higher . . .

"I screwed up bad, Trav."

"You're gonna be okay."

"Tie me off . . . go down alone."

"I'm not leaving you up here. I told you I'd get you down, and I will. Besides, aren't you forgetting something?"

"What?"

"Kanes stand together, Tom. No matter what."

Again the mounting tension relaxed slightly, then began its relentless ascent with renewed energy, building slowly, pushing toward the summit, ever upward now . . . upward . . .

"Tommy fell, Dad. He fell. I did the best I could, then went for help . . ."

"You left him? You chickenshit little bastard."

"Dad, you don't understand . . ."

"I understand fine, bucko. I understand just fine."

. . . upward . . . and then, in shattering triumph . . . it pressed at last to a passionate, soul-wrenching climax of a surprising strength and power only hinted at by the deceptive foundations laid earlier. Once more in contrasting fourths and sixths, the haunting melody started its inevitable crashing descent, shuddering with chilling precision down, down . . . falling to its penultimate resting place in preparation for the final recapitulation. Then, like wind filling calm sails after a storm, the opening melody reappeared, and a quiet restatement of the bittersweet lament was heard for the last time, ending with the serene peace and resolution promised in the opening.

Travis removed his fingers from the keys. Trembling with emotion, he clasped his hands in his lap to still their shaking. Not trusting himself to speak, he sat quietly as the final chords faded to silence.

"Thank you, Travis."

Travis looked over at his mother. He saw tears shimmering in her eyes. To his astonishment he found his own face was wet, too.

"Ain't this sweet. You girls havin' a private party, or can anybody join in?"

Travis turned. Kane stood in the doorway, an empty glass in his hand. "Dad . . ."

Leaving the door ajar, Kane lurched in. He set his glass beside the half-spent bottle on the bar, then moved to the center of the room and stood cracking his knuckles . . . smiling malevolently, hideously drunk. "You and me got a bone to pick, boy. You think you can defy me in front of people and get away with it?"

Catheryn hurried to his side. "Dan, you and Travis can discuss this later. Right now isn't the time."

"Now's the perfect time." Circling his wife with a thick arm, Kane propelled her to the couch. "And for once, you're gonna stay out. This is between me and Travis. Come here, boy."

Catheryn rose. "Dan, please . . ."

Kane whirled. "Stay put, Kate." Then, turning to Travis, "Get over here, mama's boy."

Travis walked slowly to the center of the room, stopping before his father. Kane glared down at him. With sudden violence his hand cracked across Travis's face. "How dare you stand up for Arnie today?" he barked. "That lying two-faced bastard's the reason Tommy's dead. Why'd you do it?"

"That's enough," said Catheryn, bolting forward. With surprising speed Kane intercepted her before she'd gone a step, roughly shoving her back onto the couch. "Butt out, Kate," he warned, towering over her. "I'm not gonna tell you again."

"Dad's right, Mom," said Travis. He stood with his arms at his sides, his cheek burning from the blow. "This is between him and me."

Kane turned back to Travis. "For once you ain't gonna hide behind your mama, eh?" he said. "That's something, anyway. Now, why'd you do it?"

"Because you were wrong."

"That's not an answer. Why'd you do it?"

"Tommy's death wasn't Arnie's fault, Dad."

"Not good enough, bucko."

"Stop this, Dan," said Catheryn, on her feet again, her voice as cold as a surgeon's scalpel.

"Shut up, Kate. One more word out of you, and Travis here's gonna think a house landed on him. Why'd you do it, boy?"

Travis stood motionless in the center of the room, his mouth filling with the salty taste of blood. Behind his father he could see the somber, terrified faces of Allison and Nate watching from the doorway.

Though unable to control his shaking, Travis resisted the temptation to flee the mindless demon that had claimed ascendancy in his father's eyes. "I did it because I wanted to stop you from making a mistake," he said, trembling with emotion. "I did it because you've been so drunk for the past three days, you don't know what you're doing. I did it because Arnie's my friend. You can hit me all you want, but it won't change anything. I'd do it again."

In three quick steps Kane crossed the room. He grabbed Travis's shirt, lifting him from the floor. "You ain't gonna live to do it again."

Travis held his father's fierce gaze. "This isn't about Arnie, is it? Why don't you just come out and say it? You think I killed Tommy. You think it was my fault."

"Wasn't it?"

"No. You never even let me tell you what happened. I tried to save him—"

"The hell you did!" Kane bellowed, shaking Travis with a terrible, unthinking violence born of rage and fury and loss and drink. "The only truth to your story's the part about leaving Tommy to die. You did that just fine. That's what you're good for, ain't it? That, and cryin'."

"Dan, don't do this," Catheryn begged, pulling at Kane's arm.

"You're not the only one who loved him, Dad! I loved him too!" Travis yelled, his eyes burning, his vision blurring. Using all his strength, he grabbed his father's fist and ripped free of his grasp. But instead of retreating, he stood his ground, watching as the expression on Kane's face changed from anger to surprise.

"Well, well." Kane placed his hand on Travis's chest and pushed. "Come on, boy."

Catheryn stepped between them. "This has gone on long enough. Travis, leave the room."

Kane brutally swept her aside. "Come on, crybaby," he said, giving Travis another push. "Do it."

Travis stumbled back. Again he stepped forward. "Gee, I don't know, Dad. Do I get to clean my blood off your shoes when we're done?"

With a roar of drunken fury Kane drew back his hand. Catheryn caught his arm. "No!" she screamed.

Kane shook her off with a powerful shrug sending her sprawling. "I warned you, Kate. Butt out."

"I won't."

As she rose to her knees, Kane moved toward her. "And I say you will."

"Leave her alone!" Travis lowered his head and rushed his father, releasing a torrent of anger and fury and hate and fear that had been building for sixteen long years, his 175 pounds driving in, legs pumping, catching Kane off balance, pushing him back. Kane banged into a lamp, splintering a table as he fought to stay on his feet. The element of surprise quickly gone, he brushed aside Travis's onslaught, but before he could retaliate, Catheryn once more rushed forward. Kane brutally shoved her away, again sending her crashing to the floor. Then, giving vent to his rage and despair and ineffable, bottomless loss, he waded into Travis as if he were plowing into a blocking frame, his thick forearms slamming the boy into the wall, again and again. Travis staggered beneath the blows, trying to stay upright, his breath coming in retching gasps. As he struggled against the darkness growing in the corners of his vision, he heard the sound of feet rushing across the floor. Allison.

"Stop it, Daddy!" she screamed, tearing at her father's arm. Still dazed from her fall, Catheryn rose and joined her, her arms choking Kane from behind, trying to make him stop. With no more concern than one would show flicking off an insect, Kane sent them skidding across the room. In an instant they were back, struggling to stem the tide of his rage. And Nate was there now too, eyes brimming with frustration at his weakness, his small fists delivering their inconsequential blows to a father he couldn't hurt, his cries mingling with Allison and Catheryn's, their voices ringing like dissonant chords in a room that had once known only the sound of music. Effortlessly, like a dog shaking himself dry, Kane threw off their feeble assault. Nate's face caught the corner of the fireplace as he tumbled to a stop. He rose immediately, blood flowing from his chin. Ignoring the screams of his family, Kane hunched his shoulders in fearful purpose, and with eyes turned insane by rage and alcohol, he once more moved toward Travis. And again Nate and Allison rushed in, hitting and clawing and tearing at a father who seemed as impervious to them as a raging storm. And once more Catheryn joined them, a log from the fireplace clenched in her hands. With grim and unflinching resolve she raised the wood over her head and brought it crashing down with all her strength. A dull, hollow thunk sounded as it slammed into Kane's skull.

Kane staggered back, falling to one knee. Released, Travis started to topple. Nate and Allison rushed to help him. Still gripping the log, Catheryn stood before Kane, her eyes holding his unwavering.

Slowly, Kane lurched to his feet. Leaving Travis, Nate and Allison quickly took their places beside Catheryn, closing ranks between Kane and their brother, their fragile strength now united in a bloody phalanx against the father who had turned against his family. Trembling, their chests heaving, wounded but unbowed, they stood in silence, shoulder to shoulder, waiting . . .

Kane hesitated, frozen by the look of terrible resolve on Catheryn's face. Bewildered, he raised his hand to his head. He stared at his bloodied hand, then again regarded the tear-streaked faces of his family, seeming for the first time to comprehend the enormity of his betrayal. At last the storm faded and grew dim in his eyes, supplanted by a look of astonished confusion and shame. His shoulders slumped. Without a word he turned and staggered from the room, grabbing the bottle on the bar as he left.

The rest of the family listened as he banged through the back door and crashed out to the beach. Then Nate sank weeping to the floor, holding his hand to his chin in an attempt to stem the flow of blood. Allison moved to sit with Travis until his spasms passed, her own body racked with silent, shuddering sobs. Ruby, the newest addition to the Kane household, who had decided to make herself scarce until her masters ceased their terrifying behavior, crept into the room. She gave Nate's hand a few tentative licks, then sat nervously at his feet.

Her breath coming in ragged gasps, Catheryn maintained her vigil at the door, brandishing the length of firewood like a talisman against her husband's return. After what seemed a lifetime, satisfied their ordeal had truly passed, she set it on the floor and helped Nate to his feet. "Come on, sugar," she said, examining the cut on his chin. "Let's go to the emergency center and see about getting you fixed up."

"It's mostly stopped, Mom," Nate said quietly, drying his eyes on his shirt.

"We'll let the doctor decide whether you're all right. If nothing else, I think you're going to need some stitches."

"I'll start cleaning up," said Allison. "Seems as though I've been getting plenty of experience in that department lately," she added, trying to cover the tremor in her voice.

"Thanks, Ali." Catheryn glanced over at Travis. "Trav, maybe you'd better come with us, too," she said, her eyes filled with concern.

Travis shook his head. "I'm fine."

"Please, honey. You may have some cracked ribs."

Travis shot a look at the door. "I'm okay, Mom. Really."

"Are you sure?" asked Catheryn, noticing the bleeding had started again on Nate's chin. She grabbed a wad of napkins from the bar and applied pressure to the cut.

"I'm fine," said Travis, forcing a smile. "I'll stay here with Ali. Go take care of Nate."

"Trav . . ."

"Mom, I'm staying here with Ali," Travis repeated stubbornly. "Believe me, I'm fine."

"All right," Catheryn sighed. Then, taking Nate's hand, "C'mon, tiger. Let's go get you patched up."

·   ·   ·

With no wind to dispel it, the layer of fog blanketing the beach had lowered with the setting of the sun, and now hung a mere hundred feet above the water. Travis stepped over the seawall and stood for several minutes, allowing his eyes to adjust to the darkness. Aside from the pounding of the surf, all seemed still. As he stood, the scent of the sea came to him like a musky perfume, redolent with the odors of rotting seaweed and blue-green mussels and dead starfish spewed upon the sand and exposed on the rocks by a falling tide. Finally, as dim shapes began to take on ghostly substance, he headed for the water's edge.

Topping the berm, he looked down at the hollow tubes marching the length of the beach. Four- to five-foot swells had begun rolling in from the south the previous day, and as he watched, Travis detected a curious incandescence lighting up their interiors each time they crashed in the shallows. He studied the magic luminescence, wondering whether he was seeing things. At last he realized the subtle effect was being caused by the red tide, a bloom of poisonous microscopic diatoms that glow when disturbed.

I wonder why I never noticed it before, Travis thought as he crossed the final distance to the ocean. *Maybe it's never been dark enough. Strange that something so beautiful can also be so deadly.* He stamped at the water's edge, seeing the same odd light flashing in brief, perfect circles in the sand beneath his feet.

No sign of his father.

He has to be here somewhere. Probably stumbled down the beach. But which way?

Travis searched for footprints. He found none. He hesitated, then turned and started toward the glittering lights of Santa Monica.

Although well past midnight, a number of the houses lining the ocean still had on their lights. Unlike the closed and impersonal faces most of them presented to the highway, on the Pacific side many had large, unshuttered windows, and as Travis progressed down the beach, he occasionally glanced into their interiors, stealing stealthy glimpses of other people's lives—other families, other desires and intimacies, other hurts and transgressions—peering in on their secret, dangerous worlds of passion and commitment and love and hate. *Are they all like us?* he wondered as he passed like a shadow in the darkness. He found no comfort in the thought.

A quarter mile down he reached the condos guarding the far end of the cove. There he turned back, following his own prints to the point where they turned up toward his house. He stood indecisively. Twenty yards farther on he spied a dark shape atop the berm. "Dad?" he called.

No answer. Travis approached cautiously. He found a pile of clothes—Kane's shirt, shoes, trousers . . . and the now-empty fifth of Jack Daniel's. Travis remembered that the night of the party his father had stripped to his boxers and swum to the raft. He'd had plenty of company on that excursion; tonight he'd apparently decided to make the journey alone.

Travis peered out over the rolling waves, vainly attempting to spot the raft in the dark and angry waters. "Dad?" he yelled again, cupping his hands to his mouth. Again, no answer.

With a growing sense of urgency Travis returned to the house. After a quick search he found his bodysurfing wet suit hanging by the outside shower. Hurriedly, he slipped off his clothes and pulled it on, then grabbed a pair of green Churchill fins and his Boogie board. Finding the raft in the darkness would undoubtedly prove difficult, maybe impossible; having his head above water on the swim out would help.

At the ocean's edge he paused to estimate the raft's probable location. He knew it swung a wide circle depending on the wind and current, the confluence of the two forces often acting in reciprocal and counterbalancing directions. Taking into account the lack of wind, Travis walked fifty yards left and waded into the hissing ocean, the kickboard leashed to his wrist trailing behind. When he reached knee-deep water, he turned his back to the surf. Hopping alternately on one foot and then the other, he pulled on his fins. Then, taking a deep, shivering breath, he braced for the shock of the cold and dived in.

Normally Travis would have studied the sets, waiting for a lull to make his way through. Since he could see nothing in the darkness, he simply gripped the front of his board and kicked out strongly, hoping for the best. A long minute passed as he fought through the boiling foam. Soon he reached a critical section just inside the roar of the breaking tubes. Without warning, a seven-footer rose from the inky surface before him. Abandoning his board, Travis clawed for the bottom, feeling the tug of the leash as the wave crashed above him, nearly jerking him back into the swirl. Gasping for breath, he surfaced on the far side and set out once more, kicking for all he was worth. He made it over the next wave. Barely. And then he was past.

The immediate danger behind, Travis cut through the coal-black water, feeling strangely claustrophobic in the darkness. He glanced once toward the lights of shore. Then, resisting the nearly overwhelming desire to turn back, he swam on through the roiling sea. Ten minutes of steady kicking brought him far from the shoreline, but still no sign of the raft. Cold and alone, he stopped and tried to estimate his position by taking bearings from lights on the beach, wondering whether he'd inadvertently passed the raft in the darkness. Repeatedly he called his father's name, feeling a strange sense of déjà vu. Still, nothing.

As he hung suspended in an undulating plane dividing darkness above from that below, Travis noticed his kicking feet were creating a glow from the diatoms. It looked as if someone were shining up a light from the depths beneath him. He planed his hand under the surface, leaving a scintillating trail in its wake. At another time he might have found the curious effect fascinating; now he could think of only one thing: If *he'd* missed the raft, how could his father have possibly found it? With an effort of will he pushed from his mind the chilling thought of his drunken father swimming through the darkness to exhaustion.

A faint light flickered on his left. Travis kicked toward it. Before long he could make out the amorphous, bobbing outline of the raft emerging from the blackness, its timbers outlined in sporadic glimmers and flashes by the surging waves. He approached. Slowly, as the image of the raft grew clearer, he saw Kane lying on the deck, vomiting over the edge.

Travis hesitated, his fear of his father returning with paralyzing force. More than ever he wanted to turn and kick for shore, leaving to his own fate the man who had commanded and threatened and frightened him throughout the entire course of his childhood. Numbly, he realized he couldn't. He also realized, as a renewed lurch of terror shivered through him, that he didn't have the courage to do otherwise.

What now?

Then something came back to him, something Kane had told him an eternity ago, something that hadn't registered at the time but now seemed more consequential than anything else in the world. "Everybody's afraid," Kane had said. "Courage, valor, bravery—those are just words that don't mean spit. The guys who make the cut are the ones who can do what they have to, *despite their fear.*"

Heart in his throat, Travis came to a decision. He circled the raft once more, then swam in. After flipping his kickboard on deck, he scrambled over the lee side, avoiding the full force of the chopping waves. Occupied with more visceral concerns, Kane appeared not to notice.

Once he'd boarded, Travis sat without speaking, his dread slowly diminishing as he realized his father was now powerless against him. Strangely, something in Kane's abject helplessness reminded him of Allison's story. He couldn't place it for a second. Then, his mind returning to the vengeance of a young girl on a frozen Minnesota river, he had it. Angrily, he savored the murderous image.

Kane heaved again. Groaning, he spat into the water. "Sick," he mumbled. "That took some guts comin' out here for me, Tom."

"It's Travis, Dad."

Lowering his head, Kane retched again, coughing up a thin spew of brackish yellow bile.

"Seasick?" Travis asked, taking vindictive pleasure in his father's discomfort. "You shouldn't drink so much on an empty stomach. Next time eat something first, like a couple raw oysters—nice slimy ones. Or one of those spicy pepperoni sticks."

Kane's puking noticeably increased.

"A big bowl of sea-urchin gonads might help," Travis went on with vicious satisfaction. "Raw eggs are supposed to be good for a sick stomach, too. Something about the yolk popping in your throat when you swallow."

"Shut up, Tommy," Kane pleaded between heaves.

"Did I ever tell you I once found a scabby Band-Aid in a bowl of chow mein? I thought it was a water chestnut. Had it all chewed up before I figured it out."

With a growl Kane lurched to his knees. He attempted to regain his feet, then slipped on the deck and crashed down hard, slamming his head on the wet boards. Moaning, he rolled over and again proceeded with pitiful, capillary-popping retches to bring up what little remained in his tortured stomach.

"Let's head in." Travis sighed, tiring of his petty revenge. He shook his father's shoulder. "Come on, Dad. It's getting cold out here. You can use my board and fins."

"Not yet," Kane groaned, still throwing up.

Realizing he had no choice, Travis moved to the side of the raft to await the passing of his father's spasms. He sat for several minutes leaning against the ladder, gazing at the shoreline. From his offshore vantage the streetlights tracing the course of the highway at the foot of the palisades resembled a necklace of tiny yellow pearls, arcing with even, glowing symmetry on their serpentine route to Santa Monica. Just under the ceiling of fog the string of homes lining the beach appeared small and insignificant. Travis searched, locating his own by the light still burning in the music room.

"Know somethin', Tommy?" Kane's slurred and halting words came through the darkness.

"What?" Travis answered, deciding to ignore his father's mistake.

"You're gonna have kids of your own someday. You're gonna find out bein' a father ain't all that easy."

"Maybe so."

"You'll see, son. You'll start out wantin' everything to be perfect. You'll tell yourself you're never gonna make the mistakes *your* old man did. Then things will begin gettin' in the way. Money, job, not enough time . . . and then one day, all of a sudden you'll discover that you've screwed up bad and it's too late to start over. I wanted the best for you, Tommy. I wanted the best for you all."

"You've got a strange way of showing it," said Travis bitterly.

"If I'm hard on you, it's 'cause I gotta get you ready for later. You've no idea what's out there, Tom. You've gotta be tough. You've gotta be prepared."

"Tommy's dead, Dad. I'm Travis."

A long silence followed. "Travis?" Kane said finally, peering into the darkness. "That you, boy?"

"Yeah, Dad. It's me."

"Travis? What're you doing out here?"

"I came to finish our little talk."

Kane stiffened as the memory of what had happened came flooding back. "Oh, God, Travis, I . . . I'm sorry," he choked, his words nearly incoherent with grief. "I'm so sorry."

"Like you told Arnie, Dad. Sorry doesn't cut it."

"I know." Kane shook his head miserably. "I know."

"How could you turn on us like that?"

"Lost control," Kane whispered, his voice breaking. "Didn't mean to hurt you. I swear I didn't mean to hurt you."

"You never mean to hurt any of us," Travis said coldly. "But you do—every time you ridicule Allison or bully Nate or treat Mom like shit. And Arnie, Dad. Jesus, he's your best friend."

"Didn't mean it. Lost control. Never again."

Sure, Travis thought. But to his surprise, for the first time in his life the harshness of his skepticism was somehow without sting. For the first time in his life, it didn't matter.

Kane raised his head, his eyes filled with shame. "I know I let you down. I let everybody down. But I'm gonna make it right. I promise I'm gonna make it right."

"How are you going to do that?"

"I don't know. But I will."

"You know something, Dad?" Travis said, recalling another night not far back when he'd also sat in darkness, waiting for the moon. "I've been afraid of you for as long as I can remember. So afraid that it got to be easier to just not feel anything at all."

Travis hesitated, suddenly realizing the reason he'd followed his father out to the beach. Quickly, he rushed on before he could stop himself. "You were right when you said I wasn't telling the whole truth about Tommy's accident. I didn't mention that all I could think of the whole time I was up there was what *you* were going to say when you found out we'd disobeyed, what *you* were going to do."

Travis laughed bitterly. "I was more scared of that than anything else. That's what I worried about. Not Tommy, or if I was going to be able to save him, or even myself. It was you."

Kane didn't respond.

"And then at the hospital, when Tommy . . ." Travis swallowed, fighting for control. "When Tommy died, I told myself I wanted it to be me, not him. But that was a lie, and I knew it. And do you know the thought that kept running through my mind the whole time I was there, no matter how hard I tried to block it out? I kept thinking if it *had* been me, you wouldn't have cared half as much."

Travis shrugged. "It's funny, but some of the things I thought were so important back then don't even matter anymore."

Pausing, Travis wiped his eyes with the back of his hand. Then, taking a deep, shuddering breath, he lowered his head. "You can be a bastard, Dad," he said quietly. "You can be a real shit to everybody around you. But you're also right about a lot of things. Maybe you were right about me."

Again, Kane said nothing.

Travis sat in the darkness, waiting for his father to bridge the chasm, waiting for him to grant an absolution only he could give . . . yet knowing he wouldn't, knowing he couldn't.

Long seconds passed. Still Kane remained silent. And still Travis waited.

And as he waited, he slowly began to accept the limits of the father before him, struck by the simple, shattering realization that the figure huddled on the deck at his feet—the godlike monarch who, with unforgiving hands and unbending, iron will had ruled the puzzles and doubts and fears of his childhood; the patriarch, life-giver, father—was just a man, with the weaknesses and flaws and faults of any mortal man.

At last Travis spoke. "It's okay, Dad," he said. "You don't have to say anything." He started to add something but hesitated, surprised by an emotion he hadn't allowed himself to feel for his father in a long time, sensing it unfolding and growing and swelling inside him until he thought he would burst. He struggled, wanting to express it, yet knowing he'd forever be unable to put his feelings into words they could both accept.

"Dad?"

Still no answer. Travis slid across the deck and saw that Kane had fallen asleep.

Smiling, he whispered the words to himself.

•   •   •

Travis sat long into the night. Sometimes he talked, but mostly he sat in silence, sat beside the shadowy figure sleeping on the deck. And hours later, as the fog finally lifted and a crescent moon rose slowly in the east, he brought his father home.

Epilogue

The Bronislaw Kaper Awards piano competition took place late that October. Twenty-five of the finest young pianists from California had been invited to compete, with the first round scheduled at ten-thirty A.M. and the finals set for later that afternoon. At nine forty-five on the morning of the preliminaries Travis stood in the wings of the Dorothy Chandler Pavilion, peering out into the rapidly filling auditorium.

Normally a closed event, the Bronislaw had received such a spate of publicity in recent months that the Philharmonic committee had decided to open the competition to the public. Surprisingly, attendance that morning was well on its way to exceeding even their most optimistic predictions. With forty-five minutes still to go, devoted music lovers had already filled over a third of the pavilion's thirty-two hundred seats.

Travis nervously searched the sea of faces, noticing that Catheryn, Allison, and Nate had already taken their places in the fifth row of the orchestra section, sitting left of center to obtain a clear view of the contestants' hands on the keyboard. Arnie sat to one side of Catheryn; her friend Adele, along with Christy and her parents, on the other.

In the weeks since Travis had last seen Christy, she'd cut her tawny hair to just above shoulder length, and her normally lean, athletic body had begun to bloom with the softening curves of pregnancy. She looked lovely, more beautiful than ever. Making a mental note to call her, Travis allowed his eyes to roam once again, examining the higher rows. He found McKenzie and her father sitting halfway up. McKenzie waved cheerfully as he caught her eye. Travis returned her wave. Then, continuing his search, he spotted Alexander Petrinski and several musicians from the Philharmonic, as well as a large group from the university. Petrinski appeared somber and reserved and sat without speaking, his countenance reflecting none of the buzzing, carnival-charged excitement that had infected the rest of the room. Travis looked away, deciding he already felt nervous enough without having Petrinski's intensity crank things up another notch.

Returning backstage, Travis made a determined effort to push aside his jitters and focus on his program. Originally, for his discretionary piece in the preliminary round he'd prepared the *Aufschwung* selection from Schumann's *Fantasiestücke,* a composition abounding with pianistic dazzle and quasi-symphonic textures. Exhilarating, fire spewing, and demanding, it was a perfect work with which to open, and Travis had chosen it to attract the attention of the judges right from the start. He knew that afterward they'd ask to hear portions of his other prepared works, works he would play in full if he reached the finals, but the initial impression he made would be critical. Nonetheless, just hours before the competition he'd notified the judges of a change in his program.

Although confident all his selections demonstrated ample range and virtuosity—undoubtedly sufficient to assure a position in the top finishers if he played well—at the last minute Travis had elected to replace Schumann's *Aufschwung* with a less demanding piece, albeit one that had grown to have deep personal meaning. Chopin's étude.

It was a risk, but one he wanted to take.

Running over the piece in his mind, Travis descended to the waiting area beneath the stage and checked the performance roster for the tenth time since arriving. Nothing had changed. He would still be playing late, twenty-third in a field of twenty-five. By the end of the preliminaries that number would be cut to four. Travis planned on being among them.

As he stood studying the roster, Travis heard an usher speaking to someone at the door. "I'm sorry, sir," he heard her say. "The performers' lounge is for contestants and competition organizers only."

"Police business, cupcake," a familiar voice rumbled. "We don't want to disturb the players, now, do we? Just tell me where Travis Kane is. I'll take it from there."

"Yes, sir," Travis heard the girl respond nervously.

Travis stepped around the corner just in time to see Kane pocketing his badge. "Harassing the help, Dad?" he asked.

Kane grinned, looking urbane and resplendent in an impeccable black tuxedo, gleaming patent-leather shoes, and a stylish moss-green cummerbund that quietly complemented his surprising and uncharacteristically elegant appearance. "Yeah, maybe a tad," he admitted, watching with amusement as the flustered usher hurried off.

"What are you doing here?"

Kane hesitated, shifting uncomfortably from foot to foot. "I never got a chance to wish you luck this morning," he finally answered. "I figured I'd do it now."

"I thought you had to work."

Kane shrugged. "Why have a responsible job if you can't duck out on it once in a while? Besides, the ol' dad's gotta show some support when one of his kids is tryin' to make his mark, right?"

"Thanks, Dad. I appreciate your coming."

"No problem." Kane shot his cuffs and tugged proudly on the lapels of his jacket. "Not bad, huh? I went back after we got yours and rented one myself."

"You look great, Dad."

"Damn right. Can't have you being embarrassed by your unrefined old man, can we? Gotta be sophisticated at these kinda events."

"In your case sophistication might take slightly more than a suit," Travis laughed, pleased Kane had made the effort.

Kane smiled. "I'll take that as a compliment." He seemed about to add something but hesitated again, once more appearing nonplussed.

"What, Dad?" Travis asked. Neither he nor Kane had discussed the fight since that night on the raft, but in the months since then something deep and fundamental and lasting had shifted in the family—not only between Catheryn and Kane, but between Travis and his father as well—and of one thing he was now certain: Kane's unexpected visit was more than casual.

Kane stood silent and unmoving for a long moment, staring down at the floor. Then he looked up and found Travis's eyes with his own. "I don't know if I've ever told you this, kid," he said softly, "but . . . I'm proud of you. More than I can say."

"I thought you didn't like classical."

"That's not what I mean, son."

"I know, Dad. I . . . well, thanks."

"Another thing," said Kane, not looking away, even for an instant. "Since you mention it, you know I don't really understand your kinda music. But I was wondering if someday . . . when you don't have anything else going . . . maybe you could play something for me. Somethin' a little closer to country, maybe."

Travis remained silent, astonished as much by his father's request as by the emotion he heard now in his voice.

"I'd like it if you would, Trav. I truly would."

A smile crossed Travis's face. "You know what, Dad?" he said slowly. "I think I'd like that, too."

Kane clapped his son on the back. "Good. Then I'm gonna hold you to it," he said. "Now, go out there and kick some ass or break a leg or bust a string, or whatever the hell you music types say to each other."

"Thanks, Dad. I will."

•　　•　　•

As scheduled, the competition started promptly at ten-thirty A.M. Nervously, Travis awaited his turn. Three hours later, it arrived at last.

As he stepped onstage, Travis glanced into the auditorium, surprised to see since he'd last looked that late-arriving guests had completely filled the orchestra section of the huge room, and a sizable throng had even spilled over to the founders circle, loge, and balcony levels. Although the glare of the lights made it difficult to pick out individual faces, he could feel the comforting presence of his family and friends out there, waiting in quiet expectation.

Travis made his way to the Steinway concert grand piano in the center of the stage. Slowly, he seated himself, giving the room a few seconds to quiet as he gathered his concentration. Then, as an electric hush descended on the audience, he placed his hands over the keys, barely touching, preparing the opening chords of Chopin's Étude No. 3 in E Major, the piece he'd once spurned.

In the silence that followed, in the instant before starting, Travis reflected on the family he loved, the family whose united spirit had navigated the heartbreaking treacheries of life's reefs and shoals that summer and had somehow come through inviolate. Catheryn, ruling without seeming to with her courage and her tenderness and her art; Kane, forever bound by the shackles of his own strength; Allison, cloaking her light in a veil of secrecy and metaphor and wit; and Nate, most vulnerable of all in his innocence and unthinking trust. And Tommy was there now too, joining with the others in Travis's mind. They were all there, waiting to hear the voice he would bring forth with his music.

If he could open his soul to that family; if he could speak with Tommy's candor and Catheryn's courage and Kane's strength and Nate's innocence; if he could convey his innermost thoughts and hopes and feelings with the unerring accuracy of Allison's words— what would he say? Travis knew he would tell each of them something different, but the meaning would always remain the same. And ultimately, despite his efforts, he also knew that meaning would be sadly diminished, diluted in phrases familiarity had bled of all significance, lost in language made impotent by time and repetition and overuse. Then, with a shock of insight as unexpected and startling as a falling star, Travis suddenly sensed his doubts and fears and uncertainties slipping away, and he realized, at long last, he already knew a way to speak to the secret heart of each of them—without words, or artifice, or evasion.

• • •

And so, filled with a soaring feeling of balance and power, of being alive in the truest sense of the word . . . he began.

Acknowledgments

Writing a novel is much like raising a child. Although both are born of a single womb, during development each invariably experiences the support of many helping hands, and this work is no exception. In addition to my core group of readers who critiqued earlier drafts, I would like to express my appreciation to several others whose assistance aided *A Song for the Asking* in its struggle toward adulthood.

To Detective Lee Kingsford (LAPD, retired), I owe a deep debt of gratitude. His unselfish gift of time, expertise, and friendship proved invaluable in the preparation of this manuscript. Ted Huttman, Jim Ruggirello, Ruth Desarno, Sandy Ausman and Miles Hoffman generously provided, from varying perspectives, illuminating access to the world of music and the backstage workings of the Los Angeles Philharmonic. With unflagging enthusiasm and consummate expertise, Mary Alice Kier and Anna Cottle shepherded this book from beginning to end, once again reminding me I'm lucky to have them as my agents. Last but not least, Elisa Petrini, my editor at Bantam, put her seasoned eye and perceptive mind to the task of assisting me in hammering out a final version, and her guidance is evident everywhere throughout these pages.

To these, and to all my family and friends who encouraged me in this endeavor—thanks.